BLOOD OF THE PALE LIGHT

BLOOD OF THE PALE LIGHT

Eric Linke

My sincerest thanks to my mother for using her years of experience as an editor to help me make my second novel the best it can be.

I would also like to thank my father for his invaluable feedback on my story.

Thank you Alyssa, for all of your love and support.

Neither this book nor its characters would exist without you.

Table of Contents

Part 1
The Coming Storms

Introduction

    Darkness enveloped the servant as he rushed down the creaking stairs. Though he was blinded by shadow, the servant's feet flew from step to step with the precision of a man who had made this trip countless times before. When he reached the bottom of the staircase, he lit a small candle to illuminate the way through his master's dark laboratory. The light of the meager flame cast eerie, flickering shadows across the many books and countless implements of sorcery that filled the dingy old room. The servant gazed upon the vast collection in awe, for even though he had been born into his master's service, he had never quite grown accustomed to the nature of his or his master's work.

    With little time to waste, the servant looked to the list of items he had been ordered to gather; and hurriedly set about his task. Back and forth he strode as he collected his master's possessions in the exact order and manner as he had been instructed.

    While he worked, he strained to avoid looking directly at an ancient, cursed mirror that reflected the candlelight. His master had once told him that if his eyes ever fell upon its shimmering face, his soul would be drawn within the reflection; and he would be cursed to watch the world from within the mirror's confines for all eternity. His master had later told him that this was all a joke: nevertheless, the servant had no interest in testing his master's sense of humor.

    The fearful man kept his eyes glued to the rows of bottles neatly arranged on their racks. Hundreds of dust covered vials lined the ancient wooden shelves on the wall; but the servant only needed to find a scant few of them. There was little room in the bags he was set to pack, and there were plants, powders, and other alien substances that needed their own places among the contents of his master's luggage.

    Down the list he worked as he found every item in sequence. He stopped to check the list again and his blood ran cold when his eye reached the names of the gaulderens listed. He recognized a few of them and knew that if his master felt the need for the terrible spells they contained, it meant that gruesome work lay ahead of them. But, as in all things, he ignored his own fear and set about following his master's instructions.

It took longer than the servant would have liked, but he eventually came to the final item his master had requested. It was clearly quite important, as his master had not only listed it, but had also circled the entry in bright red ink. The servant looked about the room and quickly found his prize: a small, rectangular wooden box that held the mysterious artifact. He opened the box to be sure the item in question was still inside and found but one, unusually long, silver needle. The point looked to be incredibly sharp, and to his surprise, the other end had no eye. The servant wondered about its purpose, for it seemed unlikely for such a spindly thing to have any real use. The long needle was too thin to be used for knitting, and there was only one in the case. The servant shook his head at his own musings. In the end, it did not matter what the needle's purpose was. All that mattered was that his master had told him to pack it. After he double checked that this was the correct item, he gently closed the box and placed it in the same brown bag into which all the other items had gone.

The man surveyed the dimly lit room as he double checked his work. His gaze swept across books of all sorts, stacked elegantly upon their shelves, and various talismans and other odd things that dangled from their pegs on the far wall of the dark, old laboratory. However, none of these things were on the list, so he paid them no heed.

With his work finished, the servant extinguished his flame and swiftly climbed the ancient stairs. Darkness closed upon him once more, but even without light, he had no difficulty ascending the stairs that led to his master's brooding presence.

The servant did not know what could trouble his master so, for his master was a sorcerer capable of magical feats so terrible and great that the thought of them made the servant's heart race with fright. The servant knew little of his master's grim mood, save that something had happened… something far away that only the sorcerer understood. This worried the servant greatly, for if there was something in the world that made his master as fearful as he seemed now, then he was terrified of ever meeting it himself.

His ascent up the stairs was swift and he soon stood outside his master's study. The servant opened the door as quietly as he could, for he feared interrupting the sorcerer's brooding contemplation. Red firelight poured from the doorway, bathing him in its sinister glow. The servant remained in the hallway and looked around the room for a spot where he could stand until his master chose to address him.

Countless books lined the walls. Some of them were new, while other tomes appeared to be as old as mankind itself. The study was much more comfortably lit than the laboratory had been; not just by the resplendent fire in the fireplace, but also by glowing orbs of flame that floated lazily about the room. As their shadows danced across the floor, an eerie feeling grew upon him that they celebrated the event that had brought the sorcerer to such worry.

Having finally spotted a place to stand, the servant bowed deeply as he entered the room and waited for his master's acknowledgment. It was an old routine that had become so reflexive that the sorcerer would often acknowledge his servant's presence without actually realizing he was there.

This time, his master did not acknowledge him at first, but sat perfectly still in a large arm chair. By the chair's shape and size, it might have long ago been the throne of a king; but time had worn away most of the chair's grandeur, as the decorative embellishments were reduced to fragmented scratches and missing pieces lost long ago.

The servant waited, and just as he thought he should leave again, his master emphatically gestured for him to approach. He finally rose from his bow and crept forward; his footsteps muffled by the fine furs that carpeted the floor. Some of the rugs he had purchased himself, but others had been there since before he was born. Nervously, the servant held out the filled bag for his master to take.

The sorcerer stood; his impressive height casting a great shadow across the room. The servant shrank away from his master's imposing figure. He had been afraid of the sorcerer since he was a child; and had never been able to outgrow that fear. However, his anxiety was not wholly irrational, for the sorcerer was a powerful brute of a man; broad shouldered, and barrel-chested. Adding to his fearsome visage was his long, flaming red hair and beard that matched the fires of madness that burned in his steel-blue eyes.

The master took the bag from his servant and opened it. His sharp eyes carefully inspected its contents, an action that showed Nikos how truly important these ingredients were; as his master had not felt the need to check his work in many years. Once the sorcerer was finished, he looked down at his servant and smiled reassuringly as he spoke.

"Thank you, Nikos. You found everything I asked for. I appreciate your diligence."

Nikos bowed his head and tried to broach the topic of his master's mood.

"Master, you seem very agitated. Would you like me to bring some chewing root?"

The master looked at him with a mad gleam in his fierce, blue eyes that frightened Nikos. The servant had only ever seen that look once before, and it had preceded terrible calamity. The sorcerer answered in a calm, nonthreatening tone that worried Nikos even more.

"No, thank you. I need my mind clear for what is to come."

The master took the bag to the far corner of the room where he had already arranged other bags filled with food and clothing. Nikos swayed uneasily as he grew further concerned about his master's mood. He could see how troubled the sorcerer was; and despite his own fear, Nikos wanted to do anything he could to help him.

"Master, if I may ask: what is it that troubles you so? Is it something I have done?"

The master turned and stepped within arm's reach of his servant. As he walked, he gazed upon Nikos in a manner that made him uncomfortable. It was like the gaze of a lion that had spotted its prey.

"No. It is nothing you have done." Nikos' discomfort grew as the sorcerer stared into his eyes and searched for something within them that was far beyond the servant's understanding. "I suppose no harm will come if I tell you. I have felt tremors in the cosmos… another sorcerer has learned to control the powers of chaos."

Nikos now understood his master's concern, for his predecessors had told stories of their master's old experiments with chaos and the horrors that had nearly been unleashed. They had spoken of the danger chaos posed not only to themselves, but to all of creation. It was this danger that had forced his master to cease all efforts to harness its unholy power.

"And you go now… to try to stop this sorcerer?" Nikos asked.

His master laughed in a manner that made even the warming fire recoil in terror.

"I don't need to. When the perpetrator used chaos, something *else* discovered them. Whatever it was… it destroyed them. I intend to find out what did this."

Nikos' blood ran cold with fear. If there was something so powerful it could destroy a sorcerer capable of wielding chaos, perhaps it was best left alone. However, Nikos kept his thoughts to himself and silently listened as his master spoke of what he had seen.

"I felt two occurrences of great power being called forth. The first… it was… evil, malevolent, and inhuman. *This* was when chaos was used. But the second time… it was a different power. Its aura was so impossibly bright… it felt like Caelum himself stood in the room with me, even though the source of this power was half the world away. This second power is what most intrigues me. I *have* to find out if there is a way to control it. I must make a long journey… and I must make it as quickly as possible. Others will have felt this same disturbance in the cosmos and they will seek its source as I do. If I am to make my gains I must make haste… or all will be lost to me."

Nikos' heart raced with fear, and his hands balled into fists as he struggled to contain it. Caelum was one of the three gods that had created all of the cosmos, and to trifle with anything so powerful that it could be compared to him could only end in calamity… and his master wanted to seek it out! Nikos then looked for a way to talk the sorcerer out of his plan.

"What others will come?" he asked.

"Other sorcerers; mortals bent on stealing away with power they cannot possibly comprehend."

"And, you believe you can control this power?"

Silence reigned as the master lapsed into the unfathomable memories of his lifetime. As the moments passed, the sorcerer's face gradually shifted from an expression of nervous contemplation to one of steadfast determination. Eventually, he returned to the present and answered Nikos' question.

"I have prepared for an opportunity like this longer than anyone. I am more than capable of controlling this new power. I need only learn how."

Terror gripped Nikos' heart, for it was clear to him that there was no way he could dissuade his master from taking this course. However, Nikos stuffed his fear down inside of himself and summoned the courage he needed for the journey ahead.

"Is there anything else you need before we leave, master?"

The sorcerer frowned and turned away from Nikos as though he were suddenly ashamed.

"Nikos, how long has your family served me?"

"Master?" Nikos replied.

"How long has it been? Do you know the years?"

Nikos stuttered as he tried to ascertain why his master was asking this question. Finally, he stopped trying to guess his master's motivations and answered it.

"We have served you since the time of my grandfather."

The master smiled again.

"And from even before the time of your grandfather's grandfather as well. Your family has served me diligently for generations, and I am forever in your debt."

With that, Nikos' master thrust an unseen dagger into his loyal servant's heart. Nikos cried out as the blade pierced him, and the sorcerer gazed upon him sorrowfully as he struck. "Where we go, no one must know me, for my enemies might force even *you* to turn against me." Pain tore through Nikos' body as he desperately clutched at his master's arm. The sorcerer looked deeply into Nikos' eyes and held him close as he watched his servant die. "Do not worry, you have not failed me. All who know me must believe me dead… or be dead themselves. I will do a kind deed in your name so that you may be sure of entry into the benevolent afterlife. Go… join your ancestors in paradise. Send them my thanks for their loyal service."

The master then gently laid Nikos on the floor and watched as the light left his servant's eyes forever. Once he was sure Nikos was dead, the sorcerer collected his bags. As he worked, he hummed an old and sorrowful song of mourning from his homeland; a place that he could see only in his dreams and distant memories. The lyrics of this song were too painful for him to sing aloud, but he felt the need to let the tune fill the air once more as he honored his dead servant.

As the sorcerer stepped through the front door of his house, he reached into his pocket and withdrew a gaulderen. He looked at the magic-infused object and gazed deeply into the crystal structure as it reflected and enhanced the strength of the firelight. The sorcerer then tossed the gaulderen into the fireplace and watched for but a moment as the once comforting flames now roared with the fury of a wildfire. The books were the first to catch fire, and soon even the sorcerer's old throne was no more than kindling. His house was a home no more, and now served only as a funeral pyre for his servant.

With his first task finished, the master started down the road towards his goal. He did not look back, for his mind was set only upon his homeland as he began his long and perilous journey.

Chapter 1

Earl Sigaberht sat alone in his dark bedchamber… and wept. Tears flowed down his face as a river flows down a mountain while he prayed to the god Caelum to bring his wife back to him.

There was no answer; for Caelum was a god long dead.

The mourning man reached to his arm and grasped the silver oath ring that marked him as the earl of Wulfgeld. He hoped he could remind himself of who he was, and of the stoic presence expected from a man of his station… but his arm ring brought him no resolve. When in public, he could maintain his facade as an indomitable ruler undaunted by the tragedy that had befallen him and his people, but in his moments of sorrow and darkness, he was only a man.

Sigaberht tore the oath ring from his arm and gripped it so tightly that the twisting bands of silver left painful marks upon his palm. He clenched the object of his wedding vows and secretly hoped that if he just held it tightly enough, he might bring his wife back to him.

"Erelda," he whispered in the darkness, as though that might call her to him.

After an agonizing eternity, the strength in Sigaberht's hand gave out; and to his despair, the oath ring slipped from his fingers and plummeted to the floor. When the ring struck the wooden surface, it let out a piercing sound that brought a moment of lucidity to Sigaberht's mind. In that instant, he forced himself to think of happier things in the hopes that this would drive him from his mourning and bring him back to the world around him.

Sigaberht tried to be grateful that his son, Ashveldt, was still alive. However, his mind turned even this happy thought back on itself. Recent memories of the ferocious wolves that had tried to murder Ashveldt tore into his thoughts. From this memory, his mind cruelly conjured the full recollection of his beloved Erelda's death. She had died defending their son's life against the onslaught of the vicious wolves sent to wreak havoc upon their people by foul witches known as the "Hexverat". Yet again, Sigaberht felt like he was back on that snow and blood covered battleground. He tried to shake the invasive thoughts away, but they would not budge.

Cold death surrounded him, but after much struggle, he finally wrenched his thoughts away from the painful vision of his beloved's corpse. However, his new thoughts brought little comfort. The earl's mind had drifted to the wayfaring demigod who now fought for him. Though his real name was 'Radnor', to the earl he was 'Veigarand'… the Ghost of the North. Even after Sigaberht had witnessed the viciousness of the wolves, Veigarand was by far the most ferocious thing the earl had ever seen on a battlefield. It was during the battle against the witches and their evil servants that Sigaberht had stood in awe as Veigarand nearly beat a werewolf to death right before his eyes!

Wolves again. Blood… death… Erelda. These same memories played in his mind as they had a thousand times before. Again, the earl tried to turn his mind to happier thoughts; but his only comfort was that the witches who had killed his beloved wife now lay dead. While Veigarand swore that he had no hand in their deaths, the earl had confirmed that they had perished. Sigaberht had hoped that knowledge of their deaths would have satisfied his hunger for revenge. Unfortunately, it did not. Thinking of vengeance spun the earl's thoughts back to his wife. He found himself wishing for the thousandth time that Veigarand had been there to save her. Sigaberht also wished that it had been he that had died and that she had lived.

Finally, the earl was able to turn his thoughts to the last time he touched Erelda's beautiful face. She had looked into his eyes with the same love for him that he had for her. Sigaberht's heart warmed as he basked in her memory. This was the memory that helped Sigaberht find himself once more.

After an eternity lost in overwhelming grief, the earl slowly rose from his tumultuous thoughts and remembered himself. The veil of shadow that was Sigaberht's own mind slowly lifted from him and his awareness of the world around him returned. The earl gazed out the window and upon seeing the darkness outside, realized that the sun had set since he had first entered his bed-chamber to mourn. The moon was almost full. However, his room was nearly pitch black, for even the moon seemed unwilling to disturb the earl's mourning with its pale rays of light.

After a final moment of grieving in the darkness, the sorrowful man lit a candle. The earl wished he could confide his grief to someone, but he could not allow anyone to see his weakness. Not even Ashveldt could see him in this state, for the young man needed his father's strength now more than ever before. Sigaberht took his oath ring back into his hand, and with shadows as the earl's only witnesses, swore that he would never allow any harm to come to Ashveldt, and would die before he allowed *anything* to threaten his son.

A knock on the door shook the earl's concentration. A curse formed in Sigaberht's throat, but before he could hurl it at the one whom dared interrupt his thoughts, a muffled, high-pitched voice came from the other side of the door.

"My lord Sigaberht, I have been sent to tell you that we have received word from our scouts: Piarin's army will be arriving in two days."

The spirit of Sigaberht, Earl of Wulfgeld, fully returned to the grief-torn man. He wiped the tears from his eyes and flung the door open with a vigor that belied his sorrow. It was then that Sigaberht saw a young, dark haired boy, perhaps only eleven, dressed in the livery of a messenger. The boy took a step back in fear, frightened by the hint of madness that lay behind the earls' silvery blue eyes. The boy felt like Sigaberht's gaze bored directly into his very soul, and the earl laughed in a manner that filled the boy with even greater dread.

"Then they come to their deaths," Sigaberht said. "Does the general know?"

"He is the one who sent me to you, my lord."

Sigaberht nodded and strode down the wide hallway. The messenger struggled to keep up with Sigaberht's furious pace, and were it not for his fear of the earl's dreadful mood, the boy would have given up following him altogether.

The earl headed towards his throne room where he could find some time to think alone in a more official place that would help him stay focused on the task at hand. It did not take long for him to reach the double doors that led to his great hall. The guards bowed and opened the way for their lord, though Sigaberht's distracted mind barely noticed them as he strode through the threshold and surveyed the room. He focused on his surroundings in the hope that he could further drag himself out of his sorrow.

While the throne room in Sigaberht's palace had been a place of merriment and feasting as well as business, the hall in his keep was a place for grim meetings of war. It was smaller than the one in his palace had been and its stone walls bore far fewer decorations. Only a few tables lined the walls of the room, while the middle of the hall was open for those who would stand before Sigaberht's royal presence and answer to him.

"My lord… if I may… if I may be so bold…" stammered the messenger. Sigaberht stopped to face his subject and impatiently waited for the scared boy to finish. As the earl's gaze came upon him again, the boy stuttered until he could finally utter his question. "How… can we… how can we stand up against Piarin now? We could barely defeat him before, but now… after the wolves came…" the boy trailed off, unable to finish his sentence out of fear.

Sigaberht stepped towards the messenger and clasped his shoulders.

"Fear not; they only come here because they do not know what monsters live within these walls."

The boy cast a fearful gaze at Sigaberht and replied.

"Veigarand? Is he still—"

"Yes," Sigaberht interrupted. "He will fight for us and all of our foes will know his wrath. At present, he is out on an errand of great import. Be sure that he comes to my throne room when he returns."

"Yes, my lord."

The messenger bowed and hurried off to complete his task. Sigaberht turned and rested upon his throne. He gazed upon the empty chamber and rested his hand upon a weary brow. He had much to plan before the enemy arrived. He only hoped that Veigarand would return from his task soon.

* * *

Night held dominion over the snow covered forest. Darkness smothered all hope as it shrouded the sleepless remains of the Hexverat's victims. This forest had once been a place overflowing with life; but was now a haunted haven of corruption and death. The once proud trees withered and died where they stood in the wintry world. Birds and beasts shunned the ghastly groves, for these woods had become an evil, malevolent place where few living souls dared to tread.

Despite the menace that stalked the accursed woods, two people *did* tread upon its unholy soil and braved the danger side-by-side. The pair who dared face those that dwelt in the darkness were the same people who had broken the witches' assault on Wulfgeld: Radnor and Elena. Radnor's hulking, armored form crushed fallen branches as he walked; while Elena's delicate steps gently crunched into the snow. Both kept their senses keenly aware for the dangers they knew lurked in this foul place. Neither one of them said a word for fear of alerting the enemy to their presence, until Elena finally broke the silence.

"Radnor… wait! I need to rest," she said breathlessly.

Radnor looked over at her as she worked to catch her breath and let her aching muscles regain their strength.

"We need to keep moving," he said. "This whole venture is foolhardy, even by my standards. We at least should have waited until we got you some armor that fits."

Inwardly, given the nature of their work, he was glad that she at least wore a tunic and trousers instead of the long, flowing skirts that she usually preferred.

Elena nodded.

"You know I wouldn't have asked to come here if it wasn't important. Besides, does armor do any good against these monsters?" she said.

Radnor did not answer as he kept an eye on the shadows for any signs of sinister movement. There were none… for now.

"This place is cursed. The chaos those witches released has deepened its hold here… and I don't know if I can protect you from it."

Elena's heart fluttered at Radnor's protectiveness. However, she quickly returned her focus to soothing her aching muscles.

"I know. Just try to remember that I can defend myself," she said.

Radnor shook his head in aggravation.

"I remember, but the fact remains: you don't know *how* you do the things you do."

"That doesn't change the fact that I do them. I just think… and it happens," Elena replied sharply.

"It's clearly not that simple. You haven't been able to use your powers at all since we returned to Wulfgeld."

"Which is why I need to come out here. I need to be where it first happened… where I—"

"First used your power?" Radnor finished.

"Yes, and you would do no different if you were in my shoes."

"I know. It's just… chaos is a *very* apt name for what we face. It's disordered… unpredictable. Even when the witches guided it, there was little rhyme or reason to how it functioned, or what it would do. Even under the dominating will of that… *thing* in the dead city… the power of chaos was overwhelming in its ferocity. I fear these traits will become even more extreme when nothing directs its energy."

"You think I don't know that?" Elena snapped.

Her thoughts turned to their previous battle against chaos. The terrible creatures the Hexverat had unleashed made the depraved wolves seem tame by comparison, and the things she and Radnor had faced in the ancient, dead city had been even worse.

It had been almost a month since the battle had ended, and it had been possibly the most frustrating month of Elena's life. She wished she could unravel the mystery of how she had destroyed the monsters that had attacked them, but she just couldn't discover the secret. Every time Elena had tried to channel her power since the battle, she had failed. When attacked by the monsters driven by chaos, using her powers had felt so natural that it now felt like she had lost the ability to walk. Elena could feel that the magic she had wielded was still inside of her, but she couldn't get it to manifest. She looked around and scanned for any threats. She saw nothing, and then continued.

"Besides, *Sigaberht* agrees with me. We need to learn more about my powers."

Radnor scoffed at the mention of Sigaberht.

"Do you think he cares at all for your safety? He sees you as nothing but a tool… a—"

"Weapon?" Elena finished.

Silence fell between the two lovers. Elena finally understood Radnor's *real* objection to their being in the cursed forest.

He doesn't want me to be seen and used the way he has been his whole life: as nothing but a tool for someone else… a weapon.

Elena wasn't sure how to talk to him about this; their relationship was new and she was still learning how to have more intimate conversations with him. Radnor spoke first.

"I just don't want anything to happen to you."

Elena wanted to kiss him, but now was not the time or place for romance. She would have to wait until they returned to Wulfgeld and she had him out of his armor again.

The sudden *crunch* of a breaking twig interrupted Elena's thoughts. Both of their heads snapped onto the origin of the sound, but only Radnor's demigod eyes could make out the vague outline of their humanoid foe in the darkness.

"It looks like we may have to test your abilities in a moment," he said.

Elena heard the gentle sliding sound of steel against leather as Radnor drew his sword, and she waited in fearful anticipation of what was to come.

"How do you want to do this?" she asked.

Radnor nervously glanced at Elena.

"Me? You're the one with the powers."

"And you're the one with the sword that will bail us out of trouble if something goes wrong."

Radnor looked down at the black blade of his sword. He struggled to hold his gaze upon the weapon, as the reality-defying steel seemed to twist and writhe upon itself while somehow also perfectly maintaining the shape of a straight, double-edged sword blade. This evil sword was made from the same chaos that corrupted the forest around them, and no one knew what horrors it might unleash. Even Radnor feared the blade's power. He had considered trying to destroy it, but he had no idea of how to safely dispose of something made from pure chaos. There was also another reason to keep it: this sword was the only known weapon that could slay the creatures they now faced. Radnor looked back to their shadowed foe and watched it carefully.

"It's just standing there… like it's waiting for something. I think we need to see what it does first."

"Do you know who it is?"

"Who it *was*, not who it is," Radnor corrected. "And no. I can only make out its general shape from here."

The two stood in silence and waited for the creature to make the first move. The pair feared that they might fall into an ambush if they committed to an attack of their own. However, the longer they watched, the more nothing happened.

"Does it know we're here?" Elena asked.

"I think it does. It clearly moved to our position, but why has it stopped?"

"Is it fearful of my power? Is it being… cautious?"

"Maybe," Radnor replied.

The demigod cursed under his breath. The monsters they had fought here before had been mindless killers. The only ones that had shown any intelligence were the ones controlled by the terrible, mysterious being of great power that the pair had destroyed within the dead city. If the creature that faced them now was truly showing signs of intelligence, Radnor feared to learn what manner of being controlled it.

The demigod wanted to do something to draw the monster out and start the fight, but he restrained the impulse. While Elena indeed held great power… it was just as unpredictable as the chaos they faced. If Radnor made a mistake, it could spell injury or death for the woman he loved and he would never forgive himself.

Suddenly, Elena took a step towards the monster that waited in the shadows. As soon as she moved, fleshy, black, spiked tendrils sprung from the darkness towards her. Radnor leapt forward to cut them with his blade, but he was too late! Right as the tendrils were about to strike Elena, golden light sprung from her hands and pierced through the darkness! The beams of light slashed through the tendrils, severing them. The shadow shrouded monster let out a terrible cry and finally stepped into view.

The thing had been human at one point, but almost all of that humanity had been stripped away and replaced with pure, malevolent evil. Its bones were shattered, its flesh was burned, and a host of tendrils suddenly burst from the fiend's chest!

All of the tendrils launched themselves towards Radnor and Elena, as the monster sought to gore them where they stood. Radnor stepped past a tendril aimed at him and narrowly avoided a slash from one of its deadly barbs. Elena threw up her hands and conjured a shield made of golden light. The tendrils slammed into her barrier and instantly burned to ash. Elena felt energy flow from her heart and into her arm. Guided by the power that surged through her body, Elena waved her hand, and a flare of light cascaded outward and slammed into her foe. The creature shrieked as it collapsed and burst into golden flames. A few moments later, there was nothing left of the monster but blood and ashes.

Radnor and Elena were about to breathe a sigh of relief when yet more shapes emerged from the shadows. Four more of the inhuman monsters came into view and their tendrils snaked ever closer. Before either person could respond, a great tree limb lashed out at Radnor. The demigod saw it out of the corner of his eye and spun out of the way. Radnor watched as the tree nearest him uprooted itself and marched towards him on sickened roots marked by an eerie, alien glow. Golden light flashed in the corner of Radnor's eye, which caused him to check on Elena. She was locked in battle against the four humanoid monsters.

Trusting that Elena could defeat her foes, Radnor turned to face the corrupted tree. He needed to be quick, as hesitation against so monstrous a foe meant instant death. The warrior launched himself at his abominable enemy with all his might. His sword lashed out against the whipping branches and the magic blade severed them with ease. The murderous monster retaliated with tremendous ferocity and Radnor was forced to dodge another limb aimed at his head. He suppressed the impulse to flee when he saw that row upon row of razor sharp teeth sprouted from the limb that had tried to kill him.

After dodging another fierce blow, Radnor saw an opening in the fiend's defenses and slashed his sword straight through its massive bulk. The monstrous thing let out a terrible, impossible, wooden cry as it splintered and crashed to the ground in a heap. Radnor watched the tree quickly dissolve away as the power of his sword undid the magic that held the dead thing together.

Just as Radnor spun to help Elena, something grabbed him by his ankle! He looked down and saw that the earth itself had taken hold of his foot. Panic flashed through Radnor's heart as he remembered the grisly fate that had befallen others attacked the same way. Desperately, he thrust his sword into the patch of dirt that had taken his ankle, and to his relief, the magic in his sword held true! There was another shriek, and the dirt around his ankle fell apart at the blow. The fearful man tore his foot loose from the evil maw before the twisted earth could try to attack him again. Now free, the warrior finally turned and saw that the original four monsters that attacked Elena were now smoldering remains in the snowy earth, but she was now assaulted by a pack of wolves!

Radnor rushed to her aid and saw that while she shielded herself against three of the wolves, one was about to strike her from behind! Radnor let out a deafening war cry as he approached, and as the vicious wolf turned to face him, it revealed a bloody maw filled with bony, glistening fangs that ran in rows and rows within its entire mouth.

Any other man would have gone mad at the sight of such horror, but Radnor's overpowering instincts told him to kill the creature as quickly as he could. Fear for Elena's life fueled his rage, and Radnor drove his sword straight through the creature's head, cleaving it from its body. As he turned back to Elena, the severed head suddenly sprouted several spider legs and pounced on him from behind!

Radnor spun with the blow and both went tumbling to the ground. Radnor's training saved him then as he was able to keep his shield between him and the monstrous thing. However, he dropped his sword as he fell! With the creature now on top of him, it raked at his helmet with teeth laden legs as it sought to destroy him. Radnor tried to toss the thing off of him, but the creature had somehow become impossibly heavy and had him pinned. Radnor stretched out his sword arm as he desperately reached for his weapon, but the creature saw his intent and drove one of its deadly limbs at his hand! Radnor quickly swept his hand out of the way, and saw his opportunity. In the creature's effort to stop him from reaching the sword, the monster had shifted its weight to one side of him. With one massive effort, Radnor finally hurled the monster upon its back. The demigod snatched up his sword and delivered a final, crushing blow into the spider-like skull that finally destroyed it.

Before Radnor could catch his breath, another wolf leaped at him with bone crushing force. However, the veteran warrior stepped aside as he raised his shield and redirected the monster's deadly attack away from him. The power of Radnor's deflection sent the monster tumbling into the snow. Radnor's sword flashed again and the foul beast was cut in half by the blow.

Radnor looked up from his fallen enemy to see that his efforts were in vain. More and more creatures descended upon the pair and Radnor took Elena by the arm.

"We need to leave! Now!" he yelled.

Elena nodded, but as she turned to join Radnor in his retreat, a barbed tendril wrapped around her ankle and dug its grisly thorn into her flesh.

Elena screamed in pain and dropped to the ground. Radnor's blood ran cold; most whom had been wounded by these monsters had died a grisly, painful death. Radnor quickly severed the tendril around Elena's ankle and started to scoop her up in his arms. Before he could lift her, more monsters closed in on him and Radnor found himself locked in a battle for survival against the horrific things. His sword and shield slashed and parried against the ferocious attacks of his foes, but it was no use. He would soon be overwhelmed!

Finally, in their moment of desperation, Elena felt power surge through her like never before. A barrier of golden light sprung from her body and formed a wall that separated the duo from their attackers. Everything that touched the barrier burst into flames and was quickly reduced to ash. The creatures stopped their advance, unable to reach the pair.

With an opportunity to flee; Radnor snatched Elena into his arms and ran as fast as he could. He did not look back to see if the barrier still held the monsters at bay. He only ran... for as long as he could keep his legs moving.

The creatures watched as the pair fled, their eyes guided by the malicious will of a being whose lust for death was matched only by the intensity of the hunger that drove its existence; a hunger now focused on the mortal pair. The woman held power so great it would be a dire threat should she learn to control it... but could also be the means to salvation. A scheme was formed... a design only comprehensible to that which conceived it. The man and woman would return... and as they were devoured... she would open the cosmos to its hunger.

After what felt like an eternity, Radnor finally found Darestr, his loyal horse, silently waiting for them at the forest's edge. Darestr's body language showed concern as the pair approached. He moved towards Radnor, who was grateful for the help as he lifted Elena onto Darestr's back.

"Let me look at your ankle," Radnor said, worriedly.

He had seen the influence of chaos in such wounds, and how it could transform a person and destroy them utterly.

As Radnor inspected her injury, he was relieved to find that there was no sign that chaos had started its grisly work on her. The only mark was a deep gash in her leg that would need to be examined by Sigaberht's physicians. The fact that there was no malevolent magical force in the wound that would continue to harm Elena was a testament to the power within her.

"I never thought I'd say this, but I'm thankful that this is *just* a deep cut," Radnor said.

Elena sighed. She reached out and gently touched his blood soaked shoulder. She tried to give him a gentle, reassuring squeeze. Elena only felt the slick blood and cold steel beneath, but she hoped he felt the gesture through his armor.

"I'm sorry, I thought I could handle it," Elena said.

Radnor shook his head as he swept her into his arms.

"I understand your desperation… your… *need* to understand yourself."

"But clearly it was foolish, and now look at me! Think of where I'd be if you hadn't stopped them from overwhelming me!"

"I know," he replied. "But we do know something for sure now. Your power is tied directly to chaos. The instant you were confronted with it, your powers returned."

"I don't know if I'm relieved… or even more worried," Elena replied.

There was a pause as Elena took Radnor's hand in hers. Radnor tried to enjoy the moment, but their escape was not complete until they were safely behind the walls of Wulfgeld.

"Come on. We need to get you back to the city and have that wound looked at."

Elena nodded, and the two began the trip back to their home.

<u>Chapter 2</u>

It was nearly sunrise by the time Radnor and Elena passed through Wulfgeld's towering gates. The men atop the gatehouse had spotted them from across the wide, open field that separated Wulfgeld from the edges of the forest and had already opened the great door by the time the pair reached it. Once inside the city, Radnor looked back through the gradually closing gate and scanned the tree line for any sign of the creatures; there was no hint of pursuit. It seemed that the abominations remained in their lair… for now.

Radnor knew the haunted woods needed to be cleansed, but there simply hadn't been time after the witch's attack. All efforts had been spent either repairing the damage done by the wolves or readying the defenses for the inevitable attack by Piarin, the Duke of Drakomar. Word of Wulfgeld's misfortune had traveled far; as it was known that the duke had assembled an army to strike at Sigaberht while his enemy was vulnerable.

Even without the threat of Piarin's assault hanging over their heads, ridding the forest of corruption would require powerful sorcerers to do most of the heavy fighting, and given how little *anyone* knew about chaos, Radnor was afraid even that would not be enough. Elena's situation also worried him. It was clear she was immensely powerful… but how? Why? And how did *he* factor into this power? The words of Hilda, the witch, echoed through his mind again as they had so many times in the past few weeks…

I fear the world will need her strength not just today, but again and again. Protect her Veigarand. Help her understand her power. She needs you… and you definitely need her.

Radnor looked away from the road and to Elena. He saw the way she looked back at him and all his fears fell away in an instant. It did not matter what else was happening. All that mattered was that he was here with her.

"What?" Elena asked.

"Nothing," he replied.

Elena rolled her eyes at him.

"I know that look, and it wasn't 'nothing'. You were worrying about something. Is it my ankle?"

Radnor started to reply, but was interrupted and stopped by a group of city guards. The guards were all equipped with mail armor, open-faced helmets, and spears. One of the guards, whom Radnor guessed was the leader, stepped forward. Radnor saw the weary expression on the man's face and recognized that this unfortunate soldier had probably doubled his time at the watch since the attack, as there were few adequately trained men left to replace those slain during the battle against the witches.

The guard leader held up his hand to stop the pair, and when they did, he tried to take Darestr by the reins. Darestr tore his head away and stamped his foot in anger at the guardsman. The man stopped and gave a fearful glance to the pair astride the temperamental horse. He shuddered when he saw that Radnor and Elena were still partially covered in the black blood and yellow ichor of the monsters they had fought in the woods. The sight and smell of the putrid gore made the guardsman's stomach turn. His nerves had never quite calmed down since the attack, and the way Radnor glared at him now was no help. The exhausted man was driven to silence.

Radnor made no move to calm his horse. The steel titan did not like being interrupted by one of Sigaberht's lackeys. Instead, he silently waited for the guardsman to explain why they had been stopped. The guard leader felt small under Radnor's stare, but after mustering his courage, he finally spoke.

"Veigarand, Earl Sigaberht commands your presence in the throne room. Our enemy arrives soon, and he would include you in the final battle plans."

Radnor nodded and dismounted from Darestr. He then turned to Elena.

"Please... see Sigaberht's physicians."

Elena gently touched his shoulder.

"See you at home," she said.

Radnor took one final, worried glance at Elena as she rode to get treatment before he started off alone towards the keep. He admired her bravery... most people would have been far more concerned about a wound like hers… but somehow it rolled off her like nothing.

Radnor climbed the hill at a pace that far exceeded what other men could accomplish; and realized that despite the fighting he had just done, he still felt surprisingly energetic. He mused on this for a moment, before deciding that the struggle of the recent battles had pushed him to grow stronger than ever before. Satisfied with this thought, Radnor allowed his mind to wander. His thoughts drifted to the guard he had just met, and Radnor realized that he could have been more polite to him. No matter how hostile Radnor's feelings for Sigaberht were, there was little reason for him to take it out on others.

The path Radnor took gradually rose as it followed the slope of the hill around which Wulfgeld was built. At the top of this hill lay Radnor's destination: Sigaberht's keep. The stone tower was a massive, imposing structure that acted as the last line of defense for Wulfgeld's rulers should the city's wall be breached. After a short climb, Radnor reached the end of the path and was met with the burned wreckage of the old palace.

Radnor paused as he silently honored the dead who had fallen defending this place. Radnor also thought of Erelda, and how she had given her life to protect her son. The demigod did not know Sigaberht well, but even he could tell how deeply Erelda's death had affected the earl. There was also their son to consider. Radnor had barely seen anything of Ashveldt since the attack, and he hoped the young man would hold himself together through the coming war. Radnor understood the prince's grief, for his own mother had perished when he was Ashveldt's age. She had been consumed by the fiery wrath of the Krigari war gods whom Radnor would one day destroy. He contemplated on how the young prince must feel, and knew to watch for rash behavior in the coming battles against Drakomar's army. As Radnor stood in contemplation of Wulfgeld's recent sacrifices, an old prayer from his homeland of Amaranthar, also destroyed long ago by the Krigari, came to his lips.

I find myself in sorrow,
For you have fallen this day,
The biting blades of foes,
Have torn your brave soul from you,
May it be that Hymurr,
Our great god of the earth.
Has witnessed your courage,
And carried you to his golden halls.

Once he finished the prayer, Radnor continued his trek to the keep: where the meeting would take place. The tower stood just behind where the palace had been, but thankfully, the stone walls of the keep had resisted the flames that had consumed the palace. Scorch marks were the only sign of the terrible calamity that marked the keep's exterior. Radnor quickly approached the door and passed the guards with a nod as he headed inside. One of the guards followed him through the door and went off to inform Sigaberht of Veigarand's return.

Radnor had quarters reserved for him, and there he could change out of his blood stained armor and into clean clothes. He rarely used them, as he spent most of his time at the cottage Sigaberht had set aside for Elena. What controversy surrounded his and Elena's living under the same roof while still unmarried was kept to hushed whispers and rumors. No one but Sigaberht would dare say anything directly to Radnor about it and expect to survive the conversation, and Sigaberht did not care where Radnor slept, so long as he was available for the earl's needs.

As Radnor navigated the halls and winding stairs that led to his chambers, he noticed the strange looks he got from those that busied themselves about the keep. While the blood and ichor on his armor drew more attention than usual, these people feared him regardless of his level of cleanliness. He was known to them only as a violent and wrathful figure from legend. The gore soaked armor merely highlighted the one trait of his that anyone in the keep cared about: his ability to kill.

Once inside his chambers, Radnor laid his sword and shield against the wall and closed the door. Finally in the privacy of his room, Radnor tore his helmet off and nearly hurled it against the stone wall in frustration. He hated how these people looked at him. At best, the servants treated him with fearful caution. Sigaberht treated him like a wild dog he had muzzled and always used a certain distant, basic politeness that revealed what Sigaberht thought of Radnor. He was a weapon to be maintained or livestock to be fed, nothing more. Sigaberht's disdain for him permeated the halls of the keep, and Radnor hated every second he had to be there.

In his anger, Radnor picked up an old wooden chair and flung it at the bed. Self-restraint caught him at the last second and his throw became a light toss. The chair bounced onto the bed without taking any damage. Radnor noticed this and felt some satisfaction in the realization that his control over his temper had improved. Not that long ago, he would have thrown the chair so forcefully that both it and the bed would have shattered into splinters. This positive change in him was in no small part from Elena's calming influence.

Radnor took a deep breath and finally centered himself so that his temper was better under control. He told himself that he did not care what these irrelevant people thought of him. All that mattered was what Elena and his few friends thought.

After suppressing his anger, Radnor went to the wash basin and scrubbed his face with a clean rag. There was a mirror in the room, and Radnor stopped to look at his reflection. Rage flared in him again, for in that moment, he saw himself as they saw him… a killer. No matter how much he tried to convince himself he didn't, he *did* care what they all thought. He wanted to be accepted as one of them, though this would never be.

It also did not help that he was frequently absent from the city's walls and the people here had not had time to grow accustomed to his presence. Sigaberht had sent him on several multi-day errands that took him away from the city. Early on, he had been a scout sent on the south roads that led to Drakomar. It was he who had first sighted the enemy force that was slowly marching towards Wulfgeld.

Radnor had mixed feelings about his assignments. He didn't like being away from Elena so much, especially when the mysteries of her power weighed so heavily on all their minds. However, he could not stay in Wulfgeld, or in any one place for more than six days at a time. If he stayed anywhere too long, a portal to the Krigari world of Narakim would open, and the evil gods that destroyed his homeland would send their legions of demons to his world and destroy everything he held dear. Radnor was not only a killer, but a cursed man.

The demigod gazed into the mirror and looked upon his blood soaked form. He did not see himself. Instead, he saw the Krigari blood that ran through his veins; the blood that made him the weapon he was. Overwhelmed with spite, he decided not to change clothes. He would instead attend Sigaberht's meeting dressed in his blood-stained armor. If all they saw him as was a killer, then he would go to the earl's court as a killer.

In addition to emotional self-indulgence, Radnor also had a more practical purpose for going as he was. As far as he was concerned, their top priority needed to be the eradication of the monsters in the forest. He wanted Sigaberht to get a taste of what lay in wait in those accursed woods, hoping that would convince the earl of the urgency of the situation. Radnor set the rag down, sat in an old wooden chair, and waited for notice that it was time for the meeting. He did not have to wait long.

* * *

The earl had finally fallen asleep in his bedchamber. Dreams flooded his mind with scattered, incoherent images of dark, foreboding woods. Something evil waited there… but there was something else… something—A soft voice called to him. Then, a shape in the trees beckoned to him; and his fear departed. A thought came to him from the mysterious shape… not a thought… a feeling… a promise… a promise of salvation should he venture into the woods. Sigaberht took a step forward, but the figure waved for him to stop. Not here… elsewhere. In another place… perhaps… perhaps he might find Erelda there, waiting for him?

Sigaberht sat bolt upright as a knock upon the door tore him from his dream's grasp. The guard had come to deliver news of Radnor's return. Still groggy from his hasty awakening, Sigaberht needed to be told twice of Radnor's bloodied condition before the information took. Once the words registered, he started to panic, and it took him a moment to calm down and remind himself that the blood probably wasn't Radnor's.

He then ordered the guard to assemble his ealdormen and officers for the meeting. Once the man departed, Sigaberht took a deep breath and prepared himself for the task at hand. He sent his retainers to fetch the garb he would wear for this meeting and stood to wash his face.

The earl had not had a haircut since the attack and his normally close cut, blonde hair was now long enough that it annoyed him. The retainers returned quite hastily, as they saw his mood and did not want to risk his temper. Sigaberht knew he shouldn't inflict himself on his servants, as they still aided him faithfully as always, but Erelda's calming influence on him was now gone, and he generally struggled to contain himself the way he had before.

He put on his most ornately decorated tunic. It was green, with silver stags embroidered along all the seams. He belted his sword to his waist, secured his silver oath ring around his arm, and finally, placed his crown back upon his head. As he dressed himself, he took the time to mentally prepare for the meeting. He visualized himself seated upon his throne and confidently giving out orders and decrees as need be. This mental practice helped calm him greatly.

Once he was in the proper mindset for a meeting of war, Sigaberht made his way down to the throne room, followed by a small army of retainers and servants. Once inside, the earl's eyes fell upon the empty throne where Erelda should have been sitting. Sadness filled Sigaberht's heart once more. However, there was no time for sorrow, as stoic grace was what he needed to provide for his subjects. As such, he turned his eyes to the great black banners that hung in the hall for inspiration.

Normally, his eyes would have focused on the ornately embroidered, silver wolf's heads emblazoned upon the banners. However, his gaze instead locked on the streaks of wolf's blood now spattered across them. Every drop of blood served as a memorial to those who had fallen in battle against the wolves, and as a warning against the wrath of the men of Wulfgeld. Sorrow was replaced by anger in Sigaberht's heart as he gazed upon the blood-stained banners, and through his anger, he was able make himself give off the appearance of a man steadfast in his resolve. Now that he finally felt prepared to face his vassals, Sigaberht gave the order for his chamberlain to allow the ealdormen and military officers into his throne room.

The ealdormen assembled were all handpicked by Sigaberht, or his late father Earl Godric, to rule in his name over the different shires he owned. Most were warriors of renown, and their loyalty was firm, but not guaranteed. Bringing them together like this was dangerous, for if he made too many mistakes in the coming days, it was possible they would depose him. On top of this problem, the ealdormen each had different, often conflicting personalities that could create trouble and rivalries when the earl needed them to be united in purpose. The shires from which the ealdormen came had not always been subservient to a common ruler, and old grievances still lingered in their minds. The unity they needed to survive the coming war with Drakomar was Sigaberht's responsibility to provide as their lord.

Another question on Sigaberht's mind was how Radnor would fit into the power dynamic. The wandering demigod was not an ealdorman and had no actual station in Sigaberht's court. He also had limited authority in Sigaberht's army. Radnor was considered a specialist, not an actual officer. Sigaberht also knew not only of Radnor's divine parentage, but that he was also the crown prince of Amaranthar, a kingdom in the far north that had been destroyed a decade before. While it may have seemed natural that Radnor's noble standing and unclaimed title should grant him some sort of leadership position, he was too dangerous to be given real power. Additionally, Radnor was also too useful as a weapon to be used as anything *but* a weapon. Sigaberht was thankful he had forced Radnor to take the unholy black oath to him on his oath ring; otherwise betrayal might be more of a concern. But when any disobedience would result in a fiery death, Radnor had little opportunity to attempt any sort of coup, at least not directly.

All of these thoughts, and more, poured through Sigaberht's mind as he watched the ealdormen enter the room.

The first ealdorman to enter was Daegal; a tall, broad shouldered man with a fiery temper he worked to control through rationalism. He was skilled with a spear and an effective negotiator when he kept his temper in check. He could be volatile, but he generally meant well.

Then there was Aethelstan. He was a much shorter man, though still not someone to be underestimated. While his prowess at arms was not at all noteworthy, he was an excellent administrator and politician. He was also arrogant beyond belief, and an ass kisser to the highest degree to those he deemed useful. These traits could come in handy, but were also dangerous if allowed to go unchecked.

There was also Osmund. He was the youngest of the ealdormen, and was not Sigaberht's first choice for the position. Osmund's father, Eorwic had been the true ealdorman of his shire, but he had recently died of old age and his son had taken up the position. Osmund was barely older than Ashveldt and sought to prove himself as a worthy successor to his father. If there had been time, Sigaberht would have considered either replacing him or installing someone more experienced to rule alongside Osmund until he had gained some wisdom. Unfortunately, such a replacement would create unrest among Osmund's people. There was no time to deal with such problems, so Sigaberht had been forced to reluctantly accept him as ealdorman for the time being.

Finally, there was Leif, who, despite the destruction of his own shire, was technically still an ealdorman. The older man stepped forward to stand with Sigaberht atop the royal dais. He was the oldest of the ealdormen and had endured the most hardship. He was a tall man, with sinewy muscle that seemed to stretch in unnaturally long fibers across his body. Leif had always been a fine warrior; and recent events had provided him with many opportunities to prove it. Leif had fought alongside Veigarand through near constant combat over the past two months. He had faced demons, ghouls, wolves, and other horrors that Sigaberht could scarcely imagine. Leif had faced all the same horrors Veigarand had faced, and even though he was but a mortal man, he had survived. He was also an experienced leader, having served as ealdorman of the distant, colony shire of Neugeld before it was destroyed by demons. Leif was loyal almost to a fault, and trusted Sigaberht's motives without question. It was for these reasons Sigaberht had chosen to make Leif the new general of his army.

The earl scanned the room and noted with melancholy that less than half of the military officers that had stood in such meetings a month before stood before him now. He tried not to let his disappointment show, but Leif saw it plainly. Sigaberht also noticed that a mixed group of soldiers and children stood in a line at one end of the room. These people were scouts who had come to report on their findings about the enemy. Sigaberht shook his head to himself as he noticed that there were many more children than adults in the unit. He regretted the necessity of using orphans made by the attack to do the reconnaissance he needed, but most of his scouts had been killed in the wolf attack. Sigaberht only hoped that their adult officers kept close, careful watch over them.

The earl's eyes then turned to the newcomer he was relying on most heavily to win the war for him. Radnor stood off to the side; still wearing his blood covered armor in what Sigaberht assumed was a gesture of spite. The warrior towered over everyone else in the room like a statue of the demigod he was.

Veigarand looks as fearsome as ever; I wonder what he wants, Sigaberht thought.

Veigarand, the Ghost of the North, was a legend among men that most believed was merely a myth. The stories that had traveled across the continent told of a warrior that served as the vengeful spirit of a kingdom now ash. Given everything Sigaberht had seen so far, the legends were not far from reality. Veigarand had cut his way through the wolves like a reaper through wheat, and now wielded a sword forged from chaos itself. Sigaberht had considered taking the sword for himself at one point, but thought better of it. He may not have trusted Radnor fully, but he trusted that sword even less. The earl wisely feared that the blade might somehow turn against him if he tried to seize it.

On further contemplation, Sigaberht decided that he would wait until after their primary discussion was completed before allowing Radnor to bring up his own point. If the petulant warrior wanted to stand there covered in filth just to spite him, then Sigaberht would return the spite and force Radnor to wait as long as possible.

Sigaberht then looked to his son and was surprised to see that Ashveldt was already dressed in full armor. Instead of sitting upon his own throne beside Sigaberht, the young man stood with his spear held across the back of his shoulders, which was an unusually informal posture for the heir of Wulfgeld to take. Sigaberht knew his son well enough to know this was not a good sign. The battle was still two days away, yet Ashveldt came to this meeting dressed for combat. Additionally, Ashveldt's unusually relaxed pose conflicted not only with his attire, but was also unlike his normal, contemplative self. Sigaberht feared Ashveldt's feelings of guilt over his mother's sacrifice would drive him to make reckless decisions as he tried to prove that he would never need saving again, and his presentation today proved to Sigaberht that his fears were valid.

Leif coughed abruptly, which signaled to Sigaberht that he had been lost in thought for too long. This had been happening more and more recently, and was yet another area where Erelda's passing manifested in his life. She had often helped him keep his awareness externalized when his mind wished to withdraw and calculate. Embarrassed by his mental habit, the earl cleared his throat and gestured towards the grim looking people.

"It is a pleasure to see you here in this hall. As we expected, Piarin has sent a small army to test us while he thinks we are weak. Initial estimates from our scouts put the enemy strength at around a thousand fighters. Now that they are closer, do we have any more accurate numbers?"

A short, well-dressed man whom Radnor identified as the captain of the scouts, stepped forward to answer Sigaberht's question.

"Yes, we do, though I believe one of the boys would like to tell you himself."

Sigaberht nodded and watched as a sandy-haired boy of about thirteen years stepped out from the line of scouts assembled in the hall. Sigaberht recognized him as the son of his trusted spy master, Leofric, whom had perished in the battle against the witches.

Radnor did a double take as Rolf stepped forward to speak. The demigod's anger flamed at Sigaberht for using the boy as a scout in so dangerous a manner. Radnor had tried to keep a close eye on Rolf during their travels, especially after Leofric had been killed, but Radnor had been too busy and was away too often to do as good a job as he would have liked. Radnor knew that Rolf had joined the scouts, but had expected him to get more training before being deployed. Now, Radnor fumed at what he saw as a great injustice. He had been a weapon all his life and he never wanted to see another human used in such a manner again.

"What is your name?" Sigaberht asked.

"I am Rolf," the boy replied.

"Yes… now I remember. I am glad to see you well after that horrible night. Your father served me faithfully… and I believe you shall continue that tradition."

"I believe that I already have," Rolf said.

Sigaberht noticed the confidence in the boy's manner and saw the same fierce, steely-eyed look of determination in Rolf's face that he saw in Ashveldt's. If Rolf wished to prove himself, their circumstances would provide plenty of opportunities.

"What information about the enemy force do you have?" Sigaberht asked.

"The enemy advance started very slowly. Apparently they were waiting to rendezvous with another force, and then hastened once they had converged. There are now close to four thousand men in the fighting force. We all counted about two hundred knights with their men at arms by their side." Rolf hesitated and looked back to the scout captain. The scout captain mouthed words to him that Radnor could not quite discern. Rolf then turned back to the earl to repeat what the captain had just told him. "But, with an army this size, we expect that there will be closer to five hundred knights. There also looked to be a corps of around a three or four hundred archers among them."

"How about siege equipment?" Sigaberht asked.

"There were men carrying what looked like pieces of a ram, plus what might have been protective coverings for it. There were a number of other large wooden pieces, and a few wagons carrying large rocks."

"That sounds like trebuchets," Leif added.

Sigaberht nodded and then continued his questions.

"How many different coats of arms did you see?"

"I spotted about thirty, but other scouts saw ones I didn't, and all together we saw two hundred and twenty seven different coats of arms."

Sigaberht leaned back in his throne, impressed at Rolf's confidence and memory.

"Did you recognize any of them? It could be useful to know exactly which of Piarin's knights are in the field."

Rolf shook his head.

"Forgive me my lord. I have not yet been fully schooled in the heraldry of our enemy. I am new to scouting."

Sigaberht waved his hand.

"You do not need to apologize. You have done me a great service. We will learn which knights are present when we loot their corpses."

Before he could continue, Rolf gestured for another boy to step forward. He was about Rolf's age, with brown eyes and hair that matched. He looked extremely nervous and clearly did not want to speak. Rolf recognized his friend's nervousness and leaned in to whisper in his ear.

"Go on, tell him what you saw," Rolf said.

The boy shook his head.

"No! You do it," said the nervous boy.

Rolf rolled his eyes and turned back to Sigaberht.

"This is my friend, Halig. He saw something the rest of us missed."

Sigaberht leaned forward and gave Halig a reassuring smile.

"Come forward, Halig. If Rolf says you saw something, I would very much like to hear it. Nothing will sound foolish to my ears."

Halig stepped closer to Sigaberht and made his statement in a quiet, stammering voice.

"My lord, there was another coat of arms… and banners too… they didn't show any of the coats of arms of any one knight, and not Drakomar's royal arms either. It was black… with a white circle… and some stars."

Sigaberht looked back to the scout captain; a look of concern now drawn upon his face.

"Can you confirm this?"

The captain nodded.

"My men spotted it too. About half of the enemy soldiers bore this banner: sable on an argent moon, below stars trinity."

"A silver full moon underneath three stars!" one of the children nervously blurted from the crowd.

Sigaberht peered past the men in front of him and spotted the source of the outburst. It was a little girl, no older than five, who now shielded herself from his gaze as she realized the error of her interruption.

"Thank you very much, Gilda," the scout captain said, embarrassed by the girl's undisciplined outburst. He did not need to worry, as Gilda's interruption had brought a moment of much needed levity to the mood in the hall.

Sigaberht nodded at Halig, whom sheepishly rejoined his companions in response. The earl then gestured out with his arm as he addressed his men.

"It appears that Piarin has brought a real army to our gates. Not only does he send his regular forces, he has also dispatched the Order of the Pale Light to destroy us."

A frightened murmur ran through the crowd. The Order of the Pale Light was known as an itinerant religious order of knights that wandered across the Southworld. They led crusades against those they deemed to be living "unholy" lives. These knights were fanatics fiercely loyal only to the head of their order and to the goddess Celestata. She was the goddess of love and the moon, and the daughter of Caelum. The Order of the Pale Light also had a reputation for being unperturbed by casualties in battle. The strength of their convictions also led to a tendency for usurpation of thrones that led many southern kings to deny them havens within their kingdoms, which in turn inflamed the Pale Light to even greater brutality during their holy wars. If Piarin had come to an accord with the Pale Light, this meant that there might soon be a massive upending of power in the Southworld with far reaching implications even Sigaberht could not foresee.

Sigaberht turned to one of his officers.

"Have you done as I commanded?" Sigaberht asked.

"Yes, my lord. The bodies of many wolves now line the road on the way to our gates. The enemy will certainly see their mangled corpses and know our fury."

"Good," Sigaberht says. "Let them see the gruesome fate that awaits them here."

Ealdorman Daegal spoke next.

"My lord, given the foes we face, and their superior numbers… perhaps it is best if we pay them to leave."

Sigaberht's blood boiled at the cowardly counsel he had just heard, but before he could respond, Ealdorman Aethelstan made his opinion on the idea known.

"And what would we pay them with? Do we pay them with silver? Do we pay them with crops? Or land perhaps? Whose land should we give them? Whose crops should we give them? Perhaps we should give them yours? If it truly is the Pale Light that comes for us, such bribes will hold little appeal to them."

Daegal took a deep breath and did his best to keep calm under this ridicule.

"I know what you are thinking, and it is not cowardice that brings these thoughts to my mind. It is simply numbers. Wulfgeld lost too many soldiers fighting those horrid witches. If our allies in the north do come to our aid, they will arrive too late. There has not been time to hire mercenaries to bolster our forces—"

"But we have brought our own soldiers to the aid of Wulfgeld. Our numbers are more than sufficient to throw the enemy back!" Aethelstan declared.

"We have the numbers, but not the equipment," retorted Daegal. "They have five hundred knights… *and* their professional men at arms. More than two thirds of their army will be equipped with heavy armor and strong swords and axes made for slaying men. Most of the people we brought are militia, not professional soldiers. They bring woodcutting axes and hunting spears to war. How many of your men have armor? I've issued my soldiers as much extra equipment as I could, and still only my huscarls have more than light armor."

"I for one, stand with Aethelstan!" shouted Osmund. "Better to die fighting than groveling for your life!"

"You stay out of this!" Daegal shouted back. He lost his temper as he was insulted by the other ealdorman. "You will gain the right to criticize me when you've earned a scar or two!"

"Enough!" Sigaberht yelled, rising to his feet as he did. "We will not yield to our enemy. If we buy them off now, they will keep coming back until they have taken the very shirts off our backs. What will we do then? No… we must destroy the enemy here and now if we are to survive another day!"

The earl resumed his seat at his throne. Daegal obeyed his lord's command and stayed silent, though it chafed him to do so. Sigaberht continued.

"How many men do we have?"

Leif stepped away from Sigaberht's side to answer.

"We have close to two and a half thousand men. Two hundred are your personal huscarls, with another six hundred soldiers and militia of Wulfgeld. The other ealdorman have brought a total of three hundred huscarls, and fourteen hundred militia."

Sigaberht nodded as he processed what he was hearing. Despite his anger at Daegal's cowardice, the ealdorman was not entirely wrong. They were not only outnumbered, but also out equipped. However, Sigaberht had been in similar situations before… and had triumphed. In an effort to keep the meeting productive, Sigaberht spoke again.

"Now then, if we are to win this battle, we must eliminate their siege engines. What do we have that can destroy the ram?"

"Nothing right now," Leif replied. "The weapons we had that might have countered the ram were in one of the storage buildings that burned down when the wolves attacked. We can possible pour boiling oil on it, but if it's protected by a proper covering… I don't think we can be sure of destroying it."

"Leave the ram to me," Radnor interjected. His icy voice chilled the hearts of everyone in the room, and they all turned to face his menacing form.

"Do you have a plan on how to do that?" Aethelstan asked.

"I have an idea, but I need to see our defenses… and the ram, to be sure it'll work." Radnor said.

"If you're confident, we will trust your judgment," Sigaberht said in an effort to cut off further argument. "It has been made clear that we are outnumbered, and while Veigarand may have a solution to the ram, bombardment from their trebuchets will sow chaos in the streets. We must also defend the wall, and we must break their morale if we are to break the siege. How do we target their morale?"

"We need to kill as many of their knights as possible," Radnor said.

"Oh, thank you, why didn't we think of that!" Aethelstan chided.

Radnor turned his fiery eyes on Aethelstan.

"On second thought, perhaps we could break their morale by having you switch to their side. You're always so helpful!"

Aethelstan took a step toward Radnor in anger, and then remembered who it was he was speaking to. Radnor continued to address Sigaberht and glared at Aethelstan while he did.

"If we kill their knights, their men-at-arms will flee."

"Yes, but the Pale Light will not flee from a battle lightly. How will killing their knights be a particular blow to their morale?" Sigaberht asked.

"I have an idea about how to draw them off, but for it to work; we must beat back the initial attack. We want to make them think this will be an extended siege."

"What makes you so sure it won't be?" Aethelstan asked.

"Because as Daegal said, we don't have the equipment we need to keep their siege engines from battering down the walls, nor do we have the weapons we need to hold the city should the wall be breached. We need to act decisively in the early stages of the battle, or the city will be lost."

"That's what you think," Aethelstan needled. "But we have beaten the enemy back before, and we shall do so again!"

Sigaberht nodded.

"You are right Aethelstan, but Veigarand does have a point, we need more than just high spirits to defeat the enemy."

"I do agree your grace!" Aethelstan replied. He then turned to Radnor. "But we still don't have a plan, now do we? How are we to kill their knights as easily as he makes it sound?"

Radnor stepped forward and turned his back on Aethelstan and faced only Sigaberht as he gave his answer.

"We ride out against them, threaten their trebuchets and force them to chase us away. If they pursue us we can string them out and overwhelm small groups of them at a time. If they try to fall back to their own lines, we move in and harass them again."

"That's too risky!" Aethelstan exclaimed. "One mistake and everyone you take with you would be killed!"

While Osmund started making his own hotheaded objections, a plan began to form in Sigaberht's mind. He was not sure he liked it, but he did not see any other choice. The earl decided that now was the time to bring up Radnor's bloodstained appearance.

"Veigarand, I see you come into this court wearing armor covered in blood. I have chosen to ignore it until now, but my curiosity can no longer be abated. What news do you bring back from your errand?"

All eyes turned to Radnor.

"My lord, as instructed, Elena and I traveled to the corrupted forest. Once we were deep inside, we found stiff resistance. Monsters came at us from all directions, and the very earth attempted to devour me."

Gasps echoed through the room, though Sigaberht listened silently. At first, this report disturbed him. He had futilely hoped that the remnants of the evil the witches had unleashed would just fade away on their own. However, the longer he thought about it, the more he found himself strangely glad that the chaos was not gone.

"What of Elena?" he asked. "Do her powers still harm these creatures?"

"Yes, my lord."

Sigaberht's heart raced as he grew more excited at the possibility of his plan's success. He thought of his dream… of the salvation promised within. Had it been a vision of the future? Did Caelum himself offer a guiding hand in his time of need? Sigaberht wished to consult with the priests… but they had all been killed when the wolves attacked. He had to be his own spiritual guide. The earl forced himself to remain calm. He needed to know more before he leapt to any plan of action.

"Was it her powers that allowed you to escape?" Sigaberht eagerly probed.

Radnor hesitated. He could see where this was going. If his will was still his own, he might have tried to lie to Sigaberht, but that damned black oath prevented it!

"Yes. She was able to slay the beasts even more effectively than I could. But… we were ultimately overwhelmed. She was barely able to place a barrier that hindered the fiends long enough for us to escape."

Both fear and elation clutched at Sigaberht's heart. His plan could work! But there was great risk to everyone involved in carrying it out. Radnor spoke again to dissuade him from the plan he saw forming in Sigaberht's mind, but it was too late. The earl had already made his decision.

"My lord, if I may, her powers are effective. But—"

"Veigarand, there is no time for second guesses. We need a plan of action, and I believe we have one now. Once we repel the initial assault, we will go with your plan, but with a twist. As our own ealdormen have pointed out, we are too few in number and too low on equipment to rely on our own ability to kill the enemy. So, we will lead them into the corrupted forest. The monsters that dwell within will do the killing for us."

More gasps of fear leapt across the hall, though Radnor was the first to object directly.

"My lord, how are we to prevent those monsters from killing our own people as well as theirs?"

"Simple. We bring Elena," Sigaberht replied with far more confidence than he actually felt.

Radnor felt his temper rise in his throat. Sigaberht was just going to use Elena like a weapon! The demigod felt an overwhelming need to strike the earl down right then and there, black oath be damned! But he knew he couldn't, so it was up to him to try to talk sense into Sigaberht.

"My lord, I know we are desperate, but Elena's powers are still unknown. She is powerful, yes, but she still cannot control her abilities. It's not as simple as just putting her in the area. We simply don't know enough to try something like this, not yet. It would also behoove you to know that Elena was hurt in the fighting. She may not be recovered in time to help us in the battle."

Sigaberht's hopes sank at the news.

"Where is she now?"

"I sent her to see your physicians, though now that I know your plans for her, I'm regretting that I did."

"I see why you have no rank here, you impetuous twerp," muttered Aethelstan. Radnor ignored the comment, as at least in his mind, Aethelstan was beneath his notice. Sigaberht shot the ealdorman a stern look, and then addressed Radnor again.

"Veigarand, what choice do I have?"

Radnor could only glare at Sigaberht.

"I think it is a sound plan," Aethelstan added.

It was Daegal's turn to give a rude look to Aethelstan, who turned back and gave an inquisitive glance at Daegal before speaking.

"What is it now, Daegal? Don't tell me you side with … *him*?" Aethelstan said.

"I don't side with anyone," Daegal said. "I was just checking to see if any shit was stuck to your mouth."

Aethelstan's hand went to his sword, but he did not draw it. Leif took a step forward, ready to break up the possible duel at a moment's notice. Radnor stepped back and watched, ready to see who would win a fight between the two ealdormen. Osmund stepped forward and stood alongside Aethelstan.

"Would you try to best the both of us Daegal?" Osmund asked.

"I would do so here and now, t'were it not for our earl's need of us," Daegal growled.

"Daegal! That's enough! Control your temper, or I shall have you removed from my hall! Is that understood?" Sigaberht yelled.

Daegal turned to his lord and bowed. The man resolved right then and there that he was not going to say another word for the rest of the meeting. As far as Daegal cared, Sigaberht could hang himself with these two idiots! It seemed to the angry ealdorman that Veigarand was the only one there with any sanity.

Aethelstan gave Daegal a rude look and withdrew his hand from his sword. Now that the situation had deescalated, Radnor continued trying to reason with Sigaberht.

"There is another problem. The trip to the corrupted forest is not just a quick gallop. What would make the enemy pursue us that far from the city?"

Radnor's words had barely been uttered when Ashveldt spoke for the first time in the meeting.

"I will go! The enemy would pursue the heir to the throne!"

Sigaberht panicked. He could not allow his son to so rashly throw himself into harm's way!

"No, Ashveldt! I appreciate your bravery, but you are needed here. Wulfgeld must have an earl, and you are to be that earl should anything happen to me. No, I shall go instead. Piarin's knights will be scrambling over each other for the glory and reward of being the one who captures or kills me."

Sigaberht turned his attention to Radnor.

"Whatever you may think of me, I hope you notice that I am subjecting myself to the same danger that I would Elena."

Radnor nodded, though it was not much comfort to know that the earl was so pleased to demonstrate that he was suicidal.

"Are there any further objections to this course of action?" Sigaberht asked.

Seeing that there were none, the earl rose and gestured to his soldiers.

"Gentlemen, you know what you must do. Assemble your men… and prepare for battle."

Everyone in the room bowed and turned to depart. Rolf tried to greet Radnor, but was quickly rushed away by Halig and the scout captain. He would have to talk to his friend later. Sigaberht descended from the royal dais and took Radnor by the shoulder.

"You turned the tide when the witches came… do you think you can turn the tide again?"

"You call me 'Veigarand', a name that carries with it fear and dread. Do you think that dread is unearned? Besides…" Radnor partially unsheathed his sword to reveal its black, blasphemous blade. "Any man who sees this sword and does not flee is either a fool or a madman."

Sigaberht smiled at Radnor's bravado and turned to rejoin his son.

Father and son left the throne room together with their retainers not far behind. After a few steps, Sigaberht turned and waved them off, as he wanted to speak with Ashveldt alone. Once Sigaberht was sure the retainers were out of earshot, he spoke to Ashveldt.

"My son, you were very quiet in the meeting today. What do you think of what transpired?"

Ashveldt walked in silence as he organized his thoughts. Finally, he made his reply.

"Tensions are high. All of them are scared… and showing it in their own way."

Ashveldt trailed off, unsure of how much of his opinion to share with his father. Sigaberht saw his hesitancy and egged him on.

"Good! I need your insight, especially now… with your mother gone."

Silence fell between them for a long time as both felt the pain of their shared grief. Finally, Ashveldt resumed speaking.

"Daegal's temper is shorter than ever, Osmund seeks to throw himself into whatever danger he can find, and Aethelstan is trying too hard to please you."

"What did you think of Leif's actions today?" Sigaberht asked.

"I do not know him as well as the others. He was very quiet in the meeting, only speaking to answer military questions."

"Yes, and I can tell you why. He does not feel fit to speak amongst the other ealdormen. He is not of noble birth as the others are. He was overjoyed when I made him ealdorman, and has taken the loss of Neugeld very personally. As such, he is limiting himself only to acting in the role as a general."

"Then why did *he* not come up with another plan?"

"You mean a plan better than mine?"

Ashveldt paused in discomfort upon his father's challenge. However, the prince knew this issue was too important to let fall to the side, so he returned the chiding from his father.

"Yes, I do mean that. I agree with Radnor. Your plan is too risky and relies on too many uncontrollable elements coming together perfectly."

Sigaberht took a moment to think. He noticed that Ashveldt had referred to the demigod as "Radnor" and not "Veigarand". Ashveldt formed attachments more easily than Sigaberht did. This was a trait the young man had inherited from Erelda and Sigaberht still did not know if this was a strength he should encourage his son to pursue, or a weakness he should stamp out before it was too late. Sigaberht decided to let it slide and continued with the conversation.

"What would you have me do?" the earl asked.

Ashveldt hesitated again, still uncomfortable with criticizing his father directly. Sigaberht pressed him further.

"Ashveldt, I need you to be honest with me. I do not wear my grief as publicly as you do, but my heart has been rent asunder by your mother's passing. My judgment may not be as sound as it was before."

Ashveldt looked into his father's eyes and saw not the earl, but a man in need of help.

"I personally... would have sided with Daegal's plan."

Sigaberht was shocked that his son would suggest taking the coward's way out. Ashveldt saw the harsh look on his father's face and hastily continued.

"I don't think Daegal meant for it to be a long term solution. I think his complete plan was to buy them off for now, and then hit them hard when our forces are replenished. We could hire mercenaries and enlist the aid of our allies in Ranrike and Wollendan. If given enough time, we could have an army so large we could take Drakomar by force!" Sigaberht's heart swelled with pride at his son's thinking and listened as his son continued. "There's something else... but I know you won't like it. We should give them the gaulderens."

Sigaberht blanched, surprised at his son's words.

"Ashveldt... who would we give them to?"

"You know who. There's only one person here who might be able to use them," he said.

"If we give them to Elena... Veigarand will have them too, and we cannot allow him to have even more weapons at his disposal."

"I understand father. But... you still fear his betrayal? Even after the oath he took?"

"I fear he may betray us through alternate means. He may use others as proxies."

"Father... I think you know as well as I that Radnor is a killer... but he is not a snake. He is a bear."

"I have caged the bear, and the bear does not like it," Sigaberht replied.

Despite the fact that Ashveldt disagreed with his father, he still understood Sigaberht's thinking and accepted it for the time being. He nodded to indicate his admission of defeat on this topic, to which Sigaberht smiled and replied.

"Thank you for the debate. I appreciate your honesty. Now tell me, was I too harsh on Daegal?"

Ashveldt nodded.

"I'm sorry to say… yes, I think you were. Everyone jumped on him before he could finish his thought and the conversation got away from him after that. You and I say things we don't mean when we get angry, but he doesn't say anything at all when he gets angry."

"You're right," Sigaberht said. "The way I spoke to him today was unfair and will breed resentment. I will speak to him before tomorrow and offer an apology."

He then took his son in a close embrace.

"Take your armor off. You need to calm yourself and find your right mind before the enemy arrives."

Ashveldt simply smiled at his father and returned the man's loving embrace.

* * *

As the scouts headed back to their lodgings, Halig, upset that Rolf had pushed him forward, finally worked up the courage to confront his friend.

"Rolf, why did you do that?" he asked.

"Do what?" Rolf asked.

Halig almost punched him, but kept his frustration in check.

"You made me go up and talk… in front of all those people!"

"So?" Rolf asked.

"I didn't want to."

"Why not? Now the earl knows your name! He will remember that you were the one who saw the enemy, *you* told him about it. Think: he'll remember that, and he will have more tasks for you, and if you do them well, he will reward you!"

Halig shrugged.

"But I didn't want to talk. It was so… I didn't like it. Why couldn't *you* have done it?"

"Because then *I'd* be the one who told the earl, and he'd remember me instead, and *I'd* get the reward, not *you*. That wouldn't be fair, since you saw them. And you're my friend, I just want what's best for you."

"I guess…"

Halig trailed off. The boys walked in silence for a while, and then Halig continued. "But, I still didn't want to talk in front of all those people. I didn't want everyone to look at me, but you made me do it when I didn't want to."

Rolf rolled his eyes. He tried to think of what Radnor would say.

"Halig, the road we walk is mean, and full of pain. We both are going to have to do things we don't want to if we're going to live. Someone else would have stolen your glory without a second thought. You have to be willing to kill anyone who gets in your way to get what you need to survive."

Halig shrugged again and fell silent. He didn't like arguing with anyone, let alone Rolf. Rolf was strong, forceful, and always seemed very confident of what he said. Halig wished he could be like Rolf, but he just wasn't as strong as the older boy.

Rolf saw that Halig had turned inward and interrupted his thoughts.

"Listen… I like you. You're very kind, but you have to learn when to be mean, or someone is going to hurt you."

Halig nodded.

"Like our parents," he said.

"Exactly," Rolf said. "Now come on, I'll race you to the next lamp post!"

Halig smiled, and then took off without another word.

Chapter 3

The sorcerer leaned against the taffrail of the lightly rolling ship, gazed upon the ominous storm clouds as they gathered in the distance… and cursed. Sailing had never been one of his preferred activities and the vicious weather on the horizon told him he would soon enjoy it even less. A storm was fast approaching and much to the sorcerer's frustration, not even his power could prevent it.

It had been five days since he had departed from his home on the Glimmering Isles, and four days since he had bought passage on a merchant vessel traveling to the continent. The sorcerer had journeyed with a great haste only mitigated by his desire for secrecy. However, maintaining this secrecy proved difficult, as the people local to the Glimmering Isles had very dark skin and hair, so a man with his pale skin and red hair automatically drew attention. While it was unlikely that anyone had cared to notice him beyond his superficial features, the sorcerer had traveled under an assumed name in order to quell curiosity and suspicion regarding his identity. To that end, he chose a name common to one of the continental peoples with whom the islanders frequently traded with. The men from the Glimmering Isles called this land "Ardiwa", but the people who lived on the continent broadly referred to their homelands as "The Southworld". The fact that they called it this when they resided north of the Glimmering Isles amused Dragorim greatly. There were several different cultural groups that lived along the coastline of the Southworld, but only ones who lived farther north tended to look the way he did, so the sorcerer had chosen to use one of those peoples' names: "Dragorim".

Once aboard the ship, the sorcerer had received some very odd glances from some of the ship's crew and fellow passengers, but after a few days, these glances ceased. Otherwise, most of those on board left him alone. This was to his preference, and he encouraged it by presenting a grim demeanor that helped him stay undisturbed.

The ship was large, even for a cog such as this. The owner had asked a hefty price for passage, but it had been worth every penny. The ship was sturdily built, and had tall sails that caught the wind with ease. The deck was spacious, and its vast cargo hold was filled to the brim with the finest wines produced in the Glimmering Isles.

Given their immense value, these wines were kept under strict guard. Unfortunately, the stingy wine merchant did not pay the guards well enough to ensure their loyalty; and as punishment for their low wages, these men "sampled" their fair share of wine as part of the compensation they felt they deserved. One of these guards was a man named "Farim". He was a kinder man than most the sorcerer had met in his lifetime. Farim came from a poor family and only took the job as a guard aboard the ship as a way to secure passage to the continent. Farim planned on abandoning his post on the ship once they made landfall. He hoped to find a better way to make a living in the Southworld than by keeping fine drink from the poor.

In addition to their low wages, the meals supplied to the guards were meager at best. As the days passed, Dragorim's loneliness slowly overcame his desire for solitude and the sorcerer found that he was happy to share his own meticulously prepared food with the guards. Farim and his fellows were most grateful for Dragorim's generosity. In exchange for Dragorim's sharing the food he had brought, Farim allowed the the sorcerer to fill his goblet with the fine wines they were supposed to be guarding.

At one point, the young man expressed his sorrow that he had nothing else with which to repay the sorcerer. Upon hearing Farim's lament, Dragorim had simply replied: "No one should go hungry." Thus, while most had left Dragorim to his solitude, the sorcerer had found companionship during his mealtimes where he could listen to discussions of current events. Dragorim attempted to question the guards for information about the region just north of the Morakors Mountains, as this was all he knew of where he needed to go. The guards told him of the existence of a city called

"Wulfgeld". He in turn asked them about it, as he hoped to learn as much as he could about his destination before arriving. Unfortunately, the guards had barely heard of Wulfgeld and had little information to offer. After he finally accepted that further questioning would prove useless, Dragorim had silently listened to the guard's discussions of their own lives as he drank in both wine and company.

The journey had progressed in this relaxed manner for several days. But now, Farim nervously stood beside Dragorim as he fumed at the approaching storm. Dragorim's anger was not helped by the fact that *he* was the cause of it. In the sorcerer's haste to make landfall on the continent, he had used the stored energy from a gaulderen to help him cast a powerful spell that changed ocean's current so that it sent the sailing vessel along at a pace far faster than it could have ever achieved on wind alone. The spell required so much energy that even with the help of the gaulderen, casting it caused Dragorim to be confined to sleeping in his hammock for an entire day. While this unnatural increase in speed had initially alarmed the crew, they did not seem to be too bothered by it once they realized this would save them both time and money. They rationalized it as a blessing from their god and did not examine the matter further.

However, it seemed that the change in the ocean currents had been extreme enough that it had caused a storm to appear, and the ship's course took them straight through it. Dragorim looked across the deck of the ship and watched the other passengers pray to an old sea god named "Sagonor". It was not a name Dragorim recognized, though he considered the possibility that this was a new name for the same old sea god from the last time he had passed this way. While the passengers prayed to their god, the crew frantically ran across the deck as they desperately tried to prepare the ship for the first buffeting waves of the storm.

After a short while spent staring at the angry waters, Dragorim decided it was best to go below, settle in, and wait out the storm. As he did, the first drops of rain began striking the deck and the wind howled in rage. Waves buffeted the sides of the ship and the sorcerer's anger at himself intensified as he stomped over to his hammock in the cargo hold. He had come too far and waited too long for an opportunity like the one before him to be simply drowned at sea. Dragorim considered undoing the spell that altered the ocean currents, but time was of the essence, and if he did not arrive at Wulfgeld swiftly enough to claim the power that waited for him, well then he might as well drown.

Hours passed, and the storm's intensity seemed to be ever increasing. Many people cowered in fear within the cargo hold and desperately prayed to their gods for salvation. Even Dragorim's nerves gradually started to come undone as the ship tossed and turned in the heaving waters. Farim eventually came below and updated him on the situation.

"The storm is getting worse," he said, stating the obvious in a panicked tone. "The waves are… the waves hitting us are the biggest I've ever seen. I fear we may be swamped and capsized… and our bodies left as but food for the fish."

Dragorim shook his head and issued a reply he hoped would dispel Farim's fear as well as his own.

"I do not believe so, my friend. We have shared too many meals together for us to merely become food ourselves."

Momentarily satisfied with his platitude, the sorcerer settled back into his hammock and quietly hummed a tune that helped calm his nerves. Overcome by curiosity, Farim sat on one of the wine barrels and listened intently. Finally, he asked about the song.

"I must beg you to tell me: What tune are you humming? I don't recognize it."

Dragorim laughed.

"It is an old tune… perhaps older than all others heard by mortal ears. Would you like to hear the lyrics?"

Farim nodded emphatically. Dragorim smiled, took a deep breath, and sang a lilting song of his people. The beat was based on groups of three, and almost seemed in rhythm with the ship's steady rocking. As Dragorim sang, the drum of the pounding rain and the roaring of the wind seemed to soften as though they too were eager to hear the passion of his music. Each time he sang the refrain, his mood became more deliberate and forceful; as though he was not singing a song, but swearing an oath. Dragorim's words carried through the air with unearthly force, and it was then that Farim wondered who this mysterious man *truly* was. Dragorim became lost in his music, and he sang so passionately that other people frightened by the storm gathered to listen to the power of his words.

Oh, my fair darling! My darling love!
I would come back to you, back to your arms!
But alas, my road is endless, my task eternal!
But I fear no harm!
For my wrath is infernal!

I swear to you, before ancient gods,
I shall return to you, my darling light,
I shall save our people, our people's old dream,
I shall cure our plight,
Those who impede me, fear my might!

I will find a way, a way beyond,
A way to lift the curse that haunts us so!
The curse that portends our downfall may be broken!
I wish you could know,
Of what I have spoken!

I swear to you, before ancient gods,
I shall return to you, my darling light,
I shall save our people, our people's old dream,
I shall cure our plight,
Those who impede me, fear my might!

For as I return home, to my love,
The way is shut, closed to my hurried flight,
I cannot rejoin you, cannot come to your embrace,

Dragorim looked to the crowd now assembled before him. All of the passengers had gathered to hear his song. The singing sorcerer blazed with a terrible fury that filled the crowd with dread, though it was not them who brought his rage. Ancient memories flooded his mind and his passion increased a hundredfold as he sang the final refrain.

I swear to you, before ancient gods,
I shall return to you, my darling light,
I shall save our people, our people's old dream,
I shall cure our plight,
All who oppose me, I shall smite!

Dragorim finished his song with such ferocity that even Farim recoiled from him in fear. The sorcerer's awareness of the world around him returned, and he looked up to see the awed expressions on the faces of those who surrounded him. It seemed that even the raging storm had quieted from the power of his wrathful tune. However, this silence was not to last. The strength of his words faded from the air and the timbers of the ship resumed creaking and groaning as waves crashed against the hull once more. The power of this hurricane was unnaturally potent, and Dragorim began to suspect there was more to the storm's origin than he had guessed. With the fearful passengers close behind, the sorcerer climbed the stairs and stepped back out onto the deck; where even he was amazed at what he saw.

Crewmen dashed across the deck as they frantically struggled against the crashing waves of the merciless ocean. Black clouds blotted out the sun and the rain that pelted the sorcerer's face was so hot it nearly scalded him. Dragorim then realized he had been mistaken; his spell had not caused this storm. Instead, even more unnatural forces were at play here. Red lightning streaked across the sky and triggered an old memory. Dragorim hastily withdrew a gaulderen from his pouch, and aimed it carefully. Once he spotted his submerged target, the sorcerer cast the gaulderen into the water and watched as a bolt of white lightning struck where it had landed. The water flashed with white light as it instantly boiled… then more bubbles appeared just before a titanic shape slowly rose from the ocean depths.

At first the great shape was difficult to make out in the shadow of the sunless day, but it was not long before the immense size of the creature became apparent and the screams of men pierced through the howling wind.

Finally, the leviathan rose to its full height. It was a massive, scaly creature that stood as high above the water as the ship was long. The monster was humanoid in shape, though its face was amphibious in nature, with many long, sharp teeth that protruded menacingly from the creature's open mouth. Its massive arms ended in webbed, clawed hands.

"Sagonor!" cried the men on the deck. Many prostrated themselves before the creature they worshiped as a god, but Dragorim stood his ground, for he knew full well what manner of being he faced. The sorcerer gave no sign of supplication and instead shouted up at the towering leviathan from his place on the ship.

"You! I assume you are the one to blame for this storm that assaults my ship?"

The giant monster turned its glaring eyes down upon the impudent sorcerer. As the two beings locked eyes, words echoed in Dragorim's mind with such force that they drove him to his knees.

"I forged this storm because of what was done by *your* hand. Why have you brought destruction upon the creatures of the sea? You changed the flow of the ocean… and the force of your change has torn a path of destruction through my home. Why have you done this? Answer!"

Sorrow ran through Dragorim's heart. He had not intended to harm anyone with his spell. He had not considered what changing the currents so drastically would do *under* the water. As his eyes remained locked with the sea god's, Dragorim saw visions of destruction and death under the sea… of the cataclysm *he* had wrought. They reminded him of fears and nightmares he had long held secret from all who knew him. Grief crashed into his soul, and Dragorim knew that there was no undoing what he had done to those who dwelt below.

However, even as the echoes of the dead flew through Dragorim's mind, his sorrow quickly transformed into steely determination. His own fears gave validation to his decision despite the consequences that were now laid bare to him. No matter how much remorse he felt, Dragorim knew that he had no choice. He could not fail his quest, no matter how many lives it cost. *Everything* depended on his success! By sheer force of will, Dragorim overcame the pain and grief that the sea god drilled into his mind and rose to his feet. The sorcerer looked up at Sagonor defiantly and made his answer.

"I am on a quest of grave importance. I cast my spell to hasten my journey across the sea so that I might reach my destination before *all* is lost."

The leviathan let out a cry of rage that sent men to their knees in frantic prayer. With a flash of movement, the creature brought its crashing fist down upon the wooden deck of the ship as it aimed to smash the sorcerer where he stood. A sphere of golden light enveloped Dragorim as he hastily raised a magical barrier that absorbed the power of Sagonor's blow. As Dragorim did this, he felt the energy from the god's attack flow into and around his very soul. In this moment, he was connected to his foe's own strength. Using an ancient technique of which few sorcerers or gods were even aware, Dragorim joined his own soul with the attacking energy and redirected it back into Sagonor's arm. The creature's hand was forced back off the ship with tremendous force that nearly knocked the beast from his feet. In response to this miraculous sight, the crew let out rejoicing cries as their lives were for the moment, spared. Upon experiencing effective resistance from a mortal for the first time in its long existence, the sea god's final angry statement whipped through the minds of all aboard the ship.

"You have slaughtered my people so that you might hasten your journey? You humans have always been the same! You bring death to all around you merely to make your lives more convenient! My children and I shall have our revenge!"

Even as Sagonor's words echoed through the human's minds, black shapes stealthily climbed onto the deck. These shapes were virtually undetectable in the dim light and the crew did not see them until it was too late. These creatures were men from the sea; monsters with scales, teeth, and claws. They lashed out against every man on the deck in nearly perfect unison. The monsters let out terrible cries as their fangs and claws found the flesh of their victims. The crew swiftly retaliated and a bloody battle commenced upon the deck of the doomed ship.

Knowing the sea god could not attack without risking killing his own people, Dragorim ran to help the guards battle the monsters from the deep. The humans were hopelessly outmatched by the creatures and despite their gallant efforts, were being slaughtered. Dragorim drew his own sword in one hand and a gaulderen in the other. He scraped the gaulderen along the sword's length and the blade erupted in sparks. The power of the lightning now coursed through the blade, ready to deal death among those who stood against him.

Dragorim steeled himself against the knowledge that more killing would be necessary today. He had not wanted any of this to happen, but these beings were now an obstacle he needed to remove from his path and the only way he could do that was by destroying them. With that thought in mind, he strode into battle, and his lightning-imbued blade cast death wherever he went. The beasts were unprepared for the ferocity the sorcerer brought to bear as he cut them down with ease. The steel sword by itself would have had difficulty penetrating their armored scales but the enchanted blade tore through them effortlessly. Dragorim's light footwork and dancing sword revealed to all that his martial prowess equaled his power as a sorcerer, and all who tried to challenge him met a swift demise at the end of his biting blade.

As Dragorim cut down the monsters in front of him, one foe tried to ambush him from behind. One blow from the monster's fearsome claws would end his life right then and there. But just as the beast was about to deliver the deadly blow, Farim came to Dragorim's rescue and drove the blade of his ax into the creature's back. The monster let out a desperate howl as the ax bit deeply into the soft flesh between its scales. Enraged by this attack, the creature spun and ripped the ax from Farim's grasp. Farim's eyes widened in fear as the creature pounced upon him and bit deep into his throat. Blood poured from the wound as the young man screamed in agony. Dragorim rushed to Farim's aid but he was too late. All he could do was avenge his newfound friend, an act he performed most brutally as he cut the monster to pieces.

Seeing the carnage wrought by Dragorim, the surviving creatures backed away from him in fear and retreated into the water. Many men lay dead, their corpses strewn across the deck of the ship, but thanks to Dragorim, just as many of the monsters from the deep had also been slain. A hellish, overpowering roar turned Dragorim's attention back to the god that assaulted their ship.

Wasting no time, the sorcerer drew his hand back and summoned a ball of fire that burned so brightly that it nearly blinded all that stood upon the deck of the ship. Terrible shrieks echoed through the air as both men and monsters felt the scorching heat of the flame. Dragorim gritted his teeth from the exertion and cast the spell towards the ocean god. The scorching fire flew with the speed of an arrow and struck the leviathan square in the chest.

Sagonor roared in agony and stumbled as the pain from the burning wound ripped its senses apart. Dragorim panted from exertion and assessed the damage he had done to his foe. The fireball had burned away the scales that protected the sea god's chest and the vulnerable flesh beneath was scorched and burned. If a lesser being had been struck by such a spell, Dragorim's foe would have been utterly annihilated. Instead, the monster still stood and slowly regained its senses. After a moment, the ocean god drew back its hand and summoned a bolt of red lightning that it now clutched like a sword. Sagonor let out a terrible roar and swept his lightning blade across the deck of the ship in an arc that slashed across the upper deck and the men who stood upon it. Dragorim turned his sword to parry the mighty blow and projected a shield from the blade to protect himself. His defense was successful, and the sorcerer emerged unharmed by Sagonor's fearsome attack.

However, the crew and passengers were not protected by Dragorim's barrier. All men that had stood upon the deck were slain by that terrible blow; instantly burned to ash or set ablaze. Sagonor's blade cut through the mast and sails of the ship, and the final, terrified screams of the dying men were drowned out as they came crashing down onto the deck.

Again, Dragorim felt the energy of the blow that struck his barrier merge with him, and he turned the point of his sword towards his foe. The sorcerer channeled and redirected the energy through his arm and out of the weapon. He flung the deadly bolt deep into the burning wound on the god's chest and straight into its heart. The ancient god Sagonor let out a terrible cry… and fell.

Dragorim watched with satisfaction as life left the beast's eyes and its body sank down into the black depths of the ocean. As soon as the god died, the clouds quickly dissipated, and the storm soon faded from existence. Sunlight cascaded down upon the carnage in the sea and the only sound heard was the gentle rolling of the ship as it continued on its course, steered only by the magical currents summoned by the sorcerer.

Exhausted, Dragorim fell to his knees and desperately tried to catch his breath. After a few seconds, he looked at his sword and saw that the blade had melted from the energy that had coursed through it moments before. The sorcerer then turned and saw nothing but utter destruction laid out across the deck of the ship. All who had dared face the monsters on the deck had met their end, either at the fangs of the fish-men, or by the power of their god. Blood and death stared back at Dragorim as he surveyed the scene before him.

The sorcerer's sadness grew, as he had not wished for any of these horrible events to transpire. He searched among the remains and found what was left of Farim, the man who had saved his life. Dragorim knelt before the remains of Farim's body and carefully cleaned the blood away from where his throat had been torn out. The sorcerer took time to mourn Farim and decided it was best to bring him below. Once there, Dragorim neatly laid Farim's body down and went searching for the last of his food. After a few moments, the weary sorcerer returned and gently placed the bag in Farim's arms.

"No one should go hungry, especially on the road to the afterlife," the sorcerer said.

While in the hold of the ship, Dragorim searched for other survivors and found only one; but the man had gone mad with fright. As soon as the sorcerer finally convinced the poor soul to leave his hiding place, the madman rushed across the deck and shrieked as he cast himself into the sea. Dragorim was alone on the lifeless hulk.

The current he had summoned still drove the ship onward. All he had to do was wait and rest within that ghost ship, and he would reach his destination. Consumed by sadness, the sorcerer was tempted to steal the rowboat at the ship's side and sink the cog right then and there. However, the current was strong enough that he worried that the flimsy craft would crumble the instant it touched the churning water. The sorcerer decided that he would wait until he was close to shore, and *then* he would turn the ship into Farim's funeral pyre. Once that was accomplished, Dragorim would steal the rowboat from the ship's side and row the rest of the way to landfall.

Weakened and weary from the battle, Dragorim climbed back into his hammock and began to brood over the events that had transpired. He wondered over what could have motivated Hymurr to place such a beast like Sagonor in these waters. There was much to Hymurr's creation that Dragorim did not understand; a fact that brought him immense anguish. His mind turned back to Farim and sadness again gave way to grim determination. Whether he knew it or not, Farim had died to ensure Dragorim could complete his mission, and the sorcerer resolved that he would not let that sacrifice be in vain. Upon reaching this conclusion, he was finally able to calm himself enough to allow exhaustion to take him, and he fell into a deep sleep.

<u>Chapter 4</u>

Radnor trudged down the road as he left Sigaberht's keep. His armor weighed upon his shoulders as he plodded over the snow covered slope and crossed from the grounds that separated Sigaberht's immediate domain from the homes of those that served him. Radnor made his way through the neatly arranged rows of streets and noticed how few people perused through the many shops that lined the old walkways. The taverns were filled to the brim with people who danced and drank heartily, though this was not the merriment of contented people. Many had died during the Hexverat's attack, and with both news and whispered rumors of Drakomar's imminent assault weighing upon everyone's minds, the carousing of this night was driven not by joy, but by extraordinary worry.

After a short walk made long by Radnor's fatigue, the warrior finally reached Elena's cottage. After the battle against the wolves, Elena had been taken in as a member of Sigaberht's household and was afforded accommodations befitting this position. She did not have any official responsibilities to the earl, save that she learn as much about her powers as she could. Sigaberht knew how instrumental she would be in whatever events lay on the road before them, and he made sure she had proper food and shelter to keep her healthy and ready for what was to come. Elena felt grateful for the treatment she received, but Radnor's feelings on the matter were far less charitable. To Radnor, Sigaberht was treating Elena like cattle as he sheltered and fed her until her usefulness ended. She was very aware of Radnor's feelings on the matter, and was not sure he was wrong. However, Elena chose to regard the gifted house and food simply for what they were: free food and shelter. This attitude allowed Elena to concentrate all her energy on learning about her powers, rather than about where to find basic necessities.

Radnor stepped up to the stoop of the small cottage. Happiness flashed across his face as he opened the door and saw that Elena stood on the other side of the threshold. Evidently, her injury was not too severe if she was already home and standing on her wounded leg. Radnor was just about to embrace Elena when a look of disgust played across her face.

"Radnor, wait!"

Radnor stopped in his tracks, and waited for her follow up.

"Your armor is *still* filthy! I don't want that awful stuff inside the house. Can you clean it off first?"

Radnor sighed and did as he was asked. After years of hard living on the road, he was still adjusting to domestic life. Radnor had originally planned on cleaning his armor inside, but Elena was right, and he would probably leave a mess all over the floor and furniture.

As such, Radnor walked around to the back of the small home and filled a bucket of water from the trough setup for Darestr to drink from. The weary warrior looked over to the small stables that had been erected behind the cottage and saw Darestr happily munching on a bag of feed brought by Sigaberht's servants.

Radnor set to work cleaning his armor and marveled at himself. It seemed strange to him that he, or anyone else, should care about something as insignificant as a bit of a mess at a time like this. Monsters born from malevolent forces now stalked the world and he was concerned about keeping the house clean! However, he knew what Elena would say: she would tell him that in troubled times like these, it was more important than ever to keep things tidy. It kept their minds off things they couldn't control and helped maintain a sense of normalcy in a time of madness. Radnor knew she was right... but his desire to do *something* about the monsters infuriated him.

Just as Radnor started to relax into his work, a frustratingly familiar voice echoed in the air around him.

"Hello, again."

Radnor knew the voice all too well. It was calm, collected, and filled the air in a way that no human speech ever could. He stopped washing his armor and futilely hoped that the voice would go away on its own.

"I know you heard me," the voice said.

62

Radnor turned and saw Ashrahan, the black-eyed Krigari god, standing before him.

"Do you mind? I'm busy!" Radnor snarled.

Ashrahan smirked in a predatory way that revealed too many teeth for Radnor's liking.

"I finally tear myself away from the watchful eyes of my king and come to check on you… *after* I helped you rescue the woman you now sow your seed with, and this is how you greet me?" Ashrahan sneered.

Despite his urge to respond violently to Ashrahan's presence, Radnor could only glare at the phantasmic image of the god standing before him. Instead, Radnor silently waited for Ashrahan to explain why he chose *now* to project his image to him after it had been so long since their previous encounter. Finally, the god grew impatient and broke the silence.

"Fine then. It seems you survived your battle with the Hexverat relatively unscathed… a pity it didn't change your demeanor."

Radnor still only glared at Ashrahan as he waited for him to get to the purpose of this unwelcome visit. The god stepped beside Radnor and looked down into the water. He gazed at his reflection and gingerly adjusted his hair for no reason Radnor could discern. Once Ashrahan was done preening himself, he continued.

"I am here to warn you. Things are stirring in Narakim. Adramelach is aware that someone has cracked the Great Barrier and allowed chaos to trickle in. He knows of the threat that poses, and he has begun acting strangely."

Radnor's blood ran hot at the utterance of the name "Adramelach". For years, Radnor had hoped to kill the god who ruled the Krigari, end their threat to humanity once and for all, and gain his long sought revenge.

"What does Adramelach plan to do?" Radnor asked.

"I'm not sure yet. He has redoubled his efforts to break into your world. I'm not sure what he hopes to accomplish if he succeeds, but for the moment, he is still unable to make progress. You might enjoy knowing that this frustrates him to no end."

Radnor's brow furrowed in concern.

"I guess I should be thankful for that. Under different circumstances I would welcome a chance to kill him. However, I have too many other problems to attend to."

Ashrahan dismissed Radnor's statement with a gesture.

"Problems or not, you forget, you don't have a weapon that *can* kill him."

Radnor shook his head and smiled in a way that made *Ashrahan* uneasy for a change. However, Radnor caught himself and decided to conceal the nature of his sword from the god. There was no need for an uncertain ally like Ashrahan to know that Radnor actually *did* possess a weapon that was capable of killing a Krigari. Radnor shrugged and made his reply.

"Well, you know me… always hot to the fight, and never one to think too much."

"Yes… I suppose," Ashrahan said. The god sensed that there was something Radnor was not telling him. He knew he could not force the information out of Radnor, so Ashrahan instead chose to change the subject… for the time being. "Adramelach is not the only one on the move. I've been watching, looking for signs. Something is stirring within chaos… something incomprehensibly evil."

The witch Lenora's words echoed through Radnor's mind as Ashrahan spoke.

There is something inside the chaos… something has merged with it… become a part of it!

After weighing what to reveal to Ashrahan, Radnor spoke.

"I know. I have seen firsthand what this evil would bring into the world. Something wished to open the way for it… but we destroyed it."

Ashrahan's eyes widened in surprise.

"It sounds like your encounter with the Hexverat was… eventful. Perhaps you could enlighten me?"

Radnor then proceeded to tell Ashrahan most of the details of his story. He began with the battle against the ogre, continued with the witches' attack on Wulfgeld, and finished with how they fought and killed the unknown, malevolent entity within the dead city. Radnor did what he could to avoid telling Ashrahan about Elena's involvement in the battle, and about the sword. However, keeping his story convincing without these details proved difficult; lying had never been one of Radnor's talents. Ashrahan caught on to the deception and chose this moment to press Radnor for the truth.

"I'm confused. You've told me that the witches' purpose in attacking Wulfgeld was to produce something that could defeat the entity you killed at the ancient city… but you never told me what it was or what happened to it. Where is the weapon now?"

Radnor's mind raced to come up with a convincing lie. He knew he couldn't lie about both the sword and Elena successfully. If he didn't give Ashrahan something to work with, the god would search for answers elsewhere and perhaps find the truth on his own. Radnor had a choice to make. He could either hide the sword and keep the weapon of his planned vengeance a secret, or he could protect Elena. It did not take long for the demigod to make his decision.

"It was a sword forged from chaos. The witches gave it to me so that Sigaberht would let them fulfill their mission."

"And where is the sword now?" Ashrahan pried.

"It was destroyed when I killed the entity. It is lost to time and space."

Ashrahan shook his head in disappointment at Radnor's obvious lie.

"It's quite a pity really; I had thought you were smarter than this."

"Can you blame me for trying?"

"No, I suppose not."

Satisfied that Ashrahan had taken the bait and would not ask questions about Elena, Radnor drew his sword.

Ashrahan reflexively stepped back from the menacing weapon. The black blade projected an eerie glow and the tendrils that ran along the blade's fuller twisted and writhed in sickening motions that even Ashrahan's godly eyes could not follow nor comprehend.

"I see you didn't come out of the battle empty handed. You think this sword can kill Adramelach?"

"Do you?" Radnor replied as he pointed the tip of the blade at Ashrahan's heart.

Ashrahan's gaze lingered on the blade. It seemed to Radnor that he was more than just fearful of its power. He looked almost… envious? Radnor did not have time to contemplate Ashrahan's reaction before the god spoke again.

"I can see why you have not yet parted with it. To forge a weapon from chaos such as the witches did, it was no mean feat. This is something only the creators have ever accomplished before… though they did it better. I must caution you: that sword is only loosely bound by order. Even I cannot predict what it is capable of, or if the spell that binds it to its current form may come apart and unleash death upon you."

Radnor nodded as he sheathed his sword. He was unsure how much of what Ashrahan said was true, and how much of it was lies meant to dissuade him from using it. After a moment's pondering, Radnor continued the conversation.

"That thought has occurred to me. The problem is that I need this sword to kill the horde of monsters corrupted by chaos that now infest the woods near here."

Ashrahan's eyes widened with surprise yet again.

"And yet you sit here, at home, and do not ride out to meet this foe?"

Radnor shook his head and kicked a small rock through Ashrahan's projected form. The insult was not lost on the Krigari, but he did not interrupt.

"Unfortunately, the earl I am sworn to has a desperate plan to use these monsters against his mortal enemies."

"I see," Ashrahan said. "Your lord is a shortsighted fool?"

"It would seem so," Radnor replied. "He plays a very dangerous game. He hopes to use the monsters as a trap so that he might drive his foes from his land. After this is done, I might be able to convince him to get the help we need to destroy these monsters."

"You had better hurry up with that. I doubt that which stirs in chaos will be willing to wait for you to prepare. I fear it may be too late before your lord comes to his senses." With that said, Ashrahan slowly faded away. He spoke only once more as his form gradually disappeared against the snowy backdrop of the city. "Adramelach summons me. We shall speak again soon."

With that, Ashrahan disappeared from the world and left Radnor to finish cleaning his armor.

Radnor finally entered the cottage and was quickly met with a tight hug from Elena. Radnor dropped his newly washed armor and returned the gesture, going so far as to plant a kiss on her soft lips. The two stood this way for a long time before Elena broke their hug and headed through the living room and into the kitchen. Radnor was glad when he noticed that Elena limped much less than he had feared. Upon further examination, he saw that her ankle was wrapped with a small bandage stained with very little blood. This was yet another good sign, considering how deep the wound had been.

"How's your leg?" he asked.

"It's much better. The Hexverat left some useful medicines behind and Sigaberht's physicians were mostly able to put me back together. It's a little stiff and the wound isn't *fully* healed… but it's enough that I can walk on it."

"I'm glad to hear that. But you be careful, all right?"

"Do you mean with my ankle, or in general?" was Elena's wry reply.

"Both."

Elena turned from the table where she had just started chopping vegetables and looked at Radnor.

"I'm sorry about today. I should have been more careful."

Radnor offered her his shoulder. She smiled and laid her head against it, snuggling into the hollow beneath his collarbone.

"We both should have. I could have argued with you more… but I would be lying if I said I didn't also want to know more about your powers." Radnor smiled at her. "But most of all, I'm, just glad you're okay."

"I'm glad you're okay, too," Elena said as she returned to cutting the vegetables. "Who was that you were talking to outside?"

Radnor's blood ran cold. He had not yet told her that he had been speaking to one of the Krigari. Before Radnor and Elena became lovers, Radnor had actively kept this secret from her. Since then, the only thing that had stopped him from telling Elena about it was how preoccupied they had been with the flurry of recent events. That, combined with Ashrahan's month-long absence had allowed the topic to fade from his mind. Faced with it now, Radnor decided to tell her the truth.

"I was speaking with a Krigari god named 'Ashrahan'."

Elena smiled and laughed.

"Oh come on, I'm being serious! Who was it?"

Elena's smile quickly faded when she saw the serious look on Radnor's face.

"Oh," she said. Fear and confusion filled her eyes as she looked around the house for any sign of Ashrahan's presence. "Is he here now? Are we in danger?" More questions burned in Elena's mind as she struggled to put them to words, but were driven away as Radnor answered her.

"He's not here now… not physically anyway. I know… I owe you an explanation," Radnor said.

Elena's confusion quickly coalesced into anger.

"How long have you been speaking to… to that… he's your sworn enemy!" Elena exclaimed.

"Yes, I know," Radnor said as he tried to calm her. "But, he was also the source of the information we used to find that horrid tower the witches imprisoned you in. Without him, I'm not sure I would have gotten to you in time."

Elena stood frozen in anger. Radnor put his hand on her shoulder and continued his story. As much as Elena wanted to, she couldn't quite bring herself to disengage from Radnor's touch. Instead, she calmed herself enough to listen to his explanation.

"Right before we got to Wulfgeld, he came to see me. At the time, he wanted me to help him kill Adramelach."

"Why would he want to do that?" Elena asked.

"I'm still not sure of everything, but I do know that Adramelach betrayed their creator. I think it has something to do with that."

Elena jumped back at Radnor's words.

"Wait, how do you know all this?"

"Ashrahan showed me. He came to me the day before the witches attacked. He showed me Caelum's death at the hands of both Adramelach and *his* creator, Damiros. Immediately after they killed Caelum, Adramelach betrayed Damiros and cast him out of the cosmos."

Elena stood in silent shock as she tried to process Radnor's story. *How could Caelum be dead? It was impossible!* After gathering her thoughts, Elena finally found the words to actually ask one of the many questions that raced through her mind.

"How can you trust the information he's giving you? How do you know this isn't some trick by Adramelach meant to lure you into trusting Ashrahan? Caelum can't be dead!"

Radnor retrieved a knife of his own from their cabinet and began chopping vegetables himself.

"I'm not totally certain it isn't lies, but he's given me too much true information, including where to find you when the witches took you… and about the threat that chaos posed. I don't think he's lied to me thus far."

Elena stopped as she tried to drink in everything Radnor was saying. Finally, she spoke again.

"Why didn't you tell me sooner?"

Radnor sighed. He heard the pain in her voice, and wished to undo it.

"Well, when he first showed himself, you and I weren't… together as we are now… and he hadn't shown himself since the time he helped me find you. After that, there just hasn't been time to sit and think about how to tell you, let alone actually do it." Radnor stopped and took a deep breath before continuing. "I'm sorry."

Elena shrugged dismissively and turned away from him. Her more rational mind understood Radnor's need for secrecy, but it still hurt. After a few moments, she regained enough composure to talk to him again.

"It's all right. I just need to adjust to being romantically involved with a demigod, I guess." She looked back up at him and forced herself to smile, wanting to keep the peace. "What did he want tonight?"

Radnor saw her forced smile and knew that she wanted to move on, so he did.

"He wanted to warn me. Adramelach knows something happened with chaos, and is renewing his efforts to force his way into our world."

"That's not the news I wanted to hear," Elena said.

"Nor I, though it is good to also know that he has been unsuccessful so far."

"We can thank Caelum for small miracles, I guess," Elena said. She stopped speaking, as it now sunk in that the god that she and countless others worshiped was dead. More questions about her and her people's worship… their whole religion came into her mind. She struggled to pick one to ask first. When had Caelum died? How? Panic nearly seized her, but Elena calmed herself quickly. While her questions were important, they needed to wait. Instead, Elena focused on questions more pertinent to the situation at hand.

"What else did he have to say?"

"Well, we discussed the events of our recent battles."

"And what did you tell him?" Elena asked, concern rising in her voice.

"He wanted to know more about how the witches died, and how we destroyed the being in the city. I had to tell him more than I wanted to. I told him about the sword."

Elena's face fell as she understood the implications of what he said.

"Oh, Radnor! If he tells Adramelach, you won't be able to catch him by surprise!"

"I know, but I needed him to stop asking questions. It was either tell him about the sword, or tell him about you. If I didn't give him something, he would have peered further into our world… and he might have learned about you. I couldn't let that happen."

Elena stepped forward to give Radnor another hug. He had often talked at length about how he would kill Adramelach… how he might catch him by surprise with the sword if given the chance. Now that one of the Krigari knew about the powerful weapon, Radnor's plan was in jeopardy. Elena said the only thing she could think of.

70

"Thank you."

Radnor returned her embrace and continued speaking.

"He also confirmed something you and I had already suspected: something in chaos is stirring. It seems that the evil thing the witches saw has plans of its own."

"Do you think it's angry we destroyed its servant in the dead city?" Elena asked.

"Maybe. I really hoped that would be the last we heard of it, but Ashrahan warned me that if that malevolence is stirring… then perhaps it will try to send the army of monsters in the forest against us. I think he may be right. When we fought them just hours ago, they seemed more organized than before. Something *directed* them to seek us out tonight."

"There's a nasty thought," Elena said. Then, an idea struck her that she did not like. "You told me that Adramelach betrayed his creator and cast him out of the cosmos. If he's not in the realm of creation as we understand it, where did Adramelach cast him *to*?"

Radnor felt his own fears settle and form a lump in his stomach.

"I've been having the same thought since we left the dead city, but have been too afraid to say it aloud," Radnor replied. "I'm worried that the thing that drove the Hexverat mad… and glares at us from chaos… is Damiros, one of the creators of all things."

Elena felt a chill as horror took her. If what they both suspected was true, how could they possibly hope to overcome such an overwhelming foe?

"Well, I suppose that answers one question," Elena said. "If Adramelach is anxious to break into our world, and Damiros really is the thing stirring in chaos… then perhaps Adramelach's actions are related to that?"

Radnor pondered for a moment, turning the idea in his mind.

"That does make the most sense. The question is, how would invading our world help Adramelach stop Damiros?"

Silence fell between the lovers, but was suddenly interrupted by a knock on the door that startled both of them.

Radnor headed to the door, working to regain his composure as he did. When Radnor opened the door, Daegal's furious face appeared before him.

"I would speak with you, Veigarand," Daegal said. Before Radnor could furnish a reply, Elena jumped into the conversation.

"Anyone who addresses him as 'Veigarand' is not welcome in my home," she said curtly.

"It's all right," Radnor said, turning to face Elena as he spoke. "This is Daegal, an ealdorman of Sigaberht, and I doubt he knows of me by any other name." Radnor turned back to Daegal. "My real name is 'Radnor'. 'Veigarand' is a name given to me by those who hate me."

Daegal nodded his understanding and hastily made his reply.

"I apologize. I had assumed it was your given name. *Radnor*, might I speak with you a moment?" Daegal asked.

"Yes, come in." Radnor gestured for Daegal to come inside and offered to hang his cloak for him. "My lord ealdorman, what is it that you wish to speak with me about?"

Daegal stepped through the door and bowed gently to Elena before he then turned to face Radnor again.

"I wanted to speak to you about what you saw in the forest today. I need to know if the earl's plan is as foolhardy as it seems."

"It is," Radnor replied.

"Well… then I'm glad we had this little chat," Daegal said sarcastically.

"Well, my story will take all night if you do not ask me more specific questions. Either way, you may be here a while. Please, take a seat."

Daegal bowed politely, then planted himself in one of the wooden chairs that occupied the small living space. The ealdorman took a moment to look around the room. It was a plain room with simple wooden walls and flooring. The space was filled with half a dozen cushioned chairs and a dining table at the far end. A wall divided the living space from the kitchen, and there was a short hallway that Daegal assumed led to the bedroom. When he finished surveying the space, the ealdorman looked out the window and into the darkness. It was late, and the candlelight cast eerie shadows across the walls as the company began to speak of ancient horrors.

"Vei… Radnor… What did you see? What did you fight in those woods today?" Daegal asked.

"We fought monsters… dozens of them attacked us. Some used to be men that were slain by those terrible forces but a month ago. Others were wolves and trees that had become corrupted by the evil." Radnor trailed off to think, and then continued. "Like I said during court, the ground itself came alive and tried to devour me. This is not the first time I've seen this. I once witnessed the earth in that place devour one of the men in our party when we went in after Lenora."

Daegal shuddered at Radnor's words. He tried to banish the horrible images that came to his mind, but they would not budge.

"And the earl expects us to battle in woods filled with that?" Daegal asked.

"What is this about battling in the woods? Are we going in to root the monsters out?" Elena asked.

"No, my fair lady," Daegal replied. "We are to lead Piarin's men straight into them."

Elena shook her head in surprise, and then looked at Radnor.

"I was getting to that," he said.

"I can understand why you would be reluctant to bring that up," Daegal said. He turned to address Elena. "How is your wound? Vei… I'm sorry, *Radnor*, partially based his objection to the plan on the fact that you were injured."

"It's… tolerable for now," Elena said. "I take it that I am involved in the earl's plan then?"

"Yes," Daegal said. "You and Radnor are to be a part of the force that leads the enemy into the forest, and your job is to make sure the only people slaughtered are Piarin's."

Elena stood in shock.

"Has the earl gone mad?" she cried.

"I do believe he has," Radnor said.

Daegal brought his fist down on the arm of the chair in anger.

"Given the way he spoke to me in court today, I would agree. The way he took the word of those two… loathsome opportunists! I knew he was desperate, but this is insanity! And Leif was no help at all! He just stood there, never voicing an opinion! In his own way, he's worse than the other two!"

Having said his piece, Daegal finally wound down. The room was held captive by an awkward silence that no one quite knew how to break for an uncomfortably long time; until Elena spoke up.

"Would you like anything to eat, my lord ealdorman?" she asked.

"Thank you, my lady, I would like that very much," Daegal said. He politely accepted some bread and butter that Elena offered to him and Radnor.

"So, what brings you here, *exactly*?" Radnor asked. "I doubt you came here just to hear my stories and rant."

"I'm not sure. I guess it's because you seemed to be the only reasonable one in the room today. Considering the stories they tell about you, that is a terrifying prospect."

Radnor's temper sparked upon hearing Daegal's reference to the terrible, and often inaccurate, tales told of Radnor's deeds during his years in exile.

"That was quite a backhanded compliment, given the nature of those stories," Radnor replied. The anger in Radnor's voice told Daegal he had just put his foot in his mouth again, and the ealdorman brought his hand to his head in his annoyance at himself.

"Bah! I do apologize! It seems that I have left my manners outside your threshold!"

Just as Radnor was about to accept Daegal's apology, there was another knock at the door. Radnor rolled his eyes in exasperation and proceeded to open it. Once the door was open, he found that Leif now stood at his threshold. Radnor eyed the ealdorman up and down as he wondered what had brought him here. The man looked tired and haggard. His face was gaunter than when the two had first met, and his long, graying hair now hung loose around his shoulders in what was quite a stark contrast to Leif's normally well-kept appearance.

"Leif, what brings you to my abode tonight?"

"I've come looking for Daegal, for he has been summoned by the earl. I was told he was seen heading this way."

Before Radnor could answer, Daegal's booming voice called to Leif.

"I am here, dear ealdorman! Please, take a seat and join our talk! Perhaps you will have more to say now than you did in court today!" Radnor stepped aside and allowed Leif to enter. Elena found the man a chair and placed it next to Daegal, who spoke again. "If your only purpose had been to summon me, you would have dispatched a messenger to do the job. You came yourself, which leads me to ask: what *really* brings you here?"

"I came to check on Elena." Leif then turned to Elena. "Veigara—"

Elena brusquely cut him off.

"Leif, we have talked about this: you are not to use that name in my presence!"

Leif nodded, embarrassed at offending Elena. His resentment for Radnor was strong, but he had known Elena for many years and did not wish *her* any ill will.

"Out of respect for *your* house," Leif started. The emphasis in Leif's tone told Radnor that the ealdorman did not approve of their relationship. As far as Radnor cared, Leif could go jump off a bridge. "Radnor told us that you had been hurt in the forest, and I wanted to see how you were doing. I may no longer be an ealdorman, but I still care for those I led."

Daegal snorted in contempt.

"Leif, you are still an ealdorman. Just because his lordship has seen to it that you serve him as general, does not mean that you are an ealdorman no more."

"I have no lands, no property at all beyond what my earl sees fit to give me," Leif replied.

"Stop wallowing," Daegal snorted. "From what I hear, you successfully led your people through hell to get them here, *and* you fought like a lion when the wolves attacked. And to top it all off, as a reward, our lord gave *you* command of his army! That includes *my* men, and the men of every ealdorman here. Do not be so ashamed of what happened in Neugeld that you run from any further responsibility. Now tell me, what do *you* think of the earl's plan? And do not mince words! I want the truth!"

There was silence as Leif contemplated Daegal's question, and he finally answered.

"I believe it is the best plan we have, given the circumstances."

Daegal scoffed in exasperation.

"By Caelum's light, I think we need to reserve *you* a place on Sigaberht's ass next to Aethelstan's!" Daegal shouted.

Just as the two were about to get into a heated argument, there was yet another knock on the door. Radnor again stood to answer it.

"Elena, is our house now the front gate to Wulfgeld?"

Radnor opened the door for what he hoped would be the final time that evening and found Halfdan and Rolf standing in the doorway. Rolf gave Radnor a quick hug, which Radnor gladly returned. Once they were done, Radnor and Halfdan clasped hands.

"Radnor! Rolf told me of what was said in that meeting, and we had to see you as soon as he finished his supper at the barracks. It's insane, I tell you! Sigaberht hasn't seen the horrors of…" Halfdan trailed off as he looked into the house. "I see you already have visitors. Perhaps we should come back at another time?"

Radnor laughed.

"Nonsense. If these two can *barge* into my home, you and Rolf are certainly most welcome!"

Halfdan and Rolf quickly stepped through the door and found seats for themselves. Standing a full head taller than even Radnor, Halfdan barely fit as he squeezed himself into one of the chairs. Rolf chose to sit on the floor. The two newcomers already knew Leif, and were quickly introduced to Daegal. Once the pleasantries were finished, an awkward silence took hold of the group. Finally, Rolf broke the tension.

"So, things are going well with the scouts. The other boys are nice, and we work together really well."

"So I gathered," Radnor replied in a serious voice. Rolf's face fell a little when he heard Radnor's inflection.

Radnor's disapproval of Rolf's joining the scouts had been made very clear when the boy signed up. He was even angrier about it now that Rolf was already being thrust into the fray with so little training. However, Radnor did not want to hurt the boy's feelings, and he noticed how his tone had affected Rolf just now. The would-be father figure took a breath and tried to put a more positive spin on his words.

"I'm glad things are going well for you. I saw you with the other boy, what was his name?"

"Halig," Rolf said.

"Halig. He seemed very shy in the meeting today."

Rolf turned his gaze to the floor as his mood became very melancholy.

"We're all orphans; most of us lost our parents in the attack. My home was burned down weeks before that. I had a head start on getting used to pain."

No one in the room quite knew how to respond to Rolf's statement, though Radnor made his best attempt.

"If you ever need someone to talk to, or need to spend a night elsewhere, you're always welcome here."

"I know, but my place is with the others like me, and in a place where I can do some good for Wulfgeld," Rolf replied. A thought struck Rolf, which caused him to visibly perk up. "I've been meaning to ask, when can we resume our fighting lessons? The training I'm getting for scouting is good, but it doesn't really focus on fighting."

"Oh, I see, the boy joins the scouts, and is surprised when he must learn scouting!" Halfdan commented, which got a laugh from the group assembled. However, the levity was short-lived as everyone's thoughts turned to the impending battle. Halfdan continued. "I do not know what Ealdorman Daegal here thinks of Sigaberht's plan, but based on what I heard, I for one think it is foolhardy. As I was saying when we arrived, he has not seen the true horrors that await us there, and I think if he saw it for himself, he might think differently."

"I agree," Radnor said. "And Daegal agrees with me as well, but Aethelstan and Osmund have joined Sigaberht in his madness. Perhaps Ashveldt can convince—"

"Ashveldt will always do as his father commands," Leif interrupted.

"I thought you were on Sigaberht's side?" Daegal questioned.

Leif nervously swallowed.

"I said it's the best plan we *have*, given the circumstances. I don't like it either, and I can guarantee you that even Sigaberht doesn't like it."

Radnor shook his head in disappointment before speaking.

"The trouble is, we're not going to convince him otherwise. He's made up his mind that it is the only course of action."

"I know," Leif replied. "Daegal and I have known him for many years. He is stubborn, and with Erelda gone…" Leif trailed off, but Daegal finished his thought.

"Erelda, may Caelum be kind to her soul, was always a calming influence on Sigaberht. She helped him stay present in the moment and kept his temper at bay. Without her guidance to help him adhere to his own moral compass, I suspect he will indeed be harder to reason with."

Elena spoke next.

"Well, what is it that has Sigaberht locked in to this plan?"

Leif supplied the answer.

"The enemy has superior numbers and equipment. We cannot hope to survive a siege through conventional strength of arms. We need to demoralize the enemy so much that they choose to leave."

"How long does it usually take to assemble and dispatch an army from Drakomar?" Elena asked.

"Well, it usually takes time, though Drakomar does have a sizable standing army as it is. In this case, Piarin only assembled a fraction of his force to attack us. The rest of the army that will besiege us is from the Order of Pale Light, and those fanatics never need time to gather for an attack. So, it may have only been a few days between when they decided to attack and actually sent out the army. But, I'm not sure how much that matters now. The truth is… they will be here the day after tomorrow with whatever numbers and equipment they could muster." Daegal said.

"Equipment… supplies…" Leif started. "An army needs food… and supply lines to keep food coming to them."

"Food," Radnor said thoughtfully, his and Leif's thoughts joining together. The group all turned their eyes to Radnor, and he continued. "Don't you see? They want to strike us while we're still vulnerable after the wolf attack. Their army was assembled and dispatched in a hurry. If they're in such a hurry, there's a good chance that army is marching faster than their supplies can keep up. They must be carrying a limited amount of food with them. If we could destroy their food supply… and maybe even cut their supply line… then perhaps we can get them to run away before Sigaberht's plan could be deployed!"

"That's a brilliant idea!" Daegal shouted.

Leif shook his head and spoke in a grave tone.

"Not to be the wet blanket in the room, but how are we to do this? We still have to ride out and attack them. And how are we to cut off their supply line? We would need to be able to get past the army at our doorstep to do that, which would be a great feat by itself. I'm not sure it can be done."

"Actually, I think it can be," Elena said.

Now all eyes turned to her.

"How?" Rolf asked.

"Wait one moment," Elena said.

She headed into the bedroom, and after a few seconds of rummaging, found what she sought. When Elena returned, she came back holding a mysterious object that neither Halfdan nor Daegal recognized. However, Radnor, Leif, and Rolf knew it all too well.

"Alban's cursed amulet!" Leif exclaimed.

"You kept it?" Rolf asked.

"Yes. I… I didn't know when it might be useful again. With this, I can try to gather all of the ghouls I can and sic them on the enemy at night. The ghouls will destroy their food supply for us."

"Will that work? Your powers don't normally… show themselves without chaos nearby." Radnor asked.

"Well, I was able to use the gaulderen to control them before. Maybe I can channel my power through gaulderens even if there's no chaos around?"

Radnor shrugged. Everything was still a guessing game that he did not like.

"Will someone please explain to me what that is?" Daegal demanded.

Leif shushed him. Daegal shot him an angry glare, so Leif hastily followed up.

"I'll explain later," he said. Leif then turned back to Elena. "How many ghouls do you think you can summon with this?"

"I don't know. But right now… I think this is our best chance to stop Sigaberht from doing something foolish."

"Okay, say this does work…" Leif said, half thinking out loud as he spoke. "How do you plan to attack their supply line? My previous point still stands on that."

"I think I may have a way to attack their supply line," Halfdan said. He turned and looked out the window. "The moon will be full soon."

There was a moment of silence as almost everyone understood Halfdan's meaning. Daegal became even more irritated, as he was the only one in the room unaware of Halfdan's nature.

"No, absolutely not!" Elena exclaimed.

Radnor remained silent for a moment longer, thinking over Halfdan's implied plan. Finally, he asked,

"Would you be going alone?"

Halfdan nodded.

"It's the only way to keep our own people safe. I will head out tonight and see if I can find out where their supply line is. If my plan works, their bodies and broken wagons will be blocking the road before any of them can reach their fellows besieging Wulfgeld."

"It's too dangerous!" Elena exclaimed. "Radnor, don't let him do it!"

Radnor shook his head.

"Halfdan wishes to make use of his power for our benefit. It's no more than the risk I will take on the walls, or the risk you might take in the forest if our plan fails."

Daegal shook his head and spoke.

"Again, I find myself unsure of what I am hearing. Halfdan, how would you survive attacking their supply line by yourself?"

Leif answered him.

"When Wulfgeld was attacked, the witches summoned a werewolf to aid them. And Halfdan …"

Leif trailed off and both ealdormen looked nervously up at Halfdan. The giant man waved sarcastically at Daegal.

"I am that werewolf. But before you judge me, I must have you know every sin I have committed when in that form was done against my will. I hope that by attacking this supply line, I may at least get the monster within me to work *for* me for a change."

"But… alone?" Elena asked.

"If anyone else were to go with me… I could not guarantee that I wouldn't attack them too. No… I have to go alone. Just pray that the enemy carries no weapons made from silver."

Not caring to discuss the matter any further, Halfdan abruptly stood and left Elena's objections at the door as he departed. Leif stood up next.

"I must inform his lordship of these plans. I think I can convince him to go along with them, but either way, I am duty bound to report this conversation to him."

Daegal stood to go with him.

"Well, the earl has summoned me, and I think if two of us argue in favor of the plan, maybe he'll be more willing to cooperate."

The two ealdormen left the house and the others to their tasks. Rolf finally stood up to go, but not before giving Elena and Radnor long hugs.

"I need to be getting back to the barracks. If I'm not back by curfew, I'll be in big trouble."

With Rolf's swift departure, an eerie silence fell upon the cottage. After a long time, Radnor finally broke it as he gave Elena a hug.

"I know you worry about them," he said.

"You say that as though you don't," she replied.

Elena looked up at him as tears formed in her eyes. Radnor nodded.

"It depends on who we're talking about. Rolf is the one I worry the most about. Since his father died, he—"

"He's been distant, even from us," Elena interrupted. "Well, you're right. Even with me, he's been distant. I understand wanting to be alone in a time of grief, but he's gone too far with this. He should be here, living as a boy with people who care about him, not—"

"Trying to prove himself to a lord who would sooner use him as fodder than see him as a person?"

Elena shook her head angrily.

"Not everything has to do with Sigaberht! It's not the earl he wishes to prove himself to! He thinks he needs to prove himself to *himself!*"

Radnor took a second to think and understood that Elena was mostly right. However, he disagreed with an important detail in what she said.

"He doesn't *think* he needs to prove himself. He really does need to. If he is ever to be a man, he must gain confidence in his own abilities."

"And how will he gain confidence in his abilities if you get angry every time you see he's off working for Sigaberht? Do you think he doesn't see your disapproval?" Elena asked.

Radnor sighed.

"Were you not the one who was worrying about him a moment ago? One moment, you worry; the next moment… you are supportive of his suicidal efforts!"

"I know!" Elena started back. She stopped as she understood Radnor's point. "I guess I am conflicted! I just don't want him to get hurt! But, he needs to be ready for what's coming in his life."

Radnor took Elena back into his arms.

"I feel the same way about him. I just wish I could keep him closer… teach him more. I can train him in combat far better than anyone else here."

"Then why not do it?" Elena asked.

How? He has his duties among the scouts," Radnor replied.

"Well, you're Veigarand. I'm sure you can get the captain of the scouts to do what you want."

Radnor smiled at the notion.

"Alright, that sounds like a plan. I will stop by the scout's barracks tomorrow and see if I can steal Rolf for some training."

Elena smiled back. The two then went about preparing and eating their dinner. They savored both the meal and their shared company greatly. After they were done eating, the pair went to bed in the hope that they could get enough sleep for the grueling days ahead.

Chapter 5

The sorcerer's journey had already been long and difficult; and he did not look forward to the many miles still ahead of him. Much to his relief, the unnatural ocean current had successfully brought his damaged ship within sight of land. After reaching this goal, Dragorim kept his promise to the dead and set the cog ablaze before he stole away with the ship's rowboat. While he rowed to shore, Dragorim watched solemnly as the hulking ship served as a funeral pyre for the dead within. However, once he landed, the sorcerer paid no more thought to what had transpired.

While he wished the outcome had been different, he would not change anything he had done. He did what he had to do. It was Hymurr's fault for putting him in this position, and *nothing* could be allowed to interfere with his mission.

After a half-day's walk, Dragorim stole a horse to hasten his journey to Wulfgeld. Fearful of losing time, Dragorim cast a spell on the horse that kept it running beyond mortal exhaustion and rode hard for over a week. He stopped for neither food nor sleep. As the days wore on, the spell that held the beast in its gallop gradually wore off, and finally, disaster struck. Without warning, the poor beast collapsed from the unbearable strain the spell had placed upon it. Dragorim was thrown from the saddle and nearly broke his neck in the fall. After checking for injuries and dusting himself off, the sorcerer investigated the horse's body and swore when he found it was dead. He continued shouting obscenities as he found his old bag and checked to make sure none of the contents had fallen out. He specifically checked to make sure that the precious, silver needle remained undamaged from the fall. Much to his relief, it was unharmed.

With the horse dead, Dragorim was forced to waste many hours marching on foot, cursing as he went. Finally, with his feet sore and muscles aching, he happened upon an inn beside the road where he hoped to find a bit of rest and a hot meal.

Dragorim hoped his stay would be pleasant, as he dreaded the prospect of finding the place to be nothing but a den of crime and violence. His concern was heightened when he spotted a suspicious looking man partially concealed in the bushes near the road. However, after studying the way the man sat at his post, Dragorim realized he was not waiting to ambush anyone, but rather was a concealed lookout who worked for the inn. The sorcerer briefly considered moving on from this place, but the hunger rumbling in his belly compelled him to stay.

As Dragorim drew closer to the inn, his fears were quickly dispelled by the sound of sweet music and the scent of even sweeter wines that wafted from the open windows. The sorcerer then casually pushed the door open and strode across the threshold of the brightly lit room. What he saw filled his heart with mirth. The jovial crowd laughed with glee as musicians performed a bawdy tune about the local baron's indiscretions. The aromas of hot, freshly cooked meats filled the sorcerer's nostrils, and even the simplest bread smelled especially delightful. Dragorim wasted little time as he hastily got the attention of the innkeeper and placed an order for a large, satisfying meal.

Dragorim did not have to wait long before his plate of food arrived, and after carefully checking that everything he ordered was present, he dug in. Despite his hunger, the sorcerer ate very slowly, as he wanted to take the time to properly enjoy every bite.

The chicken was spiced and seasoned in a way the sorcerer had never tried before, and absolutely relished once he did. Dragorim ate lush, green vegetables covered in a sweet sauce he could only describe as "magical". The bread came with a pat of honey butter which he delicately spread across each slice with utmost care. Finally, the wine he ordered was bold and fruity; he relished each sip with greater reverence than the last. His manners were delicate as he slowly chewed and savored each bite. Nothing went to waste as each speck of meat, each sprig of leaf, and each crumb of bread was eaten with care.

Just as Dragorim finished eating his last piece of bread, a small peasant boy came to his table.

"Please, sir," the boy started. "Please, do you have any food to spare? I am hungry, and my father has not the coin to buy food. Our crops have been bad, and everything we grew has gone to the baron."

The sorcerer turned his eye to the boy. At first, he looked for signs of weapons that the child might be concealing behind his back, but the boy's hands were at his sides, and the sorcerer saw no outline of a dagger under his clothes. The child was also clearly underfed, as Dragorim could see the points of his shoulders through his thin clothes with frightening clarity. There was little muscle on the boy's arms and his face was so gaunt and pale that he looked like he was already dead. In response to the boy's request, the sorcerer reached into his pouch, withdrew the last gold coin he had in his possession, and gave it to the child. The boy looked up at him in awed shock at the man's kindness. He stood expectantly as he waited for Dragorim to ask for something in return but no request came. Finally, the boy spoke again.

"Sir, the coin you have given me is most generous, but I have nothing to give you in return."

Dragorim nodded.

"I know. Take it. No one should ever go hungry… least of all innocent boys such as yourself. Just be sure you spend it on good food. If there's too much for you to eat, give it to others who need it, understand?"

The boy nodded, and then bowed deeply.

"I shall sing a song of you and your generosity to everyone I see! What is your name?"

Dragorim did not hesitate when he gave his answer.

"Nikos," he said.

Once their interaction ended, the boy ran to order food for himself, and was totally unrestrained in his excitement at finally being able to eat a full meal again. Dragorim leaned back as a strange mixture of both longing and worry for his homeland washed over him while he watched the boy happily order every item on the inn's menu. The sorcerer watched the boy at the front counter carefully, and once he was sure the child had received *all* the food he had paid for, Dragorim turned his attention to the musicians and laughed at their bawdy and irreverent songs.

Dragorim noticed that their songs tended to focus on either the indiscretions of lonely farmer's wives, or the atrocities committed by the local baron. The sorcerer looked around the room and saw that there were no armed guards of any kind here. The people in this tavern may have lived under the baron's oppressive thumb, but they certainly did not shy away from expressing their displeasure for it. Suddenly, the door to the inn flew open, and a shouting man rushed through the door.

"He comes! The baron's carriage comes! Quickly, silence yourselves!"

Dragorim quickly realized that this was the man that had been keeping watch outside the tavern. Silence crashed down upon the room, as no one wanted to draw the baron's attention to their festivities. It was not long before the clattering sound of wooden wheels rolling against the stone-paved road outside became audible inside the tavern. All waited with baited breath in the hope that the carriage would pass. The clattering sound of the uneven wheels stopped, and an audible rustling leaked through the walls as someone was heard exiting the unseen carriage. Footsteps grew louder as multiple people now approached the tavern, and the door soon swung open to reveal a pair of armed men. They strode into the room with the arrogant swagger of men accustomed to getting what they wanted.

"You, innkeeper!" the lead soldier barked.

"Yes, my… my lord?" the innkeeper stammered.

"Food! We demand food for ourselves and the lord baron."

"What will you have?" the innkeeper asked.

"Meat and bread. Make it fast!"

As the innkeeper hastily informed his cooks of the situation, the other soldier in the pair stalked about the room as though he was looking for an excuse to hurt someone. Dragorim had seen thugs like these many times before, and he knew the consequences for resistance.

The innkeeper nearly tripped on his way back from the kitchen as he hastily presented the soldiers with all the food he could carry.

"In a basket, you moron!" the solider berated.

Again, the innkeeper rushed to his task and quickly loaded all of the food into a nearby basket. Suddenly, the second soldier looked to his compatriot.

"Don't forget about the tax," he said.

The lead soldier smiled and looked back to the innkeeper, who began pleading with them.

"Please sir; have I not been taxed enough?"

The lead soldier laughed at the innkeeper's plight.

"If you pay no taxes, how is the baron to pay for soldiers to protect you from the bandits on the road?" he jeered.

The innkeeper nervously looked back and forth between the two soldiers and quickly reached into his coin purse for the money they demanded. Once the coins were handed over, the soldier bowed mockingly and the pair departed the inn with their ill-gotten gains. Dragorim wished he had done something to oppose the soldiers, but knew that anything he did would cause the people here to suffer under the baron's retribution.

As soon as the soldiers departed, the musicians announced the end of their long performance. However, the evening of good food and pleasant songs had made Dragorim nostalgic for the happier days of his youth… and he wanted more. The sorcerer cared little about the baron's oppressive presence outside the inn, and so Dragorim stepped forward to ask the performers for one final tune.

"My wondrous musicians! Before you go, I must beg a boon of you. There is a song from my homeland… I would very much like to hear it once more."

The musicians looked to the innkeeper as they wondered if they would be paid for this extra work. The innkeeper shook his head, as with the extra taxes taken, he no longer had the funds to pay them. However, the musicians looked to each other, and after a several seconds of whispered conversation, the singer spoke to Dragorim.

"We would love to perform one final song for you, and we will do it for free, for the baron's foul robbery should not curtail our merriment. What is the name of the tune you wish to hear?" the singer said.

The sorcerer chuckled gently.

"I am afraid this is not a tune that you would know; but I would gladly teach it to you. It is simple once you get the knack for it. Let me show you."

The sorcerer rose from his seat and his enormous frame shocked the crowd as he stepped on stage. He paid them little heed and gestured to the percussionist first.

"First, we must have the drum. Now yours is smaller… lighter than the one normally played for this song, but it will have to suffice. Here, let me show you the pattern to play."

The sorcerer drummed against the floor with his hands. The rhythm he performed fit in a simple meter based on groups of four beats. The pattern was elementary and did not take long for the drummer to master. Once the beat was established, the sorcerer turned to the harpist.

"Your harp, it is a fabulous harp, though not tuned for the music of my homeland. Let me tell you how to tune it to my needs."

After a few instructions from the sorcerer, the harpist went to work, adjusting some strings to be sharper, and others to be flatter. Finally, the harp was tuned the way Dragorim needed it. Normally the difference in pitch from string to string was tuned in even intervals, but they were now tuned so that the interval between each string was a step larger than the last. It was an odd system that created alien harmonies when the strings were played together. The audience wasn't sure how they felt about the sounds that were produced, but Dragorim loved them the moment he heard them. The sorcerer then began teaching the harpist the simple melody that went with the beat and lyrics. Like with the drummer, it did not take long for the harpist to master it. Finally, Dragorim turned to the singer.

"The lyrics are not in a language you speak, and it would be unfair of me to force you to learn them and perform the translation right here in front of your audience. If you don't mind, *I* will sing the lyrics."

The singer saw the hint of madness behind Dragorim's eyes and simply nodded at the barrel chested giant and stepped aside. Now a performer, the sorcerer turned and faced the crowd.

"The bawdy songs sung tonight reminded me of one such tune from my homeland. My voice is not my craft, but with the help of these musicians, I hope that I can share a piece of my homeland with you. I hope you enjoy the song."

The sorcerer then hummed and sang sounds that made no sense to the audience. However, he was merely warming up and reminding his ear how the tune went. Once Dragorim felt prepared, he joined his voice with the harp and the drums in full. First, he sung the tune in his native language. The audience listened to the haunting sound as it instantly grabbed the attention of everyone seated before him. It was clearly music from a culture no one had ever encountered before, and even the drunkards in the audience felt driven to listen to the curious sounds uttered by the stranger. Finally, the sorcerer stopped and spoke again.

"I'm sorry. I have wanted to hear it in my native tongue like this for a long time. Now, I will attempt to sing it for you in *your* language so that you may understand its meaning. The translation is… not exact, and the rhymes may not be consistent, but I think the punch line will still be effective."

The passionate sorcerer began to sing again, and this time the lyrics were sensible to the listeners. Dragorim stumbled some, for the form was not right; but he did not care, as the meaning of the words was what he cared for the most.

> *On one summer's morn I found lady fair,*
> *She worked in her field,*
> *She worked for her grain.*
> *She worked til her body ached with great pain.*
>
> *I found her hair was so very pretty,*
> *Her nose and her smile*
> *Were oh, so dainty,*
> *My heart ached for her touch,*
> *Her grace, my love.*
>
> *A loaf of bread was what I bore for her*

Bread was what I brought
Her heart swelled for me
Or that was what I thought.

But another man brought meat to her door,
His meat won prizes
His ham brought delight
His sausage filled her field, night after night!

With his song concluded, the sorcerer burst out laughing. Others in the crowd did not know what to make of the melody that went with the lyrics, but laughed at the punchline just the same. The sorcerer clapped each musician on the back and thanked them for the service. He then took his leave of them all and left behind a confused and bewildered crowd. The time for rest had come to an end, and Dragorim now wished to find another horse and continue his ride.

As the sorcerer headed to the back of the inn in search of stables, an audible cry of pain drove him to sprint for his destination. As Dragorim rounded the corner of the inn, he found the shadowed spot from where the cry had come, and his heart fell. The starving boy he had helped but a short while ago now lay dead. The same pair of armored men who had robbed the inn now crouched over the boy's corpse as they greedily stole the food he had intended to bring back to his family.

Dragorim's rage flamed within his heart as he summoned balls of fire to his hands and strode towards the murderers. The pair of bandits looked up from their victim to see the enraged sorcerer stalking towards them. At the sight of the fire in his hands and the fury in his heart, the murderers ran for their lives. They did not make it more than a few steps before the sorcerer cast his flame in their path and set the ground ablaze. The bandits stopped in their tracks and pleaded with Dragorim for their lives. They even offered him the food stolen from the child they had murdered.

"Please sir! Take it, it is all we have!" they cried.

Dragorim pitied them not.

"Why did you slay this poor boy? He would have shared his bounty with you, had you thought to ask. Now his blood is on your hands, and you shall pay for it dearly!"

The lead robber spoke again, begging for his life.

"We're sorry! The baron ordered the boy to give him the food, and the boy refused, saying our lord had enough. The boy ran! We just did what we were told!"

The sorcerer looked past the men who worked for the wicked baron, his eyes scanning the road for any sign of the nobleman's carriage. There was no sign of it, save for tracks driven into the dirt path. Dragorim turned his fiery gaze back to the men kneeling before him.

"Was the food taken from the inn not enough to sate the baron's appetite?" Dragorim demanded. He received no answer, and his patience ran thin. "Tell me one thing… and you *may* be spared. Where is his carriage?"

The soldier nodded and pointed back in the direction the carriage had taken along the road.

"They will not have gone far. He will have waited for us to return with his food."

More flame appeared in the sorcerer's hand, and he spoke again.

"Thank you. May your souls find redemption before your gods."

Dragorim lashed out with all of his rage and the two soldiers screamed in agony as fire consumed them. The sorcerer watched with vengeful satisfaction until all that remained of them were charred skeletons.

Now that the murderers had been dealt with, Dragorim sprinted along the dark road in the direction the soldier had pointed. Fire burned in Dragorim's soul, and he intended to inflict this fire on the baron and all those who aided the wicked nobleman. It did not take long for Dragorim to catch up to his foe, as the baron's carriage had indeed stopped to wait for the now dead soldiers to rejoin them. Several armed, torch-bearing men guarded the baron's conspicuous, gilded carriage. These soldiers wore mail armor and helmets that glittered in the torchlight, and carried various weapons and shields at their sides

Under the cover of darkness, the sorcerer withdrew a gaulderen from his bag and lined it up for a throw. Once Dragorim was confident in his aim, he hurled the object of power through the air. The small gaulderen struck its mark and the magic within exploded with such power that the carriage was hurled onto its side with splintering force. Shards of wood scattered across the road as the splendid carriage was smashed into pieces. Frightened screams filled the air as horses were sent tumbling, and men scrambled to aid the baron and find the source of the attack.

After waiting a moment to size up the enemy's response, Dragorim stepped out of the shadows and hurled a ball of flame that incinerated one of the soldiers where he stood. Another guard saw Dragorim and rushed towards him with his spear aimed at the sorcerer's heart. Dragorim turned to face the threat and deftly sidestepped the over committed thrust. The soldier tried to change direction, but fell off balance as he missed his target. He could do nothing to stop the sorcerer's assault. Dragorim grabbed the soldier by the helmet with one hand and tore the soldier's ax from his belt with the other. The soldier stumbled as he was pulled further off balance by the sheer strength Dragorim threw behind the maneuver. The sorcerer wasted no time and struck the soldier with a hard blow to his unarmored neck. The man cried out in fear as the blade sliced deep into the the his throat. The soldier sputtered and gagged as he toppled to the ground and choked on his own blood.

Another soldier ran for Dragorim. However, he was more careful than the previous man and stopped his charge before he was in range of Dragorim's ax. He adopted a practiced, effective guard with his spear and drove a hard thrust towards his opponent. Dragorim turned the soldier's attack aside with his ax and threw a counter cut, but the soldier expertly parried Dragorim's blow with the butt of his spear. Before the soldier could bring the point of his spear back on line, the sorcerer leaped upon him and seized his helmet with a hand now filled with fire. The helmet melted on top of his head and the man could only scream in agony for the final torturous moments as his life came to an end.

The third and final soldier had just succeeded in extricating the Baron from the wrecked carriage when Dragorim fell upon him. The soldier stood no chance against the sorcerer's rage and was cut down in an instant. The baron now faced Dragorim's fury alone. The fat, gluttonous ruler looked upon the sorcerer in terror. He had several cuts on his face and his clothing was torn and dirty, but was otherwise unharmed.

"What is it you want?" the baron demanded. At first, Dragorim was confused by the baron's confident attitude, until he realized that the nobleman was so complacent in his position that it simply hadn't occurred to him that Dragorim aimed to kill him. The sorcerer grinned wickedly at his prey.

"At your orders, your men killed a starving boy for the food *I* had given him. From what I have heard and seen, you have already taken the food from their farms, and yet that is still not enough for you?"

The baron tried to answer, and after a great deal of stuttering, gave his reply.

"The harvest has not been good this year. I have soldiers to feed, a castle to maintain, and—"

"And a belly to keep full, I see," Dragorim said as he roughly poked the baron's over-sized stomach with his ax.

The baron stopped talking for a moment, and then defiantly looked up at the sorcerer.

"I was hungry."

Dragorim nodded.

"Well, we shall have to fix that, won't we?"

The sorcerer tossed the ax aside and started to intone an ancient spell. The baron was frozen in fear as Dragorim rubbed his hands together and spoke in a language unknown to anyone else in the world. The sorcerer opened his hands and revealed an ominous red light that hovered in the air for but a moment before it flew into the baron's heart.

The baron's expression turned blank. All traces of fear were now absent from his face, save for his eyes, which still reflected the terror in his soul. The sorcerer spoke again.

"I have only ever used this spell once before. It only works on those enslaved to their greed, and I do not encounter them often, for I refuse to suffer such men to live. Your crimes are too horrific for a traditional punishment to be sufficient. Your will is now enslaved to mine. You said you were hungry, yet plenty of food surrounds you." The sorcerer gestured to the corpse of the nearest fallen soldier. "*Eat.*"

Horror filled the baron's heart. He wished to scream, but he could not, as the sorcerer's spell allowed him only to crawl to his former guard and devour the dead man's flesh.

"Only when you have consumed the bodies of every one of your guards will you be free to go."

Both of them knew there was no surviving this punishment. To eat that much in one sitting would cause the baron's stomach to burst, and he would die. Dragorim leaned in close to the baron's blood covered face and spoke to him one final time.

"You will never make anyone go hungry again."

The sorcerer then turned and resumed his search for a horse. The road ahead of him was long, and he wished to hasten his journey as much as possible.

Chapter 6

Daegal fumed within Sigaberht's throne room. He had been kept waiting for some time, and the longer he stood in that oppressive space, the more he found himself wishing that he was *anywhere* else. The ealdorman was sure he was in for another dressing-down regarding his temper; and the only thing that held him in the room was his oath of obedience, without which he would have long since departed.

Daegal quickly glanced over at Leif, whom silently stood beside him. Leif's impassive expression belied his anxiety, and he was uncharacteristically oblivious to Daegal's growing fury. The older man was deeply lost in his own thoughts, and nervously waited to make his report about Radnor and Elena's alternate plan to repel their enemy.

Despite Daegal's frustrations, he understood why Leif was so loyal to Sigaberht. Unlike the other ealdormen, Leif had started life as a peasant and managed to prove himself worthy of greater and greater titles. Leif was a rarity among the other nobles, and most resented him for it. Additionally, Leif had not been raised among the nobles like the other ealdormen, and as a result, had been conditioned from birth to believe he was less than the others. To combat this, Sigaberht had done what he could to make Leif feel like he was equal to the other noblemen, going so far as to replace Neugeld's previous ealdorman with him.

Daegal did not share the contempt that other ealdorman held for Leif. Ever the pragmatist, Daegal had recognized that Leif had always proven to be a strong, competent leader, especially when faced with adversity. Generally speaking, Daegal respected Leif, which was a massive improvement over how he felt about the other ealdormen in Sigaberht's court.

Osmund was a boy and had done nothing to earn his respect, nor consideration as an equal. As for Aethelstan… if Daegal thought Osmund was not truly his equal, he felt Aethelstan was *far* beneath him. Aethelstan had done nothing but draw Daegal's ire from the day they met. In Daegal's opinion, it had been a mistake to allow Aethelstan to be anything but a floor sweeper, let alone an ealdorman. But, such things were not up to him. They were the purview of the earl, and the earl was Sigaberht.

Daegal's meandering thoughts were interrupted as Sigaberht and Ashveldt abruptly entered the throne room. Daegal was pleased to see that Ashveldt looked more relaxed. The young man no longer wore his armor, and instead was clad in a dark green tunic made from soft linen.

However, Daegal's blood boiled when he saw that Aethelstan and Osmund walked with them. The ealdorman's mind raced with the possible implications presented to him as the other ealdorman entered *alongside* Sigaberht and his heir… as though they were of equal status to them. However, relief washed over Daegal when at a gesture of Sigaberht's hand, Osmund and Aethelstan stepped away from the royal presence and joined Daegal and Leif before him.

Leif cleared his throat to make his report, but Sigaberht spoke first.

"My lord ealdormen, I have summoned you all back here so soon after our last meeting… because I must make an apology. Thanks to the wise counsel of my son, I now realize that I have done one of you wrong, and as an example for my son, I must make apology to this person not in private, but in front of those who witnessed my offense." Sigaberht turned his gaze to Daegal. "Ealdorman Daegal, I was unjustly harsh with you today. The oath between a lord and his vassal runs both ways. If it is not to the benefit of both parties… then it is no oath at all. While I still disagree with your counsel, and believe that your suggested course of action will be ineffective, I should not have been so abusive in my manner towards you. Your harsh words to the other ealdormen were in response to ridicule that *I* permitted. It is unreasonable to expect a man in your position to stand idly by and accept such harsh words from his peers. I now, in front of your peers, apologize for the way I treated you."

Daegal was speechless. Just a moment before, he had almost been ready to abandon Sigaberht to Drakomar's mercy, but now, a formal apology in front of Osmund and Aethelstan? For a person in Sigaberht's position to so publicly apologize for the way he spoke to an underling -- especially in front of the other ealdormen, it was either the most genuine apology anyone had ever made, or a crafty manipulation to buy Daegal's loyalty with kind words.

Either way, it was working.

Regardless of the sincerity of Sigaberht's words, a public apology was social currency Daegal could use to gain favors from other ealdormen down the road. He didn't like playing the political game, but sometimes it was the only way to get things done.

Daegal bowed graciously to Sigaberht and spoke in kind.

"My lord Sigaberht, I am humbled by your apology, and I gladly accept it. I shall always strive to maintain polite discourse when within your court."

Sigaberht nodded politely and felt satisfied that the matter was now finished. Daegal snuck a quick glance at Osmund and Aethelstan. To his surprise, Osmund appeared pleased at the situation. Upon seeing Osmund's demeanor, Daegal began to consider that he might have misjudged the young man. He made a mental note to try to speak with Osmund at the next opportunity. If Osmund could be reasoned with, perhaps he could be turned against Aethelstan. At the thought, Daegal turned to look at his hated peer. To Daegal's delight, Aethelstan looked as though he had just bitten into a rotten apple.

Osmund spoke next.

"My lord Daegal, in keeping with our lord's example, I would also apologize to you. I was swept up in the fervor of the moment, for the stresses of being an ealdorman are so new to me. You are my senior and I, too, spoke harshly and out of turn. I hope that you might forgive me also."

Daegal was further surprised by this behavior from Osmund and wondered what had happened that caused such an open shift in Daegal's favor. He also wondered if this was a power play on Osmund's part. Was this the first sign of interest in an alliance? Was it merely an effort to stay in Sigaberht's good graces? Or was it something else?

No matter what it was, Daegal knew how to play the game. He clasped Osmund's shoulder and bowed towards the young man to demonstrate his respectful acceptance of the apology.

Daegal wondered if Aethelstan would apologize. If he did, Daegal would know that Sigaberht must have ordered their apologies, and Osmund's sincerity would be called into question.

Aethelstan was silent.

Daegal took a strange sense of satisfaction in that. He briefly considered needling Aethelstan about it, as he was now the "odd man out". However, Daegal decided against it, as any hostile remark would push the boundaries of what Sigaberht would allow, and Daegal did not wish to squander his newfound favor.

Such petty nonsense is Aethelstan's game, not mine. Daegal reminded himself.

Before anyone else could continue, Ashveldt spoke.

"We both would like to thank all of you for returning so abruptly. Ordinarily, we might have waited for a more convenient time for something such as this, but given the circumstances, we wanted to be sure the apology was made before the enemy might prevent us from doing it properly." There was a pause in his speech as each ealdorman bowed to Ashveldt. Once they were done, Sigaberht's heir continued. "Since you are all here, it was decided we should reopen the debate regarding our battle plans. Has anyone devised a suitable plan that might replace the one we have?"

Leif stepped forward and spoke.

"My lords… Daegal and I were just at Veigarand's home…"

Sigaberht leaned forward in his seat upon hearing two of his ealdormen were present at the home of a servant he did not trust. However, the earl did not interrupt Leif's speech. "A plan was formed that may accomplish the same goals as yours, but with less risk."

"Please, let us hear it!" Ashveldt said.

Leif then explained the plan while the earl and his son listened eagerly. Sigaberht bore his usual impassive, contemplative expression as Leif spoke. Ashveldt's face was marked by such surprise that he stood with his mouth nearly agape. Sigaberht noticed this and decided he would later remind Ashveldt about hiding his feelings from public view when in court. Once Leif finished speaking, Ashveldt addressed him.

"Your plan hinges on a great many unknowns. Do we know that Elena's gaulderen will work? Do we know that Halfdan will not simply abandon us the moment he is on the road?"

"Halfdan is a monster, but he is a monster like Veigarand: both are bound by moral codes of their own making. If Halfdan says he will attack the enemy supply lines, we can be sure he will do so," Leif replied.

Sigaberht sat lost in thought. Finally, after an uncomfortably long silence, he spoke.

"And what if you fail? What then?" he asked.

Daegal took the opportunity to throw his support behind Leif.

"Then… I think we can all agree to go along with the original plan. I may not like it, but if the other options prove ineffective, I find it hard to argue with," Daegal said.

There was silence as the royals considered the plan. Ashveldt spoke next.

"Father, I do believe this is the best plan available to us. I think we should pursue it to the fullest extent that we can."

Sigaberht nodded to his son, and then turned back to the ealdormen.

"My son's counsel is wise. However, I would not switch strategies without first hearing the consultation of my ealdormen. Leif, I assume you support this plan?"

Leif looked to the other ealdormen for any sign of support. No one would make eye contact with him and their faces turned to stone. They waited to see how Sigaberht would respond to Leif's answer before revealing their own positions. Leif turned back to Sigaberht and after a moment's hesitation, nodded his agreement.

"Speak up! I would not be satisfied until all may *hear* your proclamation!" Sigaberht commanded.

"Yes, my lord. I do support this plan!" Leif said.

Sigaberht turned to Daegal.

"Do you, most loyal ealdorman, support this plan?"

"I pledge my support for this plan!" Daegal enthusiastically replied.

"I also support the new plan!" Osmund shouted before he was asked.

Finally, all eyes turned to Aethelstan.

"Aethelstan, you are oddly silent. What say you?"

Aethelstan bowed graciously before his lord.

"I concur with the other ealdormen. This plan seems the safest. That being said, I will gladly support you if we must still resort to using the monsters in the dark forest."

Daegal scoffed audibly, but otherwise kept his thoughts to himself. Sigaberht shot him an angry glance that caused Daegal to bow and turn away from the royal presence to show his own apology. With the unspoken exchange with Daegal complete, Sigaberht continued.

"Then this is what we shall do. We shall hold out against our foes on the first day. I will need all of your men to accomplish this. Veigarand will be the spearhead of our defense. If he says he wants something, you give it to him. He does not command your men, but he will know best how to use his reputation to drive the enemy from our walls. They must see him for what he is, and they must flee from him in terror."

The ealdormen all nodded in agreement, though Aethelstan made a comment.

"My lord, your logic is sound, though it seems we rely on monsters to win the battle for us. Veigarand? The werewolf? And this… Elena… woman?"

Leif wheeled on Aethelstan with a near murderous rage that caught everyone in the room off guard.

"I will not hear you speak of Elena as a monster again, do you hear me?" he said.

Aethelstan took a step back from Leif, fearful of the sparks in Leif's voice. Sigaberht smashed his fist against the arm of his throne and sprung from his seat.

"Enough! Aethelstan, watch your tongue! I would not have you incite more discord!"

Aethelstan backed down like a dog with its tail between its legs. Sigaberht then spoke to the whole room.

"Do not forget, our *true* enemy is nearly at our gates. I will assemble you again tomorrow, and we will discuss battle plans in more detail. For now, you shall go. All... except you."

Sigaberht pointed at Aethelstan. The other ealdormen turned, bowed, and walked back to the exit. As they were leaving, Sigaberht turned to Ashveldt.

"Son, you are tired, and I have private business with Aethelstan. Go... get some rest."

The stern look in his father's eyes told Ashveldt that now was not the time to argue. The prince bowed to his father and swiftly left the room. Sigaberht then looked to his retainers and guards.

"Go. See that my son's needs are met. I shall be in my chambers shortly."

The guards and retainers followed their lord's command and hurried out of the room. Now alone with Aethelstan, Sigaberht turned his attention to the nervous looking ealdorman. Sigaberht rose and approached Aethelstan with his hand extended.

"I apologize for my harsh words. What I have to say to you now must not be suspected by the other ealdormen, or even my son. Is that understood?"

Aethelstan soared with elation. He had been worried he was about to be punished, but instead, his lord was taking him into his confidence!

"Yes, my lord," Aethelstan said, bowing deeply as he did. "What is it that you need of me?"

"You were not wrong when you said that we rely on monsters to win the battle for us," Sigaberht said. "I do not like this fact in the least. Moreover, I am disturbed that Daegal and Leif would hatch plans with the monsters in such an insidious manner."

"Do you fear treachery?" Aethelstan asked. He hoped the answer was "yes" so that he could leverage Sigaberht's fears into even greater favor with the Earl.

"Not yet," Sigaberht replied. "But betrayal is an unpredictable web of lies and deception. Leif and Daegal knew of my decision, and consulted with *Veigarand*. For them to have done this... they must be questioning my leadership. I cannot allow that to go unnoticed. To do so would be foolish and could lead to disaster not only for myself, but for my son." Sigaberht paused.

Thoughts turned in Aethelstan's mind. The ealdorman may not have liked Daegal or Leif, but Sigaberht's fears seemed excessively paranoid. However, Aethelstan was not going to turn aside from a chance to gain more influence, and stayed silent.

Finally, Sigaberht resumed. "I will not allow any harm to come to my son. He is all that I have left. I would give up my title and allow Piarin to claim these lands if it would keep him safe. But, alas, that is not how the world works. My son will never be safe unless the rule of Wulfgeld is securely his." Sigaberht let out a world weary sigh. "I must ask you a favor."

Aethelstan nodded as he eagerly awaited his lord's command. If he was successful in his task, he might not only gain favor from Sigaberht, but also from his heir.

"I ask that you watch Veigarand and keep me informed of his whereabouts. If there is to be treachery from the other ealdorman, it is from *him* that it will originate."

"If he is such a danger, why not have him killed?" Aethelstan asked.

Aethelstan's blood ran cold at as Sigaberht's expression turned unsettling.

"I asked myself the same question when he first arrived, when the blood of Neugeld had not yet dried upon his hands. The reason I dare not slay him, is as you have said: I must use monsters to win the day."

Sigaberht paused again and took a long breath.

"Veigarand may be the most dangerous monster here, but he may not be the most important. I must also ask that you have your men keep watch on Elena. She holds great power and may be the key to things larger and more profound than you or I could ever dream of. What scares me the most is that my son is now in the middle of this den of monsters. I fear there is knowledge about Elena's power that is being kept from me and I must know the truth if I am to protect my son. If you do these things, you will be richly rewarded. Do you understand?"

"Yes, my lord," Aethelstan replied. His eagerness and excitement were now stained with fear and apprehension. Spying on someone as temperamental and dangerous as Veigarand would be difficult to do without detection. Aethelstan doubted that Veigarand would respond to such spying in any way that didn't involve incredible violence.

"You have your orders, now go and carry them out," Sigaberht commanded.

Aethelstan bowed and hurried on his way out of the throne room. Sigaberht stood for a moment longer before collapsing into his throne. Exhaustion ate away at his will. He had been without proper sleep for some time, and he knew he would need plenty of it if he was going to survive the battle that loomed ahead. After spending a time collecting himself, Sigaberht, Earl of Wulfgeld, rose from his throne, headed for his chambers and hoped he could force himself to sleep that night.

Chapter 7

Far to the south of Wulfgeld, there was an ancient road built by an empire lost long before the current civilizations sprang to life. This road led south from the fortress-city of Drakomar, safely nestled in the Morakors Mountains, and ran down into the heart of the greatest kingdoms of the Southworld. Many people traveled along this road every day for trade, religious pilgrimage, and myriad other reasons. Now, a very distinguished traveler followed this road on a long, northward journey that took him beyond the Southworld's old kingdoms… past Drakomar's mighty walls… and would only conclude when he reached the gates of Wulfgeld.

Darkness fell upon on the trail, and so the traveler decided to make camp for the night. It did not take him long, for he was an old sorcerer of great renown, though he preferred to be called a "wizard".

With a simple wave of his hands, he had set up his tent, lit his fire, and set his dinner to roasting on a spit. The wizard's name was Ulrich. He was an elderly man known for his congeniality and grace under pressure; a reputation he had spent many years cultivating through his kind deeds and protectiveness of those who could not defend themselves.

Exhausted from his trek, the wizard leaned back in his seat in the hopes that stretching out might ease his aching bones. Even with his advanced magical powers, the sands of time had taken their toll, and Ulrich's journey had been very slow and ponderous. The old wizard spread a thin, numbing ointment on his aching legs as he eagerly anticipated the completion of his cooking meal.

However, anticipation transformed into worry as the purpose of Ulrich's journey spun back to his mind. The wizard had friends among ravens, and they had warned him of the terrible things that had been unleashed upon Wulfgeld. However, Ulrich had already known of the terrible events even before his raven friends informed him of the details; for he had seen the power unleashed from halfway across the continent. The stunning aura had revealed a kind of magic unlike anything Ulrich had ever seen before, and the old wizard was sure others had seen it from even farther away than he had. Ulrich shivered as he thought not only of the terrible power that had made its presence known to the world, but of what others might try to do with it should they reach it first.

As he sat in contemplation, Ulrich fingered an old medallion that dangled from his drooping neck. This medallion bore the shape of a star that symbolized the Order of the Starlit God. It was an old order of sorcerers and witches devoted to preventing others of their kind from abusing their power. Ulrich was the last surviving member of this order. All the other members had either been killed in battle against evil sorcerers, or had died of old age. Now, seated alone at his campfire, the apprehensive wizard found comfort in the lines engraved upon the old symbol from his youth.

In addition to his general desire to help those in need, Ulrich also had a personal stake in the events that had transpired in Wulfgeld. He was the one who had taught the Hexverat how to wield their magic, and it was he who had set them loose upon the world. Based upon what the ravens had told him, his former students had wielded yet *another* kind of magic he had never seen before; and it too was extremely powerful. Ulrich contemplated this power with tremendous fear; for the ravens had spoken of the corruption that was now consuming the woods beyond Wulfgeld, and the restless dead that stalked within.

Ulrich wrung his hands in frustration. The Hexverat's actions were a betrayal of everything he had taught them, for he had trained them as healers, not killers. Now, their old teacher was compelled to help deal with the horrors his former students had left behind, and hopefully learn what terrible thing had brought his old pupils to such madness. He shivered at the thought. If this new magic and its defilement of creation was even half as deadly as he thought it was… he wasn't sure he *could* defeat it.

The wizard sighed to himself. Such thinking was not constructive. At the very least, he could use his powers to help heal the sick and the wounded… just as the Hexverat *should* have been doing. Then another thought struck him. It was quite possible that the people of Wulfgeld would not want his help. He wielded magic just like the Hexverat, and he could become the object of a newfound fear of it. Ulrich had seen such problems arise before. One wicked sorcerer was all it took to turn an entire city against all mages. Ulrich shook his head. Again, such thinking was not helpful to his mood. No matter what, he needed to reach Wulfgeld and do what he could to repair the damage his former students had done.

Suddenly, an object dropped to the ground beside him. Ulrich jumped, startled by the sudden intrusion into his thoughts. He scrambled to his feet and realized with fright that the thing which had plummeted to the ground beside him was a dead raven. Its lifeless eyes stared up at Ulrich as he frantically scanned the trees for any sign of a threat. Almost as if on command, a black-robed figure strode from the shadows and into the firelight. The identity of Ulrich's hooded foe was impossible to make out as he stood at the dimmest part of the light. The two stared at each other for a long time as they sized each other up. After a while, Ulrich decided he had had enough of this waiting game and decided to take action. He took a step forward and challenged his opponent.

"Show yourself to me, stranger! I have no interest in tricks tonight! Show yourself and tell me what you want, or begone!"

The shadowy figure bowed gracefully and with a wave of his hand, flung a projectile of sickly green energy straight for Ulrich!

The aged wizard turned his hand and quickly summoned a barrier that shielded him from the force of the vicious spell. Ulrich gritted his teeth in pain as the force of his opponent's attack nearly shattered the barrier. He might be old, but he was not helpless. Ulrich snapped his hand and a bolt of lightning sprang from his fingertips towards his foe. The cloaked enemy did not move away from the attack, but instead threw up a barrier of his own. Ulrich watched as his foe absorbed the energy into his own body… and hurled it back at him! The aged sorcerer yelped in pain as the returned bolt shattered his shield and scorched his clothes.

The mysterious opponent had just used a technique Ulrich had only ever seen once before, and fear clutched at his heart when he realized who his adversary must be. The old wizard reached into his pouch and withdrew a gaulderen of great strength. Before the robed figure could attack again, Ulrich threw the gaulderen at his own feet. The fragile object shattered and a wall of blue light sprung from the ground. The black-robed sorcerer hurled a ball of fire straight into the new barrier, and much to Ulrich's relief, his shield repelled the onslaught.

Confident his barrier could withstand any punishment his enemy could throw at it, Ulrich took a moment to breathe and think. He closed his eyes in deep concentration and felt his awareness of the world leave his body as it entered the forest around him. The old wizard felt every leaf, every flower, and every blade of grass that surrounded his mortal form. Now connected to the life around him, Ulrich pushed energy from his soul into the plants and sent a message to any who might hear.

"Help!"

With his message sent, Ulrich snapped his awareness back onto his foe, who was now mustering strength for another assault against Ulrich's shield. However, the attacker realized the futility of another direct attack and stopped to look upon the wizard. The robed figure bowed once more, and then removed the hood from his head. Ulrich's eyes narrowed in anger as he recognized the flaming red hair and beard of his foe. Uncharacteristic malice filled Ulrich's heart as he addressed his attacker.

"I had hoped you had the decency to die in whatever hole you crawled into after we last met… Dekaros," Ulrich spat bitterly.

Dragorim chuckled when Ulrich called him by one of his old names.

"You old fool! Our last encounter was merely a minor setback, nothing more."

"Then why did you wait until now to reveal yourself… to take your revenge!"

"I have no time for the luxury of revenge, though I must admit that this battle pleases me. No, I do this for the same reason *you* travel on this road! I seek the prize that awaits me in Wulfgeld!"

Ulrich's eyes widened in fear.

"You cannot hope to control the forces that await you there. If you try, you will surely doom us all!"

Dragorim shook his head.

"I have no use for the powers of chaos that your students so clumsily wielded. I seek the power that snuffed them out! *That* is the key to *everything*!"

Ulrich did not understand what his old nemesis was saying and decided to probe further. He hoped not only to gain information, but also to stall his opponent for as long as possible.

"You talk about 'powers of chaos'? Is that what they used? How do *you* know of this power?"

Dragorim laughed; it was a laugh that betrayed madness of a kind Ulrich had never seen. It was not the laugh of a man devoured by lust for power or overwhelming sorrow. It was the madness of a man whose life had been devoid of hope for many ages… and finally grasped at hope once more; and it frightened Ulrich beyond comprehension. Once Dragorim finished laughing, he answered Ulrich's question.

"I once tried to control it myself, but great calamity forced me to give it up. It's a pity you didn't train your students better. They might still be alive today if you had done your job properly!"

Ulrich shook his head and changed the subject away from his own perceived failure.

"Others will come to Wulfgeld. They will stop you. They will not allow you to destroy all for *your* selfish ambitions!"

"By the time they are aware of my intentions, it will be too late."

There was a sudden creaking behind Dragorim that brought a malicious smile to Ulrich's lips.

"No, I believe it is too late for *you*."

As the creaking grew louder, Dragorim spun to face his new foe. Suddenly, a long, grasping vine started to wrap itself around his ankle! As the sorcerer hurriedly leaped away from its binding grip, an unknown attacker thrust a wooden object towards his face. Thinking Ulrich had launched a tree limb at him; Dragorim threw his hands over his face as he hurriedly summoned a barrier to protect himself. While the golden barrier absorbed some of the force of the blow, Dragorim had been too slow to summon it, and the limb still struck him on the head with enough force to send him tumbling to the dirt.

Dazed, Dragorim could only lie on the ground until a brilliant flash of light brought him back to his senses. He rolled to the side just in time to avoid a deadly white fireball Ulrich hurled at him. Dragorim flashed to his feet and sent fireballs of his own towards Ulrich's shield.

Much to Dragorim's annoyance, his assault had little impact on the barrier that still stood strong. He did not have time to try to find a way around Ulrich's defense before another limb from the shadows of the woods lashed out at him. Dragorim deftly ducked the blow and realized it had not come from the nearby trees, but from something else within the black woods. The sorcerer then withdrew a potent gaulderen from his pocket. He clutched it tightly and summoned a ball of flame again; with the aid of the gaulderen, this fire was far more powerful than before. Dragorim hurled it with all his might into the shadows of the forest, and his effort was met with a woody, inhuman scream of pain as the ball of fire exploded in the darkness.

Firelight now illuminated the shadows of the forest before him and Dragorim nearly recoiled in fright when he finally saw the burning outline of his attacker engulfed in the flames. It was a tall, humanoid shape made from wood. Its head looked almost like the stump of a tree, though its long, powerful antlers and glowing yellow eyes revealed it as something much more. Its hands terminated in long, spindly, clawed fingers. Ulrich's cry for help had been heard; an elemental guardian of the forest had come to his aid!

As the elemental screamed in pain, it flung its arms out towards Dragorim. Waves of force ran along the ground towards him, but Dragorim leaped out of the way before their crushing power could smash him to pieces. In response to his agility, the roots of the nearby trees burst forth from the ground and sought to ensnare him! As he ran to avoid this threat, Dragorim had to dodge yet another fireball cast by Ulrich. Dragorim instinctively tried to use the trees for cover, but caught himself as he realized that doing so would only hasten his doom at the hands of the attacking elemental. If he had any hope of winning this battle, the sorcerer needed to find a way to isolate his opponents.

Dragorim quickly stole a glance back at Ulrich as he looked for a way to penetrate the barrier. In his momentary analysis, Dragorim found his opening. The sorcerer quickly summoned a bolt of lightning to his hand as he dodged yet another attack from the fearsome elemental. Then, with precise aim, he hurled his bolt at a tree limb that hung above Ulrich's head. The lightning bolt severed the limb from the tree and it plummeted straight for Ulrich's head! The old wizard tried to move out of the way, but his old body wasn't fast enough. The falling missile missed his head… but landed hard on his shoulder. Ulrich cried out in agony as he was driven to the ground by the weight of the impact. He tried to get up, but he could not move his arm. He tried to move again, but the pain and crunching of now broken bones told him his arm was useless. The pain proved too great for his frail constitution, and Ulrich's mind slipped into blackness.

With the wizard now unconscious, Dragorim was free to battle the elemental unhindered. However, exhaustion was beginning to overtake him. Dragorim relied on another gaulderen to help him as he hurled a second great ball of fire at his woodland foe. The limbs of many nearby trees suddenly swung into the path of the fireball and formed a wall that absorbed the energy of his attack. Burning flames scorched and charred the limbs, but they held strong against the roaring fire. Dragorim stole a quick glance back to Ulrich. If he could kill the wizard now… the elemental might lose interest and go away. However, an enraged snarl turned Dragorim's attention back to the immediate threat.

Just as he looked back to the creature, the beast smashed through the burning limbs that had once shielded it. The elemental was charging at him with its antlers aimed at his heart! Dragorim tried to move out of the way, but before he could move, the tree roots around him finally caught him and held him in place for the elemental to trample.

With one final, desperate effort, Dragorim willed a barrier to form in between him and the rampaging monster. As the beast struck, the sorcerer felt the primal, unrelenting energy of his attacker's spirit join with his own soul as he absorbed the elemental's energy. After taking in the force of his opponent's attack, Dragorim focused all of the gathered energy into a single point and directed it into his opponent's head. Splintering, shattering force erupted from Dragorim's barrier and the elemental's head shattered. The elemental's now lifeless body was flung backwards by the force of Dragorim's counterattack and landed in a fragmented heap on the ground. With the elemental's death, the tree roots released their hold on the sorcerer and returned to their natural places beneath the earth. Not wanting to take any chances, Dragorim hurled a ball of fire upon the elemental's corpse. Fire crackled and sparked as the creature burned to ashes before Dragorim's eyes.

Now that the elemental was dead, Dragorim focused on calming his ragged breathing. He hated to admit it, but Ulrich had almost bested him as he did once long ago. Once the sorcerer's breath was under control, he turned his attention back to the fallen wizard, who had finally regained consciousness. Dragorim approach his defeated foe with malice in his heart.

Ulrich lashed out with his unbroken arm and sent a wave of fire cascading out in an arc in front of him which set the nearby grass ablaze. However, the spell was weak, and Dragorim merely waved the flames aside as he stalked towards Ulrich's fallen form. The old wizard tried to throw another ball of flame, but the pain was too distracting. He could not focus his mind to muster the strength he needed for his spell! Ulrich reached into his pouch for a gaulderen, but it was too late! Dragorim rushed towards him and ripped the pouch from him. The determined wizard tried to reach for the knife at his belt, but his foe simply tore the blade from his hand. Using only one arm, Dragorim lifted the now helpless wizard and hurled him into the nearest tree. Ulrich landed with a sickening thud and his head swam from the force of the blow. The brave wizard then spoke to his attacker, and he knew his end was near.

"All will know your *true* name, and they will know what you are the moment it is uttered!"

Dragorim laughed with malicious glee, for he knew an ancient quarrel was soon to be ended.

"How will they know? Will you tell them? If you knew my secret name, this battle would have gone very differently. Besides, no one alive knows any of my names, not that it matters. Getting a new name… it's like getting a new pair of shoes. I have only gone by my current name for a short while. Do you think I should change it again? Which one shall I choose? Should I steal yours?"

Ulrich shook his head.

"None of the others would believe you are me—"

"They don't have to believe I am you. There can be more than one 'Ulrich' you know. And… you are the last living person who has ever seen my face."

"Is that why you take your revenge now?" Ulrich asked.

Dragorim smirked at his prey.

"Now he puts it together. Others like you will try to stop me… and they will die. But I must have secrecy. No one must suspect that I will be the cause of their deaths. But for you… that was not an option. You know my face and would see through any method I could conjure to conceal it. I had to kill you directly before… before you could stop me from doing what *must* be done."

"Is that what you tell yourself? I've seen what you think must be done, and the consequences would be so severe—"

"That is what you said last time, old man… you and your *order*. You still do not know what my true intentions are."

"Then tell me, and perhaps we can help each other!" Ulrich pleaded as he tried to muster the strength for one final spell.

Dragorim smiled.

"No, I need not share my plans with you." Dragorim glared into Ulrich's eyes and resumed speaking. "Usually, I only kill because I *must* kill, not because I *want* to. For you, I'll make an exception."

Dragorim then wrapped his hands around Ulrich's neck… and squeezed. The red-haired sorcerer watched with satisfaction as Ulrich futilely struggled to free himself. It was no use, as the old man was no match for the muscled foe who throttled the life from him. The old wizard tried to muster his final attacking spell, but the pain was too great for him to maintain the focus he needed. After a few more agonizing moments, Ulrich lay dead at Dragorim's feet. The red-haired sorcerer looked down at Ulrich's lifeless body and muttered.

"Oh, how things could have been different… if you had just left me alone all those years ago. We might even have been friends."

Dragorim turned to the campfire and saw Ulrich's dinner still cooking upon the flames. The sorcerer uttered a prayer for his fallen foe. Despite his personal grudge against Ulrich, Dragorim respected the old wizard's spirit and compassion. Dragorim then spoke a word of kindness over his enemy's corpse.

"May this food keep your belly full as you pass on to the afterlife."

The sorcerer then looked up from Ulrich's body and gazed at the stars. With malice in his heart, he shook his fist at them.

"You will mock me no longer! I am coming, and I will regain what I have lost!"

As Dragorim started back down the road, he waved his hand over Ulrich's fallen corpse and lit the entire area ablaze with a torrent of fire. The campsite was now Ulrich's funeral pyre, and upon seeing his victory made manifest, Dragorim breathed a sigh of relief. He had successfully removed his most dangerous obstacle from the path to Wulfgeld, and he could now focus on the true task at hand. With that thought, he set out once more in search of the power he so desperately needed.

Chapter 8

The sun rose, bringing with it the final day before war came to Wulfgeld. By Sigaberht's estimation, Drakomar's army would arrive and make camp in the nearby woods later that evening. Sigaberht had hoped that Elena's ghouls could attack while the enemy was still unprepared, but she needed more time to assemble the number of ghouls needed for an assault. That being the case, Sigaberht resigned himself to holding the walls by sheer strength of arms. If he could drive the enemy back for just one day, the rest of the plan could come to fruition. However, until the enemy actually did arrive, the only thing that could be done… was waiting.

Waiting did not suit Radnor well, but thankfully, he had a plan to help him pass the time. He took Elena's suggestion and headed down to the barracks where the scouts were housed. Since Radnor had time before the battle, he was going to spend it giving Rolf a lesson in fighting. His walk was brisk and short, and he rapidly found himself nearing the barrack's threshold. Radnor inspected the condition of Rolf's living quarters as he approached.

The building showed its age, and Radnor suspected the structure was a repurposed stable. The wood-board walls were warped and left holes where they had once been solidly joined. To Radnor's comfort, someone had taken the time to fill the holes with clay. The thatched roof appeared solid enough to keep out rain and snow, and several chimneys led down to fireplaces that kept the occupants as warm as possible. There was an additional section that had been added to the original building where the officers now slept. The scout's barracks was not the most impressive building Radnor had ever seen, but the demigod saw that it provided ample shelter for orphans in need. There was a training yard just in the back of the scout's barracks that also connected to one of the barracks used by soldiers of Wulfgeld.

As Radnor approached, he saw a number of these soldiers engaged in drills on the field. To Radnor's disgust, none of the scouts were among them. He understood that some would be out spying on Piarin's forces, but the fact that none of them were out training for the coming battle seemed unusual to him.

Radnor made his way to the outer door of the officer's quarters and knocked firmly. It was not long before a thin, bedraggled man answered the door. It took Radnor a moment to realize that he was the same, well dressed captain he had seen the day prior.

The man did a double-take when he saw Radnor, for it was not often that a feared monster from horror stories told to children should be knocking on *anyone's* door, let alone *his* door. The man tried to straighten himself up, hoping to look as presentable as possible.

"I am Captain Sceotan. Can I help you?" he asked.

"There is a scout among you, Rolf Cellestan. I would like to work with him in the yard."

Surprise flashed across Sceotan's face, but quickly transformed into a warm smile.

"Good. I'll go fetch him."

The captain disappeared inside the barracks. The sounds of fierce commotion and whirlwind activity resounded through the walls. Just as Radnor was about to storm inside to see what the problem was, the main door to the barracks opened and a disorganized group of children came piling out. Both boys and girls of many ages wandered aimlessly, as they had no idea why they had been dragged out in the cold. The older ones did what they could to keep the younger ones in line, but some of the children were as young as five or six, and needed more corralling than the older children could muster. Radnor watched the crowd and noticed that Rolf and his friend Halig were among those trying to maintain some semblance of order. At first, the youths took no notice of Radnor, but as soon as Rolf saw him, he slapped Halig on the shoulder and exclaimed loudly.

"Hey look, he's here!"

Before Halig or any of the other children could comment on Radnor's presence, Sceotan shouted over the crowd.

"Scouts, is that how we are to act before the Ghost of the North!?"

After much hustle and bustle, the children quickly lined up and stood at attention, ready to receive their orders. Radnor looked past the group to the scout captain. The man shrugged at him.

"When you said you were here to train Rolf, I hoped you would be willing to train the lot of them."

Radnor's temper flared, but he refused to let it show too strongly in front of the youths.

"Why haven't *you* been training them? Should the wall be breached, they will need to defend themselves. Why are they not being prepared for the battle tomorrow?" Radnor demanded.

Sceotan dug his heels into the ground at Radnor's accusation. If he was at all afraid of the demigod, it did not show as he snapped back.

"Because my job was to train them for *scouting*, which is what I have done to the best of my ability. Now, if *you* want to teach strategies for not losing count of enemies, how to memorize coats of arms, how to estimate the number of men in large groups, what food can and cannot be foraged on the road, how to do all that *without* being seen, *and* teach them sword play at the same time, be my guest."

Radnor's temper burned even hotter at Sceotan's defiance, but he caught himself. The scout captain in charge of these boys hadn't been neglectful, he was just overworked and at his wits end. Radnor realized his mistake and quickly tried to make amends.

"I apologize… my question was unfair and implied negligence where there was none."

Sceotan nodded in reply, and then continued as if nothing had happened.

"Where would you like them to go?" he asked.

"To the yard. I would have them do drills with practice swords."

The captain nodded, and then turned to the formation of children.

"Alright then, you heard the man! Now march!"

The group of children did indeed march, and as they went, the captain turned to Radnor.

"Good luck getting those practice swords. The soldiers at the barracks mostly hoard them all. There are few good men in the lot, but most have become misers about their gear after the wolf attack."

Radnor looked out over the practice field, searching for the watchman in charge of maintaining order on the field. After a moment, he spotted the man sitting at a desk at the edge of the yard. That was the one he needed to talk to.

"Don't worry, I'm sure I can get them to cooperate," Radnor replied with icy determination.

The children waited for him at the fence just outside the training grounds. Rolf stood with a wide grin on his face. He had missed his practice sessions with Radnor, and was actually glad that he could share one with his friends. Halig, however, was less sure of the whole idea. He wanted to hold onto his childhood for as long as possible. In fact, Halig had only joined the scouts so he could receive food and shelter, and training to fight in a battle he was far too young for wracked his nerves without end.

Radnor stepped in front of the children and forcefully opened the gate in a manner that communicated to all of the soldiers already in the yard that like it or not, the children were coming in. A few of the men stopped their drills and gave odd looks to the squad of youths that came marching into their domain. One soldier looked like he was about to say something rude, but stopped when he saw Radnor step into the yard alongside the youthful invaders.

"Wait here," Radnor said to the group. He then moved over to the other side of the yard where all of the wooden swords were kept. The watchman on duty looked at Radnor at first quizzically, and then fearfully as he realized Radnor was heading *his* way. The watchman had fought alongside Radnor against the wolves and had seen firsthand what he could do to an enemy. The colossal warrior stepped up to the watchman, and spoke.

"I will need practice swords for the young scouts you see lined up over there."

118

The watchman sighed and shook his head.

"I would give them to you if I could, but they are all in use by the soldiers in the yard," he replied.

"Is there a way I could get them to let us borrow some?"

"You could try asking the sergeant. His name's Aelfric. But I warn you, he's been in a foul mood since the attack."

Aggravated, but not ungrateful for the help, Radnor thanked the watchman for his time, and then made his way over to have a chat with Drill Sergeant Aelfric.

Radnor had never met Aelfric, but Leif had spoken of him in meetings over the past month. Based upon Leif's words, the sergeant was a stern man, filled with the desire to produce the best possible soldiers he could *and* keep them sharp after their training was nominally completed. He was an experienced soldier and had fought against Drakomar's forces all of his life. The sergeant gave Radnor a scrutinizing look as he approached. Unlike the watchman, Aelfric was not afraid of Radnor's reputation. The grizzled sergeant had fought in a different area of the city during the wolf attack, and while word of Radnor's exploits had reached his ears, he still had his doubts about their accuracy. Just as Radnor nearly reached him, the sergeant spoke.

"What do you think you're doing, bringing those little urchins into my training yard?" Aelfric demanded. Instead of replying, Radnor took a close look at the man's upper arms. "What are you looking at?" the sergeant asked. Radnor then looked him in the eyes.

"You said it was *your* training yard, so I was checking to see if you had the earl's oath ring on your arm. You don't, which means *Sigaberht's* still the earl, and it's *his* yard… not yours."

The sergeant chuckled.

"Be that as it may, *I'm* the one responsible for this place, and I don't see how letting a bunch of kids run amok in here is going to do anyone any favors."

"I'm here to train the *scouts* to defend themselves," Radnor said.

"Is that so?" Aelfric said.

"Yes, it is. I know they are only children, but if the wall falls, they may have no choice but to take up arms. I came here to ask if you would be interested in doing joint exercises with them. I know the young scouts would learn a great deal."

Aelfric's eyes stared at an unknown point on the horizon as he considered Radnor's request. His brow furrowed, and he abruptly spoke again.

"You are who I think you are?" he asked.

Radnor stood silently and watched the man with cold malice in his eyes. Aelfric sighed.

"Look, you think I'm denying them the opportunity to train because it's fun for me? Look at these men!" Aelfric gestured angrily across the training yard. "Half of these men were not even soldiers before they were sent to me! Many of them are tradesmen who live in town and are wearing armor scavenged from the soldiers who died fighting the wolves. Others are the farmers and soldiers the other ealdormen brought with them, and it is *impossible* to get them to work together properly. I've broken up a number of fights already. Old rivalries do not die easily."

Radnor nodded, unsure of what the "old rivalries" were exactly. The sergeant saw by Radnor's expression that he unaware of these issues. Aelfric explained.

"Let me give an example. Estland, now ruled by Aethelstan, was once ruled by an earl of its own… that is until Sigaberht's ancestors conquered it. In fact, most of the shires here were independent until Sigaberht's forefathers established their dominion. When they were independent, they fought each other constantly. Even united under Wulfgeld, they have never really gotten over their prior grievances. So, you can see that my hands are already full with that problem and my equipment is already in use trying to bring novices up to speed, or in the excessive number of drills I've needed to run trying to get veterans who dislike each other to protect each other."

Radnor again felt sorry for how he had acted, just like he had when he first spoke to Sceotan. The weary warrior realized his own angst about his relationship with Sigaberht was still making him jump to conclusions about everyone who served the earl.

120

"Does Leif know about your problems?"

Aelfric nodded.

"Yes. He was the one who predicted they would happen before anyone else. More practice swords were made, but too many craftsmen died, so there aren't enough people to make them. There also should be more sergeants here to help me with this. Most of them are dead too, so those of us left are spread thin. No matter what Leif does, we simply don't have the equipment and manpower to train properly."

Radnor puzzled over why Leif hadn't asked him for help with this. Finally, Radnor gave up on piecing out the answer, and spoke again.

"Perhaps I can help you with that. My reputation may help get them to listen, at least a little bit. I can get some training for the scouts and you can hopefully get more cooperation from the soldiers.

The sergeant looked him over, and then nodded.

"Alright, I suppose not all the stories can be bullshit. Bring your people over, and let's get this started."

Radnor was surprised at how easily Aelfric had been convinced, but felt no need to question it. The warrior waved the children over and watched as Sceotan marched them forward. Aelfric stopped the drilling soldiers where they were and introduced Radnor to them. The demigod cringed a little when he heard the cheers and jeers that soared from the crowd as the sergeant referred to him as "Veigarand". Radnor assumed the cheers were from those who knew him from the recent battles, and that the jeers were from people who knew only hints of his reputation. One jeer was a lyric from one of the more common songs sung about his supposed misdeeds.

He will crush your spine,
He will take your head,
If you meet Veigarand,
You will soon be dead!

Anger rose in Radnor's throat as he heard them, and the demigod took the opportunity to eliminate dissent right then and there.

"I hear insults thrown at me as my name is spoken. Who among the men here dares to slight me to my face?" Silence reigned supreme as Radnor's rage burned down their bravado. "As I thought… cowards… the lot of you! So quick to turn your anger against each other instead of the enemy that comes to your doorstep!"

Upon hearing Radnor's incendiary words, one man stepped forward to challenge him.

"Who are you to speak this way? I have been told of you. You have no rank… no title! You are a caged animal! Nothing more!"

Radnor's eyes narrowed as he focused his gaze on the soon-to-be dead man, but before he could do anything regrettable, another voice came out of the crowd.

"I saw him fight the wolves! Without him, we would all be dead right now!"

"No, *you* would be dead! And *we* wouldn't have to pay taxes to Wulfgeld anymore!" cried another voice.

The shouting reached a fever pitch and was only silenced after much effort from the sergeant. Once the group had settled down again, Aelfric chewed them out.

"You call *him* an animal? Seems to me *you're* the animals! Squabbling over petty bullshit! You should be ashamed to even call yourselves men… let alone soldiers! Whether you believe the stories or not, Veigarand is an experienced warrior! I am allowing him to work with you because I think there is knowledge he can offer you! Now, if you refuse to learn from him, you might as well be helping the enemy, do you understand?"

Murmurs rippled through the crowd but they rapidly silenced. It seemed the naysayers had reluctantly agreed to work with him.

"That's better!" the sergeant shouted. "Now, I will turn things over to Veigarand."

Radnor nodded, and looked to the crowd again.

"The first thing you must do is learn to work together. All those who have never fought in a battle before, step to the east side of the yard. All those who are veterans, step to the west side of the yard."

After a few moments of shuffling, the two groups finished forming. The children stood and watched awkwardly. Radnor quickly addressed their confusion.

"I believe most of you should join the novices."

The children took the invitation and stepped over to the novice side. Interestingly, the novice men did not seem to mind having the children among them. Radnor noticed that Rolf stood near his friend, Halig, also among the novices. Seeing an opportunity to boost Rolf's confidence, Radnor called him forward.

"Rolf! It seems that you are on the wrong side. I believe you belong with the veterans."

Rolf reluctantly stepped forward, but stopped as some soldiers in the crowd laughed at Radnor's words. Before anyone could say anything directly, Radnor spoke.

"Rolf, it seems some here think I'm mistaken in my assessment. Tell me, how many battles have you seen?"

Rolf gulped nervously.

"I was there when Neugeld was destroyed, but I was there to be rescued. I was kept out of the fights with the ghouls on the road, though I very much wished to help you. My father died protecting me during the wolf attack—"

"Did you fight? Or did you cower like a baby?" Radnor goaded. He hoped the boy took the bait.

Rolf glared at him, but quickly realized what Radnor was doing. The boy strode over to the veteran's side of the yard and loudly proclaimed his deeds for all to hear.

"I fought alongside my father against the wolves! I joined Veigarand and the others when they traveled with the witches, and I survived the horrors there that drove other men mad!"

"Yes, you did," Radnor said. "And if that doesn't make him a veteran of battle, I don't know what does."

Murmurs spread through the crowd of soldiers. Hearing Rolf declare his deeds with such confidence enhanced their willingness to work with him and the other children. Seeing that there would be no further resistance, Radnor continued.

"Alright, here's the deal. We are now going to divvy up into pairs. I want one veteran and one novice per pair. It looks like there are more novices than veterans here, so some veterans will have to take two novices. You are also not to pair up with someone from your own shire, is that understood?”

Groans and complaints erupted from the groups, but Aelfric soon shut them down. Slowly, the two groups came together again, and at the incessant nagging of the sergeant, all of the pairs were formed. Radnor gave one more order.

“Talk among yourselves for a moment while I speak with your sergeant.”

Radnor turned to Aelfric, and was pleased to hear that conversation did start among the soldiers.

“Sergeant, I would like to wait a moment for them to converse, and then I would like you to gather all the pairs into two opposing sides. It is from here we will drill battle formations and tactics.”

Aelfric nodded.

“I have to admit, getting disparate groups to work together is not my specialty. I generally train only Wulfgeld’s forces. In the past, the other ealdormen were present when we needed men from their shires to work together.”

“And why are they not here now?” Radnor asked.

“Beats me,” Aelfric replied. “The only thoughts I have on the topic are for people above my station to say.”

“Please sergeant; I would appreciate it if you would share them with me.”

Aelfric looked him over, and sized Radnor up as a person. After a moment, the sergeant seemed satisfied with what he saw and answered.

“This stays between you and me. From what I can tell, Sigaberht is keeping the ealdormen close, and it seems like he’s *intentionally* keeping them away from their soldiers.”

“Do you think he suspects a coup?” Radnor asked.

Aelfric shrugged.

“I’m not sure. Like I said, that’s above my station. I just know that without their own rulers to keep them in line, the men from the other shires have been difficult to work with. They want things done *their* way. I’ve been trying to work with them in units based on where they are from, but it’s been impossible to get two units from different places to follow orders properly."

Radnor contemplated what he was told. Sigaberht's mind was an enigma, and he wasn't sure he would ever understand the earl. Satisfied with that thought for the time being, Radnor decided it was time to begin the training session. He gestured towards the soldiers in front of them as he spoke to Aelfric.

"Shall we then?"

Radnor was not surprised to see the Rolf and Halig had immediately paired up. This would be a good opportunity for both of them. Halig would get to learn how to fight, and Rolf would learn how to teach and lead.

It did not take long for the sergeant to form all of the pairs into two distinct teams. After a moment, Aelfric chose a leader for each "team". There were complaints, but after some discipline from the sergeant, the arguing ceased. Radnor and Aelfric quickly began running the two factions through drills. Some drills focused on outmaneuvering enemy formations, others trained on how to retreat in an organized way, and others taught them how to take ground from the enemy. Aelfric drilled them on unified commands so that units from different shires readily understood the different orders that could be given at a moment's notice.

Aelfric periodically switched up the team captains and members to force everyone to work with each other. Eventually, the insults and complaints transformed into jokes and friendly jabs. It wasn't perfect, but a sense of camaraderie started to form among the men. In order to keep the group mentally focused; the drills were switched over to include individualized training sessions. At first, Radnor led small groups of novices through the basics of swordsmanship. He illustrated key points about moving the sword in the most efficient ways possible, as well as simplified rules of combat that could be easily digested in a short time span. While he would never train a long term student this way, it was the best way to transmit as much information as possible to a large group of people with as little time as they had.

After a while, Radnor had the veterans begin helping
the novices. There still weren't enough practice swords for
everyone, but simple sticks were gathered to serve the same
role. Some groups of novices were given real swords and
practiced on training dummies while veterans from the
different shires sparred against each other with practice swords.
To Radnor's relief, the longer the groups trained together, the
more it seemed that the children had become almost adopted by
the men they trained with.

Radnor also kept an eye on Rolf as he worked with
Halig, and was pleased with what he saw. Rolf was proving to
be a natural teacher, and while the boy sometimes said things
that revealed gaps in his understanding of what Radnor had
taught him, there was a genuine affection behind Rolf's words
and actions that made shy Halig feel at ease with the older boy.
Radnor approached the pair, but before he could say anything,
Rolf spoke.

"Radnor! I would like you to meet my friend Halig!" As
Rolf introduced them, Radnor could see that Halig was scared
of him. The boy shrunk away even as Rolf tried to push his
friend into the spotlight. Radnor noticed how uncomfortable
Halig was and tried to smile reassuringly. It only seemed to
make things worse. Oblivious to what was happening, Rolf
kept talking. "Halig, you should learn from the man himself!
Doesn't that sound like fun?"

Halig shrugged. The child did not want to appear rude,
but he also was less than keen on working with Radnor. It was
this reticence that made Radnor decide that he should work
with Halig. He hoped that he could instill some confidence in
the boy. Radnor knelt in front of Halig and looked him in the
eye.

"I think it would be a pleasure to work with you, Halig.
Rolf, could you go work with some of the other children? I
want to work with Halig alone."

Rolf nodded sullenly and went on his way. The boy had
hoped to be able to watch Radnor teach Halig and be a part of
the process, but Rolf knew better than to argue with Radnor.

As Rolf walked away, Radnor stood and looked down at
Halig.

"Now, can you show me what Rolf was showing you?"

Halig nodded and began silently walking through some of the basics of sword work. Radnor watched with empathy as Halig clumsily swung the wooden sword through the air. The boy had clearly never held a sword before, and whatever Rolf had shown him, it had not helped. The longer Radnor watched, the clearer it became that Rolf had been introducing skills to Halig in the wrong order. Halig was too focused on where his hands should go and while he was pulling the sword along its length somewhat properly, his feet were always misaligned, and that made it much harder to control the weapon. Radnor saw what needed to be done, and got to work.

"You're doing well, but there's something you're missing that we can work on."

Halig looked up at Radnor, clearly already upset by this ordeal. Radnor continued. He tried to speak in a soft tone in an effort to alleviate Halig's fears. "It's alright. You've done some good work with the blade, but your feet need to be better aligned with your cut. Right now, you're moving the sword with just your arm and trying to turn it from your wrist. There is a better way. Let me show you..."

Radnor then demonstrated a simple sword cut without the complication of movement. He kept his feet planted and drove the blade to an invisible target in the air. Once the blade reached the target, he stopped his body, and the blade instantly stopped with him. Radnor then did the same technique again, but slowly so Halig could better see what he was doing. Radnor spoke as he slowly demonstrated the cut.

"Do you see how I move the blade? It is not just my arm that moves the weapon, but my whole body in connection with the ground. The strength and more importantly... *control* of a blow starts not from my arm, but from my feet."

Radnor then demonstrated the same blow, but now stepped as he did so. Blow after blow he threw at his invisible foe. Each strike was precisely aimed, and the blade danced through the air as though it were a part of his body. He moved with grace as his feet guided the blade to the "target". However, Halig still looked lost, so Radnor stopped as he realized he might have gotten ahead of himself with the demonstration.

"That's what you'll be able to do once you master your feet. For now, let's start with connecting to the ground while standing still."

Radnor then worked with Halig on this skill. First, he had the boy push against him with his hand and showed Halig how better to align his feet so he could direct the most force into him. After a while, the nervous boy seemed to understand the concept, and Radnor moved on to applying it with the sword. All the while they worked; Radnor noticed that Halig's mood was not improving. Even when the child was successful in his tasks, he seemed to get more upset with what was going on. However, Radnor pressed on, determined to break the child out of his nervous fear. Their exercises culminated in Halig striking a sword Radnor held in his hand. Radnor held the weapon just tight enough to provide resistance to Halig's blows, but not so much that he would keep Halig from moving it at all. At first, the boy swung wildly, and when his blade struck Radnor's it bounced off with no effect.

"You're *throwing* your weapon at me. Move from your center and *place* your sword in the same space mine occupies, and watch what happens."

Halig nodded, and tried to do what Radnor said. At first, he couldn't get it. But, after several more repetitions, the boy's body aligned with the cut, and when the blow struck, it knocked Radnor's sword out of his hand!

Radnor grinned from ear to ear and he clasped Halig's shoulders with enthusiasm.

"Excellent! Did you feel how effortless that was? *That* is how you use a sword—"

Radnor stopped short. Halig was crying. He knelt down in front of the child to get back on eye level again.

"I'm sorry; did I hurt you when I grabbed your shoulder? I was just excited. I'm sorry if it was too much."

Halig shook his head.

Radnor knelt in silence, desperately trying to figure out what to say or do to help the boy.

"Is there something I can do? I'd like to help you if I can," Radnor said.

"I… I don't… I don't want to kill anyone," Halig stammered.

It was then Radnor understood why Halig was so upset. He spoke calmly, with an empathetic tone that helped calm Halig's nerves.

"Listen… would you believe a secret if I told it to you?" Halig nodded. "I don't want to kill anyone either… not people anyway."

"But you have, haven't you?" Halig asked.

Radnor nodded.

"Yes. Many."

"But… I don't want to hurt anyone. I just want to go home. I want to be like my mom… my dad. I want to help people, not hurt them."

"What did your parents do?"

"My mom looked after old people, and my dad… he was an herbalist. He made medicine for them. I want to be like them. I don't want to kill anyone!"

"Halig, I need you to listen to me. Bad men are coming here. You understand what the wolves did? Well, these men are coming here to finish what the wolves started. If I can't stop them, you need to be able to defend yourself."

Halig shook his head.

"But who's going to take care of the sick when you're fighting? Who's going to look after the people that get hurt?"

Radnor smiled as Halig's bravery revealed itself. Despite Halig's nervousness, the boy was arguing with him.

"Is that what you would do if the wall falls? Help the sick?"

"The wall won't fall if we can save the people who get hurt."

Radnor had assumed that Halig's parents died in the wolf attack, but now he needed to know more.

"Is that what happened to your parents? Did no one help them when they were hurt?"

Halig nodded.

"They went to save the old people they looked after. My mom and dad got most of them to a guard house and locked the doors. That's where they left me too. The wolves couldn't get to us… but Mom and Dad… they couldn't save everyone. The wolves got them when they were looking for more people to help. They did all they could, but everyone was fighting or running. No one helped them."

Radnor wanted to argue with Halig. Without the people fighting, the wolves would have killed everyone in the city. However, Radnor also knew that Halig wasn't exactly wrong either. A battlefield needs healers as well as soldiers.

"So, you want to help people; even at the risk of your own life?" Halig nodded. Radnor smiled. "My friend, you are truly a brave young man. Few dare to argue with me, but in doing so, you have shown me your true heart. You are courageous and kind. Wulfgeld needs more like you."

"Rolf says I need to toughen up… that the road ahead is scary and that I need to be ready to kill."

Radnor shook his head.

"Rolf means well. But next time Rolf says that, you tell him that your road is different than his."

"Will you tell him for me?" Halig asked.

Radnor thought for a moment, and then gave his answer.

"No. I think this is something you should do yourself. Be brave, as you have already shown me you can be."

Halig nodded.

"Now what?" the boy asked.

"I think I should teach you how to use a shield, so if it comes to it, you can protect your friends while they fight. Does that sound better to you?"

Halig nodded and smiled. He liked the idea of shielding his friends much better. Radnor retrieved a shield from the collection of weapons that had been gathered during the training and began working with Halig on how to use one. Eventually, Halig got the hang of using the shield to protect not only himself, but to protect someone standing next to him. As their training wore on, Halig noticed that Rolf kept staring at them. So, Halig paused his drills.

"I think it's Rolf's turn," he declared.

Before Radnor could reply, Halig took the shield and joined another group of children to practice his newly learned techniques with them.

Rolf saw his opening and made his way back over to Radnor.

"How'd it go with Halig?" Rolf asked.

"You'll have to ask him yourself," Radnor said.

Rolf threw a cheeky sword blow at Radnor, who ducked it expertly.

"Ready?" Rolf asked.

Radnor smiled, and the two sparred and practiced together. Once they started working again, they both found that it still was easy for them to train together. They moved and practiced sword work with such grace that the sight of it caused other pairs to stop their drills and watch Radnor work with Rolf. Rolf smiled and laughed regularly as he trained with Radnor. However, Radnor had things he needed to say to the boy. Finally, the mentor broached an uncomfortable topic.

"Rolf, you should live with Elena and me. We can provide you with more safety than you can find here."

"I don't want safety," Rolf said as he parried a thrust from Radnor. "You act like I haven't already proven myself in a fight. I was there that night, remember? You even said it just a bit ago: I fought the wolves just like the soldiers did *and* I fought beside you at the dead city."

Radnor shook his head as he turned aside a cut from Rolf. He returned to thrust again and watched as Rolf mechanically parried it once more.

"If you really believed what you say, you wouldn't feel the need to throw yourself into harm's way just to prove something to yourself."

Rolf shrugged and went silent. The pair continued with their exercises in silence for a long time. They practiced their thrusts and parries with a remarkably regular rhythm that Radnor quickly realized was in error.

Hoping to avoid training themselves into complacency, Radnor changed the timing of his thrust slightly. This change in timing caused Rolf's parry to go wild and allowed Radnor's blade to gently poke him in the chest. Radnor then continued his speech.

"Rolf… I know I'm not your father, but he died protecting you. That will all go to waste if you throw your life away needlessly."

"If I die fighting against my enemies, it will not have been thrown away."

Radnor grew frustrated.

"Let me rephrase it then: Your father died so that you would have a chance to live a long, full life. If you go down this road, I won't be able to protect you, and frankly, I don't trust that anyone else here can. Your scout captain can try, but he could easily fail. And Sigaberht cares nothing for you."

Rolf rolled his eyes in frustration.

"Why does it always come back to Sigaberht with you? Give it a rest. My serving has nothing to do with him. You may not have had a choice in how you spent your life… but I do… and this is what I've chosen."

Radnor nodded.

"I'm sorry Rolf. I just care about you, and want to see you stay safe."

"I know Radnor, but I have to find my own path… my own place in the world. I can't do that while living in someone else's shadow. I still haven't been told the truth of what my father did… how he *really* served Sigaberht, and I'm still trying to understand him. I've asked Leif, but he wouldn't give me a straight answer. I would ask you, but I bet you know even less than I do. No matter what I learn about him, I know I loved my father and I know that he loved me… but I don't want to live in *his* shadow either. I have to accomplish things on my own if I ever want to be seen as my own man, and that means I have to do it without your protection."

Radnor sighed. In a way, he was proud of the way Rolf stood up for himself and his own beliefs. The recent hardship he had endured had forced him to mature very quickly. He sometimes looked at Rolf and saw a mirror of himself at that age. He knew the rage that drove the boy, and Radnor hoped that Rolf's heart had not hardened so much that he could never be happy again.

"Very well, just know that my invitation will always stand, and I'm always happy to train you."

Rolf smiled.

"Thank you."

The two shared a short hug and then resumed their drills.

Hours passed, and the training session gradually came to a close. Things had gone rather well. While not everything was perfect, the group had improved in all areas, and the men from different shires were working together far better than before. No one was celebrating or drinking together yet, but people were more willing to follow orders and watch each other's backs. They didn't need to like each other; they needed to fight together, which they were doing much better now.

Aelfric eventually gathered the group for closing questions before ending the day's training. Radnor waited, and at first, no questions were asked, but then a small boy finally spoke up.

"Are the stories true? Did you really kill all those people?" he asked.

Radnor sighed.

"Yes and no. I have killed many people. The stories tell of my deeds as though they were crimes… but those I slaughtered were… not unlike the soldiers who shall besiege us soon. I didn't kill random people."

"How many people have you killed?" came another boy's question.

"Only as many as I had to."

One of the adults chimed in with a more relevant question.

"What are we expecting from the enemy tomorrow?"

"We're expecting a sizable force with around five hundred knights, plus support troops. As for siege engines, we believe they have the parts needed to assemble trebuchets, and also at least one covered ram."

"So we're looking at what, three or four thousand troops?" one of the men said.

Before anyone could answer, another man asked his question.

"How are we to deal with the ram? We don't have the weapons needed to penetrate that kind of armor."

Radnor smiled.

"I can't comment on that, other than to assure you that there is a plan in place to deal with the rams, and there is a plan of defense in addition to what you're being prepared for. I can't say anything else right now, but just know that I will be fighting on the front lines of this battle with you, and the number of Southworlders I kill tomorrow will make the stories you've heard of me seem like cheery tales of mirth," Radnor said.

Laughs and cheers cascaded from the group when he said that.

"I think that is the statement to end on. Company, dismissed!" Aelfric yelled.

It was not long before the troop disbanded. Morale was high as the soldiers all headed off for food and drink. Sceotan, who had been watching the training from afar, came over and shook Radnor's hand.

"I must thank you for what you have done today. You have given me some hope that we might survive this."

Radnor smiled.

"Thank you for allowing me to work with the scouts. They are all fine children."

The scout captain smiled back and turned to face the gaggle of children gathered before him. He quickly got them lined up and proceeded to march them back to their own barracks. Radnor turned to make his goodbye to Aelfric, but found that the man had already gone. With that, Radnor made his way back home.

* * *

"So, what did Radnor teach you?" Rolf asked.

Halig shrugged. Unsatisfied with this response, Rolf pressed his friend further.

"You must have learned *something!*"

Again, Halig shrugged. He was tired, and didn't want to argue with Rolf about it, but Rolf kept pushing anyway. He was used to getting his own way where Halig was concerned. While

Rolf didn't mean to hurt Halig's feelings, his constant pressuring and nagging finally forced Halig's temper.

"I learned that I don't need to be like you. I can be like me."

Rolf was stunned and confused. He had expected Halig to tell him about learning footwork, or something along those lines.

"What does that mean? What about fighting?" Rolf demanded.

Halig shrugged again.

"He showed me how to use a shield, how to protect people."

"Nothing about the sword?" Rolf asked.

Again, Halig grew impatient.

"I didn't want to learn how to use a sword. I don't want to hurt anyone."

Rolf sighed.

"I told you… the world isn't kind to… we need to be ready—"

"Radnor also told me to tell you that my road is different is yours. If you want to be my friend, you have to let me be me."

Silence fell between the two boys, and then Halig, ever the peacemaker, spoke again.

"What did Radnor teach you?"

It was Rolf's turn to shrug.

"Nothing new. We drilled a lot of the old stuff. It was good practice though."

Halig shook his head.

"I wasn't talking about sword stuff."

Now Rolf grew uncomfortable with where the conversation was heading, but after a moment's hesitation, he answered Halig's question.

"He said I shouldn't get too focused on proving myself and that if I'm going to honor my father's sacrifice, I need to stay safe."

"Are you going to listen to him?" Halig asked.

Rolf shrugged.

"I would listen to him," Halig said.

"Like you said, my road is different from yours," Rolf replied.

"Yes, but what of tomorrow? What will happen?" Rolf shrugged again. Halig continued. "Both our families died to keep us safe. Whatever happens tomorrow… we'll keep each other safe. If we do that, our parents won't have died for nothing. Deal?"

Rolf smiled.

"Deal!"

The boys clasped hands and felt ready to face the world anew.

As the exhausted children piled into their barracks, they found a most unexpected sight. Several of the earl's personal guards stood silently at the front entrance. The children were stunned by their presence, as the warriors of Sigaberht's personal household had never before ventured down to their barracks. Now not one, but three of them stood in the room. They all carried spears and shields in their hands and wore swords on their belts. Their shields bore the wolf's head sigil of Sigaberht's house, but like all other examples of this old sigil, wolf's blood had been intentionally spattered across the shield's faces to commemorate those who had fallen against the wolves' onslaught and intimidate the invaders from Drakomar. Before Sceotan could offer a word of greeting, the leader of the trio spoke.

"We come here in search of the one named 'Rolf Cellestan'. He is said to be here with you."

Everyone in the room turned to Rolf. The boy gulped, fearful of what they could want with him. Despite his nervousness, he stepped forward.

"I am Rolf. What business do you have with me?" he asked, as he worked his hardest to sound confident.

The leader of the soldiers peered down at Rolf through his helmet and sized the boy up. The look the man gave him reminded him of the way Radnor looked at him when they were training, and Rolf felt more at ease. The man spoke.

"You have been summoned to a meeting at the keep. You will come with us."

136

Rolf nodded and quickly joined the armored men as they left the scout's barracks. Together, the group made the slow climb up the hill to Sigaberht's keep.

Chapter 9

Upon arriving at the door to Sigaberht's throne room, Rolf found himself quickly ushered inside by an officious looking retainer. Rolf quickly noticed that no one lead or followed him inside and when he turned to see where his escort had gone, one of the men gave him a reassuring wave right before the door was shut.

Rolf looked around the large room and carefully eyed his surroundings. He had been here just yesterday, but Sigaberht's great hall felt entirely different today. After a moment, Rolf realized the difference was that unlike yesterday, he was alone. There were no ealdormen, no other children… and no Radnor. It was just him. Rolf's thoughts raced to find a plausible purpose for his being brought here. Nothing reasonable came to his mind, and Rolf's nervous tension quickly grew to outright worry. It was then that he began to wonder if Sigaberht had some nefarious plan for him, for Rolf knew of the animosity between Radnor and the Earl. *Will Sigaberht want me to spy on Radnor for him?* Rolf thought. *Well, if he does, Sigaberht is going to have another thing coming.*

Rolf's line of thought was broken by the entrance of a lone man dressed in simple, unadorned clothes. His pants were brown and his tunic was dark blue, and neither looked like the kind of garb one would wear to court. The simple clothing the man wore belied his true nature, and it took Rolf an extra second to recognize that this simply dressed man was none other than Ashveldt. The boy almost gasped at seeing Ashveldt so modestly dressed. The prince was not even wearing his crown! Ashveldt spoke before Rolf's thoughts could race away.

"Come! Come! There is nothing to be afraid of! I wish to speak with you, not as lord to subject, but son to son."

The prince gestured for Rolf to step towards him. Rolf tentatively did as he was bidden, but stopped at the edge of the royal dais. Ashveldt shook his head.

"No… come here… sit with me. I would not speak with you as your lord, but as your companion in fate."

Rolf looked again at the edge of the dais and hesitantly started to climb up. Impatient with Rolf's slowness, Ashveldt took him by the arm and hoisted him up. The prince then gestured for Rolf to sit on his throne. The boy's eyes grew wide.

"Where will you sit then, my lord?" he asked.

Ashveldt smiled.

"I shall sit on the dais. My throne is quite comfortable, but I have grown weary of comfort. I shall find this spot to be a fine seat, and I believe you will find my throne to be *very* fine indeed."

Rolf stared uncomfortably at Ashveldt's throne for a moment, but after a reassuring gesture from the prince, he sat down. Ashveldt had been right… it was a comfortable seat. After easing into the chair, Rolf grew more comfortable with the situation and finally allowed himself to truly relax for the first time that day.

"By the look on your face, I see that you find it pleasing," Ashveldt commented. Rolf nodded. "Good. Now then, I suppose you are wondering why I brought you here."

Rolf took a long moment to prepare an answer in the best, most formal speech he could muster.

"Yes, I am. My lord, I have not the slightest idea of why you have asked me to come. At first, I thought I was summoned to perform some task for the earl, but given that you alone have come to see me… I now believe I have been summoned for some other purpose."

Ashveldt smiled again.

"You are correct. You and I are on the eve of a great battle… or at least it might have once seemed great to me. The one we have already faced together makes all other battles seem insignificant by comparison… don't you agree?"

Rolf shrugged. Despite his youth, he had seen many terrible battles in the last month, and the horrors of war had become "normal" to him. Ashveldt was taken aback by Rolf's indifference. Finally, the prince got to his point.

"You and I share something in common… we both lost a parent that terrible night. I know your father died saving your life… and my mother died saving mine."

Rolf nodded, but Ashveldt's words sent his thoughts elsewhere. Rolf tried to keep himself together as visions of his father's death against the blood-soaked fangs of wolves flooded his mind. Ashveldt saw the boy turn inward and hastily spoke again.

"But… there are differences between us. You were able to avenge your father… and I was not allowed to avenge my mother. For this, I envy you. But at the same time, I also owe you a gift for your service."

Rolf looked into Ashveldt's eyes and saw the sadness within them. He then realized what Ashveldt was looking for. Unfortunately, he could not give Ashveldt the story he sought.

"My lord, do you speak of what happened after we left Wulfgeld? When I fought alongside the witches? I'm afraid I must tell you, I did not get my revenge. One of the witches was slain by the evil we sought, and the other cast herself into chaos before I could drive my blade into her heart."

Ashveldt nodded.

"I know. But the witches are dead, and you were *there*… you were a *part* of it. I was not allowed to join you in your battle. *You* were given a chance to prove yourself. I wish I had been given that opportunity. As I said, I envy you."

Rolf nodded, though his thoughts turned against himself.

I had the opportunity, and I failed.

The boy tried to dispel the intrusive thought and shook his head. After regaining himself, Rolf tried to speak words of comfort to the grieving prince.

"It must have been difficult to stay behind when you knew there were others continuing to fight elsewhere."

"It was agonizing," Ashveldt said. "The only thing that kept me sane was helping to pick up the pieces in Wulfgeld. I was at least able to fulfill my duty as my father's heir, even if I could not fulfill my duty as my mother's son."

Silence reigned between the grieving sons for a moment, and then Ashveldt continued.

"There is another difference between us. I believe an injustice has been done to you… one I intend to rectify. You see… I knew who my mother was. You… you did not know who your father was, and I intend to change this."

Rolf braced himself for what was to come. All his life, he had believed his father was a trade master who guided caravans to Wulfgeld's trading partners in the Northworld; but the way his father fought and led other fighting men into battle proved that there was much more to Leofric Cellestan than he had ever known. Ashveldt saw the anxious look on Rolf's face and spoke again.

"It appears you already know something?"

Rolf shrugged again.

"Your highness, I am no fool. A simple trade master does not fight in the manner he fought, nor does he lead men into battle with such authority. Please, I have wondered at this so much that my heart has ached… who was my father?"

Ashveldt nodded.

"Your father was a great man. He served us as master of spies. He and his men traveled far and wide, spying on our enemies in Drakomar. The information he gave us was invaluable. Five years ago, it was *he* who warned us of Drakomar's impending attack. If it had not been for his advance warning, we might not have been able to drive them off as we did. The enemy believed him to be a spy for them, and so did not question his frequent trips to Wulfgeld and Neugeld. He served us loyally and fearlessly until the day he died. You should be proud of him. He loved you very dearly, and I know that no matter what he did for my family, I know that in his heart… he served us to serve you. When the time comes, I pray to Caelum that I might be as dedicated a father to my children as Leofric was to you."

Tears formed in Rolf's eyes, but were never shed. After the night his father had died, Rolf had sworn never to cry again. He didn't quite know what to make of this revelation about his father. Part of him was angry with his father for keeping this secret from him; but Rolf knew that he had always loved him. Rolf blinked away the tears and spoke.

"Why was I not told of this before?"

"Because your father feared for your safety. He played a most dangerous game with our enemies; one mistake could have put you in great peril."

Ashveldt stopped and gazed upon Rolf's face for a moment.

"You know, you look very much like him. I hope you take the compliment when I say: I do believe something of Leofric lives on in you."

Rolf smiled a little at that thought. His feelings were a tumultuous mess, but in the end, he loved his father very dearly, and would do everything he could to honor his memory.

Ashveldt stood and retrieved a mysterious item from his pants pocket.

"I don't know why, but something gives me the feeling that you might need this."

Ashveldt held out a mysterious object to Rolf, who looked at it quizzically. It was a large medallion strung onto a necklace strap. It appeared to be gold with the image of three stars and a crescent moon aligned with a small sun etched upon its face.

 Rolf looked at it closely, unsure of what it was. Ashveldt then explained.

"It was your father's. The medallion is one of but a few that were made in the forges of Drakomar. This medallion is something Leofric carried on him in secret whenever he was in Drakomar, as it would mark him as a man of authority in the city. The marking on the front: it's a variant of the symbol they use to represent the will of both Caelum and his daughter, Celestata. Keep this medallion with you. If things turn foul tomorrow, you may be able to trade this in exchange for your safety, or perhaps there is some truth to the Southworlder's beliefs, and Celestata might guide you when you need it. Either way, take it as a final gift from your father."

Ashveldt handed the necklace to Rolf, who bowed as he gripped the heirloom tightly. Ashveldt then bowed to Rolf and gestured for the door. The pair made their goodbyes, and Rolf headed back to the barracks, medallion in hand. As he walked, the boy reminded himself that he had sworn never to cry again, so it was impossible for those drops of water that now fell from his face to the snow covered path to be tears.

* * *

As Radnor walked home from his training session with Rolf, he found himself lost in thought. Rolf's words poured through his mind, and he wished he could do more to help the boy. He knew in the end that Rolf needed to find himself on his own. Radnor just wished he could provide him with more guidance.

In addition to the problems with Rolf, Radnor was also disturbed by the fact that he had heard nothing of the dissent among the soldiers until now. The warriors of Wulfgeld were even less prepared than Radnor had realized. Daegal's original plan of bribing the enemy to go away seemed much more sensible now.

He was also disturbed by the fact that Leif had said nothing about it in court, or to Radnor privately. Had he said anything about it to Sigaberht at all? Or was Leif trying so hard to prove his worth that he hadn't told anyone of the problems he was having? Radnor did not get to truly finish any of these thoughts as his mind wandered worriedly from problem to problem. As he approached his home, he at least knew one thing was certain: he could count on Elena to be a rock for him to lean on.

As Radnor stepped across the threshold of his home, he quickly found himself in Elena's embrace. He settled into her arms for a moment, but then gently pulled away to look upon her face and eyes full of love. However, weariness clouded her gaze. Before Radnor could say anything to express his concern, Elena spoke.

"I can't talk long. I've been trying to gather the ghouls all day. If I don't maintain control of them, they start to wander off."

She led him by the hand to the bedroom. Once inside, Radnor saw Alban's gaulderen sitting in the middle of the floor.

"How do you know that?" Radnor asked.

"It's almost like I… I see through their eyes sometimes. I can feel their thoughts, their… desires. I hate it. They're such… primitive creatures; their minds are limited and barbaric."

Curiosity piqued Radnor's interest.

"How are they limited?" he asked.

"They're… if you can't eat it, sleep under it, or have sex with it, they don't care."

"Is that the only thing that's bothering you?"

Elena sat down on the bed.

"No. Despite everything I just said, I… they aren't just animals. They are a little more than that. Looking into their minds… I can see why Alban went insane, but at the same time, they're a sort of… *people* too. I don't like doing this. It feels immoral."

"Do you think we should stop?" Radnor asked.

He hugged her, crushing her against his powerful chest as he did. Elena nestled in and found comfort in the way he held her.

"I would if I could, but we don't have a choice. It's us or them, isn't it?"

Radnor nodded.

"I'm afraid so."

Elena gave him a final squeeze before letting go.

"Could you get me some food? It looks like I'll have to keep at this all night if I'm to gather the numbers we need."

"Of course."

Radnor went to the kitchen to prepare a small meal for Elena. He wished he could tell her to stop gathering ghouls; but the people of Wulfgeld needed her to do this if they were to have any chance of surviving what was to come. As Radnor re-entered the bedroom with Elena's food, he found her nervously clutching a piece of parchment in her hand. She smiled at him, and spoke.

"Radnor, I know how much you hate those stories and songs they sing about you… about the man they call 'Veigarand'. So, I decided to write one of my own for you."

With that, Elena started to sing.

144

By a name, by a name,
They call you by a name,
Veigarand, they call you,
And your deeds, they try to shame.

But I know the great truth,
I know what you have done,
I know you by your name,
Radnor, you are the one,

You are my one heart thief,
My life now rests with you,
You make my days brighter,
My love for you is true.

Elena looked up from her parchment, embarrassed at what she had sung. Radnor smiled, and took her into his arms once more.

"Do you like it?" she asked.

"What do you think?" he replied gently.

Elena took a moment to silently enjoy being enfolded within Radnor's warmth before she spoke again.

"Just know… whatever happens, tomorrow, or hereafter: I love you."

Radnor broke from her just slightly, just enough to look into her eyes. When his eyes locked with hers, their souls met.

"I love you, too."

Elena sighed and settled back into him for a few more moments. Finally, she broke their embrace.

"I have to get back to it. Otherwise, all my work will have been for nothing."

Elena then sat cross legged on the floor. Her eyes were closed as she concentrated on what she was doing. Her work clearly took a substantial effort to accomplish, and Radnor saw that completing this task would push her endurance to the limit. So, Radnor sat on the bed behind her, ready to take care of anything she needed or wanted.

As the two lovers sat together, night drew on for an eternity as the people of Wulfgeld waited with bated breath for their enemy to come. Rumors of the Pale Light's brutality swept across the city and dread stalked the streets.

The soldiers from Drakomar marched along the forest path, and all bore witness to the gruesome remains of wolves' heads mounted along the winding, woodland road to the city. Fear ran through the hearts of the invaders as they saw the grisly spectacle that greeted them. Some of the men in Piarin's army tore their eyes from the path, and instead found their gazes resting upon the snow covered, gambrel roofs of the old city. Veterans who had previously assaulted Wulfgeld gasped when they saw that Sigaberht's old palace, that great building the invaders had years before seen resting atop the high hill within the walls, was now only a pile of charred lumber. These men could only guess at the number of dead that now lay buried inside the city. Rumors spread among them of the terrible deeds that had happened in Wulfgeld… and of the curses that still lingered upon the wretched city.

Despite their fears, the men-at-arms knew of the eternal shame that would forever plague them should they retreat from these lands, and the glorious reward that awaited them if they took the city. Plunder alone was enough motivation for many of them to stay and fight. For the others, the Knights of the Pale Light, gold and plunder meant nothing. They fought for the glory of their goddess, and the homes they longed so dearly to have and so they paid no heed to the rumors of sorcery plaguing Wulfgeld.

The army of Drakomar arrived outside the gates of the city. Its soldiers stuffed their fears deep within their hearts and dutifully erected their camp in preparation for the siege ahead. Their work was slowed only by the creeping, gnawing feeling that some unholy thing was watching them from the space between moonlight and shadow. Most rationalized this feeling as nothing more than stressed nerves on the eve of battle, but those with more sensitive minds could not shake off their fear… and were visited by dreams so vivid and haunting that they drove them to screaming in the night.

Part 2
The Siege

Chapter 10

The sun rose over the tree-shadowed horizon, and its rays brought dread to those who witnessed its arrival. The watchmen of Piarin's army wondered at the eerie lights and shadows that danced among the trees and ran across the snow covered field that separated them from Wulfgeld's imposing walls. Most disregarded what they saw as tricks of the light in an unfamiliar land, but others feared that the dancing lights were harbingers of the insidious presence they had felt watching them from umbral corners.

Drakomar's encampment was divided in two: one half was occupied by men native to Drakomar, and the men of the Pale Light dwelt within the other. Such an arrangement was necessary for their continued allegiance, and it had been no mean feat to bring the two factions together. By the Pale Light's doctrine, the men born in Drakomar were heretics and blasphemers; and the warriors of Drakomar saw the Pale Light as nothing but murderous fanatics. This hostility forced the two factions apart even as they slept and prepared to battle side by side.

On Drakomar's side of the camp, men-at-arms grumbled about the cold as they rose from their slumber. The smell of cooking eggs and soups filled the air around them, and men lined up to receive their morning rations. Waiting soldiers glanced fearfully at the chaos-defiled light of the sun as it painted the trees with its uncanny glow. The sight sparked fearful thoughts of the terrible, unseen things that lay in wait within the woods beyond Wulfgeld, though none dared to speak these thoughts aloud.

On the other side of the camp lay a different scene. The knights and men-at-arms of the Pale Light knelt in long lines as their priests read a sermon. The warriors of belief committed themselves to their worship and opened their souls to the spirit of their protective goddess. There were no complaints, for they were engrossed in prayer. There was no food, for hunger was replaced with discipline. There was no fear… only faith.

At the center of this grand camp rested the pavilions occupied by the commanders of the army. As Drakomar's soldiers toiled all around this cluster, a lone man strode from his tent. This man, clad in only a thin undershirt and pants, took in a deep, contented breath as the cold air stung his lungs and skin. He was a knight of Drakomar, and he wasted little time as he began his daily exercises to prepare his muscles and mind for the battle ahead.

While the knight stretched his body, he looked to his left and right as he inspected the activity of the soldiers under his command. The pride that swelled in his chest blinded him to the fear and apprehension that clutched at the hearts of his men.

The man looked to the walls of Wulfgeld and saw that few warriors guarded the battlements. His knightly posture grew taller as confidence in victory soared to new heights. The knight looked to his belt and fingered the white, silk favor given to him by Princess Isabeau, daughter of Duke Piarin, Lord of Drakomar. The knight had sworn an oath upon this favor, in both the names of Isabeau and of Celestata, goddess of love and daughter of Caelum, that he would only return home as the herald of victory… or as a corpse.

The knight cared little for the material spoils of war that waited within the city. He would of course take his share of loot, but his ambitions lay upon another prize: Isabeau's hand in marriage. He had been assured by the princess' stepmother that if he led their army to victory, Isabeau would be his bride. Even now, as the knight stood at the edge of the soon-to-be battlefield, his thoughts lay only upon this objective… this prize. However, his fantasy was soon broken when his thoughts were interrupted by a friendly voice.

"Sir Legier, glad to see you are up and about!"

Sir Legier turned to discipline the one who had dared interrupt his musings, but his anger quickly dissipated when he saw that it was Sir Arnulf, his second-in-command and closest friend, who had banished his pleasant fantasy. The two knights exchanged a warm embrace before they both stopped to listen to the furtive prayers of the holy order of knights that joined them in their expedition. Arnulf spoke first.

"Should you not be among those in prayer?"

Legier sighed in annoyance, as the two had had this argument twice before since the two armies had rendezvoused on the road.

"My induction into their order was purely symbolic."

"Yet important enough that the Primarchus felt it necessary to induct you before we left."

Legier waved his hand dismissively at Arnulf's concern.

"A matter of convenience. As I said, it was merely symbolic of my dedication to preserving their right to plunder."

Arnulf shook his head and his tone took on a firmness that Legier disliked.

"The Primarchus *insisted* you be inducted into their order because none of them will listen to anyone who *isn't* in their order. Your 'symbolic' action will not hold their loyalty for long if you don't at least pretend to be one of them."

"They will be loyal to me because our lord has what they want."

"They bow only to Celestata."

Legier snorted.

"Then why do they bow to the Primarchus?"

"He speaks for Celestata."

"Does he?"

Arnulf shrugged.

"They say he does,"

Legier laughed mockingly at the Pale Light's beliefs.

"I'm sure they do. Stealing wealth from people must feel easier when you always believe you're in the right, no?"

"And what exactly is it we're doing here?" Arnulf asked.

Legier turned back to his friend.

"We are here for much more than wealth. Wulfgeld is our chance at freedom!"

Arnulf nodded.

"Perhaps you are right… that their beliefs are just an excuse. But if that's true, we are *their* chance at freedom from exile."

"Bah! They doomed themselves by their own actions!"

"That's not my point. We assault Wulfgeld because we need their farms if Piarin ever wants to be free from his vassalage, and the Pale Light fights for us so that they might have a home once more."

Legier threw his hands in the air in frustration at Arnulf's coded words. Arnulf rolled his eyes and explained.

"What I'm trying to tell you is that underneath all of their facades and sophistry, we're the same as them. Yet *they* certainly don't believe we're the same. You should go to prayer."

Legier shrugged. He didn't like the way the argument had shifted, and decided that the topic was beginning to bore him.

"It doesn't matter if I attend their prayers or not. They don't want to mix with anyone else. They worship Celestata as their chief goddess, while we mainly worship her father. You'd think that would appease them. Yet we're not good enough for them still! Because of that, they will always be guests that have overstayed their welcome."

Arnulf smiled.

"That I can understand. They are… difficult to get along with. They're so—"

"Quick to kill anyone who disagrees with them?" Legier interrupted.

Arnulf smiled and nodded.

"However, all I'm saying is that we need their numbers for the coming wars as much as they need Drakomar for a home. If we want to keep their allegiance, we need to play by their rules too."

Legier nodded. He didn't like it, but Arnulf's words rang true. Legier wished to change the topic, so he gestured for Arnulf to follow him as he walked to the edge of the camp. Once past the rows of tents, they began their assessment of the terrain. The open field that surrounded the city was large and covered with a thin layer of snow. This would make the ground slicker than normal, but the snow was thin enough it wouldn't hamper movement more than that. The city walls stood within clear view, and the pair looked them over with the precision of experts of war. After studious observation, Legier pointed towards the city and spoke.

"Look to the battlements. See how few men stand upon them? The walls are nearly devoid of all guards. If the city has so few defenders, our victory is most assured!"

Arnulf shook his head in disappointment at his over-eager commander.

"Yes, 'assured'… unless Sigaberht has held the rest of his men in reserve. It has been nearly a month since word of his tragedy reached us. He must have anticipated this attack and he has had time to gather his ealdormen and their warriors."

Legier sighed in frustration at his discouraging friend.

"Do you believe me a fool? Despite what you may think, I do not take this siege lightly. And despite how you tell it… you were not the only survivor from our last attempt to take the city."

Arnulf grunted.

"I have never claimed to be the only survivor. However, enough of us were killed that day that I am quite concerned. We lost nearly a hundred knights at our last attempt, and hundreds more men-at-arms were slaughtered by our enemy. Do not think yourself invincible just because our lord appointed *you* as the marshal of this army."

If any other man had uttered those words to Legier, the marshal would have thought the speaker jealous of his newfound position as the army's leader. However, Legier knew Arnulf to be a true and steadfast friend, who only ever looked out for his well-being. However, Legier's confidence in victory was unshakable.

"Ah, but you see, that's why we brought *them* along. Their blood will bring our victory."

Arnulf disagreed, and spoke even more emphatically as he tried to drive his point home.

"Do not forget what happened to Sir Mercadier when *he* was the marshal and champion of Drakomar. He even killed Earl Godric himself, and what was his reward? Death at the hands of Sigaberht's spear. The sons of Godric were a merciless and fearsome trio that day."

Legier laughed at Arnulf's concerns and answered with a swift rebuttal.

"Ah! But have you not heard? There is but *one* brother now, for the other two have perished. With only one of the brothers left to lead… we slay him, we slay any hope they have at defeating us!"

Arnulf shook his head yet again. He always hated it when Legier was in a stubborn mood. He respected Legier… but the man could be truly insufferable sometimes.

"But, you forget Sigaberht's son. Ashveldt is a man now and Sigaberht is no fool. He will have done everything he can to solidify Ashveldt's position as his heir. If the earl dies, he will die a martyr and the people *will* rally to Ashveldt's banner."

Legier scoffed at Arnulf's remark.

"Bah! Ashveldt may be a man, but he is young, and will be foolhardy. He will be eager to prove himself on the battlefield. I think we may strike him down even before his father."

"I hope you're right," Arnulf said. "History oft repeats itself, and if Sigaberht is killed first, it might be an omen of our doom by Ashveldt's hand."

Arnulf's words grated on Legier as they poked holes in his fantasies.

"Why must you ruin my mood?" Legier asked.

"I would not be doing my duty as your second if I allowed your marital ambitions to cloud your judgment before victory is secured. You must also recall, the Primarchus has a line of suitors ready to marry our princess and solidify Drakomar's ties to the Pale Light forever more."

While Legier did not believe that Piarin would ever allow his daughter to marry one of those fanatics, he again knew that Arnulf's main point was correct: they needed to act with utmost caution. The marshal sighed in annoyance at himself and smiled at Arnulf.

"My friend, I thank you for your service to me. As always, you are not the friend I want, but the friend I need." Arnulf bowed at the compliment and Legier resumed his speech. "Are there any other words of caution you have for me?"

Arnulf hesitated as he sought the right words for his thoughts.

"There is something that has been bothering me, but I have not spoken of it until now, because the thought was not fully formed until last night. We have heard of the battle that has now weakened Sigaberht. We know Wulfgeld was assaulted by a vicious army of wolves emboldened by the power of the Hexverat." Legier grew bored at Arnulf's repeating of known facts, and his gaze started to wander. Arnulf noticed the impatient look in Legier's eye and hastened to his point. "But, what we don't know is… how were the witches defeated? What power did Sigaberht muster to drive back such a relentless and deadly enemy within his walls?"

Legier considered his friend's words carefully. Somehow, despite the terrible forces thrown against Sigaberht, the earl had claimed victory against a foe that should have been his downfall. This raised a question: what was it that Sigaberht had used to turn the tide in his favor? Legier looked Arnulf directly in the eye.

"That's quite a question… and I don't know the answer. Therefore, our first task must be to test Sigaberht. We must see if we can draw out any secret weapon he could use to destroy us as he destroyed the witches. Come; help me draw up the plans for how we shall do this."

Legier gestured for Arnulf to return with him to his tent. Once inside, they gathered around a large table arranged for battle planning. Legier quickly unrolled a map of the area and the city's known defenses and laid it out before them.

After studying the map, it was decided that they should start with a probing assault on the walls. Archers would cover the advance of siege ladders carried by groups of knights and men-at-arms who would attempt to storm the battlements. Volunteers would be gathered to be among the first wave of the assault. It was dangerous work, but the pair knew that there would be no shortage of knights who would kill for the chance to be the first up the ladders and onto the walls. Even for the men-at-arms, the glory and reward that awaited success far outweighed the fear of death.

The two commanders also decided that the men from Drakomar would assault the wall on one side of the gate house, while the knights of the Pale Light would keep to the other side. This would provide both factions the perception of equal of risk and inclusion while also keeping the two different command structures out of each other's way.

Thankfully, the rest of the plan did not hinge upon which faction's men were at the front. While the soldiers on the ladders kept the defenders distracted, the covered ram would be brought to assault the gate. Arnulf objected to this part of the plan at first. While the ram itself could be replaced, the armored covering could not. However, Arnulf relented when Legier pointed out that if they were going to make Sigaberht reveal any secret weapons he might have, they would need to present a threat capable of forcing the earl's hand.

Once the assault was underway, Legier and Arnulf would watch and see how things turned out. Neither of the knights liked the fact that they had to sacrifice some of their men in order to learn the enemy's capabilities, but both knew that this was war, and fully committing to an assault that *might* win the day could turn foul and cost everyone's lives if a secret weapon was brought upon them at the wrong time. The pair hoped that if Sigaberht did have some sort of weapon, that it had already been exhausted in the battle against the Hexverat.

At the same time the battle was to commence, the siege engineers were to begin assembling the handful of trebuchets they had with them. After the day's probing assault was completed, these weapons of destruction would hurl their deadly boulders among the buildings in the city to sow chaos within the walls.

No sooner had the plan been agreed upon, than a small, black-robed man stormed into the tent. Before either Legier or Arnulf could speak, the man threw his hood back, revealing a bald head, pale complexion, and dark, brown eyes that revealed his anger at the Grand Marshal.

"So, I see you do still live, Legier. I did not see you at this morning's prayers, and was concerned that you might have died in the night."

Legier suppressed the impulse to draw his sword at the priest's disrespect and merely smiled before making his reply.

"Archpriest Venatus, I am glad to see you here in my tent. I had grown worried that you had forgotten we must prepare for the battle that is upon us."

Venatus smiled. Legier's barb demonstrated some measure of intelligence on his part, and actually raised Venatus' opinion of the brash knight.

"Preparation of the soul takes precedence, for the body cannot be truly prepared if the spirit lacks in devotion. Is *your* soul prepared, marshal?"

"I prayed before Celestata on the eve of our departure from Drakomar. I don't feel the need to do so again, as I'm sure her eternal presence heard me the first time."

"Bold of you to assume she heeds the words of an unbeliever like you."

Arnulf stepped between the pair before the hostility escalated further.

"Archpriest, we appreciate your concern for our souls, but know that we have not dallied, nor made light of our labors. We have forged a plan of battle that we hope will provide us with the information we need to properly besiege the city."

Venatus stopped only to glare at the commanders.

"Do these plans involve the use of my knights?" he asked.

"Of course. We would not want you to feel left out," Legier answered.

"Then why was I not a part of this meeting?" Venatus demanded.

"Because, as you said… your soul was not yet prepared, and we have no time to dawdle."

Venatus reflected for a moment. He knew that exchanging insults with Legier would get them nowhere, and so decided to concede the matter.

"My people's inability to adapt has been our undoing. I shall not make the same mistake. I ask that I be informed of when such a meeting is taking place in the future. I believe I can trust my priests to deliver the sermons without my help."

Legier smiled in surprise at how easily he had won the debate. He considered that the Pale Light might be more cooperative than he had thus far believed.

"Well, in that case, please, listen to our plan and see if it suits you as well as it suits us."

Venatus drew up a chair, looked at Legier's map, and listened to the plan with great attention. He saw nothing wrong with it, and while he believed Celestata would protect them from any unholy weapons Sigaberht might unleash upon them, she had also been known to test his people with great adversity, and so he agreed that it was wise to be cautious. He eventually approved of their plan, and when the trio left the tent to assemble their soldiers, it was not as foes, but as allies.

* * *

Atop the walls of his city, Earl Sigaberht watched dispassionately as his enemies scurried to and fro like ants… ants that he would soon crush beneath his boot. The earl had been informed of their arrival in the night, and despite the possible advantages of attacking them before they were settled in; he had chosen not to launch an assault on their encampment. While the thought of hitting the enemy before they were rested from their journey was tempting, the simple fact was that such an attack would likely result in many casualties for Wulfgeld, and Sigaberht could not afford to take heavy losses so early in the siege. Instead, he had opted to take a defensive stance, and had even gone so far as to *reduce* the number of guards on the wall that night so his men would be as well-rested as possible. They were going to need every advantage they could muster if they were to hold the walls that day.

The earl turned and faced his son. Ashveldt gazed upon the gathering enemy force with extreme concern. Sigaberht could see that the prince was worried that this day might be their last.

Ah! Were it only my last day! To join Erelda and leave the agony of life to others would be a great blessing! Sigaberht thought.

The earl was shocked when he caught his own forlorn mood. He did not like the dark place where his mind had gone, and he knew that if he allowed himself to die today, the only thing he would accomplish would be to thrust tremendous responsibility and pain upon Ashveldt. When thinking of the harm his death would bring to his son, Sigaberht's will was steeled with resolve. The earl spoke to his son and gestured out towards the enemy that assembled at the far end of the snow covered field.

"Do you see how they organize themselves? They have taken the time for a full meal in the morning and only now do we begin to see them assemble for an attack. They've left themselves only a half-day's light for the battle. What does that tell you?"

Ashveldt studied the movement among the trees with stern concentration before answering his father.

"They have no plans to take Wulfgeld today. They are not committing to a full on attack, and today's assault will be a measured one designed to test us."

Sigaberht nodded.

"I believe you are correct… good work. I had been hoping our enemy would be overconfident, but this arrangement tells me we are unlucky in that regard. Their commander intends to prod us and see what we are made of before devising further plans."

"If we're right, he will be happy for this to be a long siege, which we *don't* want," Ashveldt said.

"Again, I believe you are correct. However, if previous engagements are any indicator, I do not think this patience will last long. In the past, Piarin's men have been overzealous in the ferocity of their assaults. Their knights commit men and arms too quickly. For them, there is more glory in short sieges won by decisive battles. Sooner or later, they *always* try to force wars to end with a dramatic flair. They have put on a facade of caution for now, but it will only be a matter of time before we can bludgeon them back into their normal way of thinking."

Sigaberht's eye fixed on the Pale Light as they joined the formation of enemy troops. They marched in disciplined, well ordered units that marked them as experienced soldiers. However, Sigaberht also noticed something that he quickly pointed out to Ashveldt.

"Do you see how they gather? The banners of the Pale Light are grouped to face only one portion of the wall, and the banners of Drakomar are grouped to face another. They do not mix. They are not truly one army. Perhaps this division will bring us the victory we need."

"We can hope but I am afraid our plan might falter. What little we know of the Pale Light is by reputation only, and that reputation is of fanatics that never flee or surrender. Are you sure that our plans to break their morale will succeed? Or will our plans merely whip their knights into a frenzy?"

Sigaberht smiled.

"It's hard to be whipped into a frenzy when you're dead."

Ashveldt nervously turned to his father.

"What do we do?"

Sigaberht met his son's worried gaze and forced himself to project confidence.

"We will man the walls and meet whatever the enemy throws at us. When the time is right, we will unleash Veigarand upon them, and we will see how much their faith is worth."

* * *

Radnor sat beside Elena. She had not slept the whole night, as gathering the ghouls required constant attention. Servants sent by Sigaberht had come to their home several times during the night. They brought food and water to help keep Elena as healthy and focused as possible. As was typical for him, Radnor resented the treatment Sigaberht gave, likening it to the care a farmer gave to useful livestock. In contrast to Radnor's feelings, Elena felt nothing but gratitude. She had graciously accepted the offerings and ate and drank heartily throughout the night. The food had been extremely helpful in keeping her awake and focused.

Now, daylight had come and Radnor knew it was time for him to join the defense of the wall. In an effort to avoid breaking Elena's concentration, Radnor tried to slip out unnoticed. Clad in his armor, Radnor opened the front door to his cottage and was just about to step outside, when Elena's hand gently pressed upon his shoulder. He turned to face Elena and she smiled tentatively as she spoke to her lover.

"Did you think I would let you go without a kiss?"

Radnor shook his head.

"I'm sorry; I didn't want to disturb you."

"I know, but if something happens—"

"Nothing will happen," Radnor interrupted.

Elena sucked in a tense breath as she tried to calm her nerves.

"I know. You have lived through many battles… but I'm still worried about what might happen to you. I don't know what I would do without you. We haven't been together long, but I almost don't remember a time when you weren't by my side."

Radnor smiled, hoping to reassure her and calm her worries.

"It's strange, but in a way, I feel the same. It's like you were always with me, even during my long years in exile."

"Do you ever wonder why?" Elena asked.

"Why what?"

"Why we feel this way? You said it yourself the night we decided to embrace our feelings… it all happened so suddenly, and my love for you is so strong… so overwhelming. It's like something is *guiding* us to this point."

Radnor shrugged.

"What can we do with such thoughts? As I recall, *you* pointed out to me that in the end it doesn't really matter *why* it is, only that it is."

Radnor took Elena in a loving embrace and the two stood in silence as they felt the energy of their shared love. Finally, Elena separated from his grasp and fiddled with the chinstrap of his helmet.

"If I am to give you that kiss, this needs to come off," she said.

Radnor chuckled and swiftly removed his helmet. The two embraced again and their lips joined together. After another long moment, the pair finally parted. Elena spoke again.

"I have to get back to it. Stay safe."

Elena turned and walked back into the cottage. Radnor gently closed the door and hurried to his station on the wall. As he walked, the demigod steeled himself for the battle that was to come; and determined that if it was needed to keep Elena safe, the world would run red with Drakomar's blood.

Chapter 11

Cold air whipped into Radnor's helm as he impatiently waited for the battle to start. The enemy forces had finished gathering for their assault long ago; and the impatient demigod wished that they would just get it over with. As Radnor watched the enemy mill about, he caught himself nervously clutching the hilt of his sword in his tight fist. Surprised at his tension, Radnor forced his fingers to loosen their hold on the weapon. The nervous warrior took a few deep breaths and reminded himself that there would be no time for fear today. Experience told him he would calm down once he was in the thick of the fighting, but anticipation was driving him insane. In an effort to calm himself, Radnor turned his attention to the details of the defenses.

The stone wall was tall and thick; with a walkway wide enough for three armored men to walk abreast, though they would be tight pressed to reliably use their weapons in the space. Many staircases led up from the courtyard to the upper walkways of the wall, which made it easier for the defenders to replace fallen comrades. One flaw was that the battlements atop the wall were shorter than Radnor would have liked. While the mortal defenders could stand behind them, *he* needed to crouch in order to completely avoid hostile arrows or thrown spears.

Radnor was posted on top of the gatehouse with Sigaberht; and his job was to deal with the enemy battering ram. However, until it came within range, the demigod was supposed to stay at least partially concealed to avoid drawing arrow fire. Thankfully, the battlements atop the gate were taller, and Radnor did not have to duck as low to stay behind them.

Leif stood nearby with a grim look drawn across his face as he surveyed the foes laid out before him. He had barely acknowledged Radnor's existence since they had gathered atop the wall, which was something that had disappointed Radnor greatly. He had hoped that his and Leif's shared experiences would have helped alleviate the resentment Leif felt for him over Neugeld, but the ealdorman's anger seemed to have only strengthened with time.

The main gate was the focal point with which the enemy aligned themselves. There were other gates set in other sides of the wall that surrounded Wulfgeld, but these were much smaller and if they were breached, would provide only narrow, easily defended openings that would still prove immensely difficult to push an army through. Therefore, Drakomar's forces had opted to focus their energy on breaching the main gate.

Radnor's assessment of the defenses did not help his nerves the way he had hoped, so the demigod brought his attention to his allies positioned along the wall. Ashveldt stood to Radnor's left, guarded by a group of Sigaberht's personal huscarls. Radnor watched for a moment as the young prince paced along the wall. Radnor hoped that Ashveldt would find his center again once the fighting began, otherwise, his anxieties might be his undoing.

Radnor then turned to look at Sigaberht; whom leaned casually against the back side of the wall. Radnor was unsure if Sigaberht's calm demeanor was due to his familiarity with battle, or a well-acted ruse meant to keep others from seeing his fear. Either way, Sigaberht's seemingly relaxed mood proved effective at helping calm not only the nerves of the nearby soldiers, but Radnor's as well.

To the right of the gatehouse, Osmund and Daegal stood guard over their own sections of the wall, each accompanied by soldiers from their shires. A significant number of their troops also waited in the courtyard below as reserves to replace those slain atop the wall. Aethelstan and his entire force were among those reserves should any portion of the wall be overwhelmed. Radnor then spotted Sergeant Aelfric as he led a company of Wulfgeld's soldiers. They were also to be held in reserve, though their role was quite different from the others. Their job was to keep Radnor alive once he entered the battle. Radnor recognized many of the soldiers in Aelfric's unit as men he had met and trained with the day before. Their attitudes towards him were clearly still positive, as Radnor exchanged polite nods and greetings with a few of them as they assembled for the battle ahead.

Radnor then looked over the men who stood with him at the gate house. Most of them were archers positioned to loose deadly arrows upon any hostile bowmen foolhardy enough to try to shoot at Radnor when he eventually revealed himself. Leif had arranged them in two solid lines so that he might coordinate their deadly arrow fire against specific targets.

Radnor then looked to the pile of heavy stones that rested at the wall's edge. He hoped his plan would work, as it required precise timing and aim for him to accomplish his task. Sigaberht had been dubious of Radnor's plan at first, but after a short conversation, the earl had become convinced Radnor could pull it off. It was certainly the only option either of them could think of.

Radnor's heart sank as he looked to the courtyard below and saw Rolf and other child-scouts had assembled there. The warrior turned to Sigaberht and demanded an explanation.

"Why are they here? The wall has not yet been breached. Are we already so desperate as to call forth children?"

The earl gave him a stern answer.

"By your tone, you are angry with me for risking children in this battle. To this, I must say that they are not here to fight. They are here to provide water and bring our wounded to safety, nothing more. And before you argue with me about 'putting them at risk at all'… This is not just a raid. Piarin intends to take all of our land from us for his own use. He doesn't want us here. He will replace us with his own people working *our* farms and living in *our* houses. With that in mind, what do you think will happen to these orphans should Drakomar take the city? I say it is better to let them help prevent that from happening."

Radnor shrugged and turned away. He was angry at the situation, but he found it difficult to argue with Sigaberht's logic. The children could save lives that day and Radnor supposed he should be thankful that Rolf and his friends were not being handed swords and thrown up on the wall to face battle hardened knights who would slaughter all who stood in their path.

The sudden blowing of a signal horn interrupted Radnor's thoughts and he looked up to see a trio of horseman riding out from the enemy formation towards the gate. Sigaberht hurried over to the front of the wall to glare down at them menacingly. The horsemen were messengers sent by the enemy to offer terms of surrender before the battle commenced. Both leaders knew this was not going to be a fruitful conversation, but starting a siege by exchanging terms was a time honored tradition that neither Sigaberht nor Legier would see broken. Additionally, Sir Legier believed that it couldn't hurt to ask… and Earl Sigaberht eagerly awaited the chance to prove him wrong.

Some of the archers near Radnor made cutting remarks about filling the enemy with arrows, though none dared violate the sanctity of wartime tradition. By the time the riders had finished trotting to the base of the gates, Sigaberht had chosen to stop glaring, and was now making a show of looking as bored as possible from atop his high place on the wall. Ignoring Sigaberht's body language, an unarmored but well-dressed rider spoke in loud, short bursts to be sure Sigaberht could hear him clearly.

"Lord Sigaberht, Earl of Wulfgeld. My own lord… Sir Legier, Marshal of the Army of Drakomar… bids that you surrender Wulfgeld to us. If you do… your life… and the life of your son will be spared. You and anyone who wishes it… will be granted safe passage to your allies in the north. Once there, you may retire however you see fit. However… if you do not surrender now… and defiantly spill the noble blood of Drakomar… then your life… the life of your son… and the lives of all who fight beside you… shall be forfeit. Do you accept these terms?"

Sigaberht glowered down upon the enemy messengers. After a moment of study, the earl guessed that the best dressed and most heavily armored man in the trio was the marshal of the army. Sigaberht had seen the coat of arms emblazoned on

Legier's shield before, and once he recognized it fully, the earl laughed heartily. He then spoke directly to the enemy knight.

"I pity you, Lord Marshal, for it seems you and your people have such short memories. I recognize your coat of arms, and as I recall, I personally flung you from the walls the last time you were here. Do not forget, Sir Legier, that the only reason you hold the title of "marshal" is because I butchered the last marshal of Drakomar who dared challenge me."

Legier bristled with anger at Sigaberht's words, and his tongue released a boastful reply.

"Then perhaps you would face *me* now! I do believe you shall find that my skill with a blade far outmatches that of my predecessor's."

Sigaberht peered down at the man beneath him and laughed.

"A duel? I might indulge such pleasure were it a different day. However, I do not feel like climbing down from my comfortable wall at the moment. Do yourself a favor: withdraw from my lands. Or better yet, perhaps you can save us all a bit of time and just fall on your sword? The men you lead to the slaughter would be most grateful."

Legier lost his temper then.

"You… your arrogance knows no bounds! By the oath I have taken to Princess Isabeau, and to Celestata, goddess of love, I shall tear down your walls and feed my hounds with your corpse!"

With that, Legier and his men turned and galloped back to their own lines. Radnor turned to Sigaberht.

"You let him have the last word?" Radnor asked.

Sigaberht chuckled.

"I will have the last word when I plunge my spear into his heart."

Radnor laughed heartily as Sigaberht returned to his spot on the wall. Horns sounded in the distance, and the enemy forces started their slow advance on the city.

A company of archers protected by heavily armored infantry equipped with even heavier shields decisively marched forward while blocks of men-at-arms carrying siege ladders advanced behind them. The archers pushed a fair distance ahead of the ladder crews, and expertly maintained this distance so as to better provide covering fire in response to any ambush the defenders might have lying in wait. No attack came, as Sigaberht had positioned all of his troops behind the walls. Radnor observed that the ladders Drakomar deployed were not as strong or protective as siege towers would have been, but wood boards did line their sides to protect the men climbing them against arrows fired into their flanks.

The enemy archers stopped just outside of range from the defending archers atop the walls and waited for the men with the ladders to overtake them. Radnor saw clusters of heavily armored knights marching behind the ladders. He could tell by their body language that they eagerly awaited the chance to scale the walls. These men would be the main source of trouble for Wulfgeld's defenders, as the first knights up the ladders would be wearing multiple shirts of mail and heavy helmets that would make them nearly impervious to all but long-sustained attack. As Radnor watched, he noticed that Drakomar's regular forces had been arrayed against the portion of the wall guarded by Ashveldt, and the forces of the Pale Light were soon to assault the area guarded by Daegal and Osmund. Radnor prayed that they were ready for the brutal fighting that was soon to come.

Once the ladder crews passed Drakomar's archers, the archers crossed into shooting range and loosed a volley of arrows at the defenders on the wall. Wulfgeld's archers quickly ducked behind the battlements as most of the vicious arrows clattered harmlessly against the stone wall. However, a few arrows hit their marks and several of the defenders cried out in pain as the murderous missiles pierced their bodies. Nevertheless, the defending archers were not broken by this initial assault, and Leif's orders rallied them to their feet once more.

"First line… Loose! Loose! Loose!" Leif yelled to his scrambling archers.

The front line of archers atop the gate unleashed an answering volley at Drakomar's archers. This volley was less effective as nearly all of their arrows bounced harmlessly off the shields of the enemy infantry. Seeing an opportunity to return fire while Wulfgeld's archers were notching new arrows, Drakomar's archers popped out from behind the shield wall and prepared to unleash a vicious volley. However, Leif had been waiting for the enemy to expose themselves in this exact manner.

"Second line… Loose! Loose! Loose!"

At his command, the second line of archers atop the wall loosed their arrows against their foes. Arrows pierced hearts and throats as the lightly armored bowmen were caught out in the open and punished for their recklessness. Their guarding infantry scrambled to place their shields between their allies and the fiendish arrows that sought to kill them. In their haste, the formation was broken, and Leif was only too happy to take advantage of it.

"First line, ready! Fire at will! Slaughter them!"

The archers from the first line promptly unleashed a continuous barrage of arrows against their foes. They expertly worked in pairs as they sought to kill every man who stood against them. One archer in each pair aimed for any opportunity they could find to wound an enemy soldier. As soon as anyone tried to bring the wounded behind the shield wall, the second archer would shoot the would-be rescuer. This tactic was extremely deadly, as the group from Drakomar desperately struggled to survive the onslaught. The enemy infantry's heavy armor and shields proved an effective deterrent against arrows. However, being struck by them was still extremely painful. As a result, Drakomar's infantry bunched and clumped together as they tried to both avoid being struck as well as aid their more vulnerable comrades.

Just as it seemed that the block of Drakomar's archers was about to panic and flee, more bowmen from the Pale Light that marched among the ladders struck with accurate counter-fire that forced Wulfgeld's archers to seek cover. This gave the main block of Drakomar's archers a chance to reform their lines. Now regrouped, the enemy archers of the main block were more cautious. They took greater care to stay behind their bodyguards' tall, heavy shields as they peppered the wall with deadly arrow fire.

While the archers battled back and forth, Drakomar's ladders continued their steady advance upon the wall. Radnor was about to warn Sigaberht of their impending danger, when to his relief, more archers clustered at several points on the wall loosed their arrows upon the men carrying the ladders. It was then Radnor realized that they had been intentionally waiting for the ladders to get closer, as the harrowing arrow fire would be ever more accurate and deadly as the range shortened. The enemy armor was heavy, but when they were in such close quarters, it was much easier for the archers to find the gaps in their foes' protection. The archers nearest Radnor expertly concentrated their fire on one group of men-at-arms carrying a ladder and within moments, enough of them were dead or wounded that the group abandoned the ladder entirely and retreated from the wall. However, Wulfgeld's archers were met with a swift rebuttal from enemy bowmen, and several of their number were dead before the rest could duck behind the safety of the battlements. Knights from the Pale Light charged forward, picked up the fallen ladder and continued their advance. Arrows slammed into them, but their armor was too thick for the projectiles to pierce flesh, and there were no easily exploitable gaps. As such, the enemy knights advanced through the hail of arrows with the same amount of concern they would give to being struck by hailstones.

The battle continued in this way for some time, as the archers from Drakomar sought to cover the advance of the ladders, and the archers of Wulfgeld did everything they could to end their assault.

Radnor watched as the ladders finally reached the wall. Once they started to secure themselves, the demigod stepped forward to aid the other defenders. Before he had made it far, Sigaberht took him by the shoulder.

"We need you *here*! The ram will be coming and I will not have you risk your life until we need to."

Radnor looked at the onrushing enemies that now scaled the ladders and grudgingly accepted his role.

"A dead weapon isn't a very good weapon," Radnor growled.

"Exactly. I'm glad to see you know your place… stay in it." Sigaberht replied.

Radnor nearly struck Sigaberht right then, but forced his temper down. The demigod turned this focus back to the battle and resigned himself to waiting for the right moment to join it. As he grappled with his feelings of powerlessness, Radnor could only watch as the knights of Drakomar assaulted the walls of Wulfgeld.

Osmund could only watch as the ladders latched onto the battlements and enemy knights swiftly clambered their way up. The ealdorman and his men had tried to push the ladders back down, but arrows from the Pale Light's archers forced them back. Other than Osmund and his huscarls, the defenders here had only light armor that offered little protection against the heavy longbows carried by the Pale Light.

Soon, several enemy knights stormed atop the wall and heavy fighting broke out as Osmund's warriors fought to crush the soldiers that stood against them. However, the first knights over the ladder wore three full shirts of mail, along with padded garments that rendered all but the most crushing blows utterly useless. Even arrows fired at point blank range didn't seem to faze the knights as they slaughtered the militia that defended Wulfgeld.

Men-at-arms quickly scaled the ladder as well and joined their knights to form an unbreakable shield wall. As the Pale Light took more and more ground, Osmund soon found himself fighting against a horde of nigh-unstoppable killers. The ealdorman stepped forward from his own line and attacked one of the men-at-arms with a sundering thrust from his spear… but it was turned aside by another foe's blade. The man-at-arms replied with a spear thrust of his own that Osmund barely ducked. Just then, an enemy knight swung his sword for Osmund's head, which was barely defended by the intervening shield of one of Osmund's huscarls.

As Osmund battled for his life, the knights of the Pale Light advanced upon the defenders. The rampaging army seized ground foot by foot, and for every man they lost, they killed ten of the defenders. The only reprieve for the men of

Wulfgeld was that the enemy bowmen had stopped firing for fear of hitting their own men. The militia forces Osmund had brought to Wulfgeld panicked and fled from their foes. They knew that to face such a relentless enemy meant only death.

As he observed Osmunds's battle with the Pale Light, Sigaberht noted that their vicious knights seemed a relentless juggernaut. They feared nothing and their will was unbreakable. The earl knew then that if they were to drive such a ferocious foe to retreat, that he needed to snatch victory from their grasp in the most dramatic way possible. The enemy needed to believe they were winning right up until the moment Veigarand could be sent to crush them.

Just then, Sigaberht noticed that Aethelstan had started marching his men to reinforce Osmund's position. Sigaberht turned to Leif and gave his orders.

"Send a messenger. Tell Aethelstan to hold his position in the courtyard. They must believe they are about to crush us before we drive them back. Aethelstan is not to reinforce Osmund until we can make the enemy believe he has taken the wall. Osmund and his men are to fall back to the gatehouse and the inner stairs until we can send Veigarand at our enemy."

Leif was shocked at Sigaberht's order. He wanted to protest, as ceding so much ground presented a huge risk. But, Leif did as he was told. He relayed the orders to a messenger that stood on hand, and the man sprinted to Aethelstan's position down in the courtyard. Aethelstan was just as surprised by the command as Leif had been. However, he was oath-bound to follow his earl's orders, and so his men stood by and waited for their chance to strike back at the enemy that now swarmed atop the wall. Having delivered the orders to Aethelstan, the messenger sprinted up the stairs towards Osmund's position. Understanding the importance of haste, the messenger sprinted across the top of the wall. However, as he did, he left himself exposed, and an eagle-eyed archer put an end to him with an arrow to the throat that scattered his words and blood upon the cold stones.

Ashveldt winced as the first ladders latched upon the walls of his home. He almost felt a strange sense of pity for the enemy that came clambering up to their deaths. The prince waited at the top of the ladder, his spear lined up with the head of the knight climbing the ladder. Once the man was in range, Ashveldt thrust his spear straight for the top of the man's helm. However, the steel guarding the knight's head was thick, and he shrugged off the blow as a minor nuisance. Ashveldt's huscarls began to pound away at the knight's armor, and soon the prince's pity turned to rage as the knight steadily climbed, unhindered by the blows. Arrows from below flew up into the faces of the defenders and left several dead. Ashveldt leaped back from the deadly missiles and hurriedly struggled to remove an arrow that had become caught in his mail. Taking advantage of the disruption, the knight finished climbing onto the wall; and after unslinging his shield from his back and drawing an ax from his hip, he began to hack and slash his way through the lightly armored defenders. Other knights soon joined him, and Ashveldt's huscarls found themselves fighting for their very lives. Seeing the carnage his foes wrought, Ashveldt leapt to the fray and desperately thrust his spear towards the first knight's throat.

Ashveldt's blow was expertly blocked by the knight's shield, which was followed by a counter-cut that Ashveldt narrowly parried with his spear. Hostile men-at-arms clambered up onto the wall and engaged the defenders as Ashveldt was locked into a duel with the enemy knight. The knight advanced on him, ax raised high for a powerful blow. Ashveldt stepped back and swung a preemptive strike at the knight's exposed arm. Again, the knight turned the corner of his shield to block Ashveldt's attack. As he did, the knight turned slightly to better place his shield to protect his arm and stomach against follow up attacks. This movement gave Ashveldt a chance to step around him and attack past the outer edge of the shield.

Striking with the butt end of his spear, the young prince delivered a bone crushing blow around the knight's shield and into his knee. The knight stumbled for a moment, as the blow had caught him where he was without armor. Ashveldt then

whipped the spear around in an arc and slammed the blade
against the knight's back, causing him to stumble forward.
However, the knight's mail was undamaged and the Ashveldt's
blade did not meet flesh.

Ashveldt had just lined up a cutting blow at the knight's
legs when one of the knight's men-at-arms swung a fierce blow
at Ashveldt's head. Ashveldt ducked the attack and drove his
spear into the man-at-arm's exposed face. Having killed his
attacker, the prince turned to find that the knight was on him
once more. Ashveldt tried to remove the spear from his fallen
foe, but the blade was stuck! Despair filled his heart as he
anticipated what would be a killing blow.

Time seemed to slow for Ashveldt as he again felt the
helplessness he had experienced when the wolves had cornered
him. Memories from that night flashed into Ashveldt's mind…
and rage consumed him. He let go of his spear and leaped upon
the knight with all of his strength and fought like a wild
animal. The knight was caught off guard by Ashveldt's berserk
ferocity and stumbled as he was driven backwards by the force
of the prince's charge. Both men tumbled over backwards, and
Ashveldt landed on top. The prince quickly drew his dagger
from its sheath and drove the blade deep into his foe's
unarmored throat.

The knight's grip on his weapons loosened as he choked
and gurgled on his own blood. Ashveldt stared coldly into the
knight's eyes as he watched him die, and in a gargantuan effort,
the warrior prince lifted his fallen foe high into the air. Driven
by his wrath, Ashveldt cast the knight's bloody corpse from the
wall and onto the men-at-arms below. Ashveldt then picked up
the dead knight's ax and shield and rejoined his men who
battled another group of knights and their men-at-arms.

One of these knights recognized Ashveldt and
shouted…

"It is the prince! Their prince has slain Sir Childeric! A
hundred gold ducats to the man who avenges him!"

The enemy men-at-arms surged toward Ashveldt and he
soon found himself driven behind his shield by a torrential
onslaught of attacks. The prince guarded and parried with his
shield as he frantically fought for his life. Blows rained upon

his armor, and it was only a matter of time before it broke, and his body was torn to pieces. However, as quickly as the onslaught had started, it stopped, as more of Ashveldt's men flew to his aid and drove Drakomar's men-at-arms away from him. As the battle raged around them, the knight that had issued the bounty stepped forward and challenged the prince to a duel.

Ashveldt had no time to play at heroics with his foe. There was no fancy footwork, no tactics, only brutal, ferocious violence. As the knight swung a powerful sword blow, Ashveldt threw a counter cut into the man's arm with his ax. This knight was not as skilled as Sir Childeric had been, and he cried out as Ashveldt's ax smashed into his arm. Though the blade did not penetrate the strong mail he wore, the pain was so severe that he lost all the feeling in his arm. Ashveldt followed up with a strong blow to the man's sword shoulder. The knight was stunned by the pain as he felt bones break under his armor. Twice more, the vengeful prince cut into the knight's shoulder as he desperately tried to bring his shield up to defend himself.

It was no use, for the knight's shield became tangled against the spear of one of Ashveldt's allies. The pain became overwhelming, and the knight withered under the prince's berserk rage. Ashveldt threw a third and final blow into the knight's shoulder and the armor finally gave way to the biting blade. The knight could only scream out in pain as the ax drove deep into his chest. One of Ashveldt's men slashed into the back of the knight's unarmored leg and severed it at the knee. The knight's men-at-arms rushed to his aid, but were driven back or killed by the ferocity of the defender's counterattack. One more knight stood alone, and after seeing two of his fellow knights killed before his eyes, he called for aid. He did not have to wait long, as nearly a dozen more knights and their men-at-arms quickly stormed up the nearby ladders. Ashveldt took a deep breath, and strode forward to mete out death once more.

Osmund's men fell around him. The enemy shield wall was too strong to be pierced by the points of spears or the blades of axes. They needed to break up the enemy formation if they were to have any hope of defending the wall. The inexperienced ealdorman decided that their only hope was to charge headfirst into the enemy and send them into disarray with sheer force of violence. To this end, Osmund threw down his spear, drew his short hand-ax, and shouted his orders.

"Piercing charge! Go! Go! Go!" Osmund shouted.

Without hesitation, the ealdorman and his huscarls hurled themselves against the Pale Light. However, their charge aimed to penetrate the enemy formation, not push it back. Chaos reigned as Osmund and his men forced their way between the rows of enemy soldiers as both sides hacked and slashed at each other. The ealdorman's senses were overwhelmed by cacophonic sound as steel clashed against steel and orders were shouted over screams of agony.

The ealdorman saw the exposed face of an enemy man-at-arms, and lashed out with his ax. He had no time to confirm the kill as he ducked a sword aimed for his head. As he moved, he saw the unarmored ankle of an enemy knight and slashed at it. His blow struck true and he felt great satisfaction as his ax severed the man's foot from his leg. The knight clutched at his wound and collapsed to the ground. Before the knight's allies could help him, one of Wulfgeld's spears struck his exposed throat, and a knight of the Pale Light died upon the wall.

After seeing that their foes could be killed, Osmund's militiamen found new courage and returned to drive against the enemy force. But, it was no use. Every enemy that died upon the wall died a martyr and was replaced by another man willing to perish for his goddess. For every man Osmund and soldiers killed, five or more of Osmund's men died with them; and the ealdorman soon found himself overwhelmed.

He tried to signal for help, but the enemy assault was so relentless that all his efforts became focused on survival. Osmund became locked in battle against another one of the enemy knights. He looked to his huscarls, but they were all dead or desperately fighting for their own lives. No help would come to the ealdorman.

The knight was armed with a sword and shield, and the ealdorman watched in awe as the glint of the sword's jeweled hilt flashed in front of his face. Osmund started a blow towards his foe, but the answering counter-cut came so swiftly that Osmund was forced to turn his weapon to block the knight's attack. The knight swiftly followed up with another sword strike and the biting blade cut deep into Osmund's shield. Seeing an opportunity, Osmund quickly turned the shield in his hand and wrenched the sword from the knight's grip. Before the ealdorman could take advantage of this, the knight's armored hand crashed into Osmund's jaw like a hammer and dashed him to the ground. There was no time for the wounded man to collect his senses before the knight rammed his shield into Osmund's throat. The ealdorman gasped in pain and choked as his windpipe was crushed by the heavy blow. The ealdorman desperately reached for his dagger and vainly slashed at the knight's ankles, but the man merely leapt away from the blow, and after scooping up Osmund's ax, killed the young ealdorman where he lay. Terror swept across the nearby militia and they fled from their foes. Cheers erupted from the warriors of the Pale Light. The wall had been taken.

Chapter 12

Discomfort grew in Arnulf's throat as he watched the battle unfold. The side of the wall assaulted by Drakomar's knights had met stiff resistance, and their attack had been stalled. The knight looked to Legier, who appeared frustratingly impassive regarding the casualties their countrymen were sustaining. Arnulf's gaze turned to the portion of the wall assaulted by the Pale Light. So far, they had proven to be a devastatingly effective army. It appeared to all who watched the battle that Wulfgeld's defenders on their side of the wall would soon be forced to abandon it entirely. Arnulf then glanced to Venatus, who stood beside them. The archpriest met Arnulf's gaze with a subtle, gloating smile. Anger flared in Arnulf's heart; and he forced himself to remain silent regarding the archpriest's impudence. He would have a discussion with Legier about it later.

"Why so tense, when victory is so clearly near?" Legier asked.

Venatus broke in before Arnulf could answer.

"He stands upon the precipice of victory delivered not by his countrymen, but by my brothers in light."

"Jealousy has nothing to do with it," Arnulf growled.

"Then why do you not answer your commander's question?" Venatus prodded.

"Enough!" Legier shouted.

The grand marshal turned to face Arnulf.

"My friend, the Pale Light has stormed the wall. Victory is almost upon us! I must ask again, why do you seem so afraid?"

"The battle is not yet won, and I fear the cost of your victory," Arnulf said.

Legier nodded, as there was wisdom in Arnulf's words. Legier realized he was getting ahead of himself, and had let himself get swept up in Venatus' fervor. Legier turned his attention back to the wall and made a tactical assessment of their situation.

On and on the Pale Light drove, and there was still no sign of any foul sorcery sent by the earl to drive them back. It was possible that his and Arnulf's concerns about Sigaberht's secret weapon were unjustified. To top all of this off, the ram was now advancing upon the gate, and if all went well, the defenders of Wulfgeld would have to face an assault not only atop the walls, but through their very gate! Victory really might come swiftly after all! Venatus turned to Legier.

"See how they flee from our might! Sigaberht must have committed all of his reserves by now, and yet they still cannot deter us from our holy purpose!"

Confident bravado swelled in Legier's breast, and he made his decision about how to proceed.

"We shall soon know for sure," Legier replied. "Signal for others to advance. I want fifty more knights and their men at arms to join the assault on the wall."

"Fifty?" Arnulf objected. "We've already committed a hundred to this assault!"

"Yes," Legier replied. "If Sigaberht had a secret weapon, he would have unleashed it once the ladders touched the walls. He has not. We have a chance to take Wulfgeld *now*, and I plan on doing so!"

Venatus smiled, and nodded.

"I agree with Legier. The glory and grace of Celestata is with us today. I say we pursue the attack to the fullest; the Pale Light shall gladly provide the men you desire. Would you like us to reinforce the men whom have been stalled?"

Legier was surprised at Venatus' willingness to commit more men to the battle, but was happy for the support. He nodded, as he understood that if both sides of the wall fell, the city would be theirs whether the gate was destroyed or not.

Arnulf could only shake his head in frustration, but his friend was also his commander, so Arnulf was forced to obey. The worried knight gave the instructions to the trumpeters, and they blew the calls that signaled for more men to join the battle. Once this was done, Arnulf prayed to Caelum that Legier and Venatus were right.

* * *

The battle raged on across the wall for an agonizingly long time as the ram slowly advanced towards the gate. The snow covered terrain proved difficult for the ram to cross, and Radnor's impatience grew as he impotently watched from his spot atop the gatehouse.

The situation atop the wall was dire. Sigaberht realized he had miscalculated, and that the timing of the battle was now against him. The enemy was taking ground atop the wall at an unmanageable rate, and so he finally gave the order for Aethelstan's reinforcements to be allowed to join the fight. He also saw that more knights of the Pale Light now marched across the field towards where his son fought, and Sigaberht knew he could not stand idly by.

Sigaberht left commanding the field to Leif and personally joined the fray as he desperately fought his way to Ashveldt's position. The earl and his huscarls fought tooth and nail for every inch of ground, as the knights and men-at-arms of Drakomar were a steadfast and determined foe. However, the wrath of Sigaberht and his son drove them to feats of arms unmatched upon the wall, and the soldiers of Drakomar soon found themselves fighting to hold on to what little ground they had taken.

On the opposite side of the wall, the battle was still going against the defenders. Aethelstan's and Daegal's forces were too lightly equipped to properly deal with the heavily armed and armored soldiers of the Pale Light. The ealdormen and their huscarls did what they could, but they were too few in number to hold out against the power of the Pale Light. Both ealdormen called reinforcements from their reserves several times. Even Sergeant Aelfric abandoned his original orders and brought his men to the ealdormen's aid, but none were sure how long they could hold the line.

As the battle raged, Rolf and the other scouts were hard at work dragging Wulfgeld's wounded away from the fighting. The dangerous work often required them to crawl among the battling forces to reach someone in need of their help. Several children froze when faced with the horror of war and had died for their hesitation. To the Pale Light, the children that aided the enemy were naught but more foes to be slaughtered; such was their devotion to the benevolent goddess of love.

When they realized how dangerous the battle atop the wall really was, Rolf and Halig dragged one of the dead enemies from the wall and stole as much of the man's armor as they could wear. Rolf, now clad in the helmet and ill-fitting mail of the fallen man-at-arms, did everything he could to help Halig find armor that could fit him. Halig was younger and smaller than Rolf, and it was nearly impossible to find anything that could be made to fit. As Halig saw men dying around him, he grew emboldened with the resolve of his own convictions. The boy took up a sturdy shield and headed back towards the wall with Rolf in tow. Rolf took Halig by the arm, but the boy would not be dissuaded from returning to the wall unarmored. Finally, Rolf spoke, hoping to break Halig out from whatever trance he seemed to be lost in.

"Will you at least let me go in first? I have the armor."

"Fine! You drag the people to safety; I'll cover you with the shield!"

With that agreed upon, the pair finished climbing the stairs and rejoined the chaos upon the wall. Three times they dove into the tumult and successfully dragged wounded men from the line. Someone always tried to kill them, but Halig's practice with the shield paid off, and he successfully protected himself and Rolf from the blades of the Pale Light.

The fighting grew even fiercer, and while Rolf hesitated to plunge into the line once more, Halig did not falter, and in his desperation to save as many people as he could, he hurled himself to the aid of yet another wounded man. Rolf followed him, and the two boys soon struggled to drag none other than Captain Sceotan from the carnage. The man had been there to direct the scouts, and it was his duty to keep them as safe as possible. When he saw the enemy knights attacking the children, he had rushed to their rescue. Sceotan had been wounded as he protected his charges, and now it was up to Rolf and Halig to rescue him.

Sceotan managed to get back behind the shield wall
formed by the men of Wulfgeld, but he needed medical
attention, and he needed it now. Just as Rolf and Halig were
about to reach him, the knights of the Pale Light charged and
broke through Wulfgeld's shield wall. Chaos erupted around
them as men smashed and trampled each other. Both boys were
kicked and stepped on, but they still struggled to rescue their
fallen ally.

As the enemy broke through Wulfgeld's lines, a
righteous knight of the Pale Light stopped to kill Sceotan. Even
as the knight's blade fell upon the helpless man, his gaze came
upon Rolf and Halig. Without hesitation, the knight attacked
the boys; his blow aimed directly for Rolf! Rolf tried to move
out of the way, but his foot was caught under Sceotan's corpse!
The boy prepared to meet Caelum in the afterlife, but Halig
blocked the blow with his shield! Rolf struggled and finally
freed his foot. The knight howled in rage at Halig's
interference and slammed his shield into the boy's shoulder.
Halig cried out as his bones broke. He tried to lift his shield,
but his arm would not move. The knight gave no quarter and
drove his blade into Halig's skull. In his final moments, Halig
felt almost glad, for he died saving his friend.

Grief stole Rolf's heart, but it was quickly replaced by
rage as he scrambled to his feet. Remembering Radnor's
training, Rolf successfully evaded another blow meant for him.
Before the holy knight could strike again, a Wulfgelder's spear
struck the knight in the chest and knocked him to the ground.

With vengeance in his heart, Rolf swiftly drew his
dagger and flung himself upon his foe. The knight cried out in
fear as Rolf drove his blade into the man's unarmored throat.
The boy watched as blood flowed from the wound and the light
of the man's soul left his eyes.

Rolf looked around him, and felt a strange sense of
sorrow as the gravity of killing another human being now
weighed on his soul. He shook the feeling aside, as this man
had murdered both Sceotan and Halig in cold blood. He
collapsed atop the dead knight and tears welled in Rolf's eyes
as he witnessed the battle around him. The enemy took him for
dead, and the battle passed him by. Rolf lifted himself from the

dead knight, and his gaze fell upon the bodies of the other children who had died trying to rescue their fallen comrades. Rolf's heart became consumed by such rage that even Radnor would have feared him.

Rolf ceased trying to aid the wounded, for the enemy was doing their best to make sure there were none to rescue. These people came here to steal and murder; and Rolf resolved to punish them for their crimes. The boy dropped back down, pretending he had died until he was sure all of the enemy knights had pushed past him and would take no notice of him.

He checked to see that he was now behind the main line of Drakomar soldiers, and that reinforcements were still making their way up the ladder. Blinded by rage, Rolf saw his opportunity for further revenge. He slowly crawled over to a wounded man-at-arms bearing the coat of arms of the Pale Light. The wounded man had a deep slash across his leg that prevented him from standing. At first, the man looked grateful for the help he thought was coming. Just as the wounded man realized Rolf was not a friend, the boy slit his throat. Satisfied with his work, Rolf left the man gurgling and bleeding against the battlements. Crawling still, Rolf found another wounded man, and again, slit his throat just as he started to cry out for help. Rolf then saw another wounded enemy and started towards him. This man may have been too wounded to fight back, but he had seen what Rolf had done and screamed for help as the murderous boy approached him.

Realizing he had been caught, Rolf rushed to the man and left his dagger buried in his neck. More enemy soldiers finished clambering from the ladders and onto the walls, and Rolf realized then that his anger had doomed him. Rolf quickly snatched up a shield and an ax from the ground and again prepared to meet Caelum in the Hall of Kings. One of the enemy knights strode forward to face him.

Rolf was no match for a foe such as this, but he didn't care. The boy stood against the knight and all the men behind him, and issued a challenge to his foe.

"Is this why you came here? To murder us? If so, then fight me, and die upon these walls!"

The knight hesitated for a moment. Rolf couldn't see the man's expression behind his helm, but there was a glimmer of recognition in the knight's mind that stayed his hand. Rolf took advantage of the hesitation and lunged for the knight, but he expertly parried Rolf's attack. The knight lashed out with his sword, but Rolf punched out with his shield and struck the knight's arm with enough force that the sword nearly came out of the man's hand. Despite the pain, the knight did not hesitate to reply with a shield strike of his own. Rolf staggered backwards and tripped over the corpses behind him. He landed hard, slamming his head against the stone floor. His fighting spirit undaunted, Rolf threw himself back to his feet. He was still dizzy from the fall and stumbled forward as he rushed the knight once more. However, the knight simply stepped aside and shoved Rolf as he tumbled by. With the extra force the knight added, Rolf slammed into the battlements at a low spot, and found himself tumbling over the edge. Down to the ground he plummeted, and landed hard. Thankfully, the snow outside the wall served to cushion his fall, and so he survived. As the world faded to black, Rolf felt several pairs of hands grab him and start carrying him away.

Leif grew more and more worried as the battle progressed. He had already sent reinforcements to the other ealdormen, and it looked as though he may need to commit even more of their reserves to that side of the wall, which would leave few to help Sigaberht should he and Ashveldt need it. Then Leif beheld a terrible sight. Through the fray, he saw Rolf on the wall as the boy fought against one of the enemy knights. Panic flashed through Leif's heart and he turned to Radnor.

"Veigarand! Rolf is in trouble! You must fly to his aid!"

Radnor saw where Rolf was and almost ran for him, but then he remembered his oath to Sigaberht. Sigaberht had ordered him to stay and wait for the ram and no matter how much he wanted to, he could not help the boy. If he even tried, the power of his oath would kill him on the spot. Leif shouted at him again.

"Damn it! Why do you not go?"

Radnor spun on the ealdorman.

"I would if I could, but Sigaberht ordered me to stay here and deal with the ram. I *cannot* disobey that order."

"Why do you suddenly care so much about what Sigaberht wants?" Leif demanded.

"If I disobey his order, the consequences would be calamitous in ways I cannot speak of," Radnor said.

The nature of Radnor's oath to Sigaberht was a closely guarded secret. No one knew of the unholy black oath that held Radnor in the earl's sway, and revealing this secret would cause Radnor's instant death. He hoped that his carefully chosen wording would get Leif to understand that he did not stay at his post by choice. Leif shook his head and wondered what calamity to which Radnor referred. The ealdorman saw the look on Radnor's face and knew the demigod spoke truly. What had Sigaberht done that could force Radnor to act this way? If what the demigod said was true, Leif wanted to know more. However, there was no time for further contemplation, as the enemy ram finally reached the gate.

"It is time, Veigarand. Destroy the ram!"

Radnor tore his gaze from Rolf's struggle and reached for the array of heavy stones just as the ram's first blows struck the gate. The ram's head was made of solid steel and struck with such force that it shook the masonry beneath Radnor's feet. Radnor peered out over the battlements and studied the great ram as it continued slamming into the gate below. It was protected by a covering made of heavy steel plates supported on a wooden frame. The plates overlapped which prevented boiling oil or other attacks to penetrate the covering. This protection was what Radnor needed to destroy.

An arrow whizzed past Radnor's head, but a returning arrow loosed by a friendly archer found its mark and silenced the enemy bowman forever. With the coast now clear, Radnor bent over and lifted one of the enormously heavy stones beside him. He quickly checked his aim and hurled it down towards the armored ram with all his might. Radnor did not watch to see the result of his work as the stone crashed down with meteoric force. Instead, he relied on the frightened and agonized screams of dying men to tell him that the stone had found its mark. Without any hesitation, the steel titan hurled another meteor upon the ram. This stone smashed through its armor like it was made of paper and crushed another one of the men underneath into naught but blood and gore. The soldiers inside the ram panicked, unsure of what to do against Radnor's assault. As the demigod hurled yet another stone into the siege engine, the enemy soldiers fled and abandoned their weapon in terror. Leif did not waste the opportunity to strike at his foes and ordered the archers to fire upon the fleeing men. One by one, the retreating soldiers were skewered and slaughtered by the deadly barrage.

Then, a rallying cry echoed over the battle. The men of Wulfgeld chanted in honor of their newfound champion.

"Veigarand! Veigarand! Veigarand!" they shouted. The men of Drakomar heard this rallying cry, and even the most stoic of their knights wavered, for if these cries were true, it meant a monster from legend and nightmare fought for Wulfgeld.

Now that the ram was destroyed, Radnor could join the battle on the wall without defying Sigaberht. Leif shouted to him.

"Veigarand! I will find Rolf! You must help Daegal and Aethelstan!"

Leif ran for where Rolf had been before Radnor could even start to argue. Radnor looked to the wall where the other ealdormen fought, and understood their dire need for his help. Radnor wasted little time and after drawing his fearsome sword, made his way to the join the fighting.

The tides of the battle continued to ebb and flow. Even as Radnor destroyed the enemy ram, Sigaberht and Ashveldt managed to stabilize their defense against the reinforcements from the Pale Light. Ashveldt had killed nearly a dozen knights from both Drakomar's and the Pale Light's armies, and his berserk rage would not be satisfied until all of them lay dead at his feet. Sigaberht had rescued his son multiple times, and each time, Ashveldt returned to the fray more enraged than the last. However, Ashveldt's fury had stemmed the flow of enemy soldiers, and they grew ever more cautious for fear of the strength and ferocity of the prince. Leif soon joined them with the rest of Sigaberht's huscarls, and they now had the numbers to not only hold the line, but gradually drive the enemy back.

On the other side of the wall, Aethelstan and Daegal battled side by side as they struggled to hold their ground. The Pale Light's assault on the wall continued ferociously, and Daegal's men had borne the brunt of the attack until Aethelstan and his men had come to their aid. However, Aethelstan's rear guard had fallen, and the knights of the Pale Light now attacked the defenders on multiple fronts. Aethelstan and Daegal fought back to back, and the two groups of defenders were slowly suffocated by the endless assault from all around them.

Radnor finally joined the battle on the wall as he rushed to bolster the ealdormen's withering defenses. He towered over the men whom he came to help, and all his foes knew him then. Radnor brandished his sword before his enemies, and its black blade cast ominous, unholy light across the blood soaked stones. One of the knights of the Pale Light strode forward to do battle with the strangely dressed warrior whom now opposed him. Radnor grinned and met the knight with a brutal assault. The northern warrior lashed out with his sword with ferocious force and speed. The knight tried to block the blow with his shield, but it was effortlessly torn asunder by Radnor's blow. The knight cried out in shock as his shield shattered in his hand. Before the knight could do anything else, Radnor threw a fierce blow for his neck. What happened next surprised everyone, even Radnor.

The instant the blasphemous blade struck the knight's mortal flesh, the man exploded into a shower of blood. The men-at-arms near him cried out and fled in terror. Even Radnor hesitated, shocked at the blade's unholy power. However, one of the few men-at-arms that had not fled threw a panic driven thrust at Radnor. The demigod turned the blow aside with his shield and struck the man with his sword. This time, the man did not burst into blood, but was instead engulfed in black flames. The man-at-arms screamed as he was incinerated in hellfire. The blade of Radnor's sword glowed with malevolent energy; as though it was gleeful at the profane destruction it wrought upon the battlefield. Radnor almost cast the sword aside, for its power was now repugnant to him.

However, an enemy knight saw Radnor's hesitation and charged for him, desperate to destroy the horror that had descended upon them. Radnor had no choice but to defend himself with the baleful blade. The knight drove his ax straight for Radnor's head, but the demigod threw a counter-cut at his opponent's weapon and the chaos sword neatly cut the enemy's sword in two. The knight staggered back and fled as the horror of Veigarand stole the last wisps of his courage. From behind Radnor, the chants of "Veigarand" grew ever louder. With no more enemies directly ahead of him, Radnor's mind flashed to his concern for Rolf. Radnor let out a cry of grief, as he believed Rolf's lifeless body lay buried beneath the other corpses on the wall. Rage surged through him, and the Wayfaring Death advanced upon the enemies that were still assaulting the beleaguered ealdormen. These foes were still unaware of the horror Radnor had unleashed upon the wall. Radnor showed no mercy as he descended upon his enemies. The terror brought by the name "Veigarand" became more potent than ever that day.

Radnor's onslaught turned the attention of the remaining enemies onto him and away from the ealdormen they had sought to overwhelm. Terror swept through the enemy force as Radnor slaughtered two more of their knights. Yet another pair of knights faced their foe bravely, but even together they were no match for Veigarand and his cursed sword. Radnor smashed through the defenses of the first knight and when his blade met flesh, the man dissolved not into blood, but instead into a swarm of vicious spiders. The spiders descended upon the second knight, crawling inside his armor and devouring him where he stood. After a few moments, the spiders themselves dissolved into blood, leaving only the desiccated remains of their victim behind. Nothing could stand before Radnor's might, and even the most stalwart of the holy warriors turned to flee. Those who could not reach the ladders hurled themselves from the walls, risking injury and death to escape the terror of Veigarand. Radnor gave them no quarter, and blow after blow rained upon his foes, wreaking panic in all those who stood before him.

It was not long before horns blew in the distance. The enemy commanders had seen the rout, and now signaled for a retreat. One knight and a handful of his men at arms were trapped on the wall, but upon seeing Radnor's blood soaked form, they surrendered without resistance. As the enemy ran back across the field, Wulfgeld's archers unleashed a withering volley of arrows, killing many of the panicked soldiers as they fled back to their camp. Radnor sheathed his sword and took a deep breath. They had won the day.

The crowd of men around him cheered even more intensely than before. They still chanted his hated name, "Veigarand! Veigarand! Veigarand!" as Radnor strode back to the gate. He caught Aelfric's eye, and the sergeant saluted him with his blood-coated sword as they passed each other. Radnor did not stop to speak with him, as Sigaberht and Ashveldt waited for him. Sigaberht's armor was covered in the blood of their enemies, and Ashveldt's mail was torn to pieces, with entire sections of rings missing. Ashveldt's face was twisted in a blood soaked grimace as Sigaberht held him closely. Unsure of what had happened between the pair; Radnor stopped in his tracks and listened. He found that Sigaberht was admonishing his son, but was trying to do so quietly enough that others would not hear.

"My son, stop! The enemy is beaten!"

"But father…" Ashveldt protested. He struggled to get out of Sigaberht's grip as he yelled. "The enemy will attack us again! We must drive them from our lands forever! We should replace the heads of the wolves with the heads of men before the day is out!"

Sigaberht shushed him as he tried to calm his enraged son.

"You are brave, but this battle will not be won by heroics alone. You fought well today… and we have our victory." Ashveldt still struggled. The berserk rage that had stolen Ashveldt's reason away was a temporary madness of which Radnor had long ago learned to be fearful. If left unchecked, it made warriors just as dangerous to their allies as they were to their enemies.

Sigaberht took his son's head in his hands, looked him dead in the eye, and spoke from his heart. "Remember who you are, Ashveldt. This rage… it is not you. Come back to me."

Ashveldt finally stopped struggling and met his father's gaze. In this moment, the prince remembered himself, and his madness subsided.

Emotions ran high between father and son as they embraced. All the men around them tried to keep their distance and pretend they were not seeing the private moment in front of them. Finally, Sigaberht and Ashveldt stepped apart. Ashveldt smiled when he saw Radnor. Sigaberht stepped forward and clasped the demigod's shoulder.

"Veigarand! Your power was on full display for all to see! If the enemy does not flee from our lands after what happened today… then they are fools indeed!"

Even as Sigaberht spoke these words, a cold fear gripped his heart. He finally became aware that the warriors of Wulfgeld did not cheer his name, but Veigarand's. An ordinary man might have been merely jealous of this attention, but Sigaberht was not jealous… he was worried. He was fearful that his plan of using Veigarand was a weapon had been *too* effective, and if Veigarand turned the tide of battles too often, it would soon be *him* who commanded the loyalty of the men, not Sigaberht. The earl tried to conceal his worry from the others, but he found it difficult to hide this from his face in his battle-weary state. However, an opportunity to redirect his emotions soon presented itself as Daegal and Aethelstan approached while bearing Osmund's body. Sigaberht channeled his fears about Radnor into grief over the death of Osmund.

"My fair ealdorman! Oh, woe! Here, we celebrate victory upon the battlefield when we have lost one so dear to us! How did he die?"

Daegal and Aethelstan laid Osmund down before their lord and stepped back in honor of their fallen comrade. Only then did Daegal answer.

"He died fighting the enemy that stormed our walls. Their assault was too great… and I was so locked into my own struggles that I did not see his. He died protecting us and protecting Wulfgeld. There is no better death!" Daegal shouted.

"Why was he not withdrawn when I commanded it? He and his huscarls were to have joined the counterattack with Veigarand!" Sigaberht demanded.

There was only silence until Leif finally tried to supply an answer.

"Much can happen in the chaos of battle."

"Yes," Daegal agreed. "And his sacrifice was not in vain. He held the line against our foes, and gave me the time I needed to regroup my own forces."

Sigaberht noted these words from Daegal. The earl would be sure that Osmund was remembered as a fallen hero that day.

"Praise, for Osmund: the victorious dead!" Ashveldt shouted.

"Praise!" shouted the men of Wulfgeld.

Sigaberht bowed his head in respect before Osmund's body. The earl's apparent grief may have been exaggerated, but he truly respected the sacrifice the youthful ealdorman had made. The man's death also brought a certain clarity to Sigaberht's mind, and he looked at the corpses around him. Although this had technically been a victory, the earl saw that more of his own people lay among the dead than his enemies. They could not afford a victory such as this again. Sigaberht turned to Leif, his mind now only focused on the battles ahead.

"I want the walls cleared. Bring our own dead down to be mourned and buried. We shall seek payment from the enemy dead. Seize their weapons, wrest the jewels from their *knightly* swords, and cast their corpses to the field below."

The earl then spoke to Radnor.

"I hope Elena's plan comes to fruition."

Radnor turned to face Leif.

"Did you find Rolf?" he asked.

Leif solemnly shook his head.

In response, Radnor wordlessly began combing through the dead, hoping beyond a hope that he would somehow find Rolf safely tucked away in some odd corner. Radnor also feared that he would find the boy's body lying amongst the dead. He vowed to himself that he would not stop searching until Rolf was found. However, Sigaberht had other plans.

"Veigarand! For whom do you search? Is it Rolf?"

Radnor turned to the earl and almost drew his sword once more.

"I warned you!" he screamed. "I warned you of the dangers of bringing the children into this battle! Many of them have been slain, and I cannot find Rolf!"

Sigaberht sighed with sorrow.

"Veigarand, you must remember, it was not I who killed these boys. It was the enemy. *They* came here to pillage my city. *They* brought death to my doorstep. We have lived here peacefully for generations, and *they* brought this savagery here; in the same manner the Hexverat brought *their* savagery. I am sorry you cannot find Rolf; I know you cared for him dearly. But, take heart, for if you cannot find him here, he might still live! I will make sure my people search for him. Once we are finished, I will personally tell you if he has been found or not. Now, I must order you to go home and get rest. We will need your strength again before this war is won."

Radnor glared at Sigaberht as he wished the man would burst into flames right there.

"A dead weapon is a useless weapon?" Radnor asked.

"Exactly."

Chapter 13

Sunset came upon the lands of Wulfgeld, and the warriors of Drakomar were finally ready to give the grand marshal their accounts of the day's events. Legier had wanted to start this process as soon as the battle was finished, but Arnulf had wisely counseled him to wait until emotions were no longer at a fever pitch. They wanted their reports to be as accurate, logical, and as unclouded by emotion as possible. Now that several hours had passed, Legier gathered all of the surviving knights and other officers to tell their stories.

Arnulf sat next to Legier and they listened intently while man after man gave their account of the battle. Venatus stood shadowed in the back corner of the command tent. He had already spoken with some of the knights of the Pale Light and had found their testimony most disturbing. In the spirit of cooperation, Venatus summoned several of his knights to join Drakomar's, so they might also give their accounts to Legier. It didn't make much difference, for no matter if the knights were from Drakomar or the Pale Light; they all shared the same, terrifying story.

Out of over a hundred and fifty knights that had assaulted the wall, nearly half lay dead, maimed, or captured. Legier counted many of their casualties not only as the best fighters among Drakomar's army, but also as friends. Legier struggled to keep his temper under control as the list of slain knights was read to him. In addition to the knights, the men-at-arms had also taken heavy casualties. Hundreds had been slain atop the wall, and the field that separated the camp from the city was littered with the bodies of men skewered by arrows as they fled.

It was oddly still as the army's commanders listened to the reports from the men atop the wall. It seemed the voices of the speaking men were the only sounds for a hundred miles. At first, the accounts followed the patterns of a normal siege. One man who gave his report was Sir Reginder, who had fought directly against Sigaberht and Ashveldt.

"Sir, the earl and his heir are fierce warriors indeed. I did not see it myself, but the word among my men is that Sigaberht's son killed Sir Childeric *and* Sir Ransome in single combat atop the wall, and killed many others. Several of Childeric's men-at-arms told me they witnessed the heir to Wulfgeld fling their lord's body from the wall after he was slain."

Legier grimaced at this news. He took a deep draught of wine from his mug, and then spoke to the reporting knight.

"Truly barbaric, these men are. Did no one try to single either of them out?"

"We did at first," Reginder replied. "Sigaberht's heir fought not only ferociously, but with reckless disregard for his own life. We almost had him in our grasp several times… but Sigaberht's huscarls are just as well armed and equipped as we are. They are trained, professional soldiers, and they rose to the defense of their lords *every* time we thought we could pin them down and slay them."

"What of the earl himself? Did he stand and fight as it seemed he would when I spoke with him?"

Reginder nodded.

"Yes, he did. He kept a cooler head than his son and directed his forces with skill and expertise. If it wasn't for the fact that he was trying to manage us *and* his son at the same time, I fear the earl and his men would have slaughtered our men-at-arms before they could even finish climbing the ladders."

"What of the archers that should have been covering you?" Legier demanded.

A different man stepped forward from the crowd and identified himself.

"I am Captain Folcard, my lord. I was in command of those archers. We did what we could… and our arrows slew many men of Wulfgeld, but once our own men were atop the walls, we could not fire without hitting our own troops. On top of that, the enemy archers proved most efficient in their fire, especially the ones atop the gate. They were well organized and anticipated our tactics. A number of our archers were killed in the initial exchanges, and as such, our total ability to suppress the enemy was severely reduced. If it were not for the bowmen brought by the Pale Light, we would have been slaughtered."

Legier dismissed the captain, and then looked to Venatus.

"What of your knights? What do they have to say?"

Venatus waved for his knights to speak. Five knights of the Pale Light stepped forward and hurled themselves to their knees before Legier. One man spoke for the others.

"My lords, we must offer our lives for our failure today. We were cowards upon the field this day, and ask that we be allowed to give penance of our blood so that our souls may be cleansed of our sin!"

Legier did not know how to respond to this, but thankfully, Venatus stepped in. He in turn knelt before the disgraced knights, and offered kind words of solace.

"Sir Frodris, the time for penance is not yet at hand, and I can assure you that your desire for it enshrines your soul in the eyes of our beloved goddess. Please, if you would but tell the tale of the day, we might yet overcome our foes!"

Sir Frodris cautiously turned his eyes towards his archpriest and clasped the clergyman's hands with his own. With a reassuring smile from Venatus, Frodris stood and faced Legier's questions.

"Now tell me," Legier said. "What happened atop the wall?"

"We… we took the wall. The soldiers who faced us were mostly farmers… peasants that dared to stand against us. I think we killed one of their ealdorman, for he was well-armed and led other well-armed men into battle. The enemy poured down upon us like locusts, but still we took ground. But then *he* came… the evil one."

As soon as Frodris finished his sentence, fear for his soul overtook him, and he wept uncontrollably before the assembled crowd.

Legier was again at a loss for words. He had seen men distraught after battle, but Frodris' uncontrolled outbursts were something beyond his experience. Again, Venatus intervened. He stepped forward, took Frodris by the arm, and led him to stand beside his comrades. Once this was done, Venatus turned and faced the marshal.

"Sir Legier, if I may, I would like to be sure we understand the full details of the events that transpired in chronological order. If I recall, after the walls seemed to have been taken, the ram was destroyed. May we hear about that next?"

Legier nodded. Venatus' idea made sense to him. He looked to the faces of the men in the room and saw their grim expressions. None wanted to speak of what needed to be discussed.

"Tell me about the ram," Legier said.

Another man stepped forward.

"My name is Sergeant Charibert, my lord. I am the only survivor from the ram's crew. Everything was going according to plan... we marched on the main gate… and we struck it. The gate shook, but held. It's a strong gate, sir, a very strong gate indeed."

"Get to the point," Legier interrupted. "What happened *after*?"

The siege engineer swallowed nervously before he continued.

"Something hit us. At first, we didn't know what it was. It just came hurtling down onto us as if the wall itself had collapsed upon us. But it wasn't that. It was only after the second stone hit… that we realized *something* was throwing boulders at us. They came in so fast… we didn't have time to pull the ram out of range. I don't know how they did it, but they were throwing… *throwing* those stones at us like they were pebbles! When they hit… all that was left of us was blood! At that point, we did all we could do, and ran. We couldn't save the ram. It was crushed into dust even as we started to flee. I'm not sure which was better, dying to their arrows as we fled, or being crushed beneath those horrible stones."

Arnulf broke in next.

"Did you see what threw the stones?" he asked.

The sergeant could only shake his head.

Legier waved him off and the man stepped back into the crowd with his head bowed in shame. Silence dominated the room once more. No one wanted to proceed, but finally, Legier asked about the other side of the wall. Venatus nodded, and a different knight of the Pale Light stepped forward. He stood taller and appeared less emotionally fraught than Frodris.

"My name is Sir Ebroin. My lord marshal, we were overwhelming the wall on that side. As Frodris said, we're sure we killed one of Sigaberht's ealdormen, though we do not know which one. We also had the other ealdormen surrounded as we cut down their men around them. If Sigaberht's huscarls are strong, professional warriors, the men the ealdormen brought with them are enthusiastic amateurs. They are not well equipped, with little to no armor. As such, the only thing that slowed us down on that side of the wall was their superior numbers. Even so, we were winning. I do believe that if… *Veigarand* had not arrived; we would have taken the wall, and been able to encircle Sigaberht."

Hushed whispers ran across the room as Sir Ebroin uttered the name "Veigarand". The knights of the Pale Light traced the image of the moon across their breasts when the unholy name was spoken.

Legier did not know what to make of the fear surrounding this name and pressed for details.

"We have discussed all aspects of the battle, save this very one. This name is unfamiliar to me, so I must ask: who is this "Veigarand"? How was one man able to turn the tide of battle against us?"

"Because he's not a man!" shouted a voice from the crowd.

Legier waved his hand to silence whoever had spoken.

"I would have order in this room! If he be not man, what is he? A sorcerer? It seems some of you recognize the name, but I do not."

Sir Reginder returned to the front and joined Sir Ebroin.

"Veigarand is a character from stories these northerners tell. Supposedly, he is the vengeful spirit of Amaranthar, the kingdom now ashes."

"A vengeful spirit?" Legier started. "Are you telling me that Sigaberht's secret weapon is a phantom from a kingdom destroyed by civil war over a decade ago?"

"Not civil war," Venatus corrected. "The stories tell of a war against demons, monsters of the underworld, that came to destroy them. The priests of my order have followed the rumors for nigh on ten years. Some rumors say *he* summoned the demons that destroyed his homeland. Others say he seeks vengeance against them. Not much can be proven, but one thing is consistent from story to story: wherever he goes, death follows."

Legier turned back to face Sir Ebroin.

"You were on the wall. What do you believe about these stories?" Legier asked.

Ebroin hesitated, unsure of whether or not to answer.

"Answer the question," Arnulf calmly ordered.

Venatus nodded and Ebroin gulped before giving his answer.

"Until today, I had barely heard a whisper of Veigarand. I was aware of the tale, but knew little other than what the priests have said… but now, I would believe *anything* told to me about Veigarand."

Gasps erupted among the men assembled as Ebroin so directly stated his beliefs on the matter. Arnulf waved his arm and silenced the fearful warriors.

"What exactly did you see?" Legier asked.

"A man… clad in armor not of the others from Wulfgeld. He carried a steel shield with a sharpened edge. I saw him cut a man's head nearly clean off with that sharpened shield. But it was not his shield that was most terrifying… it was his sword. Its black blade glowed with a sinister light, and he cut through our shields and armor like they were nothing. And the things that weapon did to us… it was horrible. There is terrible sorcery in that blade…" Ebroin trailed off, unable to speak further. Another knight, Sir Oderic, who fought on that part of the wall, stepped forward.

"What Ebroin says is true. I witnessed one of our men-at-arms challenge Veigarand, and he was incinerated by flames black as coals the instant the blade touched him."

200

Shock ran through the room, but Oderic continued. Even Venatus stood in horror at the words he heard.

"When Veigarand struck Sir Grimbald with his sword… there was nothing left. Grimbald… dissolved into a torrent of blood. By Celestata… whatever horrors are spoken of Veigarand, they are true!"

Commotion and chaos erupted among the men in the tent as they panicked over the prospect of having to fight Veigarand themselves. Arnulf pounded on his shield with such force that it drew everyone's attention to him.

"Cease this at once! You are the warriors of Drakomar! You shame yourselves as simpering children!" he shouted over the crowd.

It did not take long for Arnulf to get the room quiet again. Legier sat silently as he considered his options. Arnulf then asked a question.

"Did anyone see anything else during the fight? Some weakness we can exploit?"

There was silence for a moment, and then Sir Oderic replied again.

"I saw what happened to our men, but one of my men-at-arms told me he saw what Veigarand did when he killed Sir Grimbald. When Grimbald… When Grimbald died in the *way* he did… Veigarand hesitated. My man-at-arms swore our enemy was just as shocked by the weapon's effect as we were. It was like he didn't know his sword was cursed."

Before anyone could internalize this information, the door to the tent suddenly flew open and a messenger rushed inside. He bowed to Legier and abruptly extended his arm and revealed a letter in his palm. The marshal took the note from the man's outstretched hands. After reading its contents, Legier scribbled his own instructions upon the parchment and sent the messenger away with his reply. The marshal then looked back to the knights assembled before him, and spoke.

"We anticipated that Sigaberht might have had a secret weapon, and we now know what it is. His weapon is a man with an enchanted sword, meant to evoke a figure from legend. Sigaberht intends to scare us off. He knows that without this 'legend' fighting for him, all is lost. Were it not for this man's interference, we would have won today. Because of your sacrifice, we know how to destroy the threat." Legier waved the letter in front of the men. "The messenger bore good news. The trebuchets are prepared, and will begin bombarding the city as soon as they receive my orders. We will pound the city into submission ere the sun rises, regardless of this 'Veigarand's' involvement. Even if they do not surrender to us, I can also assure you that when we next attack, every effort will be done to draw this man out and slay him with arrows from a distance. I believe he should be easy to pick out. He does not wear the armor of Wulfgeld. Did anyone get a good look at the coat of arms emblazoned upon his shield?

"It was a green field, emblazoned with a golden dragon," came Ebroin's reply.

"Good," Legier started. "We shall hunt him down, and if he dares show himself again, any power his sword might have shall be eliminated by the hundred arrows that will skewer him. Now, is there anything else I should know about before we adjourn for the night?"

Arnulf spoke next.

"My lord, we took a single prisoner from the walls… a boy. He was fighting for the enemy. *He* may know something about Veigarand."

Legier stood, smiling as he did.

"You see? The siege shall turn to our favor yet. Please, take your rest. You are tired, and this has been a grueling day. Know that the sacrifices of those who died today will not be in vain."

At this dismissal, the knights and soldiers of Drakomar departed from the tent, their hearts lighter than they had been at the start of the meeting. Hope filled them now as they made for their own tents to eat, drink, and rest in preparation for the days to come. Venatus spoke to Arnulf and Legier.

"I must go speak with my priests. They must be informed of what we have learned. I suspect many will seek guidance for their souls in the coming days."

With that, Venatus strode out of the tent and headed back to his side of the camp.

Arnulf then headed for the exit of the tent and was halfway through the doorway when he realized that Legier had not followed him.

"Do you not wish to speak to the prisoner?" Arnulf asked.

Legier shook his head.

"It is cold, and I am tired. We will interrogate him later, when he has had a chance to stew for awhile."

Legier then gestured for Arnulf to sit beside him. The knight did so and waited for Legier to continue. A crashing sound rang in the distance, and Legier smiled.

"It appears the bombardment has begun. Let the people of Wulfgeld see the price of resistance."

The marshal of Drakomar leaned back in his chair and enjoyed the sounds of rocks smashing against the buildings in the city of Wulfgeld.

* * *

Radnor stood at the door to Elena's and his home, but he could not bear to enter. He waited at the threshold as he grasped for the words he would use to tell Elena that Rolf had almost certainly died upon the walls. Pain wracked his soul, and he wasn't sure he had the heart to tell her that her would-be brother was dead. After an age of internal struggle, Radnor finally found the resolve to do what had to be done, and entered their cottage. All was quiet and still.

Radnor saw that Elena was fully occupied with summoning the ghouls, so the weary warrior decided to take this opportunity to clean himself up. He headed back to the water trough behind the cottage. After shedding his armor, Radnor stood in the cold air and approached Darestr. His loyal horse sensed Radnor's grief and proceeded to gently nuzzle his beloved master with his snout. Radnor replied with pats, and the two stood silently for a time. Radnor looked down to the old ring on his finger and sighed. He looked back to Darestr, and spoke.

"I don't know how well this ring works. I don't know if you'll understand me when I tell you that Rolf… you remember Rolf, right? Rolf…” Radnor stammered, unable to say the words aloud. “Rolf… is dead.”

With the aid of Radnor’s ring, Darestr understood his master’s words perfectly, and groaned in sorrow. Radnor patted Darestr on the shoulder, and the two mourned him together in the cold night air. It was a long time before Radnor spoke again.

“Thank you, my friend. Your company is always appreciated.”

Then, a sinister voice emanated from the shadows.

“Why thank you! I didn’t know you cared!”

Radnor spun and was met with Ashrahan’s impish, grinning face.

“Get the fuck away from me!” Radnor snarled.

Ashrahan took a step back as he feigned injury.

“I come to check on you, and this is the thanks I get?”

Radnor spun away from the god, hoping he would just go away.

Ashrahan rolled his eyes in disgust at Radnor’s behavior.

“You’re not going to get rid of me that easily. We have business to attend to.”

Radnor turned back to face the Krigari god and glared.

“Fine, what do you want?” he demanded.

“I want to talk to you about Adramelach,” Ashrahan replied. “He is more determined than ever to break into your world. We need a plan of action, should he succeed.”

“You told me this last time we spoke. It is of little concern to me now. Besides, do you even think that’s possible?” Radnor replied.

The serious look on Ashrahan’s face answered Radnor’s question.

“This is a being that defeated Damiros. If there’s anyone that can find a way, it’s him.”

Radnor patted Darestr again.

“Then what chance do you think we have of stopping him?”

“This is why I come to you. We need a plan.”

Radnor shrugged, annoyed at Ashrahan's badgering. Finally, Radnor started talking again.

"Have you any idea *why* he wants access to our world so much? You've shown me that there are hundreds, maybe *thousands* of worlds. Would one of them not be as useful to him?"

Ashrahan shook his head.

"For a long time, I believed that his interest in your world stemmed from the fact that it's the only one he can't reach."

"Huh?" Radnor said.

Ashrahan quickly clarified.

"We have spoken of barriers. There is a barrier that separates the cosmos from the ocean of chaos."

"I know that, already." Radnor interjected.

Ashrahan nodded.

"Yes, you know about the one that the witches so dangerously toyed with. But, there is another barrier that separates your world from all the others too."

Radnor cocked his head in surprise.

"Wait, so you're telling me that the Krigari can walk freely from one world to another?"

"Yes, to every world except yours."

Just then, a female voice broke into the conversation. It was soft, yet filled the air with sound in the same, unearthly manner that Ashrahan's did. Radnor spun around, frantically searching for the source of the other-worldly voice. Ashrahan grinned.

"He seems confused. Is he always so slow to catch on?" the female voice said.

"I'm sorry to say, yes, he is," Ashrahan said.

"It's a pity. Such a handsome man, yet so few brains to match the brawn."

Radnor's temper flared.

"Enough! Ashrahan, cease this trickery! I am tired from a day of slaughter, and unless you want to join the dead, I suggest you leave me alone."

The female voice laughed.

"Empty threats. I can see why you like him though. He is faced with beings greater than himself, and yet still, he challenges us."

Ashrahan sighed.

"All right, you've had your fun. Come out."

"Fineeeeee," said the female voice.

With that, a woman gradually materialized before Radnor's eyes. She was tall and thin, and dressed only in wispy robes that barely concealed the rise and fall of her voluptuous breasts. She stood in a pose most men would have found inviting and provocative, but given that Radnor guessed her to be one of the Krigari, he found her display off-putting. Her long black hair tumbled down across her shoulders, with a streak of golden blonde hair that ran alongside her face and curled around her neck like a serpent. Her amber eyes shone dully in the dim light as though they glowed with a light of their own. She smiled playfully and showed off her bright red lips against her pale skin. Her beauty struck Radnor thoroughly, but he knew what she was, and his heart turned cold to her despite her fair appearance.

"Is this another conspirator?" Radnor asked.

Ashrahan nodded.

"Allow me to introduce… Lashmatu."

The Krigari goddess bowed mockingly at Radnor before resuming her previous pose. Radnor was unimpressed.

"Great. I'm going to have *two* of you dropping in on me, exactly what I always wanted."

Lashmatu laughed.

"Do not worry. I am only here at Ashrahan's request. Otherwise, I would not waste my time with you."

Radnor glared ineffectually before speaking again.

"Then why come at all? What do you have to offer to our little alliance?"

Lashmatu smirked, revealing a smile that was somehow even more predatory than Ashrahan's toothy grin.

"Do you remember what Ashrahan showed you? The vision of the final battle between Damiros and…" She paused, as though she was hesitant to say the name that came next. "Caelum?"

"Yes," Radnor said. A chill of terror ran down his spine as he recalled his vision of the worlds destroyed by the awesome powers of the creators and their servile war gods.

"Well, I am the witness to those events. Ashrahan told me that he showed you a vision of that final battle. That was *my* memory."

Then I guess I have you to thank for the nightmares, Radnor thought. He took a deep breath, then spoke again.

"So, the information you provided has turned some of the Krigari against their master, but if I am correct, you are all still enslaved to Adramelach's will. How can either of you help me in any way?"

"Well…" Ashrahan started. "We are all sworn to obey him under the power of a black oath, forged on an oath ring of Caelum's own making. We must obey his commands without question *and* cannot lift a finger to harm him directly. However, there is still a narrow window for us to help *you* kill him."

"How so?" Radnor asked.

"Well," Lashmatu started. "Since he hasn't ordered us *not* to help you, we have an opportunity to find a way to trap him for you, so you can deal the final death blow."

"What sort of trap did you have in mind?" Radnor asked.

"We're not sure yet," Lashmatu replied. "It partially depends on how many of us we can bring to our side. If enough of us move against him all at once, the prison we forge might prove most effective."

"I'm hearing a lot of 'ifs' in your plan, which does not improve my confidence in your ability to hold up your end of the deal," Radnor said.

Lashmatu held her hand to her breast in mock shock and Ashrahan laughed at Radnor's barb. The demigod continued. "It sounds like what you need is a way to keep him from giving you any commands. If he orders you to kill me, you're compelled to do so, correct?"

"Yes," Lashmatu said.

"Well, it seems to me that the trap would need two components… one to bind him, and one to gag him."

"Like trapping a wolf," Ashrahan said.

"I wouldn't know," Radnor said. "I've mostly just butchered them."

Lashmatu laughed.

"Ashrahan! You misled me! I was under the impression that I wouldn't like him!"

Ashrahan shrugged and replied.

"It's not my fault you have bad taste in men."

Lashmatu laughed again, further annoying Radnor. Just then, Elena's voice came from the house.

"Radnor! Is that you?" she called.

"*Oh*! Who's this?" Lashmatu asked.

Radnor's temper flared as he sought to protect Elena from harm.

"No one for you to concern yourself with!" he growled as his hand instinctively reached for his sword.

Lashmatu noticed his threatening gesture and grinned.

"How gallant. Perhaps I should meet your lover and compare notes. I wonder what she would reveal about your…" Lashmatu clearly gazed at Radnor's groin. "Prowess."

Lashmatu's goading proved successful, and Radnor instinctively stepped forward so that he might deliver a killing blow. However, he knew full well he could do nothing to harm Lashmatu's projection.

Ashrahan spoke again.

"Veigarand, your woman's involvement says that it is time for us to depart. It is for the best, as Adramelach will be looking for us to help him again."

"What?" Radnor asked.

Lashmatu smiled.

"He's ordered us to help him break into your world. I hope your mortal war ends soon, because if we succeed before you're prepared, all our lives will be forfeit."

With that, the gods faded from Radnor's vision. The demigod turned and found Elena coming toward him from inside the cottage.

"What are you doing out here?" she cried as she ran to him and hugged him tightly.

"I was… I was waylaid by our Krigari friend again."

Elena looked up at him, eyes filled with fear.

"What did he want?" she asked.

"Nothing that matters right now. I… I have something I need to tell you."

Elena saw the look in his eyes, and knew something terrible had happened.

"What? What do you need to tell me?" Radnor turned his gaze away from her and refused to make eye contact again. "Radnor… please tell me." Elena's mind raced with fear as she ran through the possibilities in her mind. "It's not Rolf is it?" she pleaded.

Radnor could not respond with words, and simply nodded his head.

"No!" Elena cried out. Tears streamed down her face as grief crashed into her.

She looked back up at Radnor.

"How did it happen?"

"I don't know for sure… we haven't found his body yet. He was atop the wall, trying to help the wounded. He got cornered, and fought valiantly. I wanted to help him, but I had orders that I could not defy—"

"Why in Caelum's name was he atop the wall? And what the hell does 'could not defy' mean? What are you talking about?" Elena demanded.

Radnor shook his head.

"*Sigaberht* is why he was on the wall," he spat. "The bastard sent the children into the fray to rescue the wounded." Radnor paused to gather breath before continuing. "As for what I mean by 'could not defy'… I would explain myself if I could, but like I said to Leif at the time, the consequences for disobeying my orders would be so severe, I simply cannot risk it."

Elena took a step back from him.

"What hold does Sigaberht have over you that he could make you do this?"

"*I can't tell you!*" Radnor cried. "But it is the thing that prevented me from saving Rolf!"

Radnor broke into tears he had not shed since the day he went into exile. Elena clung to him, and the pair wept together for their fallen friend.

After a time, Elena spoke.

"I must get back in the house. My work is not done, and if I allow my grief to make me fail, Rolf's sacrifice will have been for nothing."

Radnor nodded.

"How close are you?"

"Close," Elena answered. "I only wait for the cover of darkness."

Radnor sighed.

"Then, when it is over… would you help me look for Rolf's body? Sigaberht promised his men would look for him, but I do not trust him."

"Are you sure he's dead?" Elena asked.

"I don't know, but I promise you this. Dead or alive, we will find him… together."

Elena nodded, and the pair walked hand in hand as they reentered their home.

Unknown to the lovers, Lashmatu and Ashrahan had only stopped projecting their forms into the world and still spied upon them. As Radnor and Elena disappeared into the house, the Krigari faced each other. Lashmatu spoke first.

"He is a dedicated one, I'll give him that," she said.

"Yes, now do you see why I asked you to come with me this time?"

"You believe he was lying to you when he told you of his battle against the Hexverat?" Lashmatu asked.

Ashrahan nodded.

"He wasn't telling me the whole truth. He was clever. He dangled information about that sword in front of me and hoped I would stop asking questions. He's trying to shield her from me, and I want to know why."

"It could be that he doesn't like you," Lashmatu suggested through an impish grin.

Ashrahan gave her a fierce look that could have killed mortal men.

"I think she's the key to his tale. Things don't add up. How could he have defeated the witches by himself? How could he have slain that which dwelt in the dead city?"

"We don't even know what it was he killed. Perhaps the threat it posed was exaggerated," Lashmatu replied.

Ashrahan shrugged.

"That's not my point. Whatever it was, it wielded the dark powers of chaos against Veigarand and those that went with him, and yet somehow, a mortal half-breed managed to defeat such power by himself? Unlikely. And you heard them talking just a moment ago, she's using *my* gaulderen to summon an army of ghouls to their aid."

"You sound quite pleased with yourself over that gaulderen," Lashmatu chided.

Ashrahan grinned.

"Of course. It has more than proven its value."

Lashmatu rolled her eyes and then gazed at the cottage door.

"Should we peek inside?" she asked.

Ashrahan shook his head.

"No, he will not bother her as she works, and we won't be able to learn anything until she's done anyway."

"Then why are we bothering with this?"

"Because… I think *she's* what Adramelach's looking for, and I need your help to prove it."

Lashmatu paused for a moment as the implications of Ashrahan's words ran through her mind. Finally, she spoke.

"Now I see why you brought me here. Hymurr always dealt in the greatest of riddles. Alright, I'll help you with this one. But we must do things my way, or we stand no chance of success."

Ashrahan grinned eagerly as the pair discussed their plans to uncover the truth.

Chapter 14

Rolf was tied to a stake in the middle of the enemy encampment. He had been largely ignored by the men of Drakomar; save for the lone soldier that guarded him. Rolf was pleasantly surprised at how well he had been treated by the enemy; though receiving any treatment kinder than torture would have surprised him.

Rolf now sat on a short wooden stool and gazed into the small fire nearby. He was grateful for its presence, as the calming flames kept him from freezing to death. He still had all his clothes, and no one had struck him since he'd been chained up.

Not everything was perfectly comfortable though. The rope that held him to the stake was tied around his neck, and while the loop was loose enough he wouldn't choke on it, it was tight enough that he was always acutely aware of its presence. His hands were tightly bound by separate lengths of rope. The enemy had intentionally left his legs free so he could walk about within the short distance he was afforded by the noose around his neck. They had taken the armor Rolf had been wearing, though that did not bother him. It was their armor, and he was happy to be rid of it. What did bother him was that they had also taken his father's gold medallion. It was now Rolf's sole goal to find that medallion and kill the one who took it from him.

At the moment, Rolf could only sit and glare as two knights strode towards him. They both drew up chairs and seated themselves in front of Rolf, who only scowled at them with all the anger he could muster. One of the knights spoke.

"I am Sir Arnulf and this is Sir Legier, Grand Marshal of the Army of Drakomar. We would like to speak to you."

Rolf silently glared at them. Unperturbed by this, Arnulf continued.

"I see you are stubborn. You do not believe we will torture you for what we want to know?"

Rolf looked away.

"I've heard of Drakomar's knights. They say you live by a code of honor. Is there honor in torturing and killing boys like me?"

Legier spoke next.

"Interesting that you speak of honor, you *murderous child*. My men have told me that you were caught slitting the throats of the wounded upon the wall. Do you find honor in that?"

"No," Rolf locked eyes with Legier and smiled. "Only satisfaction."

Rolf's words were met with a fierce backhand thrown by Legier. The boy's head snapped back from the force of the blow, but he gritted his teeth and spat his angry retort.

"You think that hurts me? I was there with the other boys. We were only there to bring the wounded to safety, and you slaughtered us. So, I must ask again, *sir*, do the knights of Drakomar find honor in killing children?"

Arnulf took a step back in shock at what he was hearing. By the look in Rolf's eyes, he believed him. The knight's mind raced for justification, and after a moment, he made an appropriate reply.

"You were there to aid the soldiers of Wulfgeld, and as such, put yourselves in harm's way. You have no one to blame for your slaughter but Sigaberht."

Even the words spilled from Arnulf's mouth, he was not sure who he was trying to convince, the child tied to the ground like an animal, or himself.

Rolf shook his head.

"You killed a dear friend of mine. His name was Halig, and he was a kind soul. If there was anyone alive who deserved to live, it was him, but you murdered him! My vengeance shall not be fulfilled until all of you are dead!"

Legier laughed and spoke again.

"The boy thinks himself a warrior… believes himself to be immortal." Legier looked back to Arnulf. "Perhaps we will need to dissuade him of such notions. But first, I would like to try a different approach. Would you mind?"

Arnulf nodded and withdrew Rolf's medallion from his pouch. Legier took it and dangled it in front of Rolf's eyes.

Rolf lunged for the heirloom, and Legier quickly snatched it back. Rolf struggled against the rope tying him to the ground, but it was no use. Defeated, the boy sat back down on his stool.

"Give that back!" Rolf demanded.

"Not until you answer our questions," Arnulf said.

"It's mine! You have no right to take it!" Rolf yelled.

"First question: where did you get this?" Legier asked sternly.

"It was…" Rolf started. He abruptly stopped speaking as he realized that it was best not to give away his father's identity, lest he also give away that he had been a spy.

"Yes?" Arnulf prodded.

"It was on a dead man. I found it on a dead man after the wolf attack. I liked it and took it."

Legier struck Rolf again with such ferocity that Arnulf stepped between them for fear Legier would kill the boy.

"Do you know whose that was?" Legier shouted.

Rolf shook his head, continuing his lie. Legier tried to push past Arnulf, but his second kept him away.

"That belonged to a friend of ours! We had not heard from him in some time, and now we know he was robbed by you, you little maggot!" Legier snarled.

"Calm yourself! The boy cannot help us if he's dead!" Arnulf shouted.

"After everything that's happened today? I don't care!" He tried to attack Rolf again, but Arnulf restrained him once more.

"My lord, stop! Walk with me, we must speak!"

Despite his anger, Legier heeded his friend's counsel and ceased his attempts on Rolf's life. The grand marshal followed as Arnulf led him a short distance away.

"What is it?" Legier demanded.

"This medallion, it was given to Leofric, correct?"

"And?" Legier questioned.

"And take a good look at the boy! Look at his face! Don't you see it?"

Legier stopped to look at Rolf more intently, but saw nothing of interest. He looked back to Arnulf and shook his head. Arnulf rolled his eyes in frustration.

"Look closer. Do you not see the resemblance?"

Legier looked again, and with Arnulf's coaching, began to see what his friend saw. Rolf's sandy colored hair and blue eyes, the shape of the boy's face, especially the brow and nose…

"Can this be? Did Leofric *have* a son?" Legier asked.

Arnulf nodded.

"It seems that Leofric's ties to Wulfgeld were deeper than we thought."

"Yes, and it certainly calls some things into question," Legier replied.

"How do you mean?" Arnulf asked.

"If what I now suspect is true, Leofric not only had a son among these people… but he hid his son from us. Does that not strike you as odd?"

Arnulf shrugged, not yet willing to consider what Legier was suggesting. Legier pressed further.

"The boy's very existence calls into question every service Leofric did for us. What else did he hide from us? How many other lies did Leofric tell us?"

"I don't know," Arnulf replied. "And frankly, that's not something I want to think about. Regardless of what truths may be revealed, Leofric was my friend, and I will not have you beat his son to death."

Legier took a step back from Arnulf in surprise.

"Were you anyone else, I would have you flogged for standing against me so openly."

Arnulf's eyes narrowed in anger.

"Is it your wish then to kill him?"

Legier leaned past Arnulf and looked at Rolf.

"Not right now. He may not have desecrated Leofric's corpse… but, he killed our men today. He slit their throats as they cried for help. You know we can't let him walk away unpunished."

Arnulf nodded.

"I know. But, we should hold off on an execution until we find out what he knows about Veigarand."

Legier chuckled.

"True, we got so caught up in other things; we haven't even asked him yet!"

Without waiting for further debate, Legier stepped past Arnulf, and with his friend close behind, the pair resumed their seats in front of Rolf. Legier spoke first.

"We have a proposition for you. We're not sure if you're the rightful owner of this medallion or not, but we are willing to let you have it back regardless, *if* you answer our questions."

Rolf glared once more, and after considering it, gave his answer.

"Alright, fine. I'll tell you what I can."

Legier smiled.

"Tell me about Veigarand," he asked.

Rolf laughed.

"So you met him, did you?" Rolf smiled to himself before he continued. "Wait… if you had, you'd be dead."

Legier wound up to hit Rolf again, but a stern look from Arnulf stayed his hand. Instead, Legier spoke.

"He killed many of my men, and he will kill many more before the siege is won if you don't help us."

"How can I help you, exactly?" Rolf asked.

"For starters, tell me about the sword he wields," Legier said.

Rolf shook his head.

"I don't even have to lie about that one. No one knows anything about that sword; least of all me. It's a terrible weapon Veigarand has wielded for years. No one knows where he got it, or how long he's had it."

"Lies!" Arnulf shouted. Rolf looked into Arnulf's eyes in surprise, and the knight continued. "That is a lie. Veigarand could not have had the sword long. He acquired it recently… perhaps he stole it from those witches that attacked you."

"Or…" Legier interrupted. "Sigaberht defeated the witches, and in an effort to frighten us, equipped one his men with the sword and sent him against us as 'Veigarand'. Who is the man with the sword, really? He must be one of Sigaberht's most loyal servants, to be trusted with so powerful a weapon."

"I don't understand," Rolf started. "What are you *talking* about?"

"What is the real name of the man with the black sword?" Legier demanded.

"He is Veigarand," Rolf replied matter-of-factly.

Legier stood, frustrated at the lack of progress. He held out his hand to Arnulf.

"Give me the medallion," he commanded.

Arnulf withdrew the medallion again. Legier snatched it from his hands and dangled it over the fire.

"No!" Rolf cried. He lunged for the medallion but the rope caught on his neck and pulled him to the ground. Legier was too far away and Rolf was helpless to stop the knight from dropping his father's necklace into the flames and melting it before his eyes.

"We know he was your father, and how important this must be to you. Tell me what I wish to know!" Legier said.

Rolf considered telling them everything. He almost was ready to tell them the whole story, from when Radnor had first come to Neugeld, all the way to the battle against chaos in the dead city. He wanted to cry and beg for mercy from the men who held him in their power. He wanted to be like other children, with a home and chores and brothers and sisters. But he was not at home. He had no brothers and sisters, and he had but one responsibility now. It was then that the boy made a decision true to his heart.

"Do you want to know the truth? Well, here's what I *can* tell you. My father died saving my life. Every day, I wish that he had lived. I pray to Caelum to bring him back to me, and nothing happens. You believe you threaten a final, parting gift from my father. His parting gift to me was life. Halig died saving my life too. *Two* people died so that *I* might live. That medallion is not a gift from my father; it's a reminder of the people who kept him from me. You people, and your greed forced him to live a life of lies. *You* are the ones who kept him from me for so much of my life!"

Rolf paused and enjoyed the look of rage on Legier's face as he spoke. He then made one final statement.

"My father is dead, but his courage lives on through me."

Legier glared down at the boy, infuriated at Rolf's impudence.

"You will not answer my questions?" Legier asked. Rolf was silent.

"So be it."

With that, the honorable knight of Drakomar dropped the boy's keepsake into the fire, and the trio watched as the gold melted into the flames. Legier walked away and motioned for Arnulf to follow. Once they were separated from Rolf, Legier gave a chilling order.

"Tomorrow morning, I want our men to drag the boy out into the field in front of the gate. I want Veigarand, Sigaberht, and all the others called to discuss terms again, and then I want the boy's throat cut for them all to see."

Arnulf stepped back in shock at Legier's order. The marshal looked at his friend accusingly.

"Do you defy my orders? My will shall be done!"

"But, his father was our friend, we cannot simply…"

"You will do this, and it will be done tomorrow. If you wish to show him kindness… give him a final meal, but he dies *tomorrow*. Do you understand?"

Arnulf reluctantly nodded.

Legier abruptly turned and stomped back into his own tent. Arnulf started back towards his own, praying under his breath as he walked.

"Celestata, please… my friend needs your guiding light. Show him the way back to sanity. He seeks to murder a child, and I have not the power, nor the will to stop him. Please, help us keep our honor… or what little of it we have left after this day is done."

<u>Chapter 15</u>

After nearly a month of hard travel, Dragorim finally reached Wulfgeld. He stood atop a snow covered hill and gazed upon the city in all its glory, and his heart fell. He had hoped to find Wulfgeld quiet and calm, but instead, he could only stand and watch as stones and other projectiles launched from Drakomar's trebuchets slammed into the city. Given his recent experience in the nearby woods, Dragorim realized he should have expected this. Just an hour or so before, he had sneaked past an unusually large pack of ghouls. During his progress, he inadvertently allowed them to spot him and had been certain they would attack. However, to his surprise, the ghouls had not pursued him. *Perhaps I look like too much trouble* the wizard thought after he made his way past them.

It had gotten considerably colder the further north he had come, and he had spent the last several days of his journey looking forward to hot meals and a warm bed. Instead, he stood shivering on the frozen hill, blocked from his goal by the invading army. He had spent the last hour looking for a way to sneak inside the city under the cover of darkness, but he did not know the area well enough and darkness was as much a hindrance as a help. On top of that, even if he avoided the enemy army, the defenders would certainly take him for an enemy infiltrator, and that would get him nowhere.

The sudden rustling of leaves behind Dragorim broke him from his concentration. Fire flamed in his hands as he spun to face the threat. However, upon turning, he was faced not with an enemy soldier, but with a dark skinned woman who drew a gaulderen in response.

"Whoa there; are you always this jumpy?" she asked.

Dragorim stopped and sized her up. She was tall and thin, with dark eyes that matched her dark black skin. She was covered from head to toe in finely cut fur coats that were much more appropriate to the current weather than the thin robes Dragorim wore. Her body language was defensive, but she did not strike first. The sorcerer closed his hands, and the flames dissipated. In response, the woman's posture relaxed and she put the gaulderen back in her pocket.

"Do you speak?" she asked.

"When I choose to."

The woman smiled, which Dragorim found oddly calming.

"Excellent! It will be good for me to talk to someone else who knows a thing or two about magic."

Or three. Dragorim thought.

"I take it you have been on your own awhile?" he asked.

She shook her head.

"Not really. I only set out for Wulfgeld two week's ago."

By the color of her skin, she had to be from somewhere near the Southern tip of the continent, and if that was true, he had to learn how she had made the trip so much faster than he had.

"From where did you start your journey?" he asked.

"I think I see your meaning," she said. "I'm from the Kingdom of Aksum, in the Southworld, but I was acting as an advisor to our ambassador in Ranrike, which is just over two week's ride north of here."

Dragorim felt relieved. She had come from much closer than him, but it still didn't explain why it took her so long to start her journey there."

"What brings you to this desolate place?" he asked.

The witch smiled again.

"The same thing as you, I suppose."

Dragorim nodded. His hand twitched as he briefly considered killing her right then and there. She was a rival seeking the power he sought, and needed to be eliminated. But, she had done nothing to harm him so far, and killing her in cold blood did not sit well with Dragorim's conscience.

"I suppose so," he said.

The woman looked past him to the city.

"It's a pity this had to happen. I've been waiting around here for two days and still haven't found a chance to get inside."

"How long has the siege been going on?" Dragorim asked.

"I think I got here right when it started. If those fools in Ranrike had…"

She trailed off, not wanting to badmouth those she served so openly. Feeling uncomfortable in silence, she quickly changed the topic.

"I'm Imari. What's your name?"

"Dragorim," he replied.

"Well, I must say I am pleased to meet you, Dragorim. Perhaps together we can find a way inside the city."

"Together?" he asked.

"Yes. We both seek the same power. We both need to understand it, and I bet we'll both fare better if we study it together. I know others of our kind would compete for it, but that doesn't mean we have to."

Dragorim smiled. At first he liked the thought of cooperating with other sorcerers again. He had tried before, long ago. The thought soured when he remembered that in the end, things always became violent once it came time to share power. Not wanting to speak on it any further, Dragorim changed the topic.

"How did you find me?" he asked.

"Your aura is quite strong; I could see it from the other side of Wulfgeld. I just spent half the evening walking over to meet you."

Dragorim pondered for a moment. It was not uncommon for a sorcerer's aura to be visible to that of other magic wielders. What disturbed him was that she had seen his aura, but he hadn't seen hers.

"That was quite a risk. What if I was a wicked sorcerer?"

Imari shrugged.

"Given the situation with the siege, it was a risk I had to take. I can't get in the city by myself, and I'm out of food. I saw your aura, and I decided the risk was worth it."

Without a word, Dragorim swiftly reached deep into his pockets and tossed her a crisp apple.

"Thank you," she said.

"No one should go hungry," he replied.

"That's something I can get behind. Now I'm *very* glad I met you," Imari said.

Dragorim found himself smiling. Imari had been nothing but friendly so far and the longer he spoke with her, the more he liked her. Given that he was still sure that sooner or later, he would need to kill her, this fact made him uncomfortable. Wanting to banish the thought from his mind, he spoke again.

"Do you have any idea why they're here?"

Imari nodded.

"Yes. And thankfully, it's not what you're worried about."

Dragorim cocked his head to the side in confusion.

"And what am I thinking?"

"The same thing I feared at first… that some sorcerer had gathered this army himself to take the power here by force."

Dragorim nodded, and then prodded for more answers.

"You still haven't answered my question. Why are they here?"

"According to the Queen of Ranrike, there's an old struggle between Drakomar and Wulfgeld. I think this is the second or third generation that's been fighting these same wars off and on."

"In other words, normal, mortal feuds?" Dragorim asked.

"That's a good way to put it. Not that that helps us much. We still can't get in the city."

Silence fell between the pair. Imari looked Dragorim over, and her eyes widened as she realized how much he was shivering.

"I do believe I can repay you for the apple. Here…"

She quickly cleared some of the ground of snow with her hands. Before Dragorim could inquire as to what she as doing, she withdrew another gaulderen from her pocket. Imari rubbed the small stone between her palms very vigorously, and within a few moments, the object of power began to spark.

Imari gently dropped the sparking stone on the ground and it burst into a roaring campfire.

"Will the invaders not come and investigate?" Dragorim asked.

"They haven't so far. I don't think they're concerned about strays camping out around here."

Dragorim shrugged, and then sat down to warm himself. Imari came over and sat next to him. The two sat in silence and stared into the flames together. After a while, Imari shifted over to him and leaned on him. Dragorim nearly pushed her away, but restrained himself.

"What are you doing?" he asked.

"It's cold. You're shivering. I'm from the Southworld, where it is always warm. Even dressed in these furs, I shiver too. Perhaps if we stay close, we won't need to shiver anymore?"

Dragorim paused, considering their options. Finally, he relented, and gently wrapped his arm around the woman who now placed her trust in him.

It was going to be a long night, but at least it was now a more comfortable night.

* * *

Dusk fell over the old city. The eerie rays of the sun faded across the horizon, and darkness slowly overtook the land. Flying stones smashed all across the city with meteoric power, sowing panic and fear among its occupants. Buildings were smashed and people were crushed by the relentless bombardment. Some of the hurled stones were coated in burning tar, and the citizens of Wulfgeld desperately fought to prevent their scorching flames from spreading.

Sigaberht could have remained in the safety of his keep, but instead stood at the threshold of Elena's home. If he understood correctly, Elena would soon send the ghouls against their enemy. Out of respect, the earl did not barge in, but instead knocked upon the door. There was a brief rustling inside, and as the door swung open, Sigaberht was greeted by Radnor's towering form.

"What do you want?" Radnor demanded.

"If the attack is to begin, I felt it right that I be here, beside you both."

"You *mean* you want to keep an eye on the situation… on us," Radnor replied.

"It's my responsibility as earl of Wulfgeld to be present for such an action being done in my name. So yes, I do want to keep an eye on it."

Radnor nodded, and Sigaberht continued. "May I come in?"

"Could you not just demand that I let you in?" Radnor asked.

"I could, and you would have to obey. But I don't want to do that. Not now."

Radnor was taken aback by Sigaberht's unexpected politeness. The demigod stepped aside so that Sigaberht and his men could enter. However, Sigaberht waved his hand to the huscarls, and they remained outside of Radnor's home as the earl crossed the threshold. Only when the door was closed did Sigaberht speak again.

"Where is she?" he asked. Radnor pointed at the door to the bedroom. Sigaberht nodded.

"You both should come to the keep. You would be safe from the bombardment there."

Radnor shook his head.

"We can't. In the time it would take to bring Elena there and get her situated, it would force her focus away from the ghouls and delay the attack too much."

"We should have started with her there… an oversight on my part."

"Yes; and not the only one either."

Sigaberht ignored Radnor's insult.

"May I enter the room?"

Radnor nodded, and then spoke.

"She is very busy and exhausted from her work. The food you've provided her has helped, and I think she has taken some very short naps, but she may not be very talkative if you bother her."

"I understand," Sigaberht said.

The pair then entered the room and found Elena sitting cross legged on the bed. The pained look on her face told both of them how deeply she was concentrating while she clutched Ashrahan's gaulderen in her hands.

"My lady, I have come to check on things. How near are we to the attack?" Sigaberht asked.

Sigaberht's question was met only with silence. Just as he was about to give up and leave the room, Elena spoke breathlessly.

"I am mustering them for the attack now. I want to wait a while longer; to be sure the enemy is asleep. Only then will I unleash the ghouls."

Sigaberht nodded his understanding and turned to leave the room.

"I can see that I am not needed here. I will wait outside the door, if that's alright. I would like to know the outcome, when you can tell me."

Elena nodded and returned to focusing on her work.

Sigaberht and Radnor exited the room, and just as Radnor was about to close the door, Sigaberht spoke to her one more time.

"Thank you."

As the door shut, Sigaberht cast a grave look at Radnor.

"Veigarand, I find that there is a secret I must share with you; one only known by myself and Ashveldt."

Radnor's mind raced with questions. Sigaberht had never trusted him before, so why now?

"This must be quite a secret… that you would reveal it to me and not your ealdorman."

Sigaberht winced uncomfortably at Radnor's point.

"Yes, you are quite right. This is a secret that is unsafe for the ears of men who might scheme against each other. I tell you now only because I must go through you if I am to be sure that *these* reach Elena."

Sigaberht reached into a pouch he had hidden under his cloak and revealed a pair of twisted, misshapen looking stones. They were made from an unknown kind of black stone, and glowed with a sinister light that frightened even Radnor.

"Are those what I think they are?" he asked.

Sigaberht nodded and held up one of the stones.

"This is the gaulderen the Hexverat threatened to destroy Wulfgeld with. The other seems to be a copy. The witches left them here when you all departed for the dead city; I suspect as a gesture of good faith. If what the Hexverat said about them is true…"

"Then the power in even one of these gaulderens is enough to slaughter thousands."

Sigaberht remained gravely silent. The sounds of destruction reverberated through the cottage as the city was attacked. Radnor listened and understood the gravity of Sigaberht's position.

"You said you need to go through me to get this to Elena. Do you mean for her to use it?"

Sigaberht shook his head.

"I don't know. I don't know how powerful this thing really is. All I know is that if the wall falls, Elena is the only one who could use it to turn the tide of the battle."

"Why give this to me? Why now?"

"I give them to you now because we do not understand them, which means there is as much a chance of us destroying ourselves with them as there is of us destroying the enemy."

"But… how do you know I'll not have Elena use them for my own purposes?"

Radnor noticed a change in Sigaberht's expression, which suddenly turned frighteningly grave and haggard. Drawing a deep breath, the earl answered him.

"My son… he nearly died today. He… he seeks to prove himself on the battlefield. We both saw him today."

"He fought fearlessly," Radnor said.

"He fought *recklessly*!" Sigaberht said. "Wulfgeld cannot survive without my son, Veigarand. *I* cannot survive without my son, and I would see Wulfgeld razed by unholy magic before I would see him perish on the battlefield."

Radnor nodded. No matter what else he thought of the earl, his love for Ashveldt surpassed his love for anyone or anything else in the world. This was something Radnor respected.

"I will be sure that she gets it, but I cannot guarantee she'll be able to use it."

Sigaberht gently clasped Radnor's shoulder.

"I understand, but I'm not sure we'll have any choice but to try."

Sigaberht bowed, and then turned to leave the cottage. Radnor spoke again.

"Why not tell the ealdormen?" he asked.

"They are mortal… they cannot be trusted with immortal power."

As Sigaberht left the cottage, Radnor clutched the gaulderens in his fist, ever more confused and frightened by the workings of Sigaberht's mind.

* * *

Arnulf lay restlessly in his cot, for sleep oft eludes a man whose conscience pursues him. He struggled to find a way to spare Rolf's life. He wanted to release the boy right then and there or at least find some way to argue for the boy to not be executed. He knew that his loyalty would be called into question if he was too vocal about his reluctance to kill Rolf. Arnulf was willing to do almost anything it took to achieve victory… but to kill a defenseless child… it was dishonorable. It went against everything a knight of Drakomar was supposed to believe and represent.

But, Legier had given him an order, and his will could not be countermanded. The grand marshal had been adamant that the boy's killing of their wounded men was reason enough for the execution, but Arnulf sympathized with the boy's reasons. Rolf had been returning the treatment their knights had been giving to the children of Wulfgeld.

Arnulf sighed.

"Who is to blame for the crimes of war? Is it the man who kills the foe in front of him? Is it the victim who takes his revenge?" His eyes tried to look to the stars for guidance but all they saw was the blank, canvas roof of his tent. "Is it the man who kills the victim for taking revenge?"

Arnulf did not want to face the answer to his questions, but his mind would not let him avoid them.

Sudden shouts from around the camp and the clanging of the alarm snapped Arnulf out of his thoughts and back to reality. He leapt from his cot and dashed outside the tent to find men-at-arms frantically running about. It did not take long for Arnulf to spot the source of the trouble; a fire had broken out towards the rear of their encampment.

"What in the…" Arnulf muttered. Then a thought struck him. "The food!" he yelled.

Arnulf grabbed the first man he could find.

"Find Legier! The food is burning!"

The man nodded emphatically and ran for Legier's tent.

Arnulf ran for the back of the camp and once there, found that many of the wagons that had once been overflowing with food were now burning husks. Men desperately threw water and snow on the flames, but nothing seemed to be able to stop them.

"Who did this? Did anyone see them?" Arnulf yelled.

One of the men-at-arms sprinted next to him to make his report.

"Sir, we have not yet sighted—"

Blood splashed across Arnulf's face as a small black arrow pierced the man-at-arm's throat. Arnulf threw himself to the ground as more skewering arrows whizzed by him.

"To arms! We're under attack! To arms!" Arnulf yelled. He reached for his sword; only to find that he had left it in his tent. An inhuman screech erupted from the forest and a torrent of glowing yellow eyes rushed in from the darkness of the woods. Arnulf ran for his life as the men who had been fighting the fire were quickly torn to pieces by hundreds of small, but swift monsters that swarmed over them. Men screamed around Arnulf as they were cut down by the tidal wave of death.

The warriors of Drakomar hurled themselves from their beds. With swords in hand, they did ferocious battle with the monsters that now ran amok. Arnulf ran for his tent, but was stopped dead when one of the attackers leaped in front of him! Only now was Arnulf able to get a good look at the creature that assaulted him. It was a short, humanoid fiend with dull gray skin. It wore old animal furs to protect itself from the cold and snow, and its bulging eyes reflected the firelight with a sickly yellow glow. In its hand it carried a primitive, but deadly dagger with a blade carved from stone.

"Ghouls!" Arnulf shouted in surprise.

Arnulf wasted no time and immediately struck at the foe in front of him. The creature deftly sidestepped his wild punch and ran up underneath his arm as it aimed to cut his stomach open with its grisly dagger! However, years of training and combat experience had honed Arnulf's defense against such an attack, and he responded with a swift kick with his booted foot. The knight found satisfaction when his foot found purchase against the creature's jaw and he watched the ghoul tumble away and land in a heap in the snow. Arnulf saw that the ghoul had dropped its dagger. He quickly snatched it up and leaped upon his fallen foe and slashed its throat so viciously that he nearly severed the creature's head from its body.

However, Arnulf did not have time to celebrate his victory, as another ghoul leaped at him from the shadows. Arnulf rolled to the side, hoping to dodge the attack completely. Arnulf grunted as the ghoul slammed into him. Pain slashed through him as the monster brought its dagger to bear. Thankfully, Arnulf's movement caused the dagger stroke to fly wild and the blade merely grazed his shoulder. Arnulf grunted with pain and seized the ghoul's knife arm with his hand as he plunged his own dagger into its heart again and again.

The struggling pair landed in an unmoving heap upon the ground. Arnulf gasped for breath. The ghoul did not. After taking a few more breaths to help calm down, Arnulf leapt to his feet and finally made it back to his tent. Chaos reigned as the ghouls ran to and fro across the camp. Tents burned, and men cried out in pain as they were brutally killed and devoured where they slept. Arnulf had almost reached his tent when he heard a young voice cry out to him. He spun and saw a ghoul was making its way for Rolf, who was still tied to the ground. As the ghoul drew closer, Rolf tried to run to safety, but the rope around his neck held him as a ripe morsel for the hungry monster.

Arnulf knew what he had to do. The knight let out a fierce battle cry as he charged at the ghoul. The monster turned to face him, but was too late. Arnulf kicked the beast square in the face and sent it toppling to the ground. Before the creature could regain its senses, the knight leapt upon the ghoul and plunged his dagger into its heart. His work done, Arnulf turned back and faced Rolf. The boy looked up at him pleadingly, but did not say a word. Arnulf ran to the prisoner and quickly cut the rope that tied Rolf to the ground. Arnulf then handed Rolf the ghoul's dagger.

"Run, get away from here."

"What about you?" Rolf asked, suddenly grateful to the man who was saving his life.

"Legier will think the ghouls freed you, or that you freed yourself in the chaos. Now go… before I change my mind!"

Rolf ran as fast and as deep into the forest as he could.

"I hope that wherever your father is… I hope he appreciates what I've done," Arnulf muttered as he ran back into his own tent.

Within moments he was fully armed and armored. Now, clad in mail, helmeted, and bearing his sword and shield, the knight of Drakomar strode from his tent. As he made his way forward, he saw that a number of Drakomar's knights, and men from the Pale Light had also fully armed themselves and now battled through the hellish battlefield, dealing death to all that stood in their path. The ghouls proved to be vicious, unrelenting foes that fought without concern for their own safety. Several knights were brought down under the torrent of the monster's primitive blades and spears. Murderous black arrows regularly flew from outside the encampment, and some found their marks in the soft flesh of the men-at-arms who struggled against their monstrous assailants. But as the men organized, the tide of the battle turned in the favor of the warriors of Drakomar. Ghouls were cut down and slaughtered as they fell prey to the retribution of their would-be victims. Finally, their torrential onslaught ceased.

Formations of armored men began patrolling the encampment, looking for signs of any remaining ghouls. Arnulf and a group of knights strode into one silent tent, only to discover the human occupants had been slain, and several greedy ghouls now feasted on their corpses. Arnulf let out a cry of rage and butchered the closest monster before it could respond. The other ghouls fled. They crawled under the walls and disappeared into the night with chunks of human flesh still clutched in their mouths and hands as they ran. Arnulf checked the bodies and nearly vomited at the sight of the disemboweled remains strewn about the tent.

Suddenly, Arnulf heard Legier's voice outside and he ran to meet his friend. Arnulf found Legier organizing the efforts to clear out the remaining ghouls and secure the camp against any new intruders.

"Legier!" Arnulf called to his friend. Legier strode over to him, and the pair met in a close embrace.

"Arnulf, I feared that you had died in the initial attack!"

"And I you! What has happened here?"

Legier hesitated before answering.

"Somehow, the enemy has managed to muster an army of ghouls to attack us."

"Do you think one of the Hexverat still lives?" Arnulf asked.

"Possibly… it would explain where the man who claims to be 'Veigarand' got his enchanted sword."

Suddenly, Venatus' voice rang out over the conversation.

"Nay! We are beset by powers far greater than any witch!" he cried.

Legier wheeled on him.

"What are you talking about?" he asked.

"Ghouls do not muster and gather such as this, and there is no sorcery I know of that could do such a thing, save for one!"

"And that is?" Legier prodded.

"Sigaberht has betrayed Caelum! He has betrayed all that is right beneath the stars and within creation! He has made a deal with *her*!"

Suddenly, the voices of knights and priests of the Pale Light echoed against the trees in the black night.

"The Foul-Temptress! The Soul-Thief!" they cried.

"Who?" Legier asked, dumbfounded at what he was seeing.

Venatus rolled his eyes in frustration at his less-educated commander.

"Just as there is darkness and light, there is Celestata, and there is Lashmatu, the Great Deceiver, the Soul-Stealer, the —"

"I get it now. You believe Sigaberht is in league with this… Lashmatu?"

Venatus nodded emphatically.

"It is the only way such a barbarous act could have been achieved. I have informed you, and I must gather my men and inform them myself. Their souls must be guarded against the evil that lurks here and we cannot stop until it is stamped out. If you are wise, you will send your men to my priests. We will do what we can for their souls as well."

Without waiting for any further discussion, Venatus abruptly turned and rushed back to the Pale Light's side of the camp.

Arnulf looked to Legier.

"What do you think?" he asked.

Legier laughed.

"I think the fool will be most useful to us indeed. This is no longer a war for land or gold… this is now a holy war. We had been worried about the dedication of their support for us… but now… now I believe they will fight until the day has been won, regardless of their losses."

"Do you believe him… about Lashmatu?" Arnulf asked.

Legier smiled.

"No, I think it is a trick left behind by the Hexverat. But, I do not see any point in dissuading Venatus from his position, do you agree?"

Arnulf thought for a moment, and then nodded. It was time to move on to other subjects.

"Do you know what the damage is?"

232

Legier sighed in frustration, his mood turning foul again as he remembered how dire the situation truly was.

"The food is mostly gone, burned to ashes. The trebuchets have also been burned beyond repair."

"Then we have no siege engines… no means of breaching the walls of the city," Arnulf said.

"I know!" Legier growled. "I need to be allowed time to think! There must be a way!"

"A way to what?" Arnulf demanded.

"A way to win! I swore an oath, remember?" Legier said.

Arnulf blanched at Legier's statement.

"What does that have to do with anything now? We have no food, no siege weapons… no idea how many casualties we've taken… how can you possibly think we can still win this?"

"The Pale Light will fight regardless of our supplies. Besides, the first run of provisions will be here tomorrow!" Legier shouted. "We will have food, and we can send word back to Drakomar that we need reinforcements. We can beat Sigaberht! We just need to find a way to kill the witch!"

"Assuming there even is one to kill!" Arnulf countered.

"And what's that supposed to mean?" Legier replied.

"These lands are cursed! You've seen it yourself! Those awful, creeping colors in the sky? The dreams? Do you not dream of fell things in the deep of the night? Have we not been attacked by vicious monsters in our beds? I say again, these lands are cursed, and we cannot hope to stand against such foes."

Legier stepped back from his friend, surprised and embarrassed at Arnulf's cowardice.

"You… you would flee from our foe?"

"I would withdraw from the field," Arnulf replied. "Our orders were to try to take the city quickly, and with few casualties. Many have died. Sigaberht's resistance has proven to be stiff and overwhelming. Winter is upon us… we do not have the ability to maintain a long siege right now. We should leave and try again in the spring."

Legier sighed. Arnulf was making sense, but the grand marshal could not bring himself to end the siege.

"The Pale Light will not retreat now, regardless of my orders," Legier said.

"The Pale Light are madmen! Would you cast us to doom for the sake of their folly?"

Legier shook his head as anger rose in his throat. However, he kept it in check and changed his argument rather than shout at Arnulf.

"The first food shipment should arrive tomorrow morning. If there is ample food, and supplies to possibly repair our equipment, we stay, and we fight."

"And if there isn't?" Arnulf demanded.

Legier paused to think, didn't like what he came to mind, and changed the subject entirely.

"Send out patrols. They are to destroy anything unusual in the area. I will not have our camp attacked again. Is that clear?"

Arnulf acknowledged the order with a nod, and then spoke again.

"You didn't answer my question."

Legier threw his hands in the air in frustration.

"If the convoy doesn't arrive, *I* will decide what we do!" Legier shouted.

"That's no deal," Arnulf said, not wishing to see his friend throw his life away.

Legier shrugged.

"I gave my word that I would only return to Drakomar either as the victor, or a corpse."

Arnulf nodded, understanding Legier's position.

"Then I am sorry it has not turned out better, my friend," Arnulf said.

"The siege is not over yet," Legier replied. "Victory *will* be mine."

The pair then parted. Arnulf set about organizing patrols. Some were made of Drakomar's own forces, and others were manned by the Pale Light. Legier set about doing everything he could to help his men recover from the night's ordeal. Many wished to depart from Wulfgeld immediately, but promises of food from the incoming convoy, and revenge for the horrors they had endured kept the soldiers of Drakomar from fleeing. Prayers from the Pale Light filled the camp with their dull murmur. They all prayed to Celestata, begging for the terror to end. For them on that night, their ordeal was over, but a terror unlike any other awaited their fellows bearing food upon the road.

* * *

Halfdan sat alone under the snow covered tree. He watched apprehensively for the moon to rise, anticipating the dreaded change it would bring. He had hoped that he would be spending the night sealed away in some dungeon in Wulfgeld where he couldn't hurt anyone. Sadly, he instead needed to weaponize his curse and unleash his inner monster upon Sigaberht's foes. Halfdan did not know if he should be upset over this development or happy for his good fortune.

He had spent many years as a werewolf and had needed to isolate himself from the rest of mankind. He hated and feared his affliction, for it brought him unimaginable pain. The faces of his wife and friends forever haunted him. Sometimes, the screaming faces of other innocent people also flooded his dreams. He did not recognize them, but he always knew that he had murdered them as well.

The change itself was always incredibly painful. Halfdan was always lost in agony as every inch of his body transformed, until he would finally slip out of consciousness and into a dim, nightmare world filled only with an insatiable lust for death. However, on this night, he found himself strangely glad the change was coming, for he could finally put the monster within to good use. Halfdan then thought of Radnor. Radnor's curse was in a way, similar to his own. It had forced the demigod to exile himself from humanity, and brought great harm to all those around him. However, their reactions to serving Sigaberht were wildly different. Radnor resented his nature and resented that he was used as a weapon by those around him. Halfdan on the other hand, found a renewed sense of purpose as he now served Sigaberht as a weapon. After a lifetime of pointless suffering, his life had meaning again.

Halfdan had already scouted ahead and knew that Drakomar's supply convoy would be coming along this road very soon. Now, the giant man looked up from his spot upon the snow-draped earth and watched as the sun finally crept behind the horizon. Each moment lingered for eternity while the moon crept into full view against the black expanse of the night sky. As Halfdan gazed at the moonrise, he noticed that the sky was absent of stars. They would not bear witness to the monstrous violence that was soon to follow.

Then… the change began.

Pain wracked Halfdan's body as bones broke and reformed. His muscles twisted and distorted to conform to his new skeleton. In his final moments of humanity, Halfdan focused all of his thoughts on the enemy convoy. He hoped he could direct the beast that now violated his body towards his foes. Halfdan desperately clung to this notion as his thoughts turned from mortal comprehension and were consumed by the urge to hunt and kill.

Halfdan could only scream in agony as his head elongated into a snout, and all of his teeth transformed into fangs. After an eternity of torment, the man's screams became wolf howls. His transformation was complete and the monster was unleashed.

However, Halfdan's mental effort was successful. The werewolf turned in the direction of the convoy, slavering at the thought of massacring the men. Fully aware of its prey, the monster sprinted through the woods, ready to kill anyone that got in its way.

It was not long before the werewolf sighted the massive caravan. It was long and consisted of many wagons laden with food, medicine, arrows, and reinforcements for the men besieging Wulfgeld. Halfdan would soon see to it that nothing remained of the enemy before he was done.

Forward he ran, blending into the shadows as he sprinted for his foes at the front of the convoy. Two armored riders guarded the lead wagon, and they were to be his first victims. The pair spoke loudly, totally unaware of the possibility of any hostile presence. The werewolf grinned as it closed the distance to its prey. The men were complacent and oblivious of the danger that lay ahead of them.

The warriors soon regretted their obliviousness as Halfdan leapt upon them. Both men were thrown from their horses by his great lunge. Teeth, claws, and the werewolf's red eyes were the last things either of the men saw. Their screams echoed against the cold night air, bringing more riders from the front of the convoy rushing to their aid. As they barreled forward, Halfdan sped toward the lead wagon and slaughtered the driver before he could respond to the threat. Blood rushed across Halfdan's snout as he bit the man's head off with a single bite. With the front wagon now driverless and immobile, Halfdan dove back into the forest.

By the time the reinforcements arrived, three men were dead, and there was no sign of Halfdan. The convoy halted, and Halfdan watched from the shadows as the enemy soldiers searched for him. They believed they were looking for human assassins, not an unholy monster. The werewolf sneaked down the line, searching for the back of the convoy. Despite what Halfdan believed, the monster that now controlled his body was a part of him and was just as intelligent as he was. The werewolf wanted to disable the wagon at the back of the convoy, and thereby trap his foes upon the narrow road. The rear guards drifted away from their posts as they made their own fruitless search for the werewolf, and Halfdan saw his opportunity to attack the rear wagon.

In a flash, he was upon his enemy. Hunger overtook his senses, and he abandoned all pretext of stealth. Halfdan took the wagon by its wheels, and with a great effort, heaved it upon its side. Men in the wagon screamed as they were tossed about and crushed under the weight of tumbling lumber meant for building siege weapons. Soldiers ran to their aid, only to stop dead in their tracks when they saw Halfdan's terrifying form. His black fur stood out against the white snow upon the road, and the men's blood ran cold when the werewolf turned towards them and let out a terrifying howl.

One of the men bravely drew his sword and charged at Halfdan, inspiring his friends to do the same. Signal horns sounded as the men charged, alerting the horsemen to Halfdan's location. As the soldiers of Drakomar bravely fought the monster, the horsemen galloped to the battle.

The werewolf pounced upon the first soldier that reached him and tore the man's head from his shoulders before he could even swing his sword. More soldiers descended upon Halfdan and struck with all of their might. Men cried out in terror as their swords and axes bounced off the werewolf's skin without drawing even a drop of blood. Halfdan seized a man in each hand and lifted them high into the air. With a flash of his arms, he smashed the two men together and crushed them into a pulpy mass of flesh and bone. Before the soldiers around him could react, the monster hurled the dead men at the others, smashing the formation to the ground.

The clattering of hoofs upon the stone road told Halfdan that the horsemen had finally reached him. The werewolf turned to face his next victim and was met with the point of a spear that struck him hard in the face. Cheers rang out as Halfdan was knocked on his back from the force of the blow. However, he was otherwise unharmed. The cunning monster pretended to be dead and waited for the right moment to strike and drive terror into the hearts of his enemies -- for men tasted better when seasoned with fear. Several of the foot soldiers surrounded him and poked him with their weapons. The horseman that had struck him finally turned around and yelled to his men.

"Get back, you fools! We don't know if it's—"

The werewolf attacked again. The men nearest him died screaming as teeth and claws tore them to pieces. More horsemen tried to run Halfdan down, but he absorbed every blow that rained upon him. He tore both horses and riders apart as each warrior fell to his assault. Screams echoed across the convoy as more men rushed to fight him. Others men either hurried to get the lead wagons moving again or fled from the werewolf's terrible fury.

More soldiers bearing torches joined the battle, as they hoped to scare off or burn the foul monster that butchered them. In response, the werewolf laughed in a terrible, inhuman way that caused several men to flee. The first man ran forward and struck him with the torch. The beast answered by seizing the man's head in his jaws and biting it clean off. The werewolf snatched the next man in his monstrous hand and hurled him into the nearest wagon. The flame from the man's torch lingered against the canvas covering, and soon the wagon was engulfed in flames. While some soldiers desperately battled the werewolf, others frantically ran to put out the fire. Halfdan noticed this and rushed for them, trampling the men who tried to fight him.

The werewolf descended upon the fire-fighters and started hurling them into the flames. In a panic, one man threw his bucket of water at Halfdan. The monster slaughtered him as the helpless human fled for his life. More soldiers finally caught up with the werewolf, and again, attacked him with weapon at their disposal. Nothing worked, and as Halfdan slaughtered them, the men finally broke and ran. They never even looked back to see what had become of their fallen comrades.

Halfdan continued his slaughter with reckless abandon. He overturned and destroyed every wagon in the caravan, and killed anyone who remained to stop him. Soon, the werewolf was unopposed in his wanton destruction of the wagons that remained. Once this task was done, Halfdan howled in terrible triumph. The werewolf then turned his attention to the road ahead. The convoy had been broken, but many men had fled into the night. Halfdan followed their scents with one goal in mind: total, unrelenting destruction.

Chapter 16

Dragorim slept alongside Imari in the cold night. The pair cuddled for warmth as time dragged on. The trebuchets had ceased their bombardment, though neither of the mages was awake to notice. The pair also slept through the terrible cries and the sounds of battle that erupted from Drakomar's camp as the ghouls attacked. However, neither of them slept peacefully, as both had become ensnared in brutal nightmares. Imari found herself in a dark, stone hallway; pursued by something she could not understand, something evil and malicious from which she could only flee.

Dragorim's dreams were also fraught; filled with memories of dead foes and lovers. However, he too felt a dark shadow over his mind, and was aware that something was trying to ensnare him through his own nightmares. He struggled against it, but each time he thought he had broken free, his unseen foe's cold grip grew tighter, and a new, painful memory played out.

Dragorim walked along a gilded road, and smiled. He stared in awe at the massive buildings arrayed before him. They were tall, reaching so high as to brush the fingertips of Caelum himself. White sunlight washed across the great city, highlighting the bright blues, greens, and golds that painted the buildings around Dragorim as he walked. Eventually, he came upon the great market square, at the center of which lay a marvelous fountain. Pushing his way through the crowds, Dragorim finally came upon it. He gazed into the clear water, and watched as the sunlight danced within the sparkling ripples. He then looked to the sculpture that rested at the center of the fountain. The massive silver statue portrayed the great creators. On the right was a tall, thin man, with a face marked by regal, well-defined features. He wore a gold crown upon his head, and stood with his arms reaching to all those who stood before him. In his hands he offered a star, representing his gift of light to creation. This was the god, Caelum.

The sculpture of a powerful, muscular figure stood to the left. His long black hair was carved so realistically that it almost looked real. He was adorned in a black great cloak that covered his whole body. This was Damiros. He too stood with his arms extended to the crowd, but his hands held fire, a gift of many uses.

Finally, in the center, there stood a marvelous figure. While he was the shortest of the three, he was also the grandest. He was dressed all in colors that matched the greens and browns of the world. This figure smiled gently through his gray beard as he gazed upon the people in the square. He stood with his arms outstretched as though preparing to embrace those gathered to him. His hands bore no gifts. Instead, he stood with his mouth open, and water arced from his lips as he breathed life into his creation. This was Hymurr, the first of the creators, and father of all that were shielded from the ocean of chaos.

Suddenly, a woman appeared beside Dragorim. Her face was kind, and her radiant smile brought joy to his heart. She was familiar to him, but it had been so long since he had last seen her, it took him a moment to recall her name.

"Serena," he said to himself.

She smiled again and took his arm. He remembered. They had had many talks at the edge of this fountain. She had often mused about the meaning of the statue. Was the water of the fountain meant to represent creation, or was it all depicting the rise of the creators from the oceans of chaos? She had been particularly curious about Hymurr's role in story. Was the god truly blowing life into creation? Or was he adding more water to the ocean of chaos?

Then, the world around him changed. The paint on the buildings became worn and scratched, their maintenance abandoned long ago. The crowds of people out to market were replaced by massive piles of corpses. Armed warriors guarded these stacks of bodies against throngs of thin, emaciated people. These people desperately fought for access to the piles of the dead, but were denied by the guards. Moments later, the stacks of dead were set ablaze, and thousands of voices cried out in agony and woe. Dragorim tore his eyes from the grisly sight and returned his gaze to the fountain.

There was no water. Instead, there was only a black, earthy sludge within the once great pool. To Dragorim's horror, many others who stood near the pool voraciously drank from the fetid slime, choking down what they could. He looked to the statues at the center of the now decayed pool. Like the buildings, the paint had worn off them, and the faces of the gods were now scarred and deformed. Again, Serena appeared beside him, but no longer did she smile. She wept. Before he could say words of comfort to her, he was whisked away through a circle of light.

Suddenly, a nearby shout forced Dragorim out of his torturous dream and back into his own waking nightmare. The sorcerer sprung to his feet, startling Imari in the process. She was still groggy, and slowly began to sit up when Dragorim suddenly pushed her back down and snuffed out their warm fire with a wave of his hand. Surprised, Imari spoke.

"What the—"

"Quiet!" Dragorim ordered.

Imari was just about to protest when she heard the shouting of men from the base of the hill.

It was then that the pair realized that soldiers from Drakomar had found them.

"I thought you said they didn't care about random people out here?" Dragorim whispered.

"They didn't… until now," Imari replied. "What do we do?"

"Stay down, wait for my signal," Dragorim said.

Dragorim then crawled deeper into the shadows of the trees. The soldiers from Drakomar finally reached the hilltop and searched for the wizards.

Dragorim waited silently and watched as the men drifted apart to widen their search. There were seven men in the patrol. Drawing his knife from his belt, Dragorim calculated his options for attack as one of the soldiers investigated the shadows near the sorcerer. As soon as the soldier was close enough, Dragorim pounced. The soldier had no time to cry out as Dragorim buried his dagger in the man's throat. The sorcerer held onto the dying soldier and gently lowered him to the ground, hoping to minimize the noise as the man gurgled on his own blood, but it was no use. The choking and gasping of the dying man was enough to alert the others to their peril. The whole group turned to face where Dragorim rested, though they could not yet see him in the darkness. The sorcerer hastily drew the sword from his foe's scabbard and prepared for a fight. The men-at-arms drew into a loose formation that covered a wide area, but also kept them within range to protect each other against a possible new and unseen attacker.

They had not spotted him yet, and the sorcerer used this to his advantage. He waited for them to get just a little bit closer, and then made his move. He hoped Imari was of the same mind as him, but there was no way to communicate his intention, so he did what he could in the moment.

"Now!" Dragorim yelled.

Flame erupted in his hand. He launched it for his foes before anyone could react, and one of the soldiers was burned to ashes.

"It's him!" they yelled. "It's the one who set the ghouls on us!"

"Get word back to the camp, we've found him!" another shouted.

Two of the soldiers broke away and ran for their camp while the other three charged at Dragorim.

The sorcerer suddenly found himself hard pressed by the three attackers. In response, he quickly withdrew a gaulderen from his pocket and threw it at his nearest foe. As soon as the gaulderen made contact, the man's body was shattered with devastating force. However, the men of Drakomar were unfazed by this horror; the gruesome sight only spurred the surviving pair to greater violence.

Surprised by their bravery, Dragorim barely managed to parry the first attack with his sword. As he did, he stepped across the front of the lead soldier, working to keep both of them in a line so they could only attack him one at a time. His effort was successful, but the frenzied attacks of the foe closest to him proved difficult to time and parry. However, in the heat of the moment, the man leaned too far forward as he tried to strike Dragorim with his shield. The sorcerer saw his opening and shoved the soldier with all his might. Already off balance, the man-at-arm's feet slipped out from under him and he was sent into the snow. Before Dragorim could finish him off, the second man lunged for the sorcerer and desperately tried to protect his friend. Dragorim expertly parried the wild thrust and responded with a deadly slash to the back of the man's neck that severed his head from his shoulders.

The first man scrambled back to his feet and made one final attempt to kill Dragorim. The sorcerer sidestepped the man's fearsome slash and cut his hand off at the wrist. The soldier dropped to the ground and screamed in pain. Dragorim did not allow him to suffer long and quickly silenced the man's voice forever.

Panting, Dragorim breathlessly spoke,

"Thank you… for the help!" he said sarcastically. "What… was so hard to… understand about…"

The sorcerer trailed off when he realized that Imari had disappeared. He frantically looked around, and found two distinct groups of footprints. One set belonged to two different pairs of boots. These had been left behind by the fleeing soldiers. The other set was a single pair of small shoes that ran deeper into the forest. Dragorim found himself in a conundrum. Common sense told him that he needed to hunt down and prevent the fleeing soldiers from reporting back to their commanders. If word of his presence got out, the men of Drakomar would not stop hunting him. On the other hand, there was a distinct possibility that Imari knew something more than she was letting on. After a moment's consideration, Dragorim took off after Imari. He decided that no matter what he did to conceal his presence, sooner or later, *someone* was going to find out he was there, and that it might as well happen now. He wished he was better able to plan for it, but at least now there would be a change in the situation he might be able to turn to his advantage later.

So, onward he plunged, rapidly following the footprints in the snow. It was not long before Imari's shivering form could be seen against the pale moonlight. Dragorim slowed his advance and quietly crept up behind her. Suddenly, she turned around and spoke to him.

"Are you okay?" she inquired.

Dragorim cautiously approached her. He did not answer, instead keeping a hand on the sword he had concealed beneath his cloak.

Imari saw his hostile demeanor and took a step away from him.

"Why do you not answer?"

Dragorim sized her up. Was it possible she had summoned the soldiers there to kill him? If so, she needed to die, here, and now. But compassion stayed his hand, and he decided he needed to be sure his suspicions were correct before killing her.

"You sent them, didn't you?" Dragorim asked.

"What?" Imari said in disbelief.

"It all makes sense. You came to me in the night. You lured me into a false sense of safety, and then you summoned those soldiers there to kill me… remove a competitor from your grab for power."

"No, no, I didn't!" Imari cried.

Sensing Dragorim's intent, she threw up a magical barrier meant to block Dragorim from reaching her. The sorcerer summoned a bolt of lightning to his hand and hurled it into her shield, shattering the barrier instantly. Imari stumbled as she retreated but tripped and fell backwards into the snow. She tried to crawl away, but to no avail.

In a moment of desperation, Imari called upon her true power. She reached out with all of her feelings. She tried to touch him with her fear, with her desire to live. If she could just get him to empathize with her for long enough… perhaps she could stop him from killing her. He continued his advance, and Imari cried out in terror and shouted to him.

"I swear, in the name of the goddess Celestata… I did not send those men! I don't know why they came for us!"

Dragorim looked deeply into Imari's eyes, and a strange feeling came over him. He saw not a foe before him, but a woman in need of help. Within her eyes he saw the truth in her words. The sorcerer sheathed his sword, and offered her a hand to help her up. The witch stared at him, relieved to see that her spell had worked.

"I believe you," he said.

Imari took a deep breath and grasped his hand with hers.

"Your hand… it's covered in…" She gasped in fear. "What did you do?"

"I killed them," he said matter-of-factly.

Imari again stepped back in fear.

"*All* of them?"

"Not quite. Two got away from me. I had to make a choice… them or you."

"And you considered me the greater threat," she said.

Dragorim shrugged.

"You ran. I had to be sure."

Imari laughed.

"I ran because I'm not a fighter. I've… I've never killed anyone. I've barely ever been in a fistfight."

Dragorim looked her over. He realized that she had put a spell of empathy on him. He had felt one like it before, but it had been a very long time since someone had used such a spell on him. For a brief moment, he again considered killing her, but decided against it. He couldn't blame her for using such a spell on him, given that he had been ready to kill her a moment before. Instead, he chose to continue their conversation.

"What is it you do?"

"I'm a scholar. I study the history of magic. I've never been very… powerful."

Imari hung her head in shame. Dragorim patted her on the shoulder.

"It's alright. You are very admirable. You may not be as powerful as most witches, but you are stronger than many I have met." Imari looked up at him in confusion. "I've met many magic users from all over the world. There's a reason most cultures barely tolerate them. Most untalented mages murder and destroy in their pursuit of power. I believe you when you say you've never killed anyone… which means you've never succumbed to the temptations you've been faced with."

Imari smiled.

"Thank you. I… most other mages treat me like garbage once they know how limited I am."

"We're all limited," Dragorim replied. "It's also possible your talents just haven't been discovered yet." he said, knowing full well she had already revealed one of them.

"Maybe," she said.

Dragorim looked around, and then back to Imari.

"We're still too close to where I killed those men. We need to keep moving,"

Imari sighed.

"My legs are going to love this. Alright, let's go."

<u>Chapter 17</u>

The sun rose, bringing with it the third day since Radnor had returned to Wulfgeld. This meant he had three more days before he needed to leave the city, lest he risk an invasion by the Krigari. He hated the thought of leaving Elena during the siege, but if it came down to it, the only way to keep her safe would be for him to leave… at least for a time. Radnor considered several ideas about how to utilize his curse to their advantage. He briefly considered combining his need to move around with Sigaberht's plan to enter the haunted forest… but it was out of the question. Any friends he led there would be killed, and he wasn't sure even he could survive another journey into those forsaken woods.

The demigod stood at a window and looked south towards where the corrupted forest lay. Even against the bright morning dawn, he could still see hints of the ghastly, unknown colors released by the evil residing there. He wished he could do something about what was happening in that forsaken grove, but until Drakomar's army was pushed back, there wasn't much anyone could do about it.

The soft sound of footsteps brought Radnor out of his contemplation, and he saw Elena step out of the bedroom.

"Good morning," Radnor said.

"Good morning," she replied with a smile.

"How are you?" he asked.

"Tired… sore."

"Then why are you out of bed?"

"Because you are. Have the enemy turned tail yet?"

"No,"

A dark look took over Elena's face.

"Shit," she said.

"My thoughts exactly."

Suddenly, Elena pulled on Radnor's arm until he stood from his seat.

"What are you doing?" he asked.

"I need your help. We need to find a way to spark my powers again."

Radnor sighed and started to speak, but Elena wouldn't let him get a word in edgewise.

"Radnor, we need to find a way for me to help! I can't be stuck here doing nothing!"

"I know!" he said. "I just… I was hoping to give you a chance to rest before giving you these."

Radnor reached into the pouch at his belt and withdrew the black stones Sigaberht had given him.

"Are those more gaulderens?" she asked.

Radnor nodded, and then told Elena what Sigaberht had told him. Elena stared at the stones in Radnor's hand.

"And Sigaberht said he wanted me to have them?"

"Yes, it seems you're the only one who can use them."

"Use them for what?" she exclaimed. "I'm not going to burn the city down just to spite Piarin!"

"I know, but…"

"But what?" Elena demanded.

"Your powers don't work unless threatened by chaos."

"I could use the other gaulderen just fine," Elena countered.

"That's what I'm getting at. The only way for you to use your powers to help… is to use these stones."

Elena gently took the gaulderens from Radnor's palm and examined them closely. Small markings in an unknown language were etched all around them. In the center of it all lay a single symbol. It reminded Elena of Ashrahan's mark that was engraved upon the other gaulderen… but this one was different. The symbol on these gaulderens took the shape of two triangles that touched at their corners, and a line drawn between their centers. The gaulderens felt unnaturally warm in her hand, and as Elena studied them more closely, she detected a fiery glow trapped within that frightened her.

"I don't know how to use these," she said.

"I was afraid that might be the case. Do they feel different than the other one?"

"Yes. Can't you feel them?" she asked.

"No. It seems my mortal blood limits my power. The only magical item I can "feel" is the sword, and I don't like it."

Elena nodded. She both understood and sympathized with Radnor's perspective.

"The problem is, I don't even know how to learn how to use one without well… *trying* to use it… but I suspect that would get us nowhere."

"It is quite a conundrum. With these gaulderens… you might not live long enough to know if you've done it right."

Elena laughed a little.

"Why is it always like this? Why is nothing simple? Did the Hexverat not think to leave instructions with these? Did whoever, or whatever created me, forget to leave some sort of hint, or clue as to what the hell I am?"

Radnor stepped forward and took Elena into his arms. He stroked her long, dark hair, and felt her return his embrace with her own. Soon, Elena spoke again.

"Would Ashrahan know what I am?"

Radnor shook his head.

"I won't tell him about you, even if you ask me to. Telling him risks making you the target of an enemy I cannot protect you against."

"I know… I wasn't really going to ask you to do that. I just… I don't understand."

"Neither do I," Radnor said. "But, you cannot dwell on that now, just as I cannot dwell on my revenge upon Adramelach. We have to live life in the here and now, and right now, we have a mortal enemy to defeat."

"We have one more thing," Elena started. "We have each other."

As the two lovers shared their embrace, they were blissfully unaware of the being that leered at them and schemed from beyond the confines of their mortal world.

* * *

Rolf had had a truly harrowing night. First, he had believed he was set to be executed by Drakomar's knights, and then found himself desperately fleeing a horde of rampaging ghouls as he escaped his captors. Rolf had needed to zigzag and weave around so often that he had gotten totally lost in the woods. By the time Rolf had regained his bearings, he realized that it would be fruitless for him to try to get back to Wulfgeld that night, as the guards atop the walls would surely think he was an enemy spy and unleash a hail of arrows upon him. Instead, Rolf had spent the night alone in the snow.

He was desperately cold and the clothes he wore were barely adequate to stave off hypothermia, though not indefinitely. At one point, he had spotted a campfire atop a hill and had decided to head for it. However, Rolf's advance was halted as he needed to repeatedly hide from the hostile patrols that now stalked the land. Much to Rolf's dismay, one of those patrols had headed up to the top of the hill for which he headed, and shortly after their arrival, the fire had gone out. Even more to Rolf's concern, only two of the soldiers came back, and they seemed to have been fleeing from something. Rolf knew it was possible that the others had simply gone down the opposite side of the hill, but that would have brought them within range of Wulfgeld's archers, and Rolf doubted they would be so foolish. So, Rolf pondered what could have happened to the other five men as he hid in the snow.

When the dawn arrived, Rolf decided it was time to investigate what had happened, and continued the journey up the hill. After a tiring trudge, he arrived and found himself surrounded by the bodies of the Drakomar patrol.

Despite the opportunity to loot the corpses for warmer clothes, armor, and weapons, Rolf was more interested in the charred remains of one of the soldiers. The only cause that made any sense to Rolf was magic, and that meant a powerful sorcerer was running amok in the woods… and they were an enemy of Drakomar. It was then that Rolf decided to pursue this sorcerer, as he hoped that if he could find them, he might recruit them in helping Wulfgeld break the siege.

After scavenging what he could from the fallen bodies, Rolf followed the mysterious footprints deeper into the woods. He only hoped that whoever it was would be friendly when he found them.

* * *

Halfdan awoke, cold and naked in a space unknown to him. He lay in a bed made from the fur that had once covered his body. At first he was dizzy. Everything was a blur of violence, blood, and death. After several nauseating seconds, he started to regain his sense of self. Halfdan's eyes adjusted to their human form once more, and the world finally came into focus. He looked around and saw that he was inside some sort of wooden room. Halfdan sat up and groaned as his muscles protested. As he studied the space around him, he gradually realized he was in the front room of a house, probably a farm house.

"How far did I go?" Halfdan wondered aloud.

Then he grew worried that he had never reached the convoy… that the monster within had taken to its own will, and that the occupants of the house would be found strewn about the interior. However, Halfdan soon spotted the mangled remains of one of Drakomar's soldiers in a corner of the room. Despite the grisly sight, relief washed over Halfdan. He had attacked the correct target after all; but what of the house's owners?

Halfdan stood and searched the other rooms. Furniture was overturned and smashed, and the back door was nearly torn from its hinges. However, there was no sign of any other victims inside. Hopefully, this meant that the people who lived here escaped his bloody fury.

Halfdan looked out the window and saw that the sun had barely peeked out over the horizon. By his estimation, it had not been long since he had changed back into his human form.

Halfdan paused as he realized that he was freezing cold, far colder than he should have been. Clothes… he had forgotten to pack an extra set of clothes! Halfdan cursed at his own carelessness. He knew better than to make a mistake like that, but here he was, naked in a mysterious house. Looting was now his only option. He scoured through the whole house in search of anything that might protect him against the cold. The clothing found on soldier's the corpse was soaked with blood, and he found nothing else in the house to fit his gigantic frame. After a frustratingly long time, Halfdan was able to gather enough pieces of fabric around his body to keep himself from freezing to death.

He thought of food, and then realized that his belly was strangely, uncomfortably full. The realization sickened him so much that he nearly vomited. Based on what he had found, it seemed that after destroying the caravan, the werewolf within had taken one of the enemy soldiers to a quiet place where he could eat in peace. The family that lived here might have already fled when Drakomar's army passed them on the way to Wulfgeld. Or, if they had still been at home, they would have fled from him, and the werewolf was probably uninterested in pursuit when the already hunted soldier provided a satisfactory meal.

Once Halfdan was prepared, he opened the front door of the house and stepped outside. Upon seeing the beautiful, shining sun and blue sky of the outside world, the cursed man wept. He wept for the atrocities he had committed, not just here, but in other places as well. He wept for his wife. He knelt and prayed to Caelum for a solution to his curse, but just as it had been countless times before, there was no answer. Halfdan merely wept.

As the tears slowly ceased, Halfdan stood and looked north. He briefly considered fleeing that way. His task was done and he knew of isolated areas where he could disappear forever. As far as Halfdan was concerned, his debt for his unwilling involvement in the Hexverat's attack was now paid.

But, something prevented him from fleeing. He had friends in Wulfgeld: Radnor, Elena, Rolf. He couldn't abandon them, not when he could still possibly help them. He wandered through the fields and found that the house was not far from the main road that would lead him back to the besieged city. He even recognized the bend in the path where he was, and realized that he had actually traveled more than twenty miles back along the road in the night. Had the monster known he would want to return to Wulfgeld when his task was done? He did not like the thought, as it meant the beast was aware of him, and that meant he too was its prey. Halfdan quickly shook the thought from his mind, and reminded himself of his besieged friends. With his friends as inspiration, the burly man collected himself and started the long walk back to Wulfgeld.

* * *

Foul news greeted Sir Legier that morning, and he could not bear it. He screamed and raged, and nothing could calm him. He had expected to awaken to messengers from the convoy informing him of their imminent arrival. Instead of messengers, he awoke to panicked survivors of a massacre. They told a grim tale of death and terror as they recounted the werewolf's vile deeds. Arnulf remained deathly silent as Legier raged. To him it was obvious: they had no choice but to retreat. Even if this disaster was somehow a fluke, the morale of the men would be broken. If news of this got out without a positive spin on it, he feared that even the fanatical knights of the Pale Light would refuse to fight. However, Arnulf also knew that Legier's back was against a wall, and feared what his friend might do. Legier looked to Arnulf and sent him to retrieve Venatus from his morning prayers. Arnulf did so, and after a brief explanation to Venatus, the two soon returned to Legier's tent. Once the pair arrived, they found that the convoy's survivors had gone, and Legier collapsed into his chair. The air was still for a long time before the grand marshal finally spoke.

"Arnulf, it seems the rumors were right. These lands are cursed. The caravan was but thirty miles from us when they were attacked. We do not have enough food to sustain the siege, and with no quick way for us to get word back to Drakomar; I fear that you were right: our only option is retreat."

Arnulf remained silent. He knew he had been right, but he felt no urge to gloat. He wished that he had been wrong.

"It pains me to see you despair like this, but you are right. It would pain us both even more to see our men slaughtered in a battle they cannot win."

"You cannot retreat now!" Venatus cried. "These blasphemers must be punished! They are in league with the Foul-Temptress! The souls of every man, woman, and child in Wulfgeld must be cleansed of her evil!"

254

"Hold your tongue!" Arnulf shouted. "I have been tolerant of your beliefs until now, but you cannot tell me you think we can possibly win this battle?"

"Do you doubt the holy grace of Celestata? Do you claim to know more of her power than she herself?"

"No," Arnulf said. "But given recent events, I might know more than *you*."

Venatus started towards Arnulf, but Legier broke in before Venatus or Arnulf could come to blows.

"Gentlemen, save your wrath for the enemy!"

Venatus stopped and glared at Legier.

"My lord would permit him to insult me in this manner?"

"Arnulf has been a staunch defender of yours since your forces joined ours. I think you owe him the courtesy of forgiveness for a single outburst."

Venatus paused, breathed, and made his apology to Arnulf.

"Very well. I forgive your words… but do not speak to me in such a manner again… or Drakomar might soon face a war on two fronts."

Satisfied that was the best he was going to get from Venatus, Legier addressed Arnulf.

"My friend, your words to me during this siege have been wise and constructive. Perhaps you will be chosen to be the next marshal of this army after I am gone."

Arnulf shook his head.

"Don't talk like that. You are still alive, here and now."

"As a victor… or a corpse," Legier replied. "Besides, you say I have despaired, but I have not. I shall stay behind with any volunteers who wish it. We will travel the cursed countryside. We will raid and do what we can to hamper Sigaberht's recovery efforts until you return with an even greater army."

"You know as well as I do that assembling such an army will take time, and you would be caught and killed before that happens. Do not throw your life away."

"I will not break my word!" Legier shouted.

Arnulf took a step back from his friend.

"I only wish what is best for you," Arnulf replied.

Legier shook his head, more to himself than anything else.

"I know. But, for me, it is better to die with my honor intact than to live as an oath-breaker and a coward."

Venatus stepped forward and clasped his hand on Legier's shoulder.

"You are brave. Perhaps there is a place for you in Celestata's grace after all. However, The Pale Light cannot stay without *full* support from Drakomar. I agree with Arnulf now. If you are to retreat, it must be no half measure; otherwise you throw your life away for nothing."

Legier nodded and returned the gesture. Venatus looked to Arnulf.

"You say that if you retreat, it will be temporary? We will regroup and attack again? The unholy presence in this city cannot go ignored."

Arnulf nodded. Satisfied with Arnulf's answer, Venatus returned to his place in tent. Legier spoke to Arnulf again.

"Has there been any further word about the enemies our patrols found in the night?"

"No, My lord marshal. What are your orders?"

Legier smiled at the courtesy Arnulf offered by referring to him as "lord marshal" again. After a moment's contemplation, he gave his answer.

"Send out more patrols. I want them found! If these are the same sorcerers that sent the ghouls and that… werewolf at us, we need to eliminate them before we can safely withdraw. Once the patrols report back, we shall begin making preparations and leave. In the meantime, will you find volunteers to help me stay and fight in the months ahead?"

"Of course, but if no one volunteers?" Arnulf asked.

"Then I hope your term as grand marshal is more successful than mine," Legier said.

With that, he stood and faced Venatus.

"Archpriest Venatus… I believe I should go and join you for the morning prayers. Your men are a part of this army, and as such, I owe you the respect of attending your rituals."

Venatus smiled.

"Please, follow me."

Venatus left the tent, and Legier turned to face Arnulf.

"I feel I should be there when Venatus informs his men of our decision," he said.

Legier then walked out of the tent before his friend could reply. Arnulf stood alone in Legier's tent, worried about his friend's state of mind. However, the knight could not dally long, and so he left the tent and set about following his lord's orders.

Legier followed Venatus and found that the sermon was already underway when they arrived. Row upon row of the warriors of the Pale Light were gathered, heads bowed in silent prayer. Legier also noticed some of his own men were mixed into the group now. Several looked up and saw him arrive. They appeared bashful at first, but after receiving no stern look or chiding from Legier, they all comfortably returned to their prayers. Several priests of the Pale Light walked among the rows of men. For reasons unknown to Legier, they would stop and listen to whispered words of the men they led in prayer. One priest stood at the front of the formation and read from their holy scrolls. Legier paused to listen as the priest read their scripture.

"Oh, child of the holy light… grant us your blessing upon this, your hallowed vanguard, who do your will upon the world. We beseech thee… grant us the strength to overcome the foe that stands before us."

The priest stopped when he saw Venatus, and stepped aside from his place of privilege. Venatus bowed at his fellow priest and stepped forward to take his spot in leading the prayer. Legier stood still, unsure of where to go or what to do. Venatus saw his confusion, and motioned for Legier to join him at the front. Murmurs ran through the crowd as all saw this honor bestowed upon the unbeliever. Jealousy filled the hearts of the warriors assembled there, though the priests quickly silenced their discontent, for jealousy was a sin. Once Venatus and Legier were at the front, the archpriest addressed the crowd before him.

"Brothers… brothers in faith! Hear me now, for I bring news to you all! Celestata tested us, and we passed her test. The ghouls came, and we destroyed them! But our success has brought on further tests of our faith… our resolve! This morning we were to have received the first shipment of food from Drakomar… but they were met on the road by a ferocious beast! The food has not arrived, and Celestata tests us further."

Despite this news, the crowd was silent, as their discipline forced them to remain so until Venatus had finished speaking. "Because of this, there is not enough food to go around. As such, the brave Sir Arnulf will be taking the knights of Drakomar from this place... and we must go with him. But, do not despair! We do not truly flee from battle! We withdraw to gather reinforcements and provisions, and then we shall return here with even greater numbers than before! I shall personally meet with the Primarchus, and Wulfgeld shall be assailed by all of the might our order can bring to bear!"

Venatus then turned to Legier. The archpriest gestured for the knight to step forward and address the crowd.

"Tell them what your plans are. My men must have faith this retreat is not done lightly," Venatus said.

Legier nodded and turned to the crowd assembled before him.

"I, Sir Legier, Grand Marshal of the Army of Drakomar, stand before you now to tell you that it is with a heavy heart that I order this retreat. You shall know that I do this for the benefit of the army, not for myself. I, along with any volunteers from my own forces, shall remain here and hinder our enemy wherever we can. I swore an oath… directly to Celestata… that I would return either as a victor, or as a corpse, and I intend to honor that oath!"

"Indeed you shall, Sir Legier," came a female voice.

Legier and Venatus whirled around to face the source of the voice. Both men dropped to their knees at what they saw, and the crowd prostrated as low as they could. A woman now stood before them, clad in yellow silk robes and golden light. Her long, butter blonde hair complemented her amber eyes as she strode forward to join the crowd assembled. Her radiance nearly blinded all those who groveled before their goddess.

Venatus was the first to speak to her.

"My... I... not since the first Primarchus have you revealed yourself to us!"

Celestata smiled warmly and gestured for Venatus and Legier to stand. Both men hesitated, but Celestata insisted. Legier stood first, nearly dragging Venatus to his feet with him. Once they faced her directly, Celestata spoke again.

"Not since the first Primarchus has there been such dire a need as this. You cannot retreat now. You are right; my archpriest... the enemy is in league with Lashmatu."

Upon hearing the name "Lashmatu", every member of the Pale Light placed their hands upon their breasts and uttered the appropriate prayer.

"Blessed be; preserve my soul against the Foul-Temptress."

Celestata smiled upon the crowd assembled, and men wept at the sight of her beauty and holy grace.

"The situation is more serious than that alone. Lashmatu herself dwells within the walls of Wulfgeld. *She* is the source of all your woes."

Gasps erupted through the crowd. Had anyone but Celestata said this to them, they would not have believed it, but the word of their goddess was irrefutable. However, Legier expressed his doubts.

"How do I know this is not some trick of the enemy? I have seen horrors beyond imagining these past days. Are you yet another horror merely *disguised* as salvation?"

"Blasphemy!" yelled the crowd. Knights stood and were about to rush upon Legier when Celestata waved for them to return to their knees. Again, the goddess of love and life smiled upon Legier.

"Your words are wise, Grand Marshal. Venatus... you may submit me to the trial."

Venatus hesitated for a moment, and then nodded his assent.

"What did the mountain say upon first seeing the light?" he asked.

"Alas, my heart is full, for until now, I have known naught but shadow."

"What did you say to the First Primarchus when you came to him upon the mountain?"

"I come to you bearing the will of my father, Caelum. Be not afraid, for I bear news of compassion. My father and I look upon you with care, and wish it to be known that terrible forces will march against you. The world must be ready, and you must lead mankind into the light, so that they might be prepared once the evil arrives."

"And tell me, fair goddess, has the evil arrived?" Legier asked.

Venatus glared at Legier for his interruption, but Celestata again waved him down.

"That arrival is what I aim to prevent here today."

Legier nodded. He did not like the riddles with which she spoke, but Venatus seemed to be satisfied. Happy that the interruption had ended, Venatus asked the final question.

"From whence did you come?"

"First, Caelum made light, and with that light he made the moon, the sun, and the stars, and was glad, for he had brought light and warmth to all of creation. But lo! Once he had finished with his labors, he longed not for the companionship of his brothers! He longed for a child. He then gathered the unused scraps of stardust that yet lingered, and molded them into my shape. I am Celestata, Daughter of Caelum, and my word is true, for if I lie, Caelum shall strike me from this spot!"

All waited for Caelum's wrath, but nothing happened. Venatus cried out.

"All hail, Celestata, Goddess of Love and Light!"

"Hail!" cheered the crowd, and many rejoicing tears were shed.

Celestata beamed at them, and her golden light filled the hearts of every man gathered before her. Then, the goddess spoke to Legier and Venatus.

"You must find a way to break down the walls of the city. If you can do that, you will force Lashmatu to use her power, and we may yet drive her from this place. If you do this, your places in paradise will be secured."

Then, without another word, Celestata faded from existence before the eyes of all assembled. All were silent as everyone present tried to comprehend the magnitude of her visitation. Legier fell to his knees, as he was overawed by what had just transpired. Where he had had doubts before, there were none now. He was now a true believer in the Pale Light. Venatus knelt beside him and spoke.

"My lord marshal, what options have we to break down the gates?"

Venatus' words forced Legier back to his senses. He thought for a moment, and then came to an idea.

"We need to find those sorcerers, and we must do so quickly. If there is any way to break down the walls, it will be through their power!"

Chapter 18

"It was a glorious victory, oh so long ago," Ashrahan muttered as he tread upon the ancient, death-strewn battleground. The Krigari's footsteps left deep prints in black ashes that coated the ground, for where there had once been a great city, only dust remained. Millions had dwelt in this place, the home Caelum built; but now… even their ghosts had departed this barren world.

Ashrahan looked up to the blackened sky and marveled at Caelum's power. A moon had once rested among the stars… but it was no more. In the creator's final desperate act, he had wielded the moon as a weapon against Damiros. When the moon came crashing down, scores of Krigari and Malakon, and millions more had died. Ashrahan would have envied Caelum for such power, had it worked. Damiros had been unharmed by Caelum's assault. Screams of the dead echoed in Ashrahan's memory as he strode through acres of wasted potential and squandered creativity.

A sharp, unnatural wind slashed across the empty plains and whipped the ashes into the air so that they stung Ashrahan's nose and eyes. At this impetus, Ashrahan hurried to his destination. He had not come to Caelum's destroyed world to reminisce… he had come for answers. Onward he strode as he searched for his goal. When Radnor had spoken of the terrible creature he had defeated, and of the gaping void which it guarded, his words had evoked memories of the war between Damiros and Caelum; the Empyrean War, so the Krigari called it. As the gods and their creators battled among the stars, the fabric of creation itself was damaged by their power. If Radnor's words were true, the half-breed had encountered the ruins of one such battle. Ashrahan needed to understand the power of which Radnor spoke, but something blocked his gaze upon that space… and he could not bodily venture within Radnor's world.

Now, an uneasy feeling took Ashrahan's mind. Something in the air felt off… wrong… as though it were no longer air. He looked up at the sky again, and watched as the stars twisted and bent in ways that made his stomach turn. Ashrahan averted his gaze and found that he somehow stood at the very precipice of an infinite maw that threatened to swallow him whole. He did not understand how he had made it so close without noticing. Fear gripped him as the implications ran through his mind. However, he had come here with a particular task in mind, one which he intended to see through to the end. The Krigari leaned forward so that he might peer into the blackness within the unholy void. He hesitated; fearful of what might ensnare him should he look too deeply within the tides of shadow. Ashrahan shook his head at himself. While fear was not unknown to him, he had never been made timid before. The god swallowed nervously, and then brought his gaze upon the unknown things that roiled in the blackness.

Pain struck him has a torrent of vague, incomprehensible images violated his mind. He tried to scream but could not utter a sound, for he was held in the grip of overwhelming evil. As the torturous moments continued, the images became more coherent: there was to be no creation, at least none that his mind could fathom. There was only hunger. Ashrahan fought against his captor, and with great mental effort, wiggled free from his foe's grip! In that moment, anger not his own washed over him. In that moment of fury, an image was revealed to the Krigari… it was of a dark, foreboding forest, where beings forged by the malevolent entity lay in the woods near Radnor's home. There they labored to drive open the Hexverat's wound in creation… and if they succeeded… then the hunger would be sated.

This was not the information for which Ashrahan had come, but he recognized it as what he needed. The Krigari struggled further, and finally freed himself entirely from his opponent's vile grasp. Before his foe could reassert his hold over him, Ashrahan summoned a portal and fled back to his home at Narakim.

As Ashrahan departed, that which dwelt within chaos was satisfied. The final pawn had been placed… and soon the woman's power would free him from his prison!

Chapter 19

Dragorim and Imari huddled under the brush as they waited for the enemy patrol to pass them by. It seemed to them that Drakomar's forces had committed an impractically large number of soldiers to search for them. While Dragorim was confident he could reliably eliminate small groups of their pursuers, the enemy soldiers came in groups of twenty or more. Based on what the pair had overhead in the long hours spent hiding, Drakomar's forces blamed them for some sort of attack they had suffered during the night. Ghouls… and possibly even a werewolf had been summoned to attack their camp, and now they wanted revenge. Sometimes they heard words to the effect that Drakomar now sought the mages for some other purpose, though neither Dragorim nor Imari were eager to come out of hiding and ask them about it.

Both mages were exhausted, with only their innate will to survive driving them forward. They watched breathlessly as a group of thirty soldiers, led by a heavily armored knight, patrolled the area around them. The men in the group all bore a coat of arms unfamiliar to Dragorim, who had spent years in isolation on the Glimmering Isles. However, the moon and stars upon a black field was familiar to Imari and fear choked her heart even more than it had before. She wanted to warn Dragorim of their fanaticism and deeds so terrible that no king would willingly grant them harbor. However, even a single whispered word might give away their position, so, the witch remained silent and hoped that they would go undiscovered.

Imari breathed a sigh of relief as the enemy force moved on. Dragorim came out of his hiding place and helped her up. Just as they were about to start moving again, a group of mounted knights came riding along the road and spotted them. The lead rider of the pair snatched a signal horn from his belt and took a deep breath for a powerful, signaling note.

Dragorim perceived the threat and instantly cast a bolt of lightning at the lead rider, but it was too late! The note sounded, and every soldier within earshot was now aware of their presence. The lightning spell slammed into the soldier, and Dragorim took some satisfaction in killing the man who had doomed him.

Sword drawn, the second rider drove his horse headlong at the pair. Dragorim slammed his fist into the ground and the earth before the knight exploded with fiery power that sent horse and rider crashing to the ground. Dragorim rushed forward and slew the knight with his own sword before the man gained his feet.

"Look!" Imari shouted.

Dragorim turned and saw dozens of soldiers rushing for them. The sorcerer took Imari's hand and the pair fled deeper into the woods as the enemy soldiers chased them. More horns sounded, and the pair frantically searched for a way to escape. Their hearts pounded and their muscles ached, but the mages forced themselves to keep moving forward.

Arrows whistled by their legs as their pursuers sought to catch them. Imari stopped and raised a barrier that shielded them from further arrow fire. Her barrier proved effective, as the arrows left only ripples in the shield as they pinged off the blue wall of energy.

Dragorim withdrew a large, wooden gaulderen from his pocket.

"Cover your ears!" he yelled.

Without hesitation, Imari did as she was told. She watched as Dragorim hurled the gaulderen high into the air and quickly covered his own ears. Right as the gaulderen reached its zenith, it exploded with a staggering sound, as though all the power of a thunderstorm had been unleashed in a single moment.

Cries of pain rang out against the trees as the unprepared soldiers fell to the ground from the blow to their senses. Dragorim took Imari's hand once more.

"Quickly! We must make haste before they recover!"

The pair sprinted away from the group pursuing them; but it was no use. The horn calls had brought many men to their position, and warriors of both Drakomar and the Pale Light closed on them in tight pursuit. Onward they ran, slowed only by the need to climb a tall hill. Again, arrows barely missed them as they ran for their lives. Imari stopped to raise another barrier, but as she did, six horsemen galloped toward her flank. Three broke off for Dragorim while the other three barreled straight for Imari.

Dragorim tried to hurl a destructive spell at the knights bearing down on Imari, but he had no time! The other three horsemen were upon him and he needed to act fast. Exhaustion was taking its toll, and Dragorim was not sure how many more spells he could cast before his power was depleted. He had used up his supply of gaulderens which contained simpler spells. For a moment, he considered turning to his final, most potent gaulderens, but decided against it, as the objects of power needed to be saved for enemies far more dangerous than the mortal men that faced him now.

Using the last of his strength, Dragorim encased himself within a barrier and waited for the charge to arrive. However, when they collided with the barrier, Dragorim turned their energy back upon them, and all three horsemen were torn to shreds by the force of their own charge. Pieces of their mangled corpses scattered across the forest floor, and their blood added a crimson hue to the colors of the earth.

Dragorim bent over and gasped for breath. It was only a moment later that he looked up from the destruction he had wrought and realized that Imari and the other three horsemen were gone. He was alone again.

Out of energy for more spell-casting, Dragorim was forced to flee yet again from yet more pursuing soldiers. Finally, he broke the enemy's line of sight long enough to scramble up a tree. The soldiers drew closer, and Dragorim held his breath, desperate not to make a sound as the enemy swarmed the area around the tree. The sorcerer had climbed high into the branches, but he was not sure how much concealment he really had if someone looked up. Agonizing moments passed, and after an eternity of breathless waiting, the enemy soldiers continued their pursuit elsewhere, believing he was still running somewhere ahead of them.

Once he was sure they had all departed, Dragorim finally took a rasping breath. After taking time to recover his strength, he clambered down from the tree and made his way back to where Imari had disappeared. He searched for her, hoping to find some trace of her. There was none, only hoof-prints leading away from the sight of the battle. Dragorim sighed, for she had probably been captured. Given the things he had overhead the soldiers saying, Dragorim feared the worst for his new friend. He felt sorry for Imari, and he was surprised to find that he desperately hoped that she would be safe. He wondered for a moment if he was still under the influence of her empathy spell… or if his protectiveness of her was genuine. Either way, there was no time to consider it. He needed to find her as quickly as possible. So, the exhausted sorcerer started his slow walk back to Drakomar's encampment.

* * *

Sigaberht and his son sat upon their thrones, and both were displeased. The ealdormen had been brought to the throne room as well, and all pondered the words spoken by Halfdan, whom had recently returned from his destruction of the enemy caravan. Based upon what the werewolf had told them, the attack had been successful. The food had been destroyed, and hostile reinforcements had been slaughtered and scattered. Many of those Halfdan did not kill would likely freeze to death in the snow bound forests. Ordinarily, such news would have been considered glad tidings, but even though the enemy caravan had been vanquished… the bulk of Drakomar's army still remained.

Sigaberht held his hands upon his brow. It seemed that the tales of the Pale Light's fanaticism were not exaggerated. Based on the reports his scouts had given, he was sure that the ghoul attack had also been successful. The enemy had little to no food, no siege weapons, and would be trapped outside the walls forever if he so wished; yet they persisted. It was a puzzle that disturbed him greatly, and he was too tired to make any attempt to hide this fact from his subordinates. The earl looked about the room and saw the dire looks on everyone's faces. They all waited for the earl's opinion on Halfdan's story. He made up his mind on how to proceed, and addressed Halfdan.

"My faithful subject… you have done excellently in your task. If you perceive my discontent, it is not with you, it is with our enemy. They stubbornly refuse to depart from my lands… and this fact vexes me greatly. You may go, for you must be tired. Take food and rest, and my thanks for your efforts."

Halfdan bowed before the earl and made his exit. However, he had noticed Radnor's absence from the meeting. This seemed suspicious to Halfdan, and so his exit was done only for appearances. As soon as he left the throne room, he quickly took a route through the nearby halls until he arrived at the door nearest the royal dais. Thankfully, the guards normally present had been moved to patrol the wall, and so the giant man was able to push the door slightly ajar and listen to what was said in the war meeting. He came in the middle of the conversation, but made out enough to understand.

"The question is…" Ashveldt started. "How are we to break the Pale Light? I believe it almost goes without saying that the Pale Light's fanaticism is the reason the army has not yet fled from Wulfgeld. How do we convince them that it is wise to withdraw? Do any of you have an idea?"

Daegal spoke first.

"I say we stand with Radnor's words from before. We kill as many of their knights as possible." The ealdorman then looked around the throne room.

"Speaking of which, I have noticed that he is absent from this meeting. Why is that?"

"I have omitted *Veigarand* from this meeting. He has other things to attend to at the moment, and his presence is not required for the council of war at this time."

"I see," Daegal said.

"Do you have a problem with our lord's will?" Aethelstan asked.

"I did not say that. I found his absence unusual, that is all."

Sigaberht shot a stern look at Aethelstan. Aethelstan's words risked giving away Sigaberht's concerns about the loyalty of his ealdormen. Now that Osmund had died in battle, this left only Daegal and Aethelstan as true ealdormen, and despite his intention, Leif was seen as an outsider by the other two. Sigaberht knew that given the dire situation against Drakomar, he was vulnerable to betrayal from within. He had trusted the Hexverat, and they had nearly been his downfall. Now, he knew Daegal was angry at him for the way he had handled the battle upon the wall, and he knew that the only thing preventing Veigarand from openly betraying him was the black oath. All Veigarand needed to do was find a way to entice Daegal over to his side of things, and Sigaberht would risk being assassinated.

An unusually loud cough from Ashveldt told Sigaberht that he had been lost in contemplation again. The earl's eyes focused back on Daegal.

"My lord ealdorman, the question remains, *how* are we to kill their knights? Veigarand cannot slay them all for us, and we took many casualties in our first battle. What do you suggest?"

It was then that Leif joined the discussion.

"My lord, if I may… the enemy has little to no food, and will be weak from hunger very soon. I say: let them starve and freeze outside our wall. We have ample food to wait them out."

"And what of their assaults upon the walls? How are we to deal with them?" Sigaberht asked.

"Many of their ladders were abandoned during the last attack. They will have far fewer of them with which to scale the wall, and as for their other siege weapons… their trebuchets have long ceased their bombardment. I believe the ghoul attack successfully destroyed their siege weapons. They have become an impotent force. We need only wait."

"Perhaps…" Sigaberht started. "But, Legier must know his logistics better than we. Why then does he allow his army to remain here?"

"Maybe it is not really his army," Ashveldt suggested.

"How do you mean?" Sigaberht asked.

"Never before have we faced the Pale Light. We know they are devoted to their goddess beyond measure, and we know that they are not welcome anywhere in the Southworld. They would say they are persecuted for their beliefs… but from what you and I have both read… they have a habit of trying to inflict their own beliefs upon their hosts and usurp the thrones of the kings that give them shelter, all in the name of some 'holy crusade'. Perhaps something similar has happened here?"

"I like your thinking my son, but there is too much supposition for us to commit to this line of thought. What you say may very well be true, but we cannot be sure. For the time being, we must operate from the premise that the enemy has some sort of new weapon… something that changes the game against us."

"I concur," Aethelstan said, and Leif quickly agreed. All eyes turned to Daegal.

"I must admit, the reasoning is sound. How then do we parse out what this secret weapon is? I'm not sure we have any way of doing so before they unleash it."

Sigaberht nodded. Daegal was right, which put them at square one.

"Daegal, your point is excellent. Here is a compromise… we wait them out for two days. We will see if they leave on their own. If they do not, we shall lure them into the forest, and hopefully not only draw out their secret weapon, but also end this siege once and for all!"

Sigaberht looked about the room for any sign of objection. There was none. In response to the silence, he continued. "Last time this idea was brought forward, it was met with significant push-back. Now, none of you speak against it. Why?"

Daegal answered first.

"My lord, I was the most vocal against it in the beginning. We have tried every alternative, and if the enemy does not withdraw within the coming days, we will know for sure that the alternatives have failed."

Sigaberht nodded.

"It seems we are all in agreement. We shall wait them out for two days, and on the third day, we shall ride against them!"

All bowed their heads before Sigaberht's will, and Halfdan rushed to inform Radnor of what had transpired. He guessed that Sigaberht had cut Radnor out of the meeting for

reasons beyond what he had admitted, and this concerned
Halfdan greatly.

* * *

Imari struggled to free herself from her captor, throwing
elbows in every direction, but to no avail. In response to her
struggling, the horseman struck her on the back with his elbow
and the pain convinced her to stop fighting for freedom. Now,
she silently waited for death to come, but it didn't. For reasons
beyond her understanding, the soldier had taken her alive. After
a long ride, she looked up to see that the horseman was
bringing her into Drakomar's camp.

"Behold, I have the witch!" shouted the horseman.

Cheers erupted among the soldiers in the camp. Insults
were flung Imari's way, and hands grabbed at her, trying to pull
her from the horse.

"Get away, she's *mine*! I get her *first*!" the rider
shouted.

The crowd did as they were ordered, and once they all
arrived at the center of the camp, the rider roughly dumped her
on the ground. Imari groaned in pain as she landed on her
shoulder. The angry mob of soldiers descended upon her again.
They viciously kicked and screamed at her. Some men tore at
her clothing. The pain was overwhelming, and continued until
the horseman drew his sword and commanded her attackers to
retreat again. Seeing the horseman's anger, the crowd drew
back.

"Send for Sir Legier. Tell him we have a special
prisoner."

Several soldiers sprinted through the camp to summon
their commander. The horseman then dragged Imari over to an
empty chair and threw her in it. Frozen with fear, Imari could
only watch as the horseman tied her down. Suddenly, a small
rock struck her head, splitting her skin and drawing blood.

"Punish her! Burn her!" yelled men in the crowd.

The horseman strode forward and unfastened her furs.
He looked to a few men who seemed to be his friends, who
then rushed towards Imari. The soldiers forcibly disrobed her,

and their hands began to find their way into more sensitive areas. She tried to reach out with her mind as she had done with Dragorim… but there were too many men… too many groping hands for her to focus on. This, combined with her exhaustion, rendered her powers useless.

Imari started to scream, but a ball of blood soaked cloth was roughly shoved into her mouth, muting her cries. More men joined the fray, and just as it seemed the angry mob would tear her to pieces, a voice shouted above the crowd.

"All of you! Disperse at once!"

The men scattered. Imari looked over to where the voice came from, and saw a dark haired man dressed in full armor standing in front of another similarly dressed man. They were flanked by a block of imposing men from the Pale Light. If Imari had been afraid before, this sight terrified her even further. A short, bald, black-robed man spoke next.

"Celestata has chosen her, you fools! Stay your hands, lest a curse be placed upon you!"

"She sent the monsters to kill us! We should burn her!" shouted one of the angry men.

There was a chorus of agreements from the crowd; but one of the armored men stepped forward and shouted them down.

"*I* am the marshal of this army, and you *will* withdraw from her! Do you understand me?"

The knights of the Pale Light that flanked him stepped forward with their hands on their swords.

After some grumbling, the soldiers backed further away from her.

One of the other knights approached her, but instead of applying further abuse, he removed her gag, drew a dagger, and quickly cut her bonds. Once Imari was free, the man threw his own cloak over her shoulders. He took a moment to hold her shivering body to his, and then spoke to her.

"My name is Sir Arnulf. The grand marshal and I would like a word with you."

Imari nodded, knowing full well that she did not have a choice in the matter.

Arnulf looked over to the crowd assembled.

"Return this woman's clothes to her, now!" he shouted.

Several men stepped forward, bearing the remains of her clothing. The furs themselves were still intact, but many of the pieces that connected the furs had been torn apart, so that the clothes were nearly useless.

Arnulf rolled his eyes. Legier looked over to one of his servants.

"Bring this woman some clothes. Make sure they are warm enough."

The servant bowed and ran to fetch clothes for the scared witch. Legier turned back to Imari.

"Please, come into my tent. We can talk there."

He bowed slightly as he gestured for her to follow him. Arnulf led Imari by the arm, and Venatus brought up the rear. As soon as they were inside Legier's tent, Imari finally spoke.

"What are you going to do to me?" she asked.

"Let's not get ahead of ourselves," Legier replied. "We have not been introduced. I am Sir Legier, Grand Marshal of the Army of Drakomar. This here is my second in command, Sir Arnulf. And this… is Archpriest Venatus of the Pale Light. What's your name?"

"Imari."

"I do believe I am glad to have met you, Imari," Legier said. "Or, I *hope* I will be. Which, I suppose leads us back to your question."

"What will you do to me?" Imari asked again.

"Nothing," came Legier's reply. "At least, not yet. That all depends on how you answer my questions."

Imari gulped nervously.

"What happens if you don't like the answers I give?" she asked.

Legier casually opened the door to the tent and gestured outside.

"I give you back to them."

Imari shuddered at the thought. She looked to Arnulf, but he gave no sign of argument, and Venatus simply smiled at her like a wolf grins at a lamb. Legier offered her a fur covered chair to sit upon and handed her a goblet of wine. She was reluctant to take a sip out of concern for mind-altering poison, so instead asked more questions of her own.

"Why do you offer me these things? Do you not believe that I am the one who sent the ghouls after you?"

"How do you know about that?" Arnulf asked.

"The men that chased us were most vocal about it," Imari replied.

"They may believe it, but I do not. If you were the one who did it, it would have been *you* killing my soldiers out there, not the man you were with," Legier said.

Imari let out a sigh of relief, though her nervousness did not leave her.

"Then why hold me prisoner?"

"*Because* they believe it, and right now, we need someone with your abilities on our side. Right now, it's between you and your friend, and he is still out of our reach. Perhaps we could use you as bait to draw him out?" Legier asked.

"I don't know him!" Imari cried. "Not really, anyway,"

"Then why do you travel with him now?" Venatus demanded. "Who is he? What does he want here?"

"I've only known him a short while. Things happened so fast…"

"You just met him?" Arnulf asked.

"Yes, I… we both were passing by Wulfgeld on our own business. We met, camped together, and then your men attacked us."

"Strange…" Legier started. "What business do you have here in Wulfgeld?"

"I came to see how I could help, after the wolf attack. I know many people died here, and someone needs to help them."

Legier chuckled.

"So, I can assume you were not pleased to find us besieging the city?"

Imari nodded.

"I will not lie to you, as I can see that lying will only lead to a painful death. I was not happy to see you here, and I spent the last two days trying to find a way into the city. I ran into the other sorcerer, and we had hoped that if we worked together, we could get inside the walls."

Legier nodded.

"Where is your friend now?"

Imari shrugged.

"I don't know. We never discussed a plan of action. We just sort of fell in together, that's all."

"I see," Legier said. "And why should I believe you?"

Imari saw a look of self-doubt in Legier's face. He was actually looking for a reason to trust her. Judging by the look on Venatus' face, he wanted something from her as well. Given that he was from the Pale Light, she trusted his motivations even less than Legier's. So, Imari directed her entire focus onto Legier. She projected her concern and her fear onto him, but with a dash of confidence that would fill him with great pride once he got her to "agree" to what they wanted. Once she was done, she spoke again.

"Because I can provide the help you seek. The question is, what do you want from me?"

Legier smiled.

"Now we're getting somewhere. I don't believe for a second that you or your friend are the ones that orchestrated the ghoul attack. It makes no sense for Sigaberht to send such powerful magic-users outside the walls for such a task. On top of that, once the attack was over, you would have retreated behind the walls, not camped out in the woods. No, you did not plan that attack. But you are correct; we do have need of you."

"We should tell her the truth," Venatus said.

Legier laughed.

"And have her think we are madmen? I'm not sure I would believe myself, had I not seen it with my own eyes!"

"I'm still not sure I believe you," Arnulf said.

Tension caught in Imari's throat. What were they talking about? Imari probed for information.

"I am a witch of Aksum. I have seen many strange things in my time. Perhaps I might shed some light upon that which you speak."

Venatus stepped towards her ominously. There was a mad glint in his eye that told her he was liable to be unpredictable.

"We have been blessed with a grand visitation! The goddess Celestata came to us and gifted us with her holy radiance!" he said.

Imari's eyes widened in surprise and fear. These truly were madmen!

"Did all of you see this? Or was it only the Archpriest?" she asked.

Legier laughed again. He seemed to find the whole affair to be quite amusing.

"I bore witness to it as well, as did nearly every member of the Pale Light present in this camp at the time."

"Strange that the only ones who saw it were the Pale Light, and you," Arnulf said.

"Do you suggest something?" Venatus said.

"I suggest nothing beyond that it is strange," Arnulf replied.

"Gentlemen, please," Legier said. "Is this discussion truly relevant to the task at hand?"

Legier then returned his gaze to Imari.

"What would you have me do?" she asked.

"You and your friend killed a number of my men during your flight. I am willing to overlook that if you do one thing for me: use your powers to break down the gate of Wulfgeld."

Imari suppressed a gasp, for this was something far beyond her abilities.

"I… I…" she stammered.

"What is it? Do you have any moral objections to this idea?"

Imari forced her fears deep inside herself and made her reply.

"What will you do with me once the gate is down?"

"I will let you go."

"And if I fail?"

Legier leaned in closer to her.

"Then my men will leave you out in the open and let the defenders of Wulfgeld take a crack at you. But that won't be an issue, will it?"

"Why me?"

"The Foul-Temptress now dwells within the walls of Wulfgeld! Our radiant goddess has tasked us to break the city's walls and destroy her once and for all. In her infinite wisdom, she chose *you* to help us."

"Me or my companion?" Imari asked.

"Is your companion here?" Venatus asked.

"No."

"Then it is *you* she has chosen."

Imari was unsure of how to respond at first, but after a moment's hesitation, gave the best response she could muster.

"I will need food, water, and a good bed to sleep on. I am tired from the hell your men put me through."

"Fair enough," Legier replied. "You shall sleep here in my tent, under guard… in case some of the less disciplined men try to take advantage of you." Imari had a feeling that the guards were actually there to keep her imprisoned, but she pretended Legier's words were true all the same. "Food shall be brought to you, and when you are ready, we will begin the assault."

"Sir?" Arnulf said, surprised at Legier's words.

Legier ignored him and continued speaking to Imari.

"You will be ready by this afternoon. We will send you forward with a group of my best men, you will break down the gate, and we will take the city. Any objections?"

Imari gulped, knowing that any argument could get her thrown back to the wrath of Legier's soldiers.

"No, my lord. None at all. Consider the gate destroyed."

"Good," Legier said. "Sir Arnulf, Archpriest… please accompany me. I will need your help in preparing the assault."

Arnulf and Venatus both bowed and followed Legier out of the tent. Imari looked on in fear as they departed. Her mind raced as she desperately searched for a way to escape her fate. But nothing came to mind. It seemed that she had traded one death for another. For the moment, her only hope was to play along with the warriors of Drakomar. Hopefully, she would find a way to make her escape in the chaos of the battle. If she didn't… death at the hands of Wulfgeld's arrows seemed a better way to go than allowing herself to fall victim to the monstrous vengeance the men of Drakomar would inflict upon her.

As Arnulf and Legier exited the tent, Arnulf began to speak his objections.

"Sir, are you sure it's wise to launch an attack today?"

Legier shook his head.

"Despite what you have been told, you are still so eager to flee? A chance at victory has arrived, and you would just let it slip away?"

"We have been blessed by the holy presence of our beloved goddess, and you would forsake this boon with cowardice?" Venatus added.

Arnulf ignored Venatus and kept his gaze firmly locked on Legier.

"Think of your men!" Arnulf said.

"I swore an oath!" Legier retorted.

"So you keep saying…" Arnulf said.

"What was that you just said to me?" Legier demanded.

"You keep bringing up the oath you took when you set off for this siege… but you seem to be forgetting the one you took when you became grand marshal. You swore to look after the best interest of your men!"

Legier took a step back, deeply hurt by Arnulf's words.

"How dare you insult me! Everything I do is for the benefit of the men! I was ready to send you all safely home just a short while ago!"

Arnulf paused for a moment to consider his words.

"Sir, may we speak in private… beyond the ears of the Pale Light?"

Legier shook his head.

"I saw Celestata as well. She was as real as you or me. Whatever you say to me, you now also say to the Pale Light."

Arnulf was shocked. Just the day before, Legier had mocked their fanaticism, but now… he was a convert.

"Legier, listen to yourself! Something is not right! You think you are in charge, but you are not!"

Venatus scoffed at Arnulf.

"Are you implying that I have somehow poisoned the mind of your grand marshal? That I bewitched his eyes so that he might see what I saw? I assure you, I have no such power, and even if I did, the goddess forbids its use."

Arnulf threw up his hands in frustrated anger.

"I'm saying that some other force is at play here… something outside what we know. Why, after generations of absence, would Celestata appear now?"

"We told you. Lashmatu lurks behind—"

"I know what was said!"

Legier broke in next.

"Look at the evidence, Arnulf! The powers we have faced here? What else could have summoned the ghouls? The werewolf? That terrible sword? It could only be a demon like Lashmatu."

"Then why has she not come out and attacked us herself?"

Venatus jumped in with his own answer.

"She is the Foul-Temptress, the Corruptor-of-Hearts, and the Soul-Thief. She prefers to work through the actions of mortal men. She takes pleasure in twisting their hearts and minds until their wills are broken and their spirits torn asunder! Only once her foes are truly beaten will she reveal herself!"

"How convenient," Arnulf replied.

Legier scoffed at him.

"Why do you not believe us? We have witnessed terrible calamity, and many of us saw Celestata appear within this very camp. She spoke to us Arnulf. She gave us our holy task, and we must accomplish it."

"Do you know why I don't believe you?" Arnulf said.

The knight gestured back to Imari's place in Legier's tent.

"You say she is the one chosen for this task. You say that she will crush the walls of Wulfgeld? *She* could barely light a candle, let alone smite our enemies!"

"You yourself heard the reports. She and her companion killed close to thirty of our men."

"No, she killed no one. It was *he* who did all the killing. If you had brought *him* into this camp, I might believe you. But you're telling me this woman was chosen by divine powers to ensure our victory?"

Legier paused to think for a moment. Arnulf's words were starting to make sense. It was as if the longer they were out of the tent; a cloud was gradually lifting from Legier's mind. However, Venatus stepped back into the conversation.

"If it were by any other circumstance, I might believe you. But, Celestata told us what to do. Imari shall be a vessel for our goddess to act through, and the wall shall be brought down!"

"Did Celestata specifically tell you to seek out the sorcerers? Did she specifically tell you it was Imari she wanted?"

"Well… not exactly," Legier stuttered.

"What *exactly* did she say?" Arnulf demanded.

Seeing Legier was wavering again, Venatus jumped back in again.

"She told us to find a way through the wall, and this is the *only* way. This is how she has always been. She rightfully trusted us to come to the correct conclusion."

Arnulf bugged his eyes out at Legier. He desperately hoped that the inherent insanity of Venatus' words would break Legier out of the fervor into which he had been swept. He got no response, and so Arnulf turned back to Venatus.

"You just said that Celestata trusted you would come to the correct conclusion. She has asked you to perform this task for her. By your own words, you have said that Lashmatu acts through the power of mortal men—"

"Do not blaspheme before me! Celestata came to me… *me*! She blessed *me* with her holy light! Not the Primarchus in his hallowed halls! It was *me*!" Venatus' eyes narrowed as he gazed upon Arnulf. "She came to me. She came to Legier, but she did not come to *you*!"

Arnulf turned back to Legier. Arguing with Venatus was pointless, but he still saw hope for his friend.

"Think of your oath! Think of your men!"

"I am thinking of them!" Legier shouted. "Defeat was closing upon us, but now, the goddess has spoken… victory is assured!"

"You think only of your bride… the prize that awaits you in Drakomar. You see the slightest chance of success, and you fling not only yourself, but everyone around you to the grinder!"

This final comment from Arnulf pushed Legier over the edge, and he lost his temper.

"Enough!" Legier shouted. "Call the patrols back! Assemble the army! We will launch the attack as soon as the witch is ready. That is the end of discussion, do you understand?"

Arnulf fell silent. This behavior was unlike the Legier he had known for so many years. The grand marshal had become desperate and unhinged in a way that worried Arnulf greatly. However, he had sworn oaths of his own, and these included obedience to the grand marshal. Arnulf silently bowed to his commander and stormed off to carry out his orders.

Legier sighed. Venatus touched his shoulder in an offer of comfort, but Legier shrugged him off. His frustration with Arnulf did not make Venatus his friend. Legier knew in his heart that Arnulf was only saying what he thought was best. But, Celestata *had* come to them. She had given them this holy task, and they were responsible for seeing that it was done. *Right?*

Legier turned back to his tent and saw that his servants brought both food and clothes for the witch. The marshal smiled. This plan would work. It had to. There was no choice in the matter.

* * *

After a frustratingly slow climb up the same hill on which he had camped the night before, Dragorim finally reached the summit and looked out over the snow covered battlefield that separated Drakomar's encampment from the walls of Wulfgeld. He had needed to avoid more patrols, and exhaustion from that task meant that it had taken hours for him to make the trek back to the peak of the hill. Only the sudden disappearance of the enemy forces had allowed him to arrive at the hill at all. It was midday, and after nearly a full night and a day of flight, the sorcerer needed to rest. Satisfied there were no foes nearby, Dragorim allowed himself to collapse on the ground in a heap. His muscles ached and it was all he could do to stop himself from falling asleep right there on the hill. However, he needed to form a plan on how to help Imari escape from her imprisonment. The sorcerer pulled himself out of the snow, sat up, and looked out over what he could see of the enemy encampment. The camp was still a far distance off and the Drakomari had cleverly used the cover of the trees to shroud themselves from spying eyes. Dragorim could not make out many details of even the outer layers of the encampment, let alone what threats lay within.

With no easy way to get information about the enemy defenses and without the energy to muster the spells he needed to fight against such potentially overwhelming odds, Dragorim eventually convinced himself that a rescue attempt would be folly. He sat and meditated to regain as much of his strength as he could. As he sat, he wondered why he was so focused on rescuing Imari. It was an odd fixation for him. As he thought, he also realized that he still did not know why he had spared her the previous night. He knew she had used magic to influence him, not that he blamed her. He would have done the same thing in her position. He could have resisted her control with his own power and crushed her beneath his heel if he had wanted. Now, the question remained: why did he not want to? Why had he not resisted her power? He had never hesitated to eliminate a threat to him before, so what made her special?

At that thought, images of all those he had killed flooded his mind. Some faces he remembered with frightening clarity; others swam through his thoughts as distorted fragments of ancient, half-memories. He had killed many over his lifetime. Many had deserved it. Remorsefully, Dragorim had to admit to himself that some, like Nikos, had not deserved death, though circumstance had forced his hand.

However, it was not the memory of all those he had killed that brought his mercy upon Imari. It was Fatim and the hungry little boy killed by the baron that inspired him. Regardless of the sorcerer's intentions, both of them had died due to his actions. Their deaths reminded him of why he had gone into seclusion to begin with. The people he had chosen to kill were not the problem, it was the deaths out of his control that haunted him so. He had chosen to use his powers to hasten his journey… and it had cost Fatim his life. He had given the boy more food than he could eat in a sitting, and the boy had been murdered for it. *He* had chosen to kill the group of Drakomar scouts that came upon them in the night, and it was *his* decision that put Imari in danger. No matter what he did, his actions always rippled across time in ways he could never predict. But now, he had control of Imari's fate. If she was to die, it was to be by his hand, and his alone. Satisfied with his thoughts on the matter, Dragorim wrapped himself up on his cloak and finally allowed himself to fall into a deep, restful sleep atop the hill.

Chapter 20

The rays of the afternoon sun cascaded brilliantly over the snow-covered battlefield. Knights of the Pale Light saw this as an omen of good tidings, for Celestata shined her holy light upon their goal.

Elena sat alone in her cottage, a situation she resented most thoroughly. Drakomar's forces had massed for another assault, and Radnor had been called to defend the wall once more. Despite Elena's sullen mood, she did not waste her time brooding. Instead, she studied the sinister gaulderens held in her palm. The black etchings upon the stones seemed almost understandable to her, and the sinister flames within danced for her as she pondered how to release them from their prison. Despite this feeling of familiarity, there was no revelation. No method of use revealed itself to her, and Elena's frustration grew with each passing moment. Her thumb happened upon the outline of the central symbol… those conjoined triangles. Elena gently traced the shape with her thumb, vainly hoping doing so would unlock the gaulderen's secrets; but nothing happened.

Elena looked up at the ceiling and let out a worried sigh. It seemed to her that the fate of the world rested on her shoulders… and she couldn't even figure out how to use a simple gaulderen! She drew her arm back to fling the stones against the wall, but thought better of it. Instead, she turned her gaze back to the gaulderens in her palm.

"The trouble is…" she said aloud. "I don't even know where to *start*."

Suddenly, a female voice called to Elena from outside the door and broke her concentration. Elena rose from her seat and let out a frustrated sigh. Unless this person was here to tell her the war was over, she had no desire to speak to anyone. At first, Elena made no move to open the door, but the insistent voice called to her again. Gaulderens still in hand, Elena begrudgingly walked over to the door and opened it. She was surprised to find a young, dark haired woman standing before her. The woman's pale skin and raven hair matched Elena's almost exactly, and her face was similar enough she could have been her sister. Elena locked eyes with the woman's amber gaze and an uneasy feeling washed over her. Finally, the woman spoke.

"Pardon me, we just look so much alike, I thought you my long lost twin!"

Elena smiled.

"As did I; though I have no sister. Who are you?"

The woman dramatically slapped herself on the forehead, as though frustrated with herself.

"I'm so sorry! My name is Synniva! Our lord Sigaberht sent me to check on you."

"Oh. Well… thank you. Come in." Elena said as she gestured for the woman to enter.

"Thank you,"

The mysterious woman stepped across the threshold and looked around the room with an amused expression on her face. Elena noticed this, and her unease at Synniva's presence increased. She claimed that Sigaberht had sent her to check in, but acted as though she had some other purpose in being there.

"Do you have news of the coming battle?" Elena asked.

"No more than you, I'm afraid. The armies assemble, but that is all. Do you want for news of Veigarand?" By the look on Elena's face, Synniva realized she had said the wrong thing when she used Radnor's other name. "I'm sorry, did I do something wrong?"

"His name is '*Radnor*'. Veigarand is the name only used by his enemies."

"Oh, I see," Synniva said. "But his lordship always…"

"His lordship does what he will, now as you can see, I am quite well, so if you wouldn't mind—"

"My, those are pretty! May I see them?" Synniva interrupted.

Elena paused; confused by Synniva's interjection, but then she realized that she was still holding the gaulderens. Given that their existence was a secret, Elena hastily lied about them.

"These? They were a gift from Radnor. They are heirlooms of his, and he wanted me to have them."

"May I see?" Synniva asked.

There was no polite way of saying "no", so Elena reluctantly opened her palms and showed them to Synniva.

"Those markings are quite curious, are they not?" Synniva asked.

Elena nodded.

"Do you know where he got them?"

Elena shook her head in confusion. Did this woman not just hear her say that they were heirlooms? She scrambled to answer the question.

"They came from his mother… who died long ago."

Synniva smiled. "What a sad tale," she said in an almost sarcastic tone that caught Elena off guard. Before Elena could respond, Synniva continued. "Do you know how to use them?"

Elena took a step back. Suddenly, Synniva's gaze seemed different to Elena. It had become… predatory.

"Who are you?" Elena asked as she stepped back.

"An interested party," Synniva said.

"That's a half answer," Elena replied. She continued her rearwards retreat and headed for a spare sword Radnor kept in the bedroom. Synniva guessed at Elena's intention and laughed, in an icy, unfriendly manner that filled the air with unnatural power.

"Weapons are no use, but do not fret; I mean you no harm. I'm here to help you."

Elena stopped in her tracks, and sized up the woman standing before her.

"You're one of *them* aren't you? A Krigari?" she asked.

"Clever; more-so than your lover I think. My name is Lashmatu, and I have come to help you."

"How can you help me? And why?"

Lashmatu stepped uncomfortably close to Elena and leaned in so tightly that if she were physically there, Elena would have felt the goddess' breath on her face.

"I… and others… have a special interest in keeping Radnor alive. Drakomar brings forth a new means of breaking the city's defenses, and I believe they will be successful."

"And why should I believe you?

286

"You can't afford not to. If you do nothing, Radnor will die fighting against impossible odds. But if you do as I say, you can save his life."

Elena weighed her options. It did not take long for her to realize that Lashmatu was right… Elena had no choice but to cooperate.

"What can I do about it?" Elena asked.

"Wield the gaulderens. Listen carefully, and I will show you how to use them."

Elena looked down at the gaulderens in her hand, and then back to the demon goddess that stood before her.

"Alright… lead on."

* * *

Dusk fell upon Wulfgeld before Drakomar's forces finished gathering for their assault. Imari stood nervously among a cluster of knights from the Pale Light. Their goal was to bring her as close to the gates as she needed in order to use her powers to bring it down. Each man wore heavy armor and carried tall, broad shields to protect them from Wulfgeld's arrows. Companies of archers guarded by other squadrons of heavy infantry were assembled to provide covering fire for her unit. Some of these groups carried the last of the siege ladders with them, but this was only a deceptive measure. They just wanted to make Sigaberht believe this attack was merely another attempt to scale the walls; until it was too late for him to stop their real plan. Imari herself was now dressed in the armor of one of Drakomar's fallen soldiers, and while she was grateful for the protection it provided, she still was less than happy to be going into battle at all.

Despite the effort Legier was exerting to keep Imari safe, she knew that each and every one of these brave warriors had orders to kill her if she failed. She had not spent her time alone in Legier's tent idly, and had tried to construct a gaulderen that could act as an explosive. However, Imari had neither the tools nor the energy to create such a powerful magical object; she had never had any talent for building gaulderens. The one gaulderen she had ever created merely produced the light of a candle so that she could light her way in the darkness of her library at home. At the thought of her library, her heart longed for her home in Aksum, far away from these war torn north-lands. Imari scoffed at her own foolishness. It had been stupid to come here! She had been comfortable in Ranrike! She could have stayed there and enjoyed the cold northern winter in a warm, welcoming city for which this war was only distant news. Now… she was set to die on this hellish battlefield, far from home, and with no one to care about her. She wondered how long it would be before anyone learned she was dead.

The witch shook her head to herself. This kind of thinking was not what had gotten her where she was in life, and it certainly wouldn't help her now. After taking a deep breath, Imari began to meditate; and finally slowed her onrushing fears. She focused on externalizing her awareness, and in those moments, she felt the fears of those around her. The men surrounding her were terrified of what was to come, but they all had seen Celestata's grace. Their knowledge of her intentions was now beyond mere faith… their beliefs were *fact*. Despite their fear, there was no swaying them from their chosen course of action. They would accomplish their goal and slaughter all who got in their way.

Imari reached out even further with her mind, searching for a way to connect to nature and calm herself. As she stretched her mind, she felt as though her spirit walked among the snow-covered trees. Instead of peace however, she found anger. Imari focused on this anger, and her awareness was drawn to a conversation unheard by the mortal men around her. Imari focused on the voices, unsure of whom the speakers were at first, but after a moment's listening, she realized they were Arnulf and Legier.

"She's playing you!" Arnulf snarled.

"How so?" Legier demanded.

Fear gripped Imari's heart when she heard this exchange. If Arnulf could make Legier recognize her deception, she would be killed on the spot!

"If she really had the power to bring down the gates, do you not think she would have unleashed those powers on us? It's her mysterious friend that we need to enlist!"

Legier scoffed.

"What, do you think her friend killed those men single handed? One sorcerer could not have killed so many alone. She must have helped him. And besides… the witch knows that if she turns her powers on us, we will take our revenge."

"Do you not see? There is more to this than we know! Withdraw the men. We must hold our ground until we know more!"

"I will not turn back from my holy mission," Legier said.

"The dreams! Think of your dreams! Dark powers are at play here, and we are being swallowed by them!"

"Do I need to relieve you of your post?" Legier replied.

Without missing a beat, Arnulf snapped back at Legier.

"No, you do not. If you're so hell bent on this suicidal venture, I'm going to the front!"

Legier blanched at Arnulf's defiance.

"I need you back here with me! Who else is to lead the men should I fall?" Legier asked.

Arnulf snorted in disgust.

"You are the one who insists on continuing this doomed siege! These men believe Celestata is with them, but what will happen at the first sign of trouble? Will they stand and fight? Or will they flee? If you want them to fight, one of us will need to see it done, and since you have become lost in your newfound love for Celestata… *I* will lead them!"

Silence fell between them for only a moment, but to Imari, it felt as though an insurmountable gulf now separated the two friends. Then, Legier shouted again.

"Alright, then go!"

Armor clanked abruptly as Arnulf gave a final salute to his commander and angrily started towards the formation. Realizing the battle would soon commence, Imari brought her awareness back to herself. A plan was beginning to form in her mind. If the spirit of these men began to waver as Arnulf feared, it was possible she could find a way to influence them.

Or, if she couldn't use her powers to influence *them*, perhaps she could focus her attention on Arnulf and get him to order a retreat. It would take some doing, and speaking to him with the required eloquence would be difficult to accomplish on a battlefield.

Her train of thought was broken as the soldiers in her unit stepped aside for Arnulf to join them. The overwrought man made his way to the terrified witch and spoke to her.

"We will begin the assault soon. You had best make peace with your god."

"What makes you think I won't succeed?" Imari asked, doing everything she could to hide her fear.

"I spoke to the men who brought you in. They talked at length about your red-haired friend, and not so much about you. I think you're stalling for time, trying to find a way out of your situation."

Imari extended her awareness outward again, this time focusing exclusively on Arnulf. She found that he was incredibly frightened, though a strong sense of duty meant that his will would not easily be bent. However, she tried her best.

"If you believe that I am incapable of helping you, and that I wasn't the one that killed your men, why not let me go? I'm clearly no threat to you."

Arnulf's expression softened as he looked at her. Compassion filled his heart, and for a moment, he was tempted to go along with her desire. However, the consequences of such a choice came flooding into his mind and he snapped back to the task at hand. The knight of Drakomar did not quite understand what had happened to him just then, though he suspected witchcraft. If they did not still need her alive, he might have killed her right then. Arnulf wisely broke his eye contact with her and spoke in a way meant to draw her into confirming his suspicion.

"Perhaps I underestimated you. You almost had me doing your bidding."

Instead of admitting anything or directly feigning innocence, Imari instead further committed to her actual line of reasoning.

"By the look on your face, you know I'm right. I need no witchcraft for that."

Arnulf shook his head.

"I cannot blame you for trying. Perhaps I am wrong, and when forced to it, you will reveal a hidden strength and destroy the gates."

"And what if you're not?" Imari pleaded.

"Then we'll die here together."

"Are your people always so grim?" she asked.

Arnulf smiled.

"Only when faced with grim situations."

Arnulf abruptly turned away from Imari and addressed his men.

"Hear me, Knights of Drakomar! Warriors of the Pale Light! Hear me and heed my words! I know you have been hurt, you have been wounded, and you are afraid. Many of you feel shame for your fear, but believe me when I say this: you have no reason for shame! The unholy foes that have been sent against us would be insurmountable to lesser men. You have risen to the challenges our enemy has presented, and have cast them down. Beautiful Celestata has presented us with a gift, and we now have an opportunity to turn our foe's terrible weapons against them. If they knew of this, they would flee from their walls in terror! Your might shall soon be known across all northern kingdoms, and your wrath shall be unwavering as we break the enemies before us! Go now! March, and take your revenge!"

Cheers sounded from the crowd, and to Imari's horror, the spirits of the men around her soared. The formation started forward, forcing Imari to march with them. All of her hard work spent calming herself came crashing down, and fear gripped her heart once more. With the resolve of her enemy so strengthened, there was no way she could influence them to flee now.

* * *

Radnor again found himself atop Wulfgeld's wall. He watched anxiously as the enemy steadily marched to the walls.

The fact that the enemy dared attempt another assault told him that something was amiss, though he didn't know what to do about it. Radnor's one comfort was that Halfdan stood beside him. Radnor's loyal friend had told him of Sigaberht's meeting, and the earl's words disturbed him greatly.

However, now was not the time to ponder Sigaberht's plans. The enemy drew closer to the gate, and something in their manner told that they would fight to the last man. In addition to the advancing infantry formations, a block of heavy cavalry stood at the rear as though they waited for something. This troubled Radnor greatly, for as far as he was aware, Drakomar's siege weapons had been smashed, and Halfdan had seen to it that no supplies reached them. How did they expect to breach the wall?

Sigaberht seemed undisturbed by this turn of events. When Radnor questioned Sigaberht about Drakomar's capabilities, the earl's response had been less than satisfying.

"They may have a weapon, but they might also be fools. Something like this was bound to happen. Drakomar's knights are prideful and honor bound to victory. Either way, we are locked to the same course of action: hold the wall."

No matter how little Radnor appreciated Sigaberht's answer, he had no choice but to accept it. Once the enemy was close enough, Radnor and Halfdan were to reposition down to the courtyard below. Sergeant Aelfric and his men waited for him there. Together, they were to observe the battle from that position, and whenever the enemy started to achieve a foothold, Radnor and Aelfric would be sent in to slaughter them until their terror of him drove them back.

This time, Leif did not stand with Sigaberht atop the gatehouse, but instead occupied the place on the wall where Osmund had fought. Ashveldt was again on his own side of the wall, and Sergeant Aelfric led the men held in reserve.

As the enemy drew closer, Sigaberht turned to Radnor.

"It is time. Go below. I will direct you from here."

Radnor nodded, obeying his lord's command. Something still seemed off to him about the whole thing, though he desperately hoped he was wrong.

* * *

Dragorim lashed out with his sword as he woke from a harrowing nightmare. Once he remembered where he was, he tried to draw his mind from the evil dream. He had been forced to relive an old battle, while he was mocked and ridiculed by the evil presence that had sent his mind into that awful memory. Dragorim closed his eyes and breathed deeply, and once fully awake, stiffly pulled himself up from where he had lain. He grunted as pain jolted through his body, for the cold had done little to help his aching muscles.

"I must be getting old," he joked to himself.

After futilely hoping the pain would go away on its own, Dragorim gave up and stood to investigate the sounds that had broken him from his slumber. It seemed that he had awoken just at the right time. A horn sounded, signaling the start of an attack against Wulfgeld by Drakomar.

At first, Dragorim was content to simply watch as men killed each other. However, a strange sight caught his eye that took him a moment to understand. There was a familiar aura among the crowd of Drakomar's soldiers, and after a moment, he realized the aura belonged to Imari. His heart pounded, and his desire to rescue her flamed in his heart. However, there were too many enemy soldiers in that group for him to kill all at once, at least not without using spells that would likely kill Imari as well. He quickly realized that the only reason she would be among them was that they wanted her to bring down Wulfgeld's defenses… and if half of what she had told him about herself was true, this was a task beyond her powers.

Dragorim carefully considered his options, and realized that there was only one… *he* needed to destroy the gate for her. However, he could not simply ride out and join the fray. He had no armor, which meant a single arrow from Wulfgeld's defenders could be his undoing. After a moment of anxious thought, Dragorim realized he would have to cast a spell powerful enough to destroy the enemy gate from a great distance.

Dragorim quickly set to lighting a campfire; which he did with flint, as he needed to save every bit of energy he had for the spell he was about to cast. Just as the sparks took to the kindling, he began focusing all of his energy on it, directing it back down into the earth. After a few breathless moments, the flames sank into the soil. Dragorim felt the fire's power and guided it through the earth, bit by bit. As he did, the flame grew larger, brighter, and hotter. The fire drew strength not only from Dragorim's soul, but from all that it devoured beneath the surface. The stronger the flame grew, the more difficult it became for the sorcerer to control. It was like trying to hold a massive bubble of air under the water, all it took was one slip, and the flames would destroy him.

It took all of Dragorim's concentration to stop it from rising up too soon. After many agonizing minutes, the underground fire finally reached its destination beneath the gates of Wulfgeld. Dragorim then fed every ounce of energy he had into keeping it under control until the right moment. More and more did the flame consume, building its power. The spell was set and Dragorim now only needed to wait until he was sure the fire was strong enough to be effective before he released it. He only hoped he had the strength to hold on for that long.

* * *

Arrows streaked for Imari as her unit neared the gates. The tight formation marched with precise rhythm, and the helpless witch could only shake with fear as the men around her stomped their way through the hail of projectiles. Arrows stuck in shields and armor, but nothing slowed their inexorable advance. Imari was curious to see how other units in the attack fared, but she dared not stick her head out from behind the protective shields that kept her alive. Again, she extended her awareness to the feelings of the men around her. The elation which Arnulf's speech had restored had mostly waned once the arrows started flying. However, these warriors were not afraid, but were instead driven by grim determination and spite. These men no longer fought for glory or loot, or even their goddess, though that's what they told themselves. They fought for revenge.

Imari looked up and saw that they had drawn so close to the gate that she could make out every detail in the woodwork. The enemy arrows suddenly ceased their assault, but before Imari could question it, Arnulf bellowed over the group.

"Our archers are drawing their fire! Company, double time!"

The soldiers instantly doubled their pace, and Imari was hard pressed to keep up with them as they swiftly advanced. As they went, Arnulf growled in Imari's ear.

"How fucking close do we need to be? If we get much closer, they won't need bows to reach us."

"I need to be touching the gate," she lied.

Arnulf glared again.

"That puts us under their murder holes. They'll be able to drop all sorts of nasty shit on us from there. Are you sure that's what you want?"

Imari hesitated, as she considered her answer. The witch steeled her resolve, and gave her answer.

"What I want is of no importance right now. What I *need* is to touch the gate."

Imari's current plan was to lead the force directly into harm's way. She hoped that if Wulfgeld's defenders killed enough of her captors, they would flee and give her a chance to escape in the chaos. All of this hinged on a great deal of luck, but it was the best plan she could form in the heat of the moment. She had to hope everyone would be too distracted to kill her in the chaos of the battle.

Just as they were about to enter the gate house, Arnulf shouted commands in a language Imari could not understand, and the front line of soldiers lifted their shields to protect them from enemy fire coming from above. This gave Imari a chance to get a closer look at the gate, and she instantly saw that something was wrong. An unnatural heat emanated from the door; the witch felt like she was standing beside a river of lava. Fearing a trap of some kind, Imari grabbed Arnulf by the shoulder.

"Stop. There's somethi—"

Imari did not get to finish her sentence. The world shook, and the earth below the gate shattered into a pillar of fire that engulfed the gatehouse from below. The explosion carried upward, shattering not only the wooden gates, but the entire gatehouse. Screams echoed through the cold air as men were consumed in the flames or crushed under falling stones.

Imari and most of the men around her were knocked off their feet by the blast. Stones and rubble pelted the group, and Imari was glad for the armor she had been given. Many men around her were crushed by the debris, but by sheer luck, Imari remained unharmed, save for bruises from the smaller stones that had pelted her. Arnulf swiftly rose to his feet, and Imari waited for him to kill her. Instead, it seemed that he had forgotten about her. She wasted no time and ran for her life. On and on her feet took her, and luck was on her side, for both sides of the battle were locked on the events at the gate, and paid her no heed. After several agonizing minutes, Imari finally realized that she had escaped!

Radnor grunted in pain as he was knocked backwards from the force of the explosion. Debris flew everywhere as pieces of rock and stone were flung in all directions. More screams echoed in the air as shrapnel from the blast struck and killed many of the city's defenders. Radnor rolled and barely dodged a heavy stone as it nearly crushed him. The demigod then hastily stood and checked himself for injuries. Once Radnor found that he was unharmed, he looked for Halfdan, and found that thankfully, his friend also bore no wounds. Radnor unsheathed his sword and sprinted for the destroyed gate. Halfdan, Aelfric, and his soldiers did the same and quickly caught up with Aethelstan's men as they poured forth to aid the wounded.

As Radnor ran, he saw Ashveldt running atop the wall towards where the gatehouse had once stood. Men from Aethelstan's forces frantically clambered over the fallen debris as they sought to dig their friends and compatriots out of the rubble. The dust had not yet settled, and the ground around Radnor burned in a hellscape he had not seen since the Krigari and their demons had destroyed his homeland. He vowed then and there that he would not allow such a fate to befall Wulfgeld. Radnor turned to Aelfric.

"Focus on recovering the wounded. I will keep them off you!"

Radnor did not wait for a response before he and Halfdan plunged into the fire and smoke. As they stepped through, they saw the line of Drakomar's forces rushing for their position. When Arnulf and the knights of the Pale Light saw Radnor and his ghastly sword, their charge ground to a halt. Suddenly, a voice called to Radnor from beside him. Distracted, he turned to see Sigaberht laying in the rubble. His leg was crushed under a heavy stone, pinning him to the ground. He was covered in blood from head to toe. Radnor could not even begin to guess at how much of it was his own.

"Veigarand, avenge me!" he cried.

Radnor turned back the way he came and shouted for help.

"Earl Sigaberht lives! Come to me! Come to your earl!"

As a counter to Radnor's cry, Arnulf shouted from the enemy formation.

"It is him! Kill him while he stands alone! Vengeance shall be ours!"

With that, the enemy charged for Radnor. The once tightly grouped formation broke apart in their rush to climb over the rubble, which gave Radnor a chance to force the engagements into one on one fights. His evil blade flashed against the dying sunlight, and the first man that reached Radnor died before he could even attempt to strike at him. Another man rushed forward and swung a blow with his spear at Radnor. The steel titan turned the attack aside with his sword and shattered his enemy's weapon in the process. Radnor then drove the sharpened edge of his shield into his foe's neck. Blood erupted from the wound as the soldier collapsed among the rubble. Radnor turned to see Halfdan locked in combat against one of the enemy men-at-arms. The giant man fought ferociously, and it was not long before his strength overpowered the smaller man, and Halfdan's ax bit deeply into his neck.

Another knight rushed for Radnor, hoping to cut him down. Radnor expertly ducked the blow and lashed out with his sword with an attack that effortlessly cut the knight's leg from his body. However, that was not what killed him. Terrible, black thorns burst from within the knight's body and devoured him where he fell. After a moment, the thorns themselves dissolved into ash.

To his surprise, Radnor found yet another man racing to challenge him. The man rushed forward with an ax in each hand. Evidently, he had cast his shield aside in the hopes that with two weapons, one might find its mark. His hopes proved futile, as Radnor had often practiced against men armed with two weapons in his training. The demigod stepped to one side as the soldier advanced on him, keeping one of his opponent's weapons in the way of the other. Radnor then threw a blow straight into the man's lead ax. The soldier reflexively blocked it, a mistake punished by an agonizing death. Radnor's sword cut through the haft of the ax like it was made from parchment and cut directly into him. As Radnor's sword slammed into his face, all of the bones in the man's body burst forth and skewered one of his fellow knights in the process.

Radnor turned to meet his next foe, but found that the enemy had ceased attacking him. At first, he didn't not know why; but when he looked back to the enemy formation, he saw that archers now arrayed themselves against him. While he had been distracted with killing their comrades, the enemy bowmen had lined up their shots, and were almost prepared to fire. They had him out in the open, and with that many arrows aimed for him, he knew he would die. Angered at his predicament, Radnor shouted at his foes.

"I am Veigarand, Ghost of the North! Do you think you can kill me?"

The enemy hesitated with fear. Even in their advantageous position, their fear of him clouded their judgment. Radnor shouted again.

"You cannot kill me! I am the Ashen Ghost! The Wayfaring Death! I will dance upon your bones and grind them to dust!"

Terror clutched at the warriors arrayed before him. Even Arnulf was overawed by Radnor's ferocity, though for him, it did not last long.

"He is the servant of Lashmatu!" he yelled, hoping to tap into his soldier's religious beliefs to get them back into the fight. "Kill him! Loose your arrows!"

Radnor ducked behind his shield and prepared to defend against the onslaught of arrows that would soon strike him. But just as Drakomar's archers were about to loose death upon Radnor, Ashveldt suddenly yelled from atop the wall, and a torrent of Wulfgeld's arrows slammed into the enemy formation. Enemy soldiers were cut down like wheat against the defender's counterattack. The Pale Light's bowmen returned fire, forcing Wulfgeld's men back, but it was too late to change their fate. Radnor took his opportunity and sheathed his sword. He waved for Halfdan, and the two men returned to the earl.

"What are you doing?" Sigaberht demanded.

"Saving your life!" Radnor yelled.

After a moment's effort, Radnor lifted the stone from Sigaberht's leg. The demigod was just about to try to pick Sigaberht up when a shout from Ashveldt distracted both of them. Radnor looked up in time to see arrows fly into the men around him. Several arrows struck Ashveldt, but thankfully were caught in his mail shirt. The angry prince shouted a vicious battle cry and leapt from the wall. He crashed down upon his foes and sprung to his feet before any of them could react. Overtaken by rage, Ashveldt left a trail of bodies as he hacked and slashed his way through his enemies.

"Go! Save my son!" Sigaberht yelled.

Halfdan then picked up Sigaberht and began to carry him to safety as Radnor turned to rescue Ashveldt.

Radnor ran into the crowd after the reckless prince. Ashveldt had killed several of his foes, but the enemy now had him surrounded and it would not be long until they killed him. Radnor hurled himself into the fray as he cut his way to Ashveldt. More shouts came from behind Radnor, and he found that Leif, Aelfric and even more men from Wulfgeld had joined him. Radnor turned back to the foes ahead of him. He could see Ashveldt, and the sight was grim. The prince was totally surrounded by attacking foes. He spun wildly, lashing out like a frenzied animal as he fought. Blow after blow rained down on him, but they did little to slow him down as they slammed into his armor. Ashveldt paused his wild swinging for a moment, and in that moment a spear pierced his mail and skewered his shield shoulder. However, if Ashveldt felt any pain, he did not show it as he hurled his ax into his enemy's face. The blade struck true, and his foe fell backwards as his face was split open by the force of Ashveldt's throw. With a mighty roar, Ashveldt then tore the spear from his shoulder and began wielding it against his foes.

Finally, the group reached Ashveldt, and Leif had to drag him back behind their lines as Radnor danced death among their foes. However, all was not well. Even as Radnor slaughtered the knights arrayed before him, the enemy cavalry formation he had seen earlier was now headed his way. If the defenders stood their ground, they would all be slaughtered.

"Leif! We need to fall back!" Radnor yelled.

Leif agreed and quickly gave the order to retreat. Radnor had to pull Ashveldt by the arm to get him to join them. A moment later, Ashveldt came to his senses and echoed Leif's order to retreat.

As they all fell back, Sergeant Aelfric and his men formed a shield wall in an attempt to bar access to the enemy force. The warriors locked their shields in place and brought their spears to bear as their formation marched to face the enemy cavalry. Radnor stopped to help them, but Aelfric shouted him down.

"Radnor, do not stop! Get the prince to safety!"

Radnor nodded and continued to drag Ashveldt away from the battle. Daegal stopped and started to array his own forces to help Aelfric's troops, but Aelfric waved him off as well.

"My lord, our sworn duty is to protect the earl and his son."

"As is yours! What do you think you're doing?" Daegal demanded

Aelfric turned and faced the charging cavalry.

"Giving you the chance to fulfill your oath. No go! The rubble will break up their charge! We will hold them off as long as we can!"

Daegal reluctantly turned and led his men up the hill. Aethelstan and his men were not far behind.

It was but moments later that the enemy charge cascaded through the fallen debris. Aelfric and his men valiantly stood their ground as they fought to protect their home.

"Death!" cried the knights of the Pale Light.

The charging cavalry slammed into the shield wall. Horses were skewered and men were trampled. Blood flowed freely through the streets of Wulfgeld as the defender's formation was broken.

"Skirmish formations, now!" Aelfric yelled.

Aelfric's command echoed over the din of the battle, and the soldiers of Wulfgeld quickly reformed into smaller fighting units. While most of the enemy knights had driven straight through the shield wall, many of them had stopped to slaughter what they thought was a broken enemy. Instead, Aelfric's forces swiftly overwhelmed them man by man. The fighting was fierce and bloody, as each knight took two or three of his foes with him before he was dragged from his horse and butchered.

The main block of mounted knights saw the troubles of their fellows and returned to wreak bloody vengeance upon Wulfgeld's defenders. Without a sturdy shield wall to protect them, the men of Wulfgeld were helpless against the second charge. Horses crushed man after man, and the knights of the Pale Light slaughtered with reckless abandon. Aelfric dodged and rolled away from a charging horseman and drove his spear into a second. The enemy knight was flung from his horse, and Aelfric was thrown backward by the sudden jolt. The sergeant leaped to his feet and to his satisfaction, found that his spear had driven straight through the knight's armor, and the man lay skewered upon the ground. Aelfric laughed mercilessly as he drew his sword and swung wildly at the rampaging knights. They swarmed around him, though none dared face him directly. Finally, one valiant knight rode from behind Aelfric and struck the sergeant's head from his shoulders. It was the best death the sergeant could have asked for.

Radnor, Ashveldt and the ealdormen fled towards the keep. The enemy knights had not yet reached them, and it seemed to Radnor that Aelfric's delaying action had been successful. As the group reached the entrance to the keep, Radnor looked back down the path to check on the enemy's progress. There was no sign of Aelfric and his men, for they had fought to the last man. Now, the over eager knights of the Pale Light were already taking their share of plunder as they burned and slaughtered their way through the city's lower districts. They tormented the city's inhabitants with wild ferocity reserved only for the vilest of heretics.

Radnor averted his gaze, for after his home had been destroyed, he had hoped to never bear witness to such horror again. While the enemy cavalry was distracted with plunder, Leif spotted a company of heavy infantry marching their way to the keep. These men bore the coat of arms of Drakomar, and were led by Sir Arnulf. Leif turned to Ashveldt.

"Your highness, we need to get you inside the keep. That is the only way we can be sure of your safety."

Ashveldt shook his head.

"Leif, you know I cannot do that. Our people are in need. We must save them!"

Aethelstan took Ashveldt by the shoulder.

"Your highness, look upon the foe that comes to us. Your father would have us all executed if he found out we let you face this foe without him."

Just then, Halfdan emerged from within the keep. He was covered in blood and bore a dire expression upon his face. Ashveldt turned to face him.

"How is my father?"

"He is with his physicians now. Of his condition, I cannot tell."

Ashveldt nodded, and then turned back to Aethelstan and Leif.

"You would both have me follow what you *believe* to be my father's wishes, but you do not understand him as I do. I am the heir to his throne, and in my father's absence, *I* act as earl."

Ashveldt defiantly turned to face Drakomar's advancing infantry.

"Never before have the enemy come so close to destroying us… but today they shall flee before the might of Wulfgeld!"

Not waiting for anyone to join him, the prince drew his sword and rushed to meet his foes. Radnor and Halfdan were quick to follow, and within moments, all of Wulfgeld's defenders stood beside their prince.

As the two formations closed, Ashveldt shouted a great battle cry and the host of Wulfgeld charged into their enemies. Man clashed against man as sword and shield smashed against armor and parted flesh. Radnor stood beside Ashveldt, his sword dealing death wherever he struck. The prince fought with the ferocity of a wild man, and his foes soon feared the wrath of Sigaberht's heir. Ashveldt's huscarls stood beside him and fought as an immovable object against Drakomar's assault. The ealdormen and their warriors attacked Drakomar's flanks, and Arnulf's force began to wither.

Then, archers of Drakomar joined the fray, and their skewering arrows overwhelmed the battling men of Wulfgeld. The flanking men were forced to retreat behind their own lines, and Arnulf's force was able to regroup. As the battle wore on, knights of the Pale Light joined the fray. Radnor hurled himself upon them in an effort to drive them back though their fear of his sword; but the promises of their goddess overpowered their fear of the cursed blade. The warriors of the Pale Light descended upon him, and it was only through Leif's and Halfdan's intervention that Radnor made it back behind the shield wall alive.

As the battle continued, Ashveldt and his loyal fighters became outnumbered nearly two to one. Drakomar's forces drove them backwards… back towards the keep. The enemy charged into Wulfgeld's protectors and broke their defensive line. Many were knocked to the ground and slaughtered before they could regain their feet, while others were separated from their fellows and forced to fight against their foes two or three at a time. Ashveldt and his huscarls fought ferociously, and the prince's loyal men died around him to protect their beloved lord. The ealdormen and their men tried to regroup, but the Pale Light were too aggressive, and the ealdormen all found themselves fighting for their very lives. Halfdan fought back to back with Daegal as they battled to stave off the onrushing torrent of foes.

Radnor stood alone and killed men in droves. The enemy came for him three or four at a time, but his sword cleft through man and armor with such ease he could kill multiple opponents with a single blow. A spear glanced off his helmet, and an ax bit into the mail on his shoulder as more soldiers attacked him. His armor held, and Radnor soon punished those who dared strike him. More and more men descended upon him, mad with fanatical devotion to the will of their goddess. The warriors of the Pale Light saw in Radnor not a man to be feared, but an apostate to be destroyed.

Exhaustion was taking its toll, and Radnor found himself more and more on the defensive as the enemy pressed in on him. Ashveldt saw Radnor's plight and led a spectacular charge that drove a wedge in the enemy formation, forcing them to turn and face him. The prince leapt among his foes with naught but a stolen spear. He unleashed a torrent of unholy brutality upon his enemies, and for the first time since the battle started, the warriors of Drakomar were driven back.

The enemy retreated and reformed their shield wall, which gave Radnor a chance to catch his breath and survey the battlefield. To his horror, the enemy cavalry had ceased their rampage, and were now headed towards their position. Radnor looked to Ashveldt and shouted at him.

"We must retreat!" he cried.

Just then, knights of the Pale Light charged again and blasted their way through Wulfgeld's reformed shield wall. Radnor killed the first man who struck him, but two more smashed into him and he was dashed to the ground. He tried to regain his feet, but one knight leapt on top of him! Radnor barely raised his shield to defend himself as the knight rained blow after blow upon him. Rage overtook Radnor, and with his immense strength, he hurled the knight off him and leapt back to his feet. As he stood, he saw that he was surrounded by the enemy, and death drew ever closer. However, before any of the

enemy knights could attack him, a strange sight caught
Radnor's eye.

A lone rider rushed towards the enemy, and Radnor
recognized her. Elena rode Darestr as she charged into battle
against the enemy that threatened her home.

"Elena! Stop!" Radnor yelled.

Elena heard him, but did not heed him. Lashmatu's
words of warning had come true; and if she did not do this,
Radnor would die. As Elena rode forth, she held aloft one of
the menacing gaulderens, and it glowed so brightly that even
the charging knights of the Pale Light focused their attention
upon it. They saw the dark haired woman who bore the object
of power, and knew their foe.

"The Foul-Temptress!" they cried.

The rampaging knights headed for Elena. Their purpose
was certain, and they would crush all who opposed them.

Once Elena was certain the charging cavalry had
targeted her, she spoke the words whispered to her by
Lashmatu and hurled one of the gaulderens for them. Her task
done, Elena turned Darestr around as fast as she could. Darestr
understood the situation and sprinted back for the keep as fast
as he could. The glowing gaulderen landed upon the ground,
and the enemy riders paid it no heed as they pursued their most
hated enemy.

As soon as the formation of charging knights was
centered over the gaulderen, it did as Elena had commanded it.
Fire sprang forth from the small stone, and a wave of fire and
earth swept across the ground. The earth beneath the knights
was torn asunder, and men panicked and screamed as the world
shook from the power unleashed. Fire and brimstone sprung up
from beneath them, and a tidal wave of death crashed upon the
war-torn streets. In a single instant, every mounted knight died
in an explosion that rivaled that which only the creators could
produce. Debris rained from the heavens, and more men were
crushed and burned by the destructive power unleashed there.
Entire streets were leveled as buildings tumbled and fell. Fires
engulfed street after street, burning the invaders whom had
ravaged city.

The defenders of Wulfgeld were blasted from their feet, and only Radnor was able to pick himself back up to observe the destruction. However, he cared not for the deaths of his enemies. All he desired was to see Elena safe and sound, and after a moment of searching, he did. Back she came, riding his own loyal horse. Elena wasted little time in returning to him, and once she arrived, the two shared a passionate embrace.

Arnulf was silent with shock. He and his men had also been sent tumbling down, and none yet dared rise upon witnessing the destructive power that had been unleashed. Never in Arnulf's wildest dreams had he imagined the devastating power displayed before his eyes.

"Retreat!" he cried.

Many of his men did not have time to respond to his order as they were cut down by the wrath of Wulfgeld. Ashveldt led the charge, flinging himself into the fray against his foes as they died around him. The men of the Pale Light scrambled and fought nearly till the last man. The men native to Drakomar gathered around Arnulf, unsure of what to do. Ashveldt's battle lust would not be needed for long, as Arnulf and the final remnants of his men signaled their surrender.

Ashveldt stopped and watched as Arnulf threw his sword down before him. The prince ceased his relentless assault. Flanked by Leif, Aethelstan, Radnor, and Elena, Sigaberht's heir looked over the surrendering force before him. Arnulf spoke first.

"I am Sir Arnulf. I command these men who faced you on the field today. Please, we surrender. We offer ourselves as prisoners to be ransomed back to our comrades."

Ashveldt nodded, and then turned to Aethelstan.

"Seize their weapons and lock them up."

Aethelstan bowed before his lord and set about carrying out Ashveldt's orders.

Radnor watched as the ealdorman led the handful of survivors into the city. Then, Leif suddenly clapped him on the shoulder.

"For a moment, I believed it was like the time Godric died," Leif said.

"For Sigaberht… it might still be," Radnor replied.

"I know we've had our differences, but if ever there was a day… I'm glad you're by our side."

"I've saved your life how many times? And yet this is what it takes for you to see me as a fellow man?"

Leif frowned, becoming defensive at Radnor's accusation.

"I value other lives more than my own. After you caused the destruction of Neugeld, this is what it took."

"And my help against the wolves didn't count?" Radnor countered.

Leif stuttered, unsure of how to reply. He was surprised at his own feelings. Radnor was right… the demigod had long earned his redemption. What made today any different? Unwilling to argue further, Leif departed to help organize the recovery of the dead and the wounded.

Radnor turned back to Elena, who ran to his embrace.

"Radnor!" she cried.

Radnor threw his shield to the ground and accepted her affection. Tears streamed down both their faces as the pair held each other. After a long time, Elena finally stepped back. Radnor looked at her, and saw that she was now covered in blood that came off his armor. Elena noticed his gaze, looked down at herself, and then looked back at him.

"I don't care," she said.

She stepped forward and hugged him again. Radnor tore his helmet off and dumped it in the dirt below. The lovers clutched each other upon the dead strewn battlefield, their thoughts fearful of the future as the world around them burned.

Imari's eyes gazed upon Elena's aura. The witch had made a clean getaway in the chaos of the battle, and had observed the battle's outcome from a distance. Fear coursed through her heart as she gazed not only upon the destruction Elena had brought down, but upon her aura. Now that Elena was out in the open, Imari could see the immense power that coursed through Elena's very soul, and it terrified her. How had one person come to wield such strength? How long had she been here? Who was this woman? Such questions burned through Imari's mind as she considered her options. A part of her wanted to flee this place forever. Another part of her wanted to find Dragorim first. But… Imari knew that whatever was going on here was too important for her to merely run away. She *had* to stay and learn what she could about Elena.

Imari scoffed at herself. Such heroic thoughts were for those far more powerful than her. This was a task for a sorcerer like Dragorim. Imari sighed and stood. Then, much to Imari's relief, she spotted his aura on top of a hill, clear on the opposite side of the battlefield from her. It was quite clear to her that he was the one responsible for the destruction of the gate, and she hoped that one day, she could thank him.

Her eyes fell to the gates of the city. If the woman with the aura was inside, it meant that one way or another, Imari needed to gain entry. It was obvious that she couldn't just walk in through the front gate, as she knew that there would be far too many guards there for her to avoid. She couldn't go back and rejoin Drakomar's troops. She may have held up her end of the bargain in a way, but she doubted that would stop them from blaming her for the failure of their attack. Legier had already proven to be a judgmental and violent man. It seemed to Imari that rejoining with Dragorim was her best option for survival. He was the one man in these forsaken lands that she felt safe with. With that thought in mind, Imari picked herself up, and began looking for a clear path where she could get to the sorcerer without being seen.

Ashrahan looked upon the blackened battlefield, and despite the pleasure he took from the aesthetics of destruction, the god was unsatisfied.

"What an enjoyable drama… I must admit, you set the stage well… but it proves nothing, save that your talent for manipulation is still unmatched."

Lashmatu rolled her eyes at the backhanded compliment.

"How does that prove nothing? I set an overwhelming force against her, and you saw what she did!"

Ashrahan shook his head.

"Your deception was masterful. I especially enjoyed your performance in front of Celestata's flock. But, Veigarand's woman only used the gaulderen with knowledge *you* provided her… knowledge that any witch could have used to similar effect."

"Mortal witches require practice," Lashmatu said. "Elena got it right on the *first* try. Do you not comprehend what that means?"

"Luck," Ashrahan said. "If you think it was more than that, I need more proof. I need proof that she is *unique*."

"You should know, old friend, that there is no luck, only Hymurr's riddles," Lashmatu replied.

Ashrahan smiled. He thought of what he had seen at the edges of the dark pit to chaos, and spoke once more.

"You may be right, but I need more. We need to bring her to the dark forest. Only there will her powers be truly tested."

"You do it," Lashmatu said.

Ashrahan glared, tired of Lashmatu's defiance, then spoke.

"You are the only one who can see through the veil of chaos there. You are the only one who can do it, and you must do it now."

With that, the black-eyed god disappeared from the conversation. Frustrated, Lashmatu gazed back to the corpse strewn battlefield while she planned her next move; and a dark presence watched with glee, for its prey had taken the bait.

Part 3
The Blighted World

Chapter 21

Darkness descended upon Wulfgeld, and all those who guarded the remains of the sundered gate stood at the watch with apprehension and dread. Wulfgeld's defenders were extremely wary of infiltrators that might be sent by their mortal foes, but that was not all they feared. Men worked tirelessly to put out the fires that had spread through the city and rescue the survivors from collapsed buildings. Furtive glances to the southern woods revealed the inhabitant's ever growing fear of those horrors which stirred among the trees. Very few slept, and those that did, slept fitfully as nightmares of unknowable, maddening terrors awakened men screaming in the night.

At first, Radnor and Elena had tried to return to their home… but it had been destroyed in the fires summoned by Elena's spell. When he saw the burned wreckage, Radnor silently turned and led Elena back to the keep. Now in Radnor's room, Elena could only stand and watch as Radnor desperately tried to wash the blood from his face. She stood close beside him, ready to hand her lover a towel as soon as he was done. Radnor had barely spoken a word since they had returned to the keep, and Elena understood why. All his life, Radnor had dreamed of having a home once more. Despite his anger at Sigaberht, Wulfgeld had started to become his new home… and now it, too, was being torn asunder as he watched helplessly.

Radnor was also worried about Elena, for she too had been oddly silent on their walk back to the cottage. Even now, she seemed lost in her own world.

Finally, Radnor reached out his hand to take the towel from her. After drying his face and hands, the warrior turned to Elena.

"Our plan failed. Sigaberht *will* try to draw the enemy into the forest."

"That's what you're worried about?" Elena asked.

"Aren't you? We know that only death awaits us in that fucking place. We need to go there to cleanse it, not use it as a weapon. We may make Damiros stronger if we go there."

"How?" Elena asked as she took the towel back from him.

"Chaos… it repurposes the dead. Think of how many fresh corpses we will be delivering for its use."

"Not if I destroy them first," Elena grimly replied.

"Do you *know* you can succeed?" he asked.

Elena shrugged.

"No more than you know you can defeat the army sitting outside the walls, ready to rape and pillage their way through this city. Radnor, you speak as though Drakomar's people are somehow better than the monsters in the forest. Monsters or men… either way we're still dead if we lose." Radnor started to object, but paused. He wanted to argue with her, but he could see that Elena wasn't finished, so he let her continue. "If Sigaberht chooses to go into the forest, then he is right to do so. We've tried everything and nothing worked!"

"But—"

"There is no '*but*'! We have two enemies. One is a horde of monsters outside our walls that will destroy us at the first opportunity, and I can't stop them! The other… is a horde of monsters I might be able to do something about. At this point… if I can use one to destroy the other, I'll do it gladly. I don't care about the risk to myself."

"But *I* do," Radnor replied.

Elena scoffed. She was angry and frustrated at their situation, and in the moment, took Radnor's statement to imply something about her feelings towards him.

"Do you think I don't care about *your* safety? About the risks you take? Why do you think I… I did what I did today? To take in the sights?"

"I never said you didn't care…" Radnor started. He trailed off. He understood her then. Rather than continue arguing with her, he changed the subject.

"What you did today, you saved my life," Radnor said. Elena nodded silently. Her eyes watered, and Radnor could see how upset she was. "I can see there's something else bothering you," he prompted.

Elena sat down in a chair and would not look at him. Tears formed in her eyes, as the emotion she had been denying came pouring through.

Panicked, Radnor came to her and took her by the shoulders.

"Are you alright?"

She looked up at him with tears in her eyes.

"I… I killed all those people. Not just the enemy… others… innocent people. My spell… *I* killed them! I just… did what I was told… and… I used the gaulderen."

Radnor's blood ran cold. He had at first been focused on her grief for having killed so many… but her last statement brought all focus to an even greater problem.

"Wait, 'did what you were told'?"

"That's not the right way… I followed the instructions I was given."

"Whose instructions?"

Elena stopped talking. She needed a moment to collect herself before answering any more of Radnor's questions. Radnor saw what she needed and took a step back to give her space. Once Elena had collected herself enough to speak again, she told him her story. She described how Lashmatu had come to their door as a normal woman, and after her true identity was revealed, had shown Elena how to use the gaulderen. As Elena spoke, Radnor grew angrier and angrier, until he could take no more. He leapt to his feet and shouted across the room.

"Ashrahan! Lashmatu! Are you here now, watching this? If you are, I can assure you that this will not be the last you've heard of this from me!" Radnor drew his sword and brandished it threateningly in the empty air. He did not know if either of the Krigari was watching, but he was too angry to care. "Know this, that if you *ever* come near her again… all of creation will run red with your blood. Hear me, and know that I speak true!"

Elena took him by the shoulder and gently pulled him back to her.

"It's alright… Lashmatu may have frightened me at first, but she gave me what I needed to save you."

Radnor sheathed his sword.

"Lashmatu is Krigari… nothing she does will be to our benefit… only hers. She and Ashrahan… they're playing a game."

Elena nodded; her eyes still focused elsewhere. Radnor knew what the look on her face meant, and spoke to reassure her.

"The knights that died on that battlefield… you said it yourself… they were monsters coming to rape and pillage. They were going to kill us,"

"I know," Elena said through teary eyes. "I'm just… I've fought some, you know that… but I've never done anything like that before. At the wave of a hand… I killed hundreds; and not just the enemy. I killed people I was supposed to be protect."

"Don't think that way. You used the weapon at your disposal to defend those you love."

Elena nodded.

"I understand that… but I wasn't raised for this… killing… and it's different for me than for you. When you fight, you have to hit them with a sword and slay your enemy one at a time. I have the power to kill untold numbers of people in an instant… and that frightens me."

"Are you afraid you'll misuse it?" Radnor asked.

"I'm trying to decide if I already have."

Elena stopped, again too upset for words.

Radnor stroked her face and gently lifted her gaze to meet his.

"I know your heart… and you aren't capable of any such thing."

"I'd like to believe that… but…"

"There is no 'but'. There is only you, and I say again… you cannot commit any of the crimes you may fear you're capable of."

Elena finally looked Radnor in the eyes and smiled.

"Thank you."

Radnor nodded, and then took Elena deeper into his arms.

"Can I tell you something? I'm scared too… of the things we must face… not just the mortal men outside the walls, but of the gods and monsters that seek to end everything. I just… I just want to know that we'll win… that you and I will come out of this together."

Elena looked up at him and smiled reassuringly.

"Of course we will… I'll have you with me."

* * *

Darkness dominated the dungeon chamber; and the only sound within the dingy space was the fervent prayers of the surviving warriors of the Pale Light. Arnulf was glad. He found the soft sounds oddly soothing, and after what he had just seen, he was grateful for a dark and quiet place to simply sit and think.

The events of the last few hours were a blur that he was still trying to process as he sat alone in his stone cell. He did not fully understand what had happened, other than that somehow, he had fallen from the pinnacle of victory into the abyss of defeat.

He hadn't believed his eyes when the gate had been destroyed. At first, it seemed that perhaps Legier and Venatus were right, and that Celestata had indeed blessed them with holy victory. But then, something had happened. He ran through the events again as he tried to understand. A woman had rode upon them and had brought death with her. At the time, Arnulf hadn't given her presence much mind. He had been in the middle of leading his men against Veigarand when the woman came riding out. How could he have known that she would be even more destructive than *Veigarand?*

He knew what the Pale Light would say. They would say that it was Lashmatu herself that had destroyed their forces. However, Arnulf still had his doubts. If Lashmatu had indeed attacked them directly, why did Celestata not intervene? It didn't make sense to him. No, it was still far more likely that one of the Hexverat still lived and now fought for Sigaberht.

Arnulf's thoughts then turned to his own men. The regular soldiers of Drakomar that had surrendered with him had been worryingly silent since they had arrived, and Arnulf hoped that was all it was… stunned silence from soldiers shocked by their defeat. There had been significant comings and goings as the prisoners had been disarmed and stuffed into cells, so Arnulf was not sure how many cells formerly occupied by his men now stood empty. His worry about the safety of his men grew more and more oppressive, until despair took him, and he finally did something very much unlike him.

"Celestata!" he cried. "Please, if you see it as good, grant me the means to die an honorable death!"

Just then, footsteps rang out through the dark hallway, and torchlight illuminated the stone walls. Arnulf looked up from his spot on the floor and hoped that his prayer would soon be answered. The door to his cell swung open, and several men stepped through. Arnulf recognized only one of them: Ashveldt, the Prince of Wulfgeld. The others were Leif, Daegal, and Aethelstan, though Arnulf did not know them, nor did he care to. The knight of Drakomar did not wait to be addressed before he spoke to the prince.

"Your highness, I trust that my men are being treated with civility?"

Ashveldt nodded.

"Your concern for your men is admirable, though it is not your business anymore. However, as an act of mercy, I will tell you that your men are being treated as dictated by our traditional rules of war. No further harm shall come to them as long as they do not rebel against us. You have my word."

Arnulf nodded.

"Why do you come to me now? To gloat?"

Ashveldt shook his head grimly.

"I have no time for gloating. Perhaps we can come to an arrangement. Your life… and the lives of your men in exchange for your people's departure from my lands."

Arnulf laughed.

"I'm not sure they're really *my* people anymore. The Pale Light has swayed many… and they will lead them until death takes all."

"What does that mean?" Ashveldt asked.

"They fight for Celestata, and they claim she personally appeared and ordered them to take the city. This is no longer just a war for land or plunder, but a holy crusade, and the Pale Light will not stop until they have cleansed the souls of everyone here."

Leif stepped forward.

"You say that 'they' claim she appeared. Did *you* see this visitation?" he asked.

"No, but what *I* did not see does not matter. Others claim they saw her, and the grand marshal says he saw her too."

"The grand marshal… Legier isn't it?" Leif asked.

"Yes… and whatever he used to be… he is not anymore. He has joined the Pale Light in their madness."

The ealdorman's brow furrowed at this news while Daegal interjected.

"So what you're saying is that we should just kill you now and save ourselves trouble and food?" Daegal said.

Arnulf laughed. While he hadn't taken a holy oath the way Legier had, the shame of defeat tasted bitter indeed, and in the moment, death seemed like a welcome escape. But that was the coward's way out, and Arnulf was no coward.

"Nothing will stop them. They believe you have embraced Lashmatu, the Foul-Temptress. Even now, I can tell you that they believe it was she who destroyed them on the battlefield today. Those that remain will seek revenge."

Aethelstan laughed.

"Your beliefs mean nothing to us! You would seek to destroy us regardless of what we have done!"

Arnulf shook his head.

"You have faced them in battle, but have you talked to them? I have. Other armies would retreat after what happened today… *they* will not. If you wish to win this war, you will need to kill every last one of them."

"You speak as though you want us to," Leif commented.

Arnulf looked to the older ealdorman.

"They commit atrocities that are beneath the honor of a knight such as I. I had almost convinced Legier to retreat… but their poisonous rhetoric meant that my words went unheeded."

"So, our attacks would have worked, were it not for the Pale Light?" Daegal asked.

"I believe so."

Everyone waited as Ashveldt stood in thought. Finally, he broke the silence.

"It seems we have gotten all that we can from you. Thank you for speaking with me," Ashveldt said.

As he and the ealdormen turned to leave, Arnulf looked to Daegal and spoke.

"You spoke of killing me…"

Ashveldt interjected before Daegal could say anything else uncouth towards the prisoner.

"As I said, you are being treated by the rules of war. Do not rebel and you will not be harmed."

"Thank you, dear prince. I saw that your father was gravely injured when the wall fell… and I know what that could mean for you. If what I saw you do on the battlefield, and our conversation today is any measure… you will make a great earl."

Ashveldt made no reply, and instead left Arnulf in silence within his prison.

* * *

Dragorim sat perfectly still atop the tall hill. Despite the hours that had passed since the battle, he had not moved from his spot. Instead, he worriedly pondered the nature of what he had witnessed. Possibilities raced through his mind as he sat. At first he thought the mysterious woman might have been one of the Hexverat, but it seemed unlikely to him that any of the Hexverat still lived. Additionally, while most of the power the woman had unleashed had been contained within the gaulderen, some of her own energy had been used as a catalyst to unleash it's power. Dragorim recognized the power she wielded; it was the same power he had come here to find. Was this woman the one that destroyed the Hexverat?

Lost in thought, Dragorim's gaze turned southward towards the haunted forest. His heart chilled as he saw how the eerie, impossible light reflected off the low hanging clouds. If this woman had been the one to stop the Hexverat from using chaos, why had she done nothing about the growing malevolence that dwelt in the woods?

A twig snapped behind him and broke the sorcerer's concentration; but when he spun to face the source, he saw nothing. Angry at himself for allowing someone to get this close without him noticing and paranoid about another attack from enemy soldiers, Dragorim rose to his feet and slowly drew his sword. Just then, a familiar voice called out to him.

"Dragorim, it's me!"

Imari stepped out from the shadows and smiled at him.

Beaming, Dragorim sheathed his sword and stepped towards her.

"Am I glad to see you safe!" he exclaimed.

Imari stepped forward and embraced her newfound friend.

The two separated after a moment and then faced the walls.

"How did you escape?" Dragorim asked.

"Not without a little help from you. I assume you're the one responsible for destroying the gate?" she said.

Dragorim nodded.

"Unfortunately, that's all I can take credit for."

Imari nodded as she understood Dragorim's implication.

"A part of me had hoped you could take credit for the charging knights too, but it seems we saw the same thing."

"Yes, it seems we have indeed reached our goal; only to find more questions without answers."

Imari shrugged in response. The search for knowledge excited her, though she wished it was under better circumstances.

"We both knew it could be like this. Answers come only to those who dig for them,"

"That's a nice saying. Who taught you that one?" Dragorim asked.

Imari smiled.

"I did. If there's one thing I've learned as a witch, it's that."

Dragorim patted her on the shoulder, and the affectionate gesture surprised even him. He quickly shook it off and continued the conversation.

"Fair enough, and you are quite right, we are again… blocked from our goal."

"The gate has been breached and darkness has fallen. Can we not simply walk through now?"

Dragorim snorted.

"Do you think that hole won't still be guarded? There will be many men defending it, and anyone trying to enter will probably be killed on sight."

"We could tell them we're here to help," Imari suggested.

"Would *you* believe us? If we're going to get inside, we need to at least wait until daylight."

"I don't know if I can wait that long," Imari said. "I'm so hungry… I'm not sure I'll be able to keep going much longer. You wouldn't happen to have any more apples, would you?" she asked.

Dragorim shook his head. Now that Imari mentioned it, he realized how ravenously hungry he was as well.

"I guess we need to find food. The question is, where?"

Suddenly, a new voice joined them.

"I think I can help you with that,"

This time, when Dragorim turned he found a sandy-haired boy of perhaps twelve or thirteen, standing in the snow. The strange boy held aloft a handful berries that he now offered to the pair of mages. Imari stepped forward and gently took one of them.

"What's your name?" she asked.

"Rolf."

Dragorim looked the boy over, unsure of his trustworthiness.

"Those berries… where did you find them?"

"They're one of the few things that grows here during the winter. They're perfectly safe to eat."

"Why should we believe you?" Dragorim asked.

"You think I might poison you? I saw the bodies you left behind. I don't want to poison people on the same side as me."

Dragorim looked into Rolf's eyes, and something in them told the sorcerer that the boy was not lying. Relieved, Dragorim smiled.

"You're from Wulfgeld then?" he said as he and Imari both took and ate some of the berries. They were sweet and juicy. The sorcerer couldn't help but think of other foods that the berries would complement in a full meal.

"Yes, I'm one of the scouts," Rolf said.

"These berries are excellent!" Imari exclaimed. "What do you call them?"

"Well… uh… winterberries."

The two mages both chuckled at that. Then, Dragorim continued his questioning.

"Is that what you're doing out here? Scouting?"

Rolf shook his head.

"I was captured in the first battle, but got free when the ghouls attacked Drakomar's camp."

"Why didn't you go back to the city?" Dragorim questioned.

"Same reason you're not headed there now… it was dark, and the guards are jumpy."

"They'd even kill one of their own?" Imari asked.

"Not on purpose, but the archers would probably shoot before they knew who I was."

"Fair enough, but why didn't you get inside during the daytime?" Dragorim said.

"I was looking for you," Rolf replied.

"And why would you do that?"

"I found your camp and the bodies you left behind. I followed your trail all day. It was slow. There were a lot of guys out looking for you, so I had to hide a lot. Then, the battle started and I was afraid to move until it was all over."

"Did you see what happened?" Imari asked.

Rolf nodded.

"Have you seen anything like that before?" Dragorim asked.

Rolf hesitated. He knew he wanted them to help fight Drakomar, but he also did not know how much he could trust these people who stood in front of him, so he lied.

"No, nothing like that."

"Were you here when the Hexverat attacked?"

"Yes, but they didn't do anything like that."

"What did they do?" Dragorim asked.

"How is that relevant to our current situation?" Imari asked.

The sorcerer turned to her, annoyed at her interference.

"We need to find out as much as we can."

Dragorim turned back to Rolf and pointed in the direction of the haunted woods.

"Do you see that? Do you know what that is?"

Rolf nodded.

"If you don't tell us what we need to know, we can't help you stop it."

Again, Rolf simply nodded. He still didn't trust them fully. Imari spoke next.

"What happened when the Hexverat attacked?"

Rolf looked nervously from mage to mage, and then decided it was best to delay this conversation for as long as possible.

"That's for someone who knows more to tell you. Right now, we need to find more food. I can help you with that, and I can help you get inside the city in the morning. Once there, I think someone will answer all your questions."

Both mages recognized that Rolf was intentionally evading their questions. Dragorim was about to press him further when Imari spoke to cut him off.

"Thank you for your help, Rolf. Please, if you know where more berries are, lead the way."

As Rolf lead them to more food, Dragorim gave Imari a stern look, but she simply shook her head at him. She felt that pushing the boy further would only make sure that he never answered their questions without the use of force, and she did not want to hurt him.

As the group worked together, they were able to forage enough food to satisfy their aching bellies. Nuts and berries were their primary food source, though Dragorim also found a rabbit's nest in the darkness. The trio ate well enough that their hunger no longer prevented sleep.

Now, in the cold dark of the night, the group took comfort in each other's arms as they huddled for warmth. Though between Dragorim and Imari, the beginnings of genuine concern and affection now united the pair. Despite their shared worry over their situation, all three of them were so exhausted that they fell asleep almost instantly, and their dreams haunted them with evil visions that held them in an inescapable vise of torment.

Rolf dreamed of his home town of Neugeld as it was burned to the ground by terrible demons. He ran through the streets as he desperately searched for his father. He would know what to do! The boy rounded a corner and saw his father embattled with a pack of blood-mad wolves. Bit by bit, his father was torn to shreds before Rolf's very eyes. He tried to help, but his legs became encased in stone, and a vicious voice laughed at him from beyond time as his father died again and again.

Imari's dreams were haunted by dark, inhuman shapes that pursued her through the woods. Tendrils reached for her, and she did everything she could to avoid their terrible touch, but they would not be abated. One seized her wrist, and another her ankle. Then, their terrible force pulled her into a black void from which there was no escape. There was an evil presence there, something that wished for nothing more than to devour her. Imari screamed, but the only reply was laughter.

For Dragorim, his dream was more like Rolf's: direct and focused. There was a flurry of activity in his mind, and soon Dragorim found himself within yet another great city. He stood atop a hill and found there was little similarity to any place he had ever seen before. He was surrounded by massive, cyclopean buildings that each felt like a monument to some great power he could never understand. The buildings were not painted, and the art that was present was foreign, alien, and meaningless to him. The shadows cast by the yellow sun were long and deep, and Dragorim was intimidated by their darkness.

The beings that dwelt within the city there were not of his kind, but were altogether different. They reminded him of lizards, with their darting tongues and large, round eyes. Their scales were often multicolored, and despite their civilized nature, their mouths bore many sharp teeth that marked them as hunters. They wore little in the way of garb, though they did wear scarves and headdresses that seemed to mark their profession and station. Dragorim walked through the city streets and received many gawking stares, as none of these creatures had seen a being such as him before.

He was just about to ask them where he was, when the sky turned red as though filled with blood. The creatures around him cried out in terror, for they feared this dread omen. The sun turned black as night, and fire rained down upon the great city. The fine masonry used to construct the massive buildings was no match for the destructive power that had been unleashed, and the many great structures toppled under the onslaught. A great wind came from the east, and several of the massive buildings were thrown onto their sides like wheat against a breeze.

Demons appeared in the air around Dragorim, and dragons descended from the sky to burn the citizens of the great city. Screams of terror echoed around him as the inhabitants fled from their destroyers. They were cut down in droves as the demons slaughtered them. However, not all of the city's builders were defenseless.

Dragorim watched as balls of blue light ascended from behind one of the buildings in the great city. At first they floated in the air like fireflies as their blue light danced against the red fire of the sky. Then, they found their targets, and each missile streaked towards their foes with deadly accuracy. Explosions rocked the city down to its foundations as dragons were struck by the deadly projectiles. The power of these weapons was unlike anything Dragorim had ever seen, and he knew then that this was not a world that would be easily conquered. Suddenly, armies of humanoid warriors descended upon the demons, and a fierce battle commenced the city streets. These beings were not of the race that built this city, and it was then that Dragorim knew that Hymurr and his own army had come to the defense of creation.

Dragorim could only watch as Hymurr's warriors fought bravely against the invading army. Their strength matched the demons they faced, and they were just as numerous. Earth tumbled and shattered as the spells of Hymurr's followers shook the foundations of the world. Massive stone pillars erupted from the ground and hurled themselves upon scores of demons and smashed them into naught but black blood. Trees and other plants became animated and destroyed the demons that opposed them.

Then, a lone black-eyed man appeared on the battlefield. His hair was as black as the night, as was his armor. In his hands he carried a great, two-handed ax made of sinister umbral steel. As Dragorim gazed upon him, it felt as though all light had been cast out of the world. The sorcerer's eyes fixed on the man's face, and to his horror, he recognized the face of Damiros, the god that had brought the gift of fire to all of creation.

Before Dragorim could process his revelation, Damiros attacked the city's defenders. The god drove his ax into the earth beneath their feet and terrible earthquakes tore the city asunder. Fire and lava erupted from the world below, burning and destroying all those who stood against Damiros. Meteors streaked through the sky, and all fled from the power unleashed by the unstoppable god.

More blue lights appeared from the building behind Dragorim and launched themselves at Damiros. The mad god smiled evilly and raised a magical shield to protect himself. The projectiles struck the barrier and exploded with tremendous force. Nearby buildings crumbled and fell upon the god, and dust filled the air as alien screams cascaded through the city. Dragorim then saw that Hymurr himself, clad only in green and brown robes, now stood atop the building as he hurled spells upon his wrathful brother.

The god of fire was unperturbed by Hymurr's attack, and rose from the ashes that surrounded him. Damiros leapt high into the air and effortlessly surmounted one of the few buildings still standing. The evil god eyed Hymurr's form from afar, and he waved his hand at his older brother. Suddenly, the great building exploded into fire and smoke with such force that Dragorim caught only a glimpse of the dark wound torn in creation before the fire consumed him.

The sorcerer awoke screaming. Imari jumped up, prepared to defend herself against a threat. Rolf tumbled upright, also prepared to battle against unknown assailants. Only a moment later did either of them realize that they were not under attack. Once Rolf was sure the coast was clear, he laid back down and tried to go back to sleep. Imari looked at Dragorim, and in the dim moonlight saw a man shaken and upset.

"Are you alright?" she asked.

Dragorim took a few deep breaths and composed himself again.

"Yes, I… I had a dream… old memories I had forgotten."

"Would you like to tell me about them? Sometimes it helps, especially when your dreams are told to someone with my abilities," Imari said.

Dragorim shook his head.

"I appreciate your concern, but it's nothing I haven't faced before. And… some things are best kept to one's self. I'm sorry I woke you."

Imari nodded, understanding his desire for privacy. She sat next to the sorcerer and rested her head on his shoulder.

"I suppose I actually should thank you. I can't say my dreams were pleasant either."

"Would *you* like to talk about it?" Dragorim asked, echoing her sentiment.

Imari smiled at his remark before she spoke.

"It was… I don't know how to describe it. Like something was after me… not human though… like nothing I've ever seen before."

"Can you describe it to me?"

Imari paused, taking a deep breath as she did.

"I don't know. I guess 'seen' isn't the right word for it. It was like nothing I have ever *felt* before. It was this, terrible, all-consuming… *evil*. It surrounded me, chased me. It felt like it wanted to devour me… like a terrible, black flame that hungers for flesh like a vicious predator."

"I'm sorry," Dragorim said. "That sounds like a terrible dream."

"Well, I guess I have you to thank for getting me out of it. So… thank you."

Dragorim lay back down, and Imari followed him. She snuggled in close, and gingerly wrapped her arm around his broad chest as she did. Suddenly, Imari felt very nervous and she spoke again.

"Is this still alright?"

Dragorim looked over to her and smiled.

"We need to keep warm, and since a fire would only give us away, I'd have to say that yes, this is acceptable."

Contented with his answer, Imari tightened her grip on him and slowly drifted off to a now peaceful sleep.

Chapter 22

Ashveldt walked nervously as he carried water to his father. The last time the prince had seen him, the earl had been whisked away to his bed so that his physicians could work on him. Ashveldt had heard little of what had transpired since then. The one thing he did know was that the last of the Hexverat's healing ointments had been used to keep Sigaberht alive, at least for now.

Two guards stood outside the door; ready to interdict any would be assassin. As Ashveldt approached, he gestured for them to allow his passage. Both bowed more deeply than usual, as they had both witnessed Ashveldt's ferocity on the battlefield that day. Ashveldt noticed their mark of respect, and was sure to thank them as one man opened the door for him. The prince peered into the dark room and found his father sprawled over the bed. It appeared as though Sigaberht was sleeping. Ashveldt tiptoed across the threshold and the guards gently closed the door behind him. As the young man looked for a place to set down his tray, he noticed that the room was shrouded in darkness, for the only glimmering light was provided by a single candle that rested on the nightstand. The prince gazed at the candle in silent contemplation, as it seemed to him that the candle was his father: a single light in an ocean of darkness.

Ashveldt's gaze returned to his father, and worry stole his mind as he saw the deathly paleness of his skin and heard his ragged, labored breathing.

"Ashveldt?" Sigaberht said.

"Father?"

"Ashveldt… I thought I recognized your footsteps," Sigaberht said hoarsely. "I am glad you are here. Please, sit beside me."

Ashveldt placed his tray on the nightstand and drew a chair from the far corner of the room over to the bedside.

"How are you?" Ashveldt asked.

"About as well as can be. I should be dead."

"And I am glad to see you are not. I heard that it took all of the Hexverat's remaining potions to heal you."

Sigaberht sighed wistfully.

"It did. I wish they had not done so."

Ashveldt was shocked at his father's admission.

"Why? Do you wish for death at such an important hour?"

Sigaberht tried to take Ashveldt's hand in his, but the effort was too painful. He coughed violently, and Ashveldt took his hand.

"Forgive me. I would rather they had saved the medicine for you. *You* might need it before this war is over. If you are injured... and the medicine that could save you has already been used on me... I would never forgive myself."

Ashveldt nodded, understanding his father's thinking. Silence fell between them, and Ashveldt squeezed his father's hand.

"You must rest. You need not worry about me; I will be sure to defend Wulfgeld honorably," Ashveldt said.

Sigaberht smiled.

"Oh, I am very sure of that... but I am not done yet."

Fear rose in Ashveldt's throat as he anticipated his father's intentions.

"Father... your wound... can you even stand?"

"I don't need to stand to ride a horse."

Ashveldt knew where this conversation was headed and his fear was replaced by anger.

"Do not mince words, Father. Tell me directly that you intend to go through with it."

Sigaberht paused, afraid of what might be overheard by those who stood at the door. However, it was no longer the time for fear, and as such, the earl spoke openly of his plans.

"The forest... I will lead our men into the forest, and we will crush our enemies against the fury of chaos."

Even in his dazed state, Sigaberht still read the doubt that flashed across Ashveldt's face and spoke hastily to ease his son's worries.

"I see we still need to work on your ability to hide your feelings, my son. But in this case, your feelings on the topic are irrelevant to what I must do. We hoped Veigarand's plan would work. It didn't. We must now go with my plan. There is no other way!"

"I know… but… I can see plain as day that you won't even be able to sit up in the saddle tomorrow."

"Then I will have the servants strap me in."

Ashveldt released Sigaberht's hand and leapt to his feet in frustration.

"Father, you cannot! The enemy will chase me as much as they would chase you! *I* will lead our forces into the forest!"

"No! I need you here, should I fall in battle. Wulfgeld needs an heir!"

"What sort of heir will I be if I am not allowed to lead when the situation calls for it?"

Sigaberht grunted in pain as he sat up to better look Ashveldt in the eyes. His son moved to help him, but Sigaberht waved him off.

"You will be *alive*! That's what you will be! Wulfgeld will live on without me. Wulfgeld cannot live on without *you*."

Sigaberht paused for breath as pain crashed through his whole being and looked pleadingly into his son's eyes.

"*I* cannot live without you. Without you, my life has no meaning."

Ashveldt's eyes locked with Sigaberht's. There was no way to talk his father out of his dangerous plan.

"There is nothing I can say to dissuade you?"

"Nothing."

Ashveldt nodded, and then handed his father the water he had prepared.

Sigaberht took the goblet and started to drink. He barely choked down the first sip of water before a coughing fit seized him.

Out of concern, Ashveldt took his father's arm and held it tightly.

"One of my lungs was pierced by a broken rib. Through the Hexverat's medicine, my bone is reset and the lung is closed, but it's still very sore. I'm alright."

Ashveldt nodded as Sigaberht held the goblet to his lips again. In an effort to prove that he was in better health than he was, the earl drained the rest of the glass in one gulp. He sputtered and coughed for a long time before he finally turned an unconvincing smile on his son.

"You should get some sleep," Ashveldt said.

Sigaberht nodded.

"Thank you for the water."

Ashveldt stood, and opened the door. Just as he was about to exit the room, Sigaberht spoke one more time.

"Ashveldt…" The prince turned to face his father. "There has never been a father more proud of his son… than I am of you."

Ashveldt bowed and left his father in peace.

* * *

Prayer. Prayer was the Pale Light's only remaining answer after the calamity they had suffered; and the Pale Light did pray. Despite their invocations, Celestata's devout worshipers still cowered in terror. Even the priests could not shake their fear that yet another supernatural threat would reach out from beyond the darkness to slaughter them during their prostration. Those that stood guard believed they saw an eerie glow in the distance, though their eyes refused to focus on the spot where the great horrors of chaos lay. Despite their fear, they still made their prayers and sang their holy chants, for their only salvation lay in the will of their goddess.

Legier knelt among the warriors of the Pale Light and joined them in prayer. He grieved for Arnulf, whom he believed was dead, and his first prayers were for Celestata to protect Arnulf's soul as he departed for Caelum's Hall of Kings, home to all those who died in sacrifice to their duty. Once he had finished praying for Arnulf's soul, Legier tried to join the prayers led by the priests. He did not know the words, for the ways of the Pale Light were still strange to him… but he would learn.

So, Legier forged his own prayers. The grand marshal swore vengeance upon Sigaberht and all those who dwelt within Wulfgeld. Legier knew it would be only a matter of time before this came to pass. Venatus had already promised that the full might of all the Pale Light's armies would be gathered for a holy crusade. Nearly fifteen thousand knights and men-at-arms would be summoned from all corners of the Southworld, and *he,* Sir Legier would lead them. They would descend upon Wulfgeld and with a cleansing fire, save the souls of all its populace. Once this was done, Legier would return to Drakomar and claim Isabeau, even if he had to do so at the point of a sword.

Once the prayers concluded, the soldiers of the Pale Light prepared themselves for sleep. Barely half of them were fit for battle, and even fewer of Drakomar's forces were still capable of fighting. Legier wished to rest with his new brotherhood, but he was still the grand marshal of Drakomar, and so he reluctantly returned to his own tent. When he arrived, he was met by a gathering of his knights. Twelve men defiantly stood in his path. They bore neither arms nor armor, which Legier took as an ill omen, for a knight appearing in public without his jeweled sword was a sign of great outcry and rebellion.

"My friends, what troubles you on this day?" Legier asked. He knew what the trouble was, but he wanted the conversation to start on *his* terms. Sir Reginder stepped forward to answer.

"My lord marshal, the siege has been broken. The enemy wields dark sorcery that no mortal army can overcome."

Legier shook his head in disgust at the cowardice on display before him.

"Do you really believe that, Sir Reginder? There is no need to be afraid! The light of Celestata guides us! Even now, she hears our prayers and will lead us to salvation!"

Reginder's hand instinctively reached for his sword at Legier's implied accusation of cowardice, and he was thankful he bore none at his belt. Legier noticed the gesture and took a step back from his fellow knight. Reginder scowled at Legier.

"We feared you would continue this folly. The priest has poisoned your mind! The other knights and I have discussed this at length, and we are all in agreement: we are leaving *tonight*!"

"Traitors!" Legier yelled. "Traitors to your oaths! You are sworn to follow my commands!"

"For so long as you speak for Piarin, yes. But you no longer speak for our lord; you speak for the Pale Light."

"I speak for all of us!" Legier yelled.

"Then convince them to retreat with us!" Reginder shouted back. "Do not allow them to throw their lives away! We speak not as your foes, Legier, or whoever you think you are now. We wish to speak to our friend once more. Throw off whatever poisonous lies were told to you by Venatus and come back to us."

"They are not lies!" Legier shouted. "I *saw* her with my own eyes! She spoke to us, plain as day!"

Reginder paused. He was fearful not only for his own life, but for Legier's. He considered having the other knights tie Legier up and drag him back to Drakomar, but he suspected that would only result in a violent response from the Pale Light. A different knight, Sir Lothar, spoke next.

"My lord… you say that Celestata told you what to do… that she promised victory… but we found only disaster. Tell us why we should have faith when you saw with your own eyes where it has led you?"

"Because, my lord knight, he is humble, and humility is the path to salvation!" came Venatus' icy voice.

All eyes turned as the old priest stepped out of the shadows and into the conversation.

"Should you not be stealing the souls of your flock?" Reginder asked.

Venatus glared daggers.

"You… you are not humble. We cannot trust in your strength, for it has proven unworthy. Only through the grace of Celestata shall we find victory!"

"Meaningless drivel," Lothar said.

"Spoken by another man with no humility, a man who believes the strength of his arm is mightier than the goddess herself!"

"You know nothing of what you accuse me, priest. If the goddess had once given us her grace, she has surely abandoned us now. Though I doubt the Pale Light has ever known her presence… for this is not the only recent defeat your order has suffered, is it not?”

Venatus paused for just a moment, and then made a reply that Reginder felt must have been rehearsed.

“I speak of humility and arrogance, for my people and I know much of these things. Our holy order has lived long and prosperously. We have won many battles before… and we too have grown arrogant. Our belief in our own power has swayed us from the true path. I have sought to rectify this in our partnership… but I see that this was always folly. If Celestata has indeed abandoned us, it was y*our* arrogance… *your* heresy that allowed it! I offer you this one chance: join our prayers at sunrise tomorrow, and see for yourself when Celestata comes to us.”

“If we refuse?” Reginder asked.

Venatus bowed his head.

“Other Archpriests would order your deaths for such an act… but I am more progressive than most. If you do not come to our prayers tonight, I will presume that you intend to retreat from these lands… and Celestata will damn your souls.”

Reginder looked to Lothar and the others. There was a moment of discussion… hesitation, but in the end, they all came to the same conclusion.

“We are leaving. I do pray that Caelum has mercy upon you,” Reginder said. He and all the other knights turned to Legier.

“Are you coming?” Reginder asked.

Sorrow washed over Legier. No matter what else he believed… he had sworn an oath to both Celestata and Isabeau… and he would not betray that oath. He shook his head, to which Reginder gave a sad sigh. Seeing there was no use in further argument, the crowd of knights dispersed and prepared for their departure. Legier stood with only Venatus by his side.

“They have abandoned you,” the archpriest said. “But you are not alone. Come with me. Join us, and we shall welcome you as though you had always been our brother.”

Legier said nothing. He simply stared into the void where he had once led a great army. Now, these soldiers were merely men heading home after great hardship. Venatus gently took Legier by the arm and after a slight tug, got the grand marshal to walk with him back to his new family.

Chapter 23

Leif sighed, drink in hand. It had been a hard day and now it looked like he was in for a hard night. Aethelstan had summoned him and Daegal to this inn, and Leif did not know why. He had arrived first and had wasted little time in ordering food and drink. As Leif waited, he watched the others who inhabited the tavern. The people here were raucous, and Leif realized that a large number of the soldiers there belonged to Aethelstan's forces. They drank heavily and sang loudly, but Leif did not blame them. They were coping with the stress of recent events, and if they were not on duty, they were free to do anything they wanted to build up their morale once more.

Daegal then came into the inn with a sour look on his face. Leif waved him over to his table.

"What, by Caelum's beard, is this?" Daegal exclaimed as he gestured to the crowd. Leif did not answer at first, to which Daegal assumed meaning. "What? Did I offend you already?"

Leif shook his head.

"No, no offense. You have merely given words to my thoughts. Why are we here? You and I have both come to this… establishment… at Aethelstan's behest, yet he is not here."

"Perhaps he is late," Daegal suggested.

"To his own event? Daegal, you may not like the man, but even you have to admit that if our fellow ealdorman is *anything*, he is punctual."

Daegal nodded and peered into Leif's goblet.

"Joining the merriment, I see?" he asked.

"My turn leading the watch is over for the night. And if I suspect we are going to do what I think we are in… two days… then I will need the extra courage." To illustrate his point, Leif took a large gulp of his ale.

"How are things at the gate?" Daegal asked.

"Morale is low, and the men are jumpy. But otherwise, things are calm. There's been little to no activity from the Drakomar camp."

"Do you think that's it? That it's over?" Daegal asked.

Leif shrugged.

"I don't know. But either way, I still think I should finish my drink."

As Leif took another gulp, Daegal waved over a waitress and ordered a drink of his own. Once his order was placed, Daegal's thoughts turned to the area of the city that had been destroyed. He knew the numbers. Hundreds had been killed by both the Pale Light's violence and Elena's spell. Dozens of buildings had been leveled and many of the roads were impassable. Almost all of Wulfgeld's manpower was being spent on rescue efforts. Daegal wanted to discuss it with Leif… as talking about it might have helped him understand what had happened… but the normally blustery ealdorman could not find the words. So, the two men sat together awhile and simply drank until Aethelstan came into the inn.

However, they did not spot him at first, nor did he spot them. The first thing Aethelstan noticed was a beautiful, amber-eyed woman seated at a table near the middle of the room. She was eagerly chatting with several of his men, and the ealdorman envied them. By the bright colors of her clothes and the striking makeup she wore, he believed her to be a lady of the night. By the way she was acting, Aethelstan was sure either one or both of his men would be satisfied before morning came. The sudden waving from the table next to her revealed Leif's and Daegal's location to him. Aethelstan returned the wave and sat himself beside Leif.

"I apologize for my tardiness. I felt a sudden, overwhelming sense of paranoia and decided to check on the gate for myself."

"Paranoia of what?" Daegal asked.

"Spies… saboteurs," Aethelstan replied.

"Do you have reason to suspect spies are within these walls?" Leif asked.

Aethelstan remained silent as he struggled to give his answer.

"Not yet, but this is why I asked you to come here instead of meeting in the keep. If enemy spies have penetrated the walls, word of our plans will surely leak to them."

"You know Aethelstan, we are surrounded by people. Any spies will be more likely to hear us here than anywhere else," Daegal said.

"Which is why this place is full of my most loyal soldiers."

"And friends…" Leif said as he gestured to all of the women in the room.

"The more noise, the better. My men are watching for spies while we discuss the plans."

"What plans?" Daegal asked.

"I have received orders from Ashveldt… we are going into the dark forest *tomorrow*."

"I thought we had agreed to more time than that?" Daegal asked.

"The gate has been destroyed… half the city has been leveled… the situation has changed," Leif commented as he stared into his glass.

Aethelstan nodded.

"With the gate destroyed, one hard push from the enemy could lead to Wulfgeld's fall."

"I find that hard to believe," Daegal said. "Did you not see what Elena did? How can the enemy plan to continue the siege if they lose men so quickly?"

"*Can* Elena do it again?" Aethelstan asked.

Daegal did not respond.

"I doubt it," Leif replied.

"What makes you say that?" Daegal asked.

"Because her powers do not manifest without the help of chaos, not completely, anyway."

"Then how did she do what we saw today?" Daegal asked.

"I saw a gaulderen… one that looked suspiciously like the one that the witches threatened to destroy Wulfgeld with," Leif answered.

The other ealdormen gasped at Leif's words.

"Are you sure it was the one?" Daegal asked.

"I'm positive. I remember considering how to cut the witch's arm off when she threatened us with it."

"How did Elena get the gaulderen?" Aethelstan asked.

"Sigaberht," Daegal said.

"Do you question our lord?" Aethelstan commented.

Daegal looked to his fellow ealdorman with contempt in his eye.

"I do. Do you not recall at the wall? He held back your reinforcements. He sacrificed Osmund and his men so the enemy would feel their defeat even harder once Radnor joined the battle. Who else would supply a common woman with such a weapon and not tell us about it?"

Leif took personal offense at Daegal's words about both Elena and Sigaberht.

"First of all, Sigaberht did not sacrifice Osmund. He was ordered to withdraw, and did not. I think it is safe to assume the messenger never reached him. Secondly, I assure you, Elena is anything but 'common'. And besides, it could be that the witches gave it to her," Leif commented.

Daegal shook his head at himself.

"It seems that I owe an apology to the earl. But of Elena... would she not have said something about it to you?" Daegal asked.

Leif pondered over this question until Aethelstan supplied his own answer.

"What if Veigarand convinced her to keep it quiet?"

"What purpose would that serve?" Daegal asked.

"We all know how he resents being in Sigaberht's service. He certainly makes no effort to hide it," Aethelstan said.

Leif and Daegal conceded that point; and Aethelstan looked to Leif.

"He clearly resents having to do penance for what he did to Neugeld. Would it surprise you if he sought a way out of it?"

Leif shook his head, though he had doubts in his own mind. He had to capitulate to Aethelstan on this point. Daegal snorted his objection.

"Radnor has his own plans, I'll grant you, but he has done nothing but fight hard at every turn. He single-handedly turned the tide of the first battle... and without his help when the gate fell, both Sigaberht and Ashveldt would be dead."

"That is true," Leif said. "I have known the man to be of firm beliefs. Betrayal is not his nature… at least not of the type you imply."

Aethelstan shrugged.

"Well, that gaulderen had to come from *somewhere,*" he said.

The ealdormen all sat in silence as they all contemplated what had been said. Daegal then changed the topic.

"So… did his highness tell you what exactly the plan for tomorrow is?"

Aethelstan nodded.

"We are to gather all of our huscarls that still breathe. Our militia is to stay here. Ashveldt says they will be a hindrance against the things that wait there."

"I'm going to need another drink," Leif said as he waved the waitress over the refill his mug. All the ealdormen waited in silence as she poured and only resumed speaking once she had departed.

"Who is to lead the group?" Daegal asked as he took a sip from his own drink.

"Sigaberht."

Daegal immediately spit out his ale and slammed his goblet on the table.

"What in… what does he think he's doing?" Daegal exclaimed.

"The medicine of the Hexverat has worked great wonders upon him—" Aethelstan started.

"Bullshit!" shouted Daegal.

Leif gestured with a silencing hand as many eyes turned upon them. Daegal calmed himself as quickly as he could, and then gestured for Aethelstan to continue.

"He is to lead the charge tomorrow. He believes his presence to be essential to drawing the enemy into the forest."

"And what will happen when he inevitably falls from his horse?" Daegal questioned.

His words were met only with a glare from Aethelstan; who continued as if Daegal had said nothing.

"Veigarand and Elena will come with us. She will use her powers to ward the monsters away from us and leave Drakomar's men to face them alone. Once we are sure Drakomar's force is fully ensnared in the trap, we are to return to Wulfgeld as quickly as possible. We are only supposed to engage our enemies if they hinder our escape."

"That's quite some plan," Daegal said.

Aethelstan merely shrugged again.

"It seems to me that it is no more dangerous than any other plan that has saved us so far. Certainly no more dangerous than following a pair of mad witches and a murderous demigod to the end of the world to fight against things never seen before by man, don't you agree?" Aethelstan said as he looked at Leif.

Leif nodded.

"I would say that you are right… though such words come easily from one who has not faced the power of chaos. We do not know or understand what it is we will face in those woods… and I fear by feeding the enemy to them… we might only make the monsters stronger." With that thought now said aloud, Leif finished the last gulp of his second drink and stood.

"Gentlemen, if tomorrow is to be the day of my death, I wish to be rested before it arrives. I bid you all farewell and goodnight."

Leif then departed for his quarters in the keep. Daegal had no interest in keeping Aethelstan's company any longer than necessary, so he rose as well.

"Aethelstan, if you have no further business with me, I will be off. My turn watching the gate will start soon, and I need to be sure no '*spies*' sneak into the city."

Aethelstan noticed Daegal's inflection, and spoke as the ealdorman turned to leave.

"My lord, it seems you do not believe my concern is genuine."

Daegal turned back to face Aethelstan.

"I know not why you called us here to speak, fellow ealdorman. You surrounded us with your men, you seemed happy to deflect blame for Sigaberht's decisions onto Radnor, and seemed over eager to imply I was guilty of treachery when you thought you could twist words to fit. If I didn't know better, I'd say *you* sought to control the situation for your own gain."

Daegal did not give Aethelstan a chance to defend himself and strode out of the inn. Aethelstan sat alone and wished he was better at this sort of work. Daegal was partially right… he had been probing for treachery. He knew that news of their impending battle in the forest would possibly cause strife… and Aethelstan didn't trust that Radnor had not poisoned the other ealdormen against Sigaberht and wanted to test their loyalty for himself. While Leif had passed the test… Daegal's devotion was still in question. Aethelstan waved for two of his men and whispered in their ears. The two huscarls departed and followed Daegal to be sure he really did go to his duty at the gate, and not to a secret meeting with Veigarand.

Feeling that his job was done, Aethelstan turned to look upon the amber-eyed woman once more. However, he found that she had disappeared. The two soldiers still remained and Aethelstan questioned them on her whereabouts.

"I don't know," said the first man.

"We turned to order more drinks, and once we were done, she was gone," said the second.

Aethelstan looked around the room, but there was still no sign of her. A moment of fear and doubt clutched at him. With all his talk of spies… had he led the ealdormen right to one? Aethelstan quickly banished the thought from his mind, then carried on his way.

* * *

Radnor looked into the dark night… and shivered. Ashveldt had personally come to his door and informed him of the plan for tomorrow. While Radnor had appreciated Ashveldt coming there himself, he did not enjoy the news the young prince had brought. Now, both he and Elena stood in the royal stables near the keep, feeding and petting Darestr as they did. Radnor thought of the battle that lay before him and could not sleep. Demons clutched at his mind as he strained to understand how he could protect Elena through it all. The plan was too dangerous and hinged on too many unknowns. He looked to Elena, who stood beside him with her hand gently stroking Darestr's snout. She too watched the shadows and the evil colors that glowed in the distance. She was afraid, but her will was resolute. She would do everything she could to combat the monsters that attacked them; and with Radnor at her side, she felt confident they would win the day. She turned to him.

"Do not fear for me. I am ready for what is to come tomorrow."

Radnor gazed back to her.

"You don't know that."

"Did you know you were ready the first time you fought in a real battle?"

"No. That's what scares me. You think you are."

Elena looked away as she considered Radnor's words, and then spoke again.

"Perhaps I chose a bad analogy, since this is *not* my first battle and certainly not our first together."

Radnor sighed.

"No, you are right. We have faced chaos before and we made it out alive, but only barely. I am afraid our luck will run out before the day is done."

Elena nodded.

"I know, Radnor. It has been what, two months since my home was destroyed? In that short time I have seen… terrible, terrible things since the day you came to Neugeld."

Radnor turned away, ashamed of his role in the town's destruction.

"I didn't mean it like that," Elena said.

"I know," Radnor said. "But it doesn't change the truth of it either. Since I came into your life, I have brought misery and despair." He looked back up to the silvery moon. "Perhaps I truly am Veigarand… the monster from song come to bring death wherever I tread,"

Elena shook her head.

"You did not bring these terrors into the world. The only thing *you* have brought me is love and respect. Your only flaw is that you care for me so much you would keep me in a box to be sure I was safe.”

Radnor looked in Elena’s eyes, and found comfort in the warmth in them, but that was not what was needed right now.

“And what of Rolf? What would Rolf say now?”

Elena tried to smile, but couldn’t. She did not have an answer for Radnor’s question.

“I thought so,” he said. He turned to go back into the keep, but Elena took him by the arm.

“You are not to blame for Rolf. He chose his own path, and it was his responsibility.”

“No, it was mine. I should have stopped him.”

“How?” Elena asked. “Would you have knocked him out? Poisoned him with some sleeping potion until it was all over? He would have hated you for that.”

“Yes, but he would be alive now.”

“Did you ever find his body?”

“No.”

“Did Sigaberht’s people ever find his body?”

Radnor hesitated.

“No,” he said. He started to understand Elena’s point.

“Then we don’t know he’s dead,” she said matter-of-factly.

“Then where is he?” Radnor asked.

Elena took hold of him. Her embrace was warm and reassuring beyond measure.

“He’s more resourceful than you give him credit for… stronger too. I’m sure he’s out there somewhere. Once this is over, we’ll find him, together. How does that sound?”

“It sounds lovely,” Radnor said.

“Good,” Elena replied.

She looked back to the tall tower, and then gently tugged on Radnor’s arm.

“I’m cold, can we go back inside?”

Radnor gave Darestr one final pat, and then followed Elena back to their room. Once inside, Elena kissed Radnor passionately and deeply. He returned her kiss as she embraced him. His passion for her was the only thing in all creation that matched her passion for him. Elena reached for the bottom hem of his tunic and began to lift it. Radnor broke from her kiss and spoke.

"Are you sure? Tonight?"

"Why not tonight? Can you think of a better time?" Elena asked.

"With the battle tomorrow—"

"Radnor, it is in times like these that we must find the good where we can. I too fear Rolf is dead, but until we have a body, for my own sanity I must believe that he lives. I too fear that we will meet our end in the battle that is yet to come. I am afraid of what will happen to me, or you, or the countless people who I know will die tomorrow… but I can't control any of that right now. All I can do is try to feel something good. I love you Radnor, and I want to feel you once more on what may be our last night together in this world."

"I love you too," he said.

Without another word, he kissed her, and as Elena lifted off his tunic, he undid the laces on her gown. As the two worked to undress each other, their hands traveled and explored, until Radnor grew impatient and lifted Elena high into the air. They kissed as he walked them both to the bed, where he gently laid her down as she finished unlacing her clothes. Once the two were both undressed, Radnor drew her into his arms, and their lovemaking went on with such intensity that even the goddess of love would have been humbled by their passion.

Chapter 24

Dawn crept over the distant horizon, bringing renewed dread to those who knew of the battle to come. Legier rose from his bed and stepped out into the light. There were no exercises this morning, for he needed to join his brothers in prayer. He took a fleeting glance at Drakomar's side of the encampment and found that many of the tents had already been struck. They would all be gone by the time the sun finished entering the sky.

"Fuck 'em," Legier said to himself as he walked to join his newfound brothers. He was better off without them. They had been holding him back. The Pale Light didn't retreat at the first sign of trouble. *They* were still willing to fight. *They* cared if Legier's oath was fulfilled, and *they* did not wish him to return home in shame.

Just as Legier entered the makeshift church, he was greeted by Venatus. The old priest smiled at him and whispered kind sounding words in a language unknown to him. Legier did not know what to make of this, but after a slight nudge from the archpriest, Legier figured out he was supposed to join the others as they were ushered into rows and columns for their prayer. The grand marshal watched the knights and men-at-arms of the Pale Light as they arranged themselves in an orderly manner and prayed to their beloved goddess. Legier joined the group and soon found himself surrounded by other knights. He tried to follow along with their prayers, but their whispered words were too difficult for him to hear, so he fell silent.

Suddenly, a priest came beside him.

"My lord Marshal, why do you not join us at the front? You do not belong mixed with the rest of the flock."

Legier looked to the priest, and shame filled his heart.

"How could I stand before these men when I do not even know the words we worship by?"

The priest smiled warmly and knelt beside him.

"Your humility is commendable, and shall bring you glory in the eyes of the goddess. I shall teach you the first prayer, and you shall no longer feel shame. Repeat after me: Celestata, beloved goddess of the stars and the moon, I beseech you in my time of need. Protect my soul from the evils of the world, so that my heart may remain true, my actions be just, and my soul remain pure. I open now my body and mind to you, so that you may guide my hand in both war and peace."

Legier did as he was told and recited the opening prayer. He repeated it, again and again, until the words were burned into his mind. Once this was done, the priest stood and left to give spiritual guidance to the others arrayed before them. Little was needed, for their faith remained strong. Legier felt inspired, for after witnessing so much terror and death, these men were still as steadfast in their will as they were the day they arrived. There were no complaints, for they were engrossed in prayer. There was no food, for hunger was replaced by discipline. There was no fear… only faith; and in faith… Legier found peace.

After a lengthy time spent in recitation, Venatus stepped to the front of the flock and began his sermon.

"Hear me, oh hallowed knights of the Pale Light! Our allies have abandoned us! They have seen the face of our enemy, and it has frightened them! But, do not lose hope, for we have never needed them! They are naught but a faithless rabble, concerned only with plunder! It is their folly, their… *arrogance* that has caused our defeat… prevented us from destroying the Foul-Temptress when she rode against us! Now, by fleeing these lands, they have condemned not only their own souls… but the souls of all those who reside behind those walls, for the Foul-Temptress corrupts all! *You* have seen her with your eyes! As long as she remains, the souls of all those present are damned to eternal torment unless we can purge the city with holy fire!"

Then, Venatus looked to the sun, and spoke again.

"Holy Celestata, goddess of love and all that is right with the world, please, give us a sign of your will! Speak to us once more, as you did but only yesterday! How shall we vanquish your eternal foe?"

Just then, a golden light descended from the sun itself. Down and down the mote of sunlight fell to the earth, as though it were a leaf floating on the wind. The crowd gasped and waited in eager anticipation of what was to come. They were not disappointed, for when the mote came to eye level with Venatus, it flashed into overwhelming brilliance! Once everyone's vision had cleared, they saw that Celestata graced them with her glorious presence once more. All men threw themselves upon the ground in prostration before their amber-eyed goddess.

"Come now, rise, my children. Rise and draw strength from my light," she said.

The men of the Pale Light did as they were told and her beaming smile filled their hearts with gladness. Venatus spoke next.

"Oh, holy goddess, we have done as you commanded. We have fought against the Foul-Temptress… but she emerged victorious. We humbly beg for your forgiveness, for we should never have suffered the unbelievers amongst us! How might we atone?"

Celestata's golden light surrounded the men of the Pale Light and filled them with such awe that all desired to be nearer to her, though Legier was the only one who dared to actually step forward. The goddess saw his action and recognized him from the previous day.

"You are the man who leads this army, yes?"

Legier was dumbfounded, and remained silent. The goddess smiled upon him.

"Your humility is to be commended, but I do believe you are to lead these forces into battle."

Legier's heart soared. The goddess had chosen him! He was saved!

Celestata gestured for Legier to come forward and stand beside Venatus. Once he had done so, she gave her orders to them.

"Oh, my priest, you believe you have failed me. You have not. Few wars are won by a single battle, and so is the case here. Your attack yesterday accomplished more than you believe, for the Foul-Temptress exhausted her powers to drive you back. You have destroyed the gate, and Wulfgeld has too few surviving warriors to repel you. Lashmatu knows this.

Even as we speak, she is preparing to flee this place. You must not allow this! For if she escapes today, she will regain her strength and wreak untold havoc upon the world! You must pursue her and destroy her. If you do this, your souls shall be forever blessed and entry into paradise will be guaranteed, regardless of any sins committed in the past or future!"

"Blessed be, oh holy one! Your word is our will!" cried Venatus.

Just then, Legier asked a very pertinent question.

"Glorious Celestata, I must beseech thee: how are we to destroy the Foul-Temptress? Is she not mightier than any mortal man? Do we have weapons capable of slaying such a beast?"

"Fear not my loyal servant. She may be more powerful than any mortal, but she is no match for me. My power shall flow through you all in the battle today, and with strength borrowed, you shall strike her from creation itself!"

Legier glowed as he basked in Celestata's radiance. His confidence was restored, and he now only wished to don his armor and charge forth into battle once more. Celestata spoke one final time.

"Go now, and prepare yourselves! The enemy rides soon!" she cried. Even as her words echoed through the woods, she transformed once more into a single mote of light that then ascended towards the sun and soon faded from existence.

Legier turned to face the men of the Pale Light.

"To arms, my brothers, to arms! We must meet our foe the very instant she appears!"

Legier did not wait for anyone to acknowledge his order before he ran back in the direction of his tent. He desired only his armor. He did not need food, for it was replaced with rapturous joy. There was no complaint, for there was only his holy purpose. There was no fear… only faith.

Chapter 25

Even as the Pale Light's soldiers armed themselves, Radnor dreamed. He walked through the streets of his homeland, and he was in awe. The buildings seemed taller and prouder than he remembered. They were painted with bright colors that contrasted gaily against the bleak, white snowscape of Amaranthar's cold winter. He found comfort in walking the old streets again and he stood amazed as he realized that he was a child once more. He looked up to find his mother walking beside him. Her blonde hair and brown eyes bore a striking beauty that captivated him now as it had so many years ago.

Together they walked and perused the wares of merchants whom brought exotic goods from all over the continent and across the sea. Suddenly, Radnor's younger brother, Kjeltil, appeared beside him. He seemed sad, but when Radnor tried to ask him about it, he was shushed by his mother. He heeded his mother's command and spoke no more. The dream then dissolved into blackness, but his mother and brother were still beside him. A man came and told his mother that his older brother, Ulfr, had died. Kjeltil cried out and struck at Radnor, for Radnor had been the one training with Ulfr when he suffered his mortal wound. Had it been his fault that Ulfr died? Could Radnor have done something to prevent it? But… this didn't make sense. Ulfr did not die in the care of physicians, he died on the training field. Why would—

The dream changed again. Radnor now stood along the streets of Wulfgeld, but was still a child. He walked on an empty, snow covered path. Then he heard it: the growl of a wolf penetrated his ears and only afterward did he see its long fangs racing towards him. Radnor ran as fast as he could, but his body was not as strong as he was used to… for he was still but a boy. He ducked inside a nearby house, and the wolf passed him by.

But the wolf was not the only threat. No matter where Radnor looked, something evil lurked in the space just outside the corner of his vision… something in the shadows between.

Radnor crawled through the house as quietly as he could. As he crossed into the next room, he found his mother and brother sitting in chairs, facing into an open door. They were dead, and their faces bore expressions of pure terror as their glassy eyes stared into the blackness beyond the doorway. Radnor wanted to stop, but the wolf's growl returned, and he knew he needed to push through the terrible abyss in the room ahead. Inch by inch Radnor crept, as fear drove him ever closer to the black edge of the door frame. Finally, he crossed the threshold and found himself in the haunted forest. The trees were old and decayed, and their snow covered branches birthed not fruit, but only death and rot. Radnor crawled on, as he was driven by some unknowable, incomprehensible force that he dared not contemplate, for he feared a final revelation would drive him to madness. The earth itself nipped at his hands and knees as it whetted its appetite for his flesh, but still he pressed forward. He gradually became aware of a goal… a *destination* for his journey, but he still knew nothing of its nature or location, only that he must go there.

Then, a terrible, cacophonous sound stole his senses from him. It was a horrific, incessant piping that drowned out all form, matter, and order from reality. The world dissolved around him, and he fell into a mad spiral within a deep, dark void, filled only with shrieking and wailing as though he were joined by the souls of every being that had ever died. Onward he plunged, and time itself became lost to his awareness. Onward he fell… on and on… and his fear rose to even greater heights, for such a fall could only come to a sudden and bloody end.

A gigantic, tumultuous noise crashed into Radnor's senses, and he sat bolt upright in bed, now awakened from his nightmare. Breathing heavily, Radnor quickly turned to find Elena lying next to him under the blankets. The morning was cold, though his blood was colder, for in all the years he had suffered from frightening dreams of the monsters he had faced, he had never had a nightmare such as this.

Another banging noise reached Radnor's ears, and he realized that which had awakened him had been someone knocking on the door. The demigod, still breathless from his ordeal, quickly threw on a long tunic and opened the door to find Halfdan standing fully armored before him. Halfdan did not wait for Radnor to answer.

"Something has happened… something terrible. You are needed in the throne room at once!"

"What has happened?" Radnor asked.

"I do not know. I only know that I was sent to fetch you as soon as possible."

Radnor nodded and waved for Halfdan to wait for him. He returned to the bedroom to dress properly and found that Elena had also awoken. She seemed disturbed, as though perhaps she and Radnor had shared a similar dream. However, there was no time to discuss it.

"What is it?" she asked.

"Halfdan is here. He says I have been summoned. Apparently, there has been a calamity that I must see to."

"I'm coming with you," Elena said.

The two dressed as swiftly as possible, and once Radnor was fully armored and Elena was fully clothed, the pair joined Halfdan outside.

"Took you long enough," Halfdan said.

"Would you have us unprepared?" Elena remarked.

Halfdan shrugged.

"Sorry, Leif was panicking when he sent me, so it must be extremely important."

Elena lowered her eyes as the implications of Halfdan's words hit her.

"That man can worry up a storm, but panicking is not in his nature," Elena said.

"You don't think Sigaberht…" Radnor started. He trailed off as he realized that he actually found himself hoping that Sigaberht *wasn't* dead.

"I don't know," Halfdan said. "But if he is… that will sure make a mess of things."

There was no need for anyone to reply, for Halfdan had said what they all knew. Just before they left, Radnor peered out the window and looked up to the sky. Nearby clouds quickly hid the sun from his gaze as though they sought to

354

protect it from him. The demigod hoped it was not an omen of the day ahead.

Once the group arrived in the throne room, they found that everyone there seemed on the brink of outright panic. Halfdan announced their presence to the guards, and Leif rushed out from a nearby hallway to greet them. He was already dressed in his armor and his countenance was grim as he approached the trio.

"Veiga— Radnor… I must inform you of terrible news. The earl… he's… he's been poisoned."

"Poisoned?" Elena exclaimed.

Leif rushed to shush her.

"Keep it down! Very few know of what has transpired. All they know is that something is amiss… but if word gets out that Sigaberht was poisoned…"

"Word won't get out," Radnor said, as he tried to support Leif how he could.

"Thank you," Leif said.

"Does the earl still breathe?" Radnor asked.

Leif nodded.

"Aye, he does. But, he seems lost in a deep sleep from which we cannot wake him."

"That's a relief… sort of," Elena said.

"What is Ashveldt doing about it?" Halfdan asked.

Leif's expression became even more serious than it had before.

"He is preparing his remarks and will summon everyone to the throne room to make an address."

"I take it he deemed us worthy to address?" Radnor asked.

Leif shook his head.

"I do not know for sure… I asked Halfdan to bring you here because I assumed the prince would do so."

Just then, Daegal joined the group.

"How the hell did this happen?" he shouted over the crowd. Leif quickly tried to quiet him, but Daegal was having none of it. "Don't shush me! How did one of them get through our defenses? Does anyone have any idea how an assassin got through?"

"I don't know! Now will you shut up?" Leif scolded.

Daegal looked around and realized that all of the servants and huscarls in the room were now staring at him. Many of them looked quite nervous, and Daegal realized the impact his outburst was having on the crowd.

"I'm sorry Leif… I—"

"Enough, we have no time," Leif started. "Where is Aethelstan? I sent his summons nearly an hour ago!"

"I don't know," Daegal said. "What do I look like, his mother?"

"You don't think he's the one—" Radnor started.

"Unlikely," Daegal said. "He had his mouth glued too firmly to Sigaberht's ass to risk hurting him."

Leif turned to one of the many servants throughout the hall.

"Find Ealdorman Aethelstan. His absence has been noted and I would have a word with him."

The servant rushed off to do what he was told. Leif spun around the room as though such an act would make Aethelstan appear. Thankfully, the group did not have to wait long, as Aethelstan came barreling into the room shortly after Leif sent off the servant.

"I apologize for my tardiness, Leif; I was attending to other matters,"

"What such matters could be more important than *this*?" Leif demanded.

"I went to the ruins of the gate in search of answers from the men there," Aethelstan said.

Leif had had enough of Aethelstan. He and Daegal both had put up with constant disrespect from the ealdorman at nearly every turn. Now, with the earl's life in the balance, Leif had no more time for Aethelstan's games.

"I apologize that my messenger was unclear about my orders. You were summoned here to me, *now*!"

"Do you think you have authority over me?" Aethelstan asked. "You… you are barely even my equal, let alone a superior. I was the one who was first informed of the day's plans, if you recall. Do you believe you can simply bark orders at me as though I were a common soldier?"

Leif glowered down on the man who stood in his way, and spoke again.

"You were the first one Ashveldt told because you were the only one still hanging around here instead of getting things done. He used you as a *messenger*, nothing more. *I* am the general of our lord's army, not you. *I* am the one who will lead our forces in battle, should he or his heir wish it, not you. *I* am senior to both you and Daegal, and when I tell you to come to me, you will do so on my schedule, *not* yours. Is that understood?"

Aethelstan looked to Daegal for help, but was met only with a vindictive grin. He turned to Radnor and Halfdan, but they remained silent. Even Elena, who had heard Radnor's less than flattering stories of the man, refused to even give him eye contact. Realizing he had no support, Aethelstan faced Leif.

"Very well. What are your orders?"

"Since you stole the time to investigate the gate... make your report. Did you find out *anything* of interest?"

"I found nothing, I'm afraid. The men I questioned saw no sign of anyone even attempting to enter the city through there."

Leif cursed. He had hoped the other ealdorman's defiance would amount to something useful. He then looked to Daegal.

"Did you see anything unusual at all during your watch?" he asked.

Daegal merely shook his head.

"Then that leaves us with merely two options. The first is that an enemy assassin made their way inside through one of the smaller, locked gates, or, someone *here* poisoned the earl."

"You don't suspect one of us, do you?" Aethelstan asked. He was worried about the amber-eyed woman that he had seen the night before... and how she had disappeared. Had she been eavesdropping on the three of them in the inn? How could she have known about their meeting?

Both Daegal and Leif saw Aethelstan's nervousness and eyed him suspiciously.

"Do you know something?" Daegal pressed.

Aethelstan shrank back, but did not answer. Leif took notice of this and wheeled on Aethelstan.

"Answer the question, or… guilty or not… I will drag you before Ashveldt as the assassin."

Aethelstan gulped, for if he was right, it might have been his error that caused their current predicament.

"There was a woman in the inn last night…"

"The inn? What inn?" Radnor asked.

To Radnor's annoyance, Leif waved him off. Despite his momentary irritation, the demigod complied, and Aethelstan continued.

"She sat behind us. I thought she was just a whore, the way she was dressed and the way she caroused with some of my men."

"When did you notice her?" Leif asked.

"Almost immediately… I say she was a whore… but her beauty was unmatched by anyone I have ever seen. It was… enchanting."

Radnor grew uneasy as he heard Aethelstan described this woman. He looked to Elena, and she bore the same concerned expression that he did. Elena asked the next question.

"What did she look like?"

"Tall, dark hair, her breasts were… wonderful."

"How about her face?" Daegal chided.

"Her face was perfect. Smooth… her mouth… her nose… and her eyes… I have never seen eyes quite like that before."

"What about her eyes?" Radnor interjected. He gave a stern look to Leif, daring him to shush him again. Leif did not, as he could see that Radnor and Elena were looking for something specific in Aethelstan's description.

"They were amber colored, and they reflected the firelight so brightly… it was almost like they had a radiant glow all of their own."

Radnor and Elena both turned to each other.

"Lashmatu," they said, almost in unison.

"What?" Halfdan said.

Radnor addressed the group.

"Gentlemen, it seems that you were indeed eavesdropped on… but I can guarantee you that the hand that poisoned Sigaberht was not hers."

"Do you know this woman?" Daegal questioned.

Radnor turned to Elena, as he had lost focus on the rest of the conversation.

"Could she have gotten someone else to do it?" Radnor speculated.

"But why would she?" Elena responded.

Daegal pulled Radnor's shoulder and got his attention again.

"What the fuck is going on? Do you know this woman or not?"

Radnor hesitated, and Elena answered.

"You could say that… there is much to explain if we are to—"

Just then, the sounding of a horn echoed through the great hall. It signaled that Ashveldt had returned and sought to make his address.

Radnor watched as the prince marched across the dais and stood before his father's throne. The young man gestured to the herald that stood nearby, who promptly announced him to the assembled crowd.

"His highness, Wulfgeld wishes to address those who would join him in battle this day. However, he also acknowledges that the news he bears has a significant impact upon not only the warriors of Wulfgeld, but every citizen who resides here. Therefore, he bids all those who wish to hear his words, pray listen to him now."

The herald then moved aside as Ashveldt stood tall atop the royal dais.

"People of Wulfgeld, let it be known that my father, Earl Sigaberht, has been poisoned!"

Gasps went out among the hall, and Leif grew frustrated that his efforts to prevent a panic had just been squandered. Ashveldt waited for the crowd to quiet down before he continued.

"Do not be fearful, for my father yet lives! I do believe he shall recover from this vicious attempt on his life, and will soon ride against our foes once more!"

Cheers erupted from the crowd but were quickly silenced by the efforts of the ealdormen.

"However, we have another grave matter to attend to. The enemy still waits outside our gates, and when news of our beloved earl's poisoning reaches their ears, they will think us weak… and they will strike! Now, my father had a plan… he was to lead our foes away from the city and lure them into the beasts that keep us away from the southern woods! Now that he has been poisoned, he cannot fulfill this plan himself. However, I shall lead our forces in his stead and go into battle in his name! The Pale Light shall soon know the meaning of fear as we see them devoured by that which haunts our woods, and we trample their bones into the mud!"

More cheers erupted from the crowd as Ashveldt spoke. The prince stepped down from his dais and summoned the ealdormen to him. His orders were simple.

"Gather your men! We ride as soon as we are armed!"

Then, Ashveldt waved for one of his retainers to join him as he strode to Elena. Once they reached her, she saw that the retainer carried a glittering shirt of mail and a helmet. Elena looked to Ashveldt for clarification, which he quickly provided.

"You will need better protection than that gown if you are to survive today. This was my mother's armor. You are about her size, so I had it repaired for you."

Elena bowed in front of the prince, and looked upon him with sadness in her eyes.

"My prince, this is a gift most profound, for I know it holds a place in your heart which nothing can fill."

To the shock of everyone around them, Ashveldt bowed to Elena.

"My lady, you are fair and gracious. I ask of you a great service of a kind which no one should have to perform. The least I can do is equip you with the best armor I can find for you."

Elena took the armor from the retainer's arms and bowed once more in gratitude for the gift. Ashveldt then turned to Radnor.

"Are you ready to ride into battle once more?" he asked.

Radnor nodded and laid his hand upon the hilt of his sword. Ashveldt smiled.

"Gather yourselves, for today we ride to war!"

Chapter 26

The morning sun was now high in the sky, and Rolf sat wide awake. He gazed across the open field from atop a hill near the city, and all seemed quiet. He hoped it would stay that way. Rolf had watched many of Drakomar's soldiers break camp and leave, and he hoped that whatever forces remained would soon do the same. If the enemy didn't attack that day, he would finally have a chance to get back inside the city and see his friends again. Rolf looked over to his side and saw Imari and Dragorim both rising from their slumber.

"Good morning you two. I hope you slept well," Rolf said.

"I guess you could say that," Imari said as she thought of the dreams she had had that night. "Did you keep watch?"

Rolf nodded. He had slept briefly, but his nightmares woke him. When he had tried to go back to sleep, he became restless and decided to make use of the time by keeping vigil over the mages.

"You should have woken us, gotten us to take shifts," Imari said.

"I am but a boy without much use in battle. You need your strength far more than I do."

Imari was unsure of what to make of Rolf. He seemed very mature for his age, but also grim… stoic, like something had happened recently that had thrust this maturity upon him, rather than a natural coming of age. Dragorim spoke next.

"Do you think you can get us into the city today?"

Rolf looked at the sorcerer. The boy still had not decided what he thought of the man. He liked Imari better. She was softer, kinder. She honestly reminded him of Elena. But Dragorim… sometimes he reminded Rolf of Radnor… but there was also something… off about Dragorim that he couldn't quite explain.

"Possibly. It depends on if the enemy tries to make another attack on the city today. That's what kept me away the other day."

Dragorim nodded and dug through his food pouch. He found some of the nuts they had gathered the night before and handed them to Rolf.

"Take these; you will need your strength before the day is out."

Rolf accepted them and began to eat. This was a moment where Dragorim reminded him of Radnor. But, even as the sorcerer did a kind deed, there was always a calculating look in his eye, as though he saw Rolf as something besides a person… like a means to an end.

As the trio ate their breakfast, they were interrupted by an astounding sight. One of the side gates opened, and to Rolf's surprise, nearly two hundred men on horseback came barreling out of gate and galloped directly towards Drakomar's camp! Rolf stood and watched as his gaze was transfixed on the horsemen who rode out against their enemies. He tried to see if he recognized anyone… but at first he saw no one he knew… until he caught a glimpse of Radnor's steel shield in the sunlight! Rolf wanted to go to him, but was unsure how. He looked to the enemy camp and saw the knights of the Pale Light emerge from the woods. They were fully armed and armored as though they had been ready for the attack! As soon as the Pale Light made their appearance, the horsemen from Wulfgeld abruptly turned and fled southward… directly towards the haunted woods! Nearly a thousand mounted knights and men-at-arms gave chase. Arrows flew between the two groups, and while most missed their mark or were caught in sturdy armor, others struck true and several horsemen from both sides fell to the frozen earth. Men toppled as their horses were killed, but once they found their own feet they did battle with each other on the open field. It was then that Rolf knew what he had to do.

"We need to go after them!" he desperately shouted.

"No, Rolf! We do not need to involve ourselves in this battle! It's too dangerous!" Imari said.

She looked to Dragorim for support, but his gaze remained locked on Elena's aura as he saw her among Wulfgeld's riders.

"Do you have friends among those horsemen?" he asked.

"Yes, sir,"

Dragorim rose to his feet, though he never took his eyes off Elena until their force disappeared around the other side of the hill.

"We cannot allow the Pale Light to catch up with them. If they do, Rolf's friends will all perish."

Imari saw the desperate look on Rolf's face, and finally relented.

"Alright, but how do we keep up with them? We have no horses."

"Leave that to me," Dragorim said.

Chapter 27

Radnor's brow furrowed with worry as the chase dragged on. They had ridden at a hard canter for almost five miles, and the horses were growing sluggish as they became more and more exhausted. Even mighty Darestr had slowed, and Radnor worried that they could not maintain their pace long enough to reach the corrupted woods before the enemy overtook them. The one comfort he took in this moment was that he knew the Pale Light's horses were likely just as tired as Wulfgeld's, and would also have slowed considerably by this point.

However, even if they did successfully spring their trap, he was even less sure they could escape it. They warriors of Wulfgeld had all brought torches as part of their armaments, for the only mortal weapon that had ever caused their foes permanent damage was fire. This equipment did little to assuage Radnor's fears, as fire had only been tested against the corrupted plant-life, and he feared it would be ineffective against more powerful foes.

Radnor checked behind him to see if he could make out any sign of the pursuing knights. They were difficult to spot past his own allies and the surrounding trees, but he still saw several of the Pale Light's banners as they chased them down, though their numbers seemed somewhat diminished from when the chase started. Radnor hoped this meant that they were pushing their horses to exhaustion faster, thus preventing some of their number from reaching the battle entirely.

Elena rode beside him. Despite being outnumbered, on the run, and heading directly into a waking nightmare, she was unusually calm. Her eyes remained focused on the path ahead, and while she had never ridden a horse into battle before, she was a skilled enough rider to keep her horse in a straight line that followed the others in front of her.

Then, the environment around them changed so suddenly it was though they crossed from one reality to another. Color drained from all things, as though the world itself had died. Even the snow seemed to reflect less light and the only sound that could be heard in the still air was the pounding of hoofs against the frozen earth. The trees were dead and decayed, and neither bird nor animal made its presence known. It was like nothing had ever lived in these forsaken woods.

Radnor tried to signal Ashveldt to stop, but the prince kept riding forward. He wanted to draw the Pale Light as far into the trap as possible. Radnor turned again to check if the enemy still followed. The fanatical warriors paid no heed to the signs of danger around them. If anything, it seemed as though the desolation around them only spurred them on.

As they rode deeper into the blasted wasteland, the environment drew ever more sinister. Twisting, black vines overtook the landscape, and the roots of many plants stuck out at odd, impossible angles that were incomprehensible to the human eye. The limbs of the trees were now studded with row after row of razor sharp teeth. The dirt beneath them became as flesh, and blood oozed from blooming red flowers that contorted as they extended their hideous thorns ever closer to the riders. Ashveldt tried to blink the evil sights away and questioned his own sanity when they did not depart. The world was changing… morphing at the twisted will of Damiros, the God Undead.

If it were not for their recent experiences, both Radnor and Elena would have believed themselves mad. For a moment, Radnor wished he was, so that none of the horrors he saw would be real.

Just as Radnor was about to insist that they go no further, Ashveldt finally decided to stop. The trees had begun to stir in their roots, and Ashveldt knew as well as anyone that such a sign meant they were as close to the center of the infestation as they could risk. The mounted force stopped their advance and faced the Pale Light's army as they approached them. Ashveldt rode to the middle of the formation and spoke to Elena.

"Whatever it is you're going to do, I hope you do it soon. The enemy shall be upon us momentarily!"

"I've tried to tell you, it's not that simple!" she said.

Ashveldt scowled. The Pale Light grew ever closer, and Ashveldt knew that they would all be killed if they were caught. More and more enemy soldiers emerged from the trees, and Ashveldt's blood ran cold.

"Swords!" he yelled.

At his command, every warrior drew their weapons and prepared for battle.

The enemy drew closer and closer, and Ashveldt grew less and less sure of what to do. If he waited too long for the monsters to come and he absorbed the Pale Light's charge, they were likely to die right then and there. But if they fled deeper into the woods, he feared that they would be overwhelmed by the evil that lurked there. However, the decision was made for him when one of the huscarls yelled in alarm.

One of the trees uprooted itself and made its way towards him. Men cried in terror as a swarm of small, unspeakable monsters descended from the branches and sprinted towards them. These creatures were a pale imitation of life; for they were born purely from the monstrous land these mortals now tread upon. They were hideous creatures made from mismatched flesh and bone. They bore no eyes, no faces; only fangs and claws.

Elena saw the monstrous charge and rode to meet them. As they drew closer, the energy within her gathered and flowed. Radnor moved beside her, ready to cut down any monster that reached them before she could act. He watched nervously as the fiends drew closer.

"Elena… any time now…" he muttered.

The lead creature leaped for Elena with all its might. Radnor swung his sword to intercept the monster, but it did not matter! Just as his blade would have cut it in two, Elena's body suddenly glowed with radiant light. A golden barrier erupted from her and incinerated the monsters that attacked the men of Wulfgeld. Other foul fiends tried to breach the barrier, but only met the same fiery end. Radnor looked to his left and right, and saw that Elena's barrier enveloped all of Wulfgeld's forces. The creatures of chaos could not reach them! Ashveldt wasted no time, as he and the other ealdormen began helping everyone in the army light their torches in case they needed to defend themselves further.

Radnor then looked over to where the Pale Light had been, and there he saw a different, sickening sight.

Legier tumbled from his horse as the poor beast died beneath him. He struggled to find his feet while other panicked soldiers crashed into him and the unholy monsters descended upon them like rabid animals. Even as the grand marshal struggled to stand, horrible tendrils snaked around his ankles and sought to drag him into the tooth filled maw of a nearby tree. Legier desperately struck it with his sword, and was relieved to find that the blade struck true! The vines were severed, and he was finally able to stand again. He looked around him as he hoped to find a chance to regroup his forces, but there was no hope of such an act. Knights and men-at-arms all desperately fought for their very survival as the world came alive with monsters. In addition to the things that might once have been wolves and birds, other, wholly alien abominations descended upon them. No amount of force seemed to turn them back. Even as a knight severed the thorned tentacles that sought to rend him, he was met with the fangs of some other indescribable horror. Some men tried to form a shield wall, but their formation was instantly shattered as the earth beneath their feet opened and devoured them. Legier froze, as he had no idea what to do when faced with this unimaginable horror. Then, he spotted Venatus and watched as the priest desperately tried to escape the vicious fiends. Legier headed for Venatus, but as he did, one of the abhorrent monsters leaped upon him!

Legier rolled to absorb the force of the blow and quickly regained his feet. The wolf-like monster landed on its back, and in one sickening motion, reversed the direction of its legs so that it was standing again. As the creature reorganized itself, Legier had a brief moment to get a good look at it, though he wished he hadn't. At first he had thought it was wolf-like, but he quickly realized that the monster merely possessed the trunk of a wolf, but spider-like head and the legs of what he could only guess had once been human. The creature shrieked at Legier with such ferocity that he nearly dropped his sword in terror. It scuttled towards him with fangs bared to kill him.

Thankfully, Legier's years of training overcame his fear and he deftly sidestepped the monster's attack as he cut into it with his sword. The blade bit deep, and black blood issued forth from the wound he had struck. Legier tried to withdraw his sword, but found he could not; the beast's flesh had fused with the weapon! Legier struggled to pry the blade free, but the creature twisted to face him again and wrenched the sword from his hand. The monster leaped for him and Legier barely had time to deflect it away with his shield. He thought to run but knew it would be useless. His only chance was to fight, and fight he did. The creature leaped at him again, and Legier struck out with his shield and bashed it to the ground. He quickly grabbed for the hilt of his sword and once his hand found purchase, he kicked the creature with all his might as he pulled his blade from its body. With this violent act, the fiend's head was nearly torn from its body, and for a moment, Legier believed it had been slain.

This delusion was quickly dispelled as the creature resumed its assault. The knight screamed in terror as he desperately hacked and slashed at it with all his might. Each blow dug deep into the body, but still the creature came. Finally, Legier struck for its limbs as he dodged and blocked its fangs and claws. One by one, he severed the creature's limbs until it could no longer attack him. The pieces still twitched as they still sought to kill him, and Legier nearly retched at the sight. He looked around him and found that he fared better than most of his men, whom were being mercilessly slaughtered by the foul creatures. He had lost sight of Venatus. More monsters attacked him, and as he struggled for his life, Legier silently prayed for salvation from Celestata. The only reply was laughter from the shadows.

Venatus crawled. He crawled as far as he could to get away from the slaughter. There had been rumors and whispers of Lashmatu's power… but no scripture had ever mentioned something so wicked as this! The archpriest seemed to have gone unnoticed by the monsters, as though they sensed he was no threat to them. He hoped that this would hold until he could make his desperate escape. Death was all around him, and the skin-like earth he crawled upon became sticky with a strange, unknown substance. He desperately tried to pull up his hand, but found it was no use. He tried to lift a leg, but it was firmly stuck on the ground. Whatever drove this horrible power had noticed Venatus, and he was its prey. Realizing his situation, Venatus called for help, but no aid came from the knights around him, for they all desperately fought for their lives. Pain crashed upon Venatus and he looked down to find he was not just stuck to the flesh-earth beneath him, but he was now a part of it. Slowly, bit by bit, his own flesh and bone were absorbed and incorporated into the hellscape that surrounded them. The archpriest called upon his goddess in desperate hope that she would answer him.

"Celestata! Please! We need your aid! Why have you forsaken us in our dire hour?"

Only then did he notice the golden barrier that surrounded Wulfgeld's forces and protected them from harm. He wept, for he did not understand why they received Celestata's divine protection, and his people did not. Just then, the goddess' beautiful form appeared beside him and spoke.

"See what your folly hath wrought, mortal. Your arrogance knows no bounds, for you see naught but your own lust for power."

"I do not understand! Please! I must know!" he cried.

Celestata stepped so that he could see her. She knelt before the terrified man, and then revealed her true nature. Though her amber-eyes never changed, her hair transformed from blonde to black, her figure and clothes shifted from that of Venatus' idealized goddess, to that of the hated form of the Foul-Temptress.

"No! It can't be!" he cried.

Lashmatu grinned evilly before the devastated priest.

"What is it you people say? 'She prefers to work through the actions of mortal men. She twists their hearts and minds until their wills are broken and their spirits torn asunder!' See now what you have done… and weep!"

Venatus bowed his head in shame and fear as he finished the saying.

"Only once her foes are truly beaten will she reveal herself!"

"That's a good boy," she said. "You were so eager to believe what you wished to be true, that all it took was a slight push, and you became an excellent pawn!"

Venatus looked past Lashmatu and asked a fearful question.

"Is that woman… the one who stands against us… is she our true goddess?"

Lashmatu paused for a moment and considered the best answer to with which to hurt him. She smiled evilly once she had made her choice, and whispered the truth.

"No, she is not Celestata. She cannot be Celestata… for Celestata and I are one and the same."

"No, it is more tricks!" he cried.

"How else could I pass your test?" Lashmatu cackled. "I am Celestata, and I am Lashmatu. I am the Moonlit Goddess… and I am the Foul-Temptress. I am the beloved daughter of Caelum… and I am his hated betrayer. Know me for what I am mortal, and weep!"

As her words echoed in Venatus' ears, the flesh-earth absorbed him fully. Lashmatu grinned wickedly as she gloated over Venatus' remains. Once she had her fill, the goddess turned her attention away from the dying warriors of the Pale Light and over to Elena's demonstration of power.

Ashveldt and the men of Wulfgeld's feelings of satisfaction turned to horror as they watched the carnage they had unleashed upon the Pale Light. Blood flowed as freely as the ocean's waters while men were disemboweled and torn limb from limb by the horrible monsters. Those who were not devoured quickly rose again as contorted imitations of the men they had once been. Ashveldt looked to Leif and saw that the ealdorman's grave expression matched his own. Aethelstan and a number of other men had already vomited. Both Halfdan and Daegal watched through gritted teeth as men were slaughtered around them. Many knights of the Pale Light fled to Elena's barrier, but were cut down by the demonic creatures before they could make it to safety. Hordes of monsters descended upon the golden wall, but so far, none had passed through. It had only been a few minutes, but the sheer scale of what Radnor was witnessing frightened even him. The demigod stepped towards Ashveldt and spoke.

"Your highness, our task is complete. We must depart here. Elena's strength will not hold out forever. We must leave the enemy to their fate."

Ashveldt remained silent. Leif joined with words of his own.

"My lord… Radnor is right. We need to leave."

But Ashveldt could not bring himself to look away from the horror laid out before him. After a brief consideration, he spoke.

"Would you think me mad if I said we should rescue them? Bring them behind the barrier?"

Radnor and Leif looked upon the carnage but a moment longer and made their decisions. Leif spoke first.

"No, I would think you *human*. However, your father might—"

"I am *not* my father!" Ashveldt said. He turned to the other men around him. "Warriors of Wulfgeld, today we prove our worth to the world! Our fellow men are being slaughtered by demons summoned forth by the witches who so wronged us! We have fought to defend our homeland from our enemies, but even as we do so now, we feed the hunger of an even more dangerous foe. The chaos that has been unleashed here must be destroyed, and the first step is to save as many of our mortal enemies as we can! Who's with me?"

The roar from the assembled huscarls spoke to the bravery of the men of Wulfgeld. Ashveldt turned to Radnor.

"I need your sword out there on that battlefield. Do you think Elena will be safe without us?"

Radnor looked to Elena as she maintained the barrier that held the monsters at bay. The act clearly took great effort, but she seemed capable of sustaining it for now. Radnor looked back to Ashveldt and nodded.

"Ready?" Ashveldt yelled. "Charge!"

Upon their prince's command, the huscarls of Wulfgeld left the barrier, and with torches held aloft, burned all foes that stood against them. The horde of monsters quickly turned their attention to this new threat, but the wrath of Wulfgeld would not be undone. Radnor led the charge and his cursed sword drew much attention from the monstrous horde. Beast after beast came for him, but the steel titan and his mighty steed would not be halted. Most of the creatures disintegrated into ashes as soon as his blade struck them. A creature that had once been a bird tried to claw at his helmet, but a fierce blow from his shield shattered the ill-formed creature into blood and ichor. Behind Radnor's fury came the men of Wulfgeld. The huscarls did what they could to help the men of the Pale Light. Burning torches in hand, they escorted their enemies back to the safety of Elena's barrier. However, the work was slow, and Radnor could not kill every monster that attacked them. Many brave warriors of Wulfgeld died to save their fellow men.

Even as men struggled to rescue their comrades, new threats emerged from the depths of the woods. A terrible cry echoed through the trees and a colossal beast rose from the forest floor. The monster stood twice as high as any tree and seemed almost haphazardly pieced together from connected masses of flesh, wood, rock, and bone. It was man shaped in a rudimentary way. The giant bore many fleshy tentacles in place of hands. Its pulpy head looked to have been crudely forged from the bodies of several human corpses. Radnor looked at the beast in terror as it moved towards Elena's position and lashed out against her barrier! Tendrils struck and instantly collapsed into ash, but the beast did not relent. More tendrils grew to replace those lost and assaulted Elena's barrier yet again, though they too were destroyed.

Then, the monster roared with such force that men were nearly thrown from their feet by its power. Black flames enveloped the creature's hands, which it then smashed against Elena's barrier. Elena yelled in pain as she struggled to maintain her defenses. Radnor realized that this beast was something Damiros had created for one purpose... to kill Elena.

Radnor rushed for the beast, as he hoped he could strike it with his sword and destroy it. But as he did, more monsters rushed upon him and he had no choice but to stop and defend himself. The earth opened up beneath him, but Darestr felt the change coming and leapt away just in time to avoid the slathering maw. A sword swung past Radnor's head; and when he lashed out with his own blade, he found that it met the steel-infused flesh of what had recently been a knight of the Pale Light, still mounted on its now undead horse. His blade passed through the creature and it fell dead before him. However, this blow, and every subsequent blow Radnor threw took time… time he could not spend rescuing Elena. Radnor soon found himself overwhelmed by the onslaught of monstrous forces.

Darestr tried to charge through them, but was met only with pain as a tendril wrapped its terrible thorns around the horse's leg and pulled them down. Darestr cried out in agony as he struggled to regain his feet. Radnor rolled with the fall and desperately tried to save his loyal horse… but it was too late. The blade of one of the reanimated monsters pierced Darestr's neck, and Radnor screamed as his beloved horse and oldest friend passed from the world.

Radnor's fury overtook him and he hurled himself against the monster that had just slain Darestr. The fiend had no time to react before Radnor cut it to pieces. Motivated by revenge, Radnor dealt death among the demons of chaos as he struggled to help Elena, but there were too many foes to count, and he knew his strength would soon ebb. Once it did, he would be cut down by the rampaging creatures.

Elena screamed as she fought against the monster's onslaught. She had never seen anything like this beast before; and her power to defend herself was starting to wane. If she hadn't needed to protect so many others, she could have focused her power into an attack that might have slain the creature, but she did not have the strength to do both at the same time! The champion of chaos brought down another fierce wave of black flame, and Elena collapsed to her knees against its might. She looked for Radnor, but could not find him among the many men who fought on that accursed battlefield. Elena watched as the creature reared its arm back for yet another brutal strike and she knew there was no surviving it. She braced herself as best she could, and prepared for the end.

Then, someone took a hold of her outstretched arm! She looked to her side and saw that a massive, red-haired man gripped her tightly. She tried to struggle, but her eyes locked with his and she saw that his purpose was to help.

"The only way out is through!" he shouted.

Then, Elena felt a connection unlike any she had ever experienced. It was comparable to when she had helped one of the Hexverat summon a spell in a battle against chaos, but this connection was different, more intimate. Elena felt like she was connected to this man's very soul.

Just then, the black flame struck! But, instead of being consumed by the devouring flames, Elena felt the energy of the attack push through and enter her body. She screamed in pain as the power wreaked havoc on her senses. Then, she felt the power pass through her and into the man who clutched at her. She opened her eyes to see the red-haired man become wreathed in the black flame. He let go of her and with a wave of his hand, cast the power of black fire back against their attacker! All of the monster's energy was condensed into a single mote of power, and it seemed that the world shattered as his attack struck Damiros' champion. The creature cried out in agony as the Undead God's own power was turned against it and staggered backwards away from them.

"Now, you must hit it again!" Dragorim yelled to the confused Elena.

"I can't! I must hold the barrier, or my friends cannot defend themselves!"

Elena was then interrupted by a familiar voice.

"Do what he says! You have to trust him!"

Elena turned and was overwhelmed with joy when she saw it was Rolf's who spoke. The distraction did not last long, for Elena knew her job was not done. The giant monster was regaining its balance, and even as they spoke, many giant spider like monsters joined the fray against the mortal men. Horses stampeded as the massive creatures crashed across the battlefield. Ashveldt and Legier tried to rally their men as best they could, but it was to no avail, for the army of chaos was insurmountable.

Seeing that defending her friends with the barrier was now hopeless, Elena allowed her shield to fall and gathered her energy into a spear made from pure, gilded light. She reared back and hurled the weapon with all her strength. The spear of light streaked through the air and struck the massive beast with such force that it shook the cosmos to its very foundation and shattered the fiend into pieces.

With the threat now eliminated, Dragorim withdrew one of his most powerful gaulderens and cracked it open. Just then, the blade of every warrior present erupted in flame. At first this startled the men, but as Ashveldt struck one of his attackers, he saw that the creature fell dead before him. All men now had a way to kill the creatures that assaulted them! Ashveldt let out a rallying cry, and men, regardless of faction, gathered around him. Together, they charged into the terrible monsters, and with blades now capable of destroying their foes, the demons of chaos learned the fury of man.

Elena turned and saw Rolf standing behind her. He was accompanied by a dark skinned woman who radiated a strange aura that immediately told Elena she was a witch.

"What are you doing here?" Elena yelled.

"Saving you!" Rolf replied. "And anyone else we can!"

He then gave Elena a quick hug and without another word, he and Imari ran to rescue as many of the wounded as they could. Elena looked to her side to see Dragorim now engaged in battle against one of the massive spider-like creatures. Just as she was about to help him, the sorcerer summoned a bolt of lightning to his hand and used it to split the creature in two. Since it was clear Dragorim did not need her help, Elena ran across the battlefield in search of Radnor. It seemed that she wasn't the only one who had the same idea, as Ashveldt, Legier, and the remaining members of the Pale Light gathered around him.

However, Daegal, Aethelstan, and Halfdan had become separated from the group, and monsters closed in on them from all sides. Their huscarls fought valiantly, but even with their magic-infused blades, there were still too many foes attacking them at once for this to be a winning battle. Many brave men died defending their lords. Elena ran for them as she felt her power flow through her once more. With her full strength now returning, she took on her true aspect and unleashed an onslaught of gilded flame upon the monsters that assaulted her friends.

Even as Elena came to their aid, Daegal and Aethelstan fought side by side against the remaining monsters. Aethelstan fought well, with precise and practiced movements, while Daegal fought with the ferocity of a lion. Out of the corner of his eye, Aethelstan saw a deadly stinger fly for Daegal's face. There was no time to consider options, and Aethelstan did the only thing he had time to do. In an act of uncharacteristic selflessness, Aethelstan flung himself in front of the deadly barb and died knowing he had just saved his fellow ealdorman's life. Daegal noticed this only a moment later and cried out in grief when he realized that his longtime foe had just sacrificed himself. Daegal bent down to retrieve Aethelstan's body, but was stopped by Halfdan's giant hands.

"Leave him! We must regroup with the Prince!" he shouted.

Daegal tried to shake him off at first, but after further insistence from Halfdan, he finally left his fellow ealdorman where he lay. Then Daegal and Halfdan hastily led the surviving huscarls to Ashveldt's position.

Fire reigned supreme as the men felled the beasts that attacked them. The woods were ablaze as men set their burning blades against the world that tried to devour them. Rolf and Imari rejoined the group as well, for they quickly learned that anyone injured by the terrible monsters would always be consumed by the chaos that infested their wounds. Dragorim joined the group, having slaughtered his way through many of the deadliest abominations set against them.

"Who the fuck are you?" Radnor demanded as Dragorim joined their line.

"I'm the one who knows how to end this!" Dragorim yelled back.

Elena spoke next.

"You said 'the only way out is through'. What did you mean?"

"If we are to escape this, we must push forward, find the source of this corruption, and close it!"

"But how?" Elena asked.

"Do you have any more of those gaulderens you used at yesterday's battle?"

Elena nodded and withdrew the final gaulderen from her pouch.

"How will that help us now? Is there a way we can use this to destroy the monsters?"

Dragorim shook his head.

"That gaulderen was made to repair the damage done to the world by those who would meddle in chaos. The witches intended it to be used to fix what they had done."

"But I was told—" Elena started.

"You were told wrong!" Dragorim shouted over her. "I have been doing this for far longer than you have and I am the only man alive who knows how to use this properly! Take your friends and go! I must push deeper into the woods, and I will use this gaulderen to stop the evil from destroying the world!"

Dragorim then took Imari's hand.

"Thank you for your kindness. No matter what happens to me, I hope you are loved."

Without waiting for any acknowledgment from either of the women, Dragorim snatched the gaulderen from Elena's hand and hurled himself among the horde of monsters.

Elena turned to Radnor.

"I'm going after him!"

"I'm coming with you!" he replied.

Elena pushed him back.

"These people need someone to protect them! I doubt the spell that enhances their swords will last forever, and they need you to keep them safe!"

"I'm supposed to protect *you*!" he cried.

Ashveldt and Legier joined the conversation as their men fought on.

"Run!" Elena yelled to them.

Ashveldt looked to Legier, who shook his head in reply. Ashveldt looked back to Elena.

"We're going with you. Your friend has given us the means to fight back, and we will do so."

Legier saw that Elena looked like she still wanted to protest, so he chimed in directly.

"My lady, my men have seen your holy grace and power for what it is… the Pale Light will not flee from this battle today."

Elena did not understand the implications of his words, but it was clear that his resolve was unbreakable. Since argument was hopeless, Elena, Radnor, and all the others drove deeper into the corrupted forest. It did not take long to catch up with Dragorim, who had become bogged down in the swarm of monsters Damiros had set against him. He was grateful that no one had listened to his order for them all to flee, as once their forces had combined; they were drove through their foes.

More and more of the monsters descended upon them, and though the warriors bore blades blessed with holy fire, they could not kill all of the creatures that sought to destroy them. As they battled on and on, their numbers dwindled as both huscarls and knights of the Pale Light died bravely protecting each other.

Rolf scooped up one of the fallen swords and did what he could to protect the others around him. Imari did as well, and the pair soon found themselves embroiled in the thick of the fighting. Rolf hacked and slashed at one foe, but was immediately met by another! He dodged to the side as quickly as he could, but was met by a terrible barb that slashed across his sword arm. The boy yelled out in pain and collapsed to the ground. Ashveldt saw Rolf's plight, and flaming sword in hand, struck the beast down without hesitation. Leif joined Ashveldt, and the pair protected Imari as she dragged Rolf to the center of their unit. His wound was hideous, and an evil, black essence was already working its way through the boy's veins.

Elena heard Rolf's screams and cried out in horror at Rolf's injury. Radnor stepped forward to protect her from a deadly barb as she dove for Dragorim and seized him by the shoulders.

"Rolf has been wounded!" she cried. "There must be a way to save him!"

Sorrow filled Dragorim's heart. He had liked Rolf. He was going to refuse her at first, but when he looked into Elena's eyes, he saw how much Rolf meant to her. Without another thought, Dragorim left his spot in the battle line and withdrew to help Rolf.

Dragorim ran to the boy as quickly as he could, and heard Rolf scream in pain as the evil consumed him. Time was almost up. He took the boy from Imari's comforting arms and reached deep into his pocket. He hastily withdrew a long, wooden case and opened it to withdraw the silver needle. Dragorim looked at it mournfully for a single moment before he inserted it into Rolf's arm. The boy cried out, and Leif turned to face Dragorim.

"What are you doing to him?" he shouted.

"Saving his life!" Dragorim yelled.

The deeper he pushed the needle, the louder Rolf cried out, but push he did until the entire needle was buried in Rolf's flesh. Then, the evil receded from the boy's blood and collected within the confines of the needle. Elena breathed a sigh of relief. Leif wasted no time and hurled Rolf over his shoulder. Ashveldt took Dragorim by the arm.

"Thank you! Now, we must keep moving!"

Onward the army pushed, and the hordes of chaos were sent against them. Elena's power flared anew, and her very gaze caused the denizens of chaos to collapse into ash. This gave Dragorim the cover he needed to advance towards the very core of the terror, but even her efforts were not enough to stem the horrid tide. Radnor and the other mortal warriors supplied the last of the destructive power needed to bring victory as their blades brought death wherever they went.

Once they arrived at their destination, all were struck by terror-filled awe at the sight of the black vortex which greeted them. This floating portal stood a few feet above the ground, and formed the shape of a jagged circle from which a black, sinister essence poured forth. This hideous miasma filled the air and seeped into the plants and earth around them. Dragorim shouted to Radnor and Elena.

"I must stop here, and you all must retreat now!"

"We cannot leave you to die here!" Elena cried.

Dragorim smiled.

"Do not worry, as I said, I've been doing this far longer than you have. Thank you for your aid, but I cannot risk your harm now. You are both too important to die here!"

Just then, a colossal monster assembled itself from the remains of those they had already destroyed! Even as the creature was still forming, it raised a massive, black-vined arm and tried to smash Dragorim into oblivion. Only quick action by Elena prevented ultimate disaster, and the creature fell to a barrage of golden flames. Another beast appeared, but was quickly felled by Radnor's biting blade. The sorcerer smiled and reluctantly accepted their aid.

Dragorim gazed into the endless void and laughed as it glared at him.

"Remember me?" he shouted.

As he did, he held the gaulderen aloft and broke its crystal shell. The power released was enormous, but none of it struck the vortex, not at first. With all of his skill, Dragorim drew the energy from the gaulderen into his own soul. This was the first step of the spell he had himself invented to prevent his own experiments with chaos from undoing the world. Then, Dragorim intoned words in a language unheard by all but a few living beings and cast the energy upon the wound in the cosmos.

Dragorim gazed upon the fabric of creation. He could see every thread, and how they each wove in and around each other. He could also see how the strands around the void had been torn and broken. The sorcerer pulled on these threads with careful precision. Matter bent and twisted to his will as the fabric of creation was stretched to its limit. With each tug, the hole in creation grew smaller, and with each stretch, the power of chaos waned. On and on Dragorim worked, as the others behind him battled the monsters that sought to stop him. However, their work gradually became easier as Dragorim slowly closed the wound in the world. The monsters came more slowly, and were less and less powerful as Dragorim neared completing his task. Just as the sorcerer was nearly finished, a terrible, enraged roar echoed through the forest. Dragorim smiled at his foe's rage and made the final touches needed to seal the wound in creation once and for all. As soon as he did, the monsters born of chaos crumbled and withered until they faded from existence itself. With their source of power cut off, there was no force to hold the abominations together any longer.

Elena's power dwindled and she collapsed to the ground. Radnor and Dragorim rushed to her aid. The sorcerer was unsure of what to do while Radnor took her into his arms and held her close to his breast. After a moment longer, Elena's eyes opened and she gazed upon Radnor's concerned face. She smiled at him and stood on her own power once more as she spoke to Dragorim.

"Thank you… without you… we could not have won today,"

"It is my duty," Dragorim said. "The Hexverat did terrible deeds here, and as a fellow mage, I must see it rectified."

"I'm glad to see there's one of your kind who isn't mad," Radnor said. He extended his hand to Dragorim, who shook it gladly. "What is your name?"

"Dragorim," he said.

"It is a pleasure to meet you," Elena replied.

Radnor looked around.

"I don't know about you two, but I would like to get the fuck out of here."

Dragorim smiled and joined the duo as they made their way to regroup with the others.

Onward the group walked. Rolf regained consciousness and was met with tearful hugs from all of his friends, but from Elena and Radnor most of all. Once he had given Rolf his hug, Radnor started off to summon Darestr so they could ride back… then remembered his fallen horse. Grief overwhelmed Radnor's heart, and he looked to the magic ring his mother had given him. He gazed upon the green horses engraved upon the silver band. He considered throwing it away. Elena came to his side.

"Radnor… I'm so sorry," she said.

The demigod looked to her as sadness filled his heart. He held the ring for her to see.

"When I wore this ring, Darestr understood me as well as you do now. But, I think it also went two ways. I think I understood him too. We understood each other in a way I don't think I ever want to experience again."

Elena looked to the ring thoughtfully.

"Do you want to throw it away?" she asked.

"I don't know."

Elena reached for his hand and closed his fingers around the old ring.

"Keep it. Remember him by it."

Radnor nodded, and gently slid the ring back on his finger.

Elena took him by the arm, and the pair walked among their fellow survivors as they headed home.

Once they exited the forest and were back in the fields outside Wulfgeld, Legier called the party to a stop. As Ashveldt stepped forward to question what had happened, Legier, Grand Marshal of the army of Drakomar, knelt before him.

"Prince of Wulfgeld, I must humbly offer the surrender of my army to your mercy. We are beaten, and we have seen the holy light that has defeated us."

As Elena stepped into view, several knights of the Pale Light prostrated themselves before her.

"Please, we beg of you, oh great goddess, forgive us for our sins! We were tricked by the Foul-Temptress! We meant no offense to you oh great one!"

Elena took a step back, unsure of what to do. Before she could speak, Dragorim spoke for her.

"Step back from her you fools! Can you not see that your goddess has more important matters to be concerned with than your pathetic souls?"

The knights stepped back, devastated by the words of their goddess' companion. Elena felt inclined to agree, but she saw that rebuffing them might cause more problems down the road, so she smiled reassuringly.

"I am sure there is a path to make amends for your wrongdoing. For now, you must honor the surrender of your general. Give yourselves to our mercy and you shall be treated fairly."

The knights of the Pale Light endlessly praised the merciful spirit of their goddess incarnate. Then Legier stood and drew his sword. Ashveldt took a step back and drew his own in response.

"What is this? You surrendered!" Ashveldt shouted.

Legier did not attack, though he maintained his fighting stance.

"My *army* has surrendered, but *I* cannot. I swore an oath that I would only return to Drakomar as a victor… or a corpse. I *must* see that oath fulfilled."

Radnor, Halfdan, and both surviving ealdormen stepped forward to protect Ashveldt, but the young prince waved them off.

"No! This shall be a duel of honor!" Ashveldt cried.

Legier bowed before the prince.

"When I arrived, I challenged your father to a duel. I am glad then, that I might at least face his son in battle."

Now prepared, the two exhausted men started for each other. There were no tactics; there were no graceful movements, only the weighty, committed strikes of two men at the edge of their endurance.

Legier threw a heavy blow at Ashveldt's helmet, which Ashveldt blocked with the face of his shield. Ashveldt stepped past Legier's shield side, to which the knight responded by attempting to strike Ashveldt with his own shield. Ashveldt stepped back and narrowly avoided the blow. The prince brought his sword down upon Legier's tattered armor, and the blade struck true. Blood spurted from the wound as Legier gasped in pain. He stepped back as agony ripped at his mind. Legier was not yet dead, so he paid no more heed to his injury and continued to battle the prince. Legier swung another heavy blow with such force that Ashveldt gritted his teeth as he again blocked it with his shield. Legier attacked again, but in his exhaustion, his sword arm swung out in a wide arc. Ashveldt saw the opening and drove a counter-cut into Legier's sword arm. Steel met flesh, and Legier's arm was rendered useless. Legier's sword dropped to the ground, and Ashveldt stopped his attack.

"Yield! You are beaten!" the prince yelled.

Legier hurled his shield to the ground and picked up his fallen sword in his off-hand.

"*As… a… corpse!*" Legier shouted.

The grand marshal made one last charge for Ashveldt. His wild aggression was met with a final blow from Ashveldt's sword, and Legier fulfilled his oath.

Chapter 28

Sigaberht sat upon his throne. Word had already reached him of Ashveldt's success, and that the survivors of the Pale Light had surrendered to him. He had even been told that Ashveldt had defeated Legier in single combat. This deed would be remembered in song for ages to come. Sigaberht took solace in the fact that his son's bravery and skill in battle assured no one would challenge his right to the throne. However, rage filled the father's heart, for Ashveldt had defied him.

At the earl's signal, the door to the throne room was opened, and his victorious son strode into the room followed by many he knew, and two strangers he did not. As soon as Sigaberht saw his son, he suppressed his anger so that it would not show publicly. The earl grabbed his new cane, walked to his son and embraced him. Tears flowed down Sigaberht's face as he found that beyond bruises and scratches, Ashveldt was unharmed.

Sigaberht released his grip on Ashveldt and addressed the assembled crowd.

"Praise to the Prince of Wulfgeld! Praise to his victorious warriors!"

Cheers rang out across the hall, and merriment commenced. The siege was over! Radnor looked to Elena, and then back to Sigaberht.

"My lord, if there is no further business for us—"

"Go!" Sigaberht interrupted. "You have saved my son, and I am forever grateful. All of you go to your homes! There will be plenty of time to discuss the day's events! Now, go, rest, and be merry! I would speak to my son… alone."

The party disbanded quickly as everyone headed back to their own homes to rest and prepare for the joyous celebrations to come. Radnor and Elena took Rolf by the hand, and headed for their room in the keep. Daegal headed for the nearest inn where he could drink heavily and honor Aethelstan's sacrifice. Halfdan saw that Daegal needed a companion and rushed forward to join him. At first Daegal was surprised, but was quickly glad for Halfdan's friendship. Dragorim walked over and spoke to Leif.

"Where are Imari and I to go?"

Leif looked at him and the dark skinned witch, and quickly made up his mind.

"You saved us today. I will find accommodations for you both here in the keep. I am sure the earl will want to speak with you once the meeting with his son is over. How many rooms do you need?"

Dragorim turned to Imari. She smiled playfully at Dragorim, and then answered Leif's question.

"Two will be good…" she said. Imari then looked back to Dragorim. "For now."

"Very well… I will see to it now, come with me," Leif said.

The trio then departed the throne room and left the earl alone with his son. Even the guards had departed.

Now alone with Ashveldt, Sigaberht's anger surged through him and he struck Ashveldt across the face.

"You had no right!" Sigaberht yelled.

Ashveldt hung his head in shame for he knew of what his father spoke.

"Father… I… I had to do it."

"You know what I wished!" Sigaberht yelled. "You were to remain here!"

"You were poisoned!" Ashveldt said, as he deflected blame.

Sigaberht's eyes narrowed.

"I was told an assassin breached the wall. But there was no assassin. The poison came from the water you brought me, didn't it?"

Ashveldt shrank before his father's anger like he was a small child again.

"Father… it was only to save you. I meant no harm!"

"Yet harm you did!" Sigaberht roared. "Not to my body, but to my heart! Ashveldt, you betrayed me! I was supposed to be the one who went into the forest! From what I was told, you would have died today were it not for the sorcerer's intervention!"

Ashveldt nodded.

"I know, Father. But what choice did I have? You would have surely died there regardless of the sorcerer's involvement."

"That's not the point!" Sigaberht yelled. "How can you expect me to ever trust you again? My will is law, even to you."

Tears rushed down Ashveldt's face.

"Father, I only did what I did to save you…"

"Think of your mother!" Sigaberht cried. "How could I face her in Caelum's Halls? How could I tell her that her sacrifice meant nothing, because *I* allowed you to die?"

Ashveldt stood silently. He ceased all argument, for no matter how much he wanted to believe he had done the right thing, the pain he had caused his father was almost as great as when his mother had died.

"Father… I'm sorry."

Sigaberht turned away from Ashveldt. He loved his son dearly, but that only made his betrayal ever more painful.

"For the sake of the realm, this stays between us, and you will receive no punishment. Go. Leave me be. Think on this and your duty as my heir."

"Father…"

"Get out of my sight!" Sigaberht roared.

Ashveldt turned his gaze to the floor and with a heavy heart, exited the throne room and headed towards his chambers.

* * *

Upon arriving at their room, Radnor instantly threw his armor off. Radnor and Rolf went off to find clothes that fit the boy while Elena changed out of her blood soaked armor. They each bathed as quickly as they could, and once everyone was cleaned up, they had a look at Rolf's wound.

"Does it hurt?" Radnor asked.

"A little," Rolf said as they all gazed upon the black line in his arm.

"Do you think we should remove it?"

Rolf looked up to Radnor and violently shook his head.

"I can feel it inside me… the evil. The needle is the only thing keeping it from killing me."

Radnor nodded, and Elena touched Rolf's arm.

"I can feel it," she said. "It's… I don't know how to describe it… but Rolf's right. We need to leave it in."

"Where does that leave us?" Radnor asked.

"Well, for starters, don't cut my arm off," Rolf said.

"Deal," Radnor replied.

There was a brief pause, before Rolf asked a question.

"What happens next?"

"Well," Elena started. "I suggest you stay here, with us. I think it's high time you had a chance to live as a boy your age should: in the safety of his own home."

Radnor nodded.

"Rolf, you already know my thoughts on this topic. I'll teach you to fight, and when the time is right, and you feel restless, you can join me on the battlefield once more."

Rolf nodded.

"What about the scouts? I'm still one of them."

Radnor shrugged.

"You're staying here with us, and if anyone tries to argue with me about it, I'll mount their head on a pike."

Rolf laughed at Radnor's exaggerated threat. He thought about what Radnor and Elena said, and realized that he was very tired; not just this day, but he was tired of bloodshed and death.

"I think I'd like to stay," he said.

Radnor and Elena both grinned with happiness.

"Good!" Elena said.

Radnor spoke next.

"The question remains: What are we to do right now?"

"Food would be good," Rolf said.

Elena smiled.

"Let's see what they have in the kitchen," she said.

Radnor smiled and took Elena by the hand as the trio headed to the keep's kitchen to scrounge up their evening meal.

Chapter 29

Arnulf sat in his cell, unsure of what to do. The dungeon was now overflowing with prisoners from the Pale Light, and they all told of the same story. Arnulf was deeply saddened when he heard the tale of Legier's duel with Ashveldt, though was glad that his friend's end had been at the point of a sword, not the ghastly claws of one of the horrors he had faced. Arnulf also found that he had grown quite sick of the Pale Light's incessant prayers, and was even more frustrated at their insistence that the witch they faced was Celestata incarnate. They repeated to him over and over again that they had seen her golden light and that her power was absolute. None of the story made sense to him, and Arnulf had given up trying to understand it altogether. One thing was for certain… if released, these knights of the Pale Light would fight for this "Elena", and they would die for her, even if it meant fighting against their own kin.

The sounds of footsteps and the jangling of keys broke Arnulf from his thoughts. The knight stood and straightened himself out. Technically, since Legier had died, Arnulf was now the commander of the army. He wasn't sure anyone in the Pale Light saw it that way, but there were still a few prisoners from Drakomar's original army in the mix. At the very least, he knew he was responsible for ensuring *their* safety.

The keys jingled once more as the door to Arnulf's cell swung open, and Ashveldt stepped through. Arnulf found that he wished to seek revenge against Ashveldt, but restrained himself. Instead, he merely spoke.

"I wondered who had come to visit me, and I find that it is you… dread prince, who lured men to slaughter."

"I guess that means the other prisoners have told you of what transpired today?" Ashveldt asked.

Arnulf nodded.

"How many of my men are still alive?"

"It depends on how you count. As far as we can tell, the survivors from Drakomar cleared out before today's battle started."

Arnulf looked to the ceiling of his cell and thanked Celestata and Caelum both for their mercy. Ashveldt continued.

"We have nearly a hundred of those from Drakomar here in the cells. Otherwise, forty knights from the Pale Light and about three hundred of their men-at-arms remain."

"What of their Archpriest, Venatus?"

Ashveldt shook his head.

"What little we have heard of him was disparaging. Apparently, they believe he led them astray and nearly damned their souls."

Ashveldt chuckled.

"What's so funny?" Ashveldt asked.

"I tried to warn Legier… I told him something similar about Venatus."

Ashveldt nodded, though he did not fully understand what Arnulf was talking about.

"What is to become of us?" Arnulf asked.

"You and the men of Drakomar are being sent home with a message of peace."

Arnulf was shocked by this news. He had expected to be executed, or at the least, ransomed.

"You're letting us go? That is very generous."

"My father wishes for the hostilities to end. If you have listened to what has been told to you, you know our world faces an insurmountable threat. My father is willing to set aside our grievances if it is the cost of our survival."

Arnulf took a moment to process what he was being told.

"What price must Drakomar pay for this peace?"

"Drakomar is to pay reparations to us. Much of the city was damaged during the barrage from your trebuchets. Your lord will pay to repair all of the damage to our city, to our crops that you raided as you marched here, and for the lives we lost. Once that is done, Wulfgeld and Drakomar shall share in defense against enemies both mortal and immortal."

Arnulf looked into Ashveldt's eyes and saw a steely look of determination within them. Ashveldt was serious.

"What makes you think I won't just bring another army? Venatus told us the Pale Light could muster fifteen thousand men to lay waste to your city."

"Because you are not a fool, or at least I don't think you are. You already know the Pale Light can't be trusted. The ones still here now believe they serve their goddess directly. They will soon be released to act accordingly, and when word of their belief reaches the rest of their order… they will schism. No, you will send our terms to Piarin, and we will finally bring peace between our two peoples."

Arnulf paused again, and realized that every word Ashveldt had said was true.

"When do we leave?"

* * *

Sigaberht's eyes fell upon the two mages he had summoned before him. It had been several hours since the army had returned from the forest, and he had finally decided what he would do with the unfamiliar pair. Despite their aid in the forest, Sigaberht considered them a threat to himself and Ashveldt. The earl had been tempted to have them killed, regardless of the outcry it would cause. However, like Radnor, they were too valuable to simply execute. So, he decided he would handle them the same way he handled Radnor. With a wave of his hand, the earl sent away the guards, who glanced nervously at the mages before they followed his command. Now that he was alone with the pair, Sigaberht spoke to them.

"You, I am told, were instrumental in saving my son's life and ending a grave threat to my realm," he said.

Imari silently bowed while Dragorim spoke.

"My lord, it is our honor to serve, but the threat is not ended, merely contained. There is a terrible will that seeks to devour all of creation. What we faced today was but a fraction of its power. You fell into its trap… it was prepared for you… prepared for *her*."

"Is that your honest assessment?" Sigaberht asked. He contemplated what he had been told. Had his trap really been the ploy of some incomprehensible horror? He shook the

392

thought from his mind. Whatever was going on, he needed the help of these mages. "Why did you come to this place?"

Dragorim answered.

"My lord, we both know of the terrible power that has been unleashed here… though I not only speak of chaos. I speak also of the woman… her power is unlike anything the world has ever seen. I believe we can help each other."

"In what way?" Sigaberht asked. He was eager to hear the sorcerer's suggestion, though he was wary the man would simply tell him what he wanted to hear.

"Allow us to teach her, help her learn more about her nature… understand her power. If we can do that, the knowledge we will gain will be invaluable to defeating the enemy we faced today once and for all."

"What makes you think the enemy has not already been beaten?" Sigaberht asked.

Dragorim shook his head.

"The wound in creation that allowed our foe to infest the world has been patched, and only by the forethought of the Hexverat. If they had not left you that gaulderen, we would all have died today."

Sigaberht nodded in understanding.

"If you teach Elena, and learn of what she is, how can I be sure you will not use this knowledge to depose me?" he asked.

Dragorim smiled.

"You can't."

Sigaberht then shook his head and removed his oath ring from his arm.

"That is where we disagree. You will swear upon my oath ring… you will swear upon my ring under pain of death that you will not betray me."

Imari gasped.

"That is against Caelum's holy law!" she shouted.

Sigaberht waved her concerns aside with a gesture.

"It is… but… these are desperate times, and I need every assurance of not only my safety, but my son's safety as well. You can either swear this oath, or I can summon Veigarand here to kill you both."

Imari gasped again, but Dragorim made no move to protest. Instead, he held out his hand to take the oath. Imari looked at him nervously. Dragorim looked back to her.

"We have no choice, and given the circumstances, I'm not sure the earl's demand is unreasonable."

Imari looked at her friend. She was still reluctant to take the oath ring, but she saw she had little choice. The witch chose to trust in Dragorim's judgment and took hold of Sigaberht's oath ring.

"Now, repeat after me." Sigaberht said. "I swear upon this oath ring that I will seek the truth about the powers that threaten Wulfgeld, protect the earl of Wulfgeld and his heir, and obey their every command until we are released from this oath."

Dragorim and Imari both repeated the words given to them by the earl. However, Caelum was wise when he forged the power of his holy oaths, and had created a way for those forced to swear under duress to negate the oath's power undetected. Few knew of this holy sign, for those who wielded the oath rings trusted their makers absolutely, and the makers concealed this weakness from them.

Even as Dragorim gripped the oath ring and swore the oath, his other hand dipped into his pocket and flashed with rapid movement as his fingers formed a small, curious sign. Once the sign was formed, Dragorim kept his hand in his pocket as he spoke the words.

Sigaberht continued. "Upon this ring, you have sworn to uphold these oaths. The penance for oath breaking is death."

Dragorim and Imari spoke these words, and as the binding flames of the oath entwined their souls, Dragorim knew he was free to continue his work as he pleased. Nothing would stop him, and soon, he would have the power he needed to finally fulfill his life's purpose!

Epilogue

Ashrahan and Lashmatu strode together through the courtyard of the royal palace. Adramelach, king of all Krigari, had called them to his hall. When word of his summons had reached them, they had been fearful, but they were oath-bound to join him. As the pair met on the way to the palace, they spoke hastily and realized what they needed to do. They knew Adramelach's purpose and were prepared for their master's questions. As the pair crossed the stone courtyard and reached the door to the throne room, they paused to look at the night sky, and gazed upon the worlds that burned among the stars. Lashmatu commented upon them.

"They were beautiful, those flaming cinders of the creations that once were."

Ashrahan smiled as he gazed upon the handiwork of his kind. Such was the way of the Krigari, for war was their only calling, and fire was their instrument.

Their conversation was interrupted as the door to the throne room swung open. They glanced at each other and without another word; the pair stepped towards the royal presence.

As they drew closer, they saw the weary expression on Adramelach's face as he sat upon the blood-throne. The king of all Krigari heard their footsteps and lifted his head to them. He straightened himself and gazed upon them with a cold, calculating look that made both Ashrahan and Lashmatu uneasy. Blood flowed in and around Adramelach's throne as he gazed upon them with his frigid stare. Lashmatu and Ashrahan bowed before their king and then finished the final approach to his royal presence.

"Do you know why I have summoned you?" Adramelach asked.

"I do," Ashrahan said.

"You two have been meddling in the mortal realm. Does my son yet live?"

Ashrahan smiled.

"Veigarand lives. He believes we work to destroy you, and we have proven to be reliable allies to him. He will trust us when the time is right."

"Good… but be sure he does not grow suspicious. Keep your visits short and do not give too much away," Adramelach cautioned.

"Do not worry, for he believes that each time I depart, it is to keep you unaware of my 'true plans'."

Adramelach took some comfort in the knowledge that at least part of his plan was working.

"Very well. What other news do you bring me?"

Lashmatu spoke next.

"Your son… he has a lover."

"Why would I care?" Adramelach scoffed.

"His lover… I believe *she* is what you have been searching for."

Adramelach's gaze locked onto Lashmatu's. This news was quite deserving of his full attention.

"Are you sure?"

"That is what we were meddling in," Lashmatu said. "We have seen her power unleashed upon chaos… and she rivals even Caelum's overpowering might. I think with the proper training, she might even surpass him."

"Given your parentage… that is high praise," Adramelach commented.

The king sat lost in thought until Lashmatu broke him from it again.

"Is it possible she is Caelum reborn?"

Adramelach laughed.

"Perhaps, though I doubt it. Hymurr learns from his mistakes, and I believe this woman is the product of what he has learned."

"Is she him? Is she Hymurr?" Ashrahan asked.

Adramelach considered this for a moment, and then dismissed it.

"Also doubtful. I do not think he would reveal himself at such an early stage of the game. No. Nothing is straightforward with Hymurr. He only deals in riddles.

However, one thing is now certain. We *must* gain entry into his world.”

He paused, and gazed upon his subjects with delight at the news they had brought him.

“This woman is the key, and with her, *we* shall open the door.”